Wade Garrison's Promise

First Book in the Wade Garrison Series

By Richard J Greene

Manybooks Editorial Review: Wade Garrison's Promise by Richard J Greene

Posted on 11th of November 2020 by Heinrich Bolton

Wade Garrison's Promise by Richard J Greene is a western novel that even readers who are not normally fans of the genre will enjoy.

Wade Garrison is a young man who grew up on a farm in South Carolina, but the cheap western novels he read as a child compel him to go out and seek his adventures. His dreams land him in eastern Colorado, where he finds employment on a ranch and becomes best friends with a man named Emmett Spears. Wade is soon faced with the harsh realities of the west when Emmet is gunned down in a saloon by four strangers. Leaving the love of his life and everything he has known behind, Wade sets out to avenge the death of his friend and bring the killers to justice.

Wade is a sympathetic protagonist, and unlike a lot of western heroes, he is not a cold-blooded killer. His mission for revenge weighs heavily on his conscience, but the further he tracks the outlaws, the more atrocities he discovers in their wake. It makes for harrowing reading but leaves no doubt that unless Wade stops them, they won't cease their carnage.

Wade Garrison's Promise is not just the story of Wade, even though it is told from his perspective. Along the way, he also encounters a stellar cast of supporting characters. These include two aging sheriffs as well as a U.S. Marshall. Unlike Wade, they are no strangers to the business of killing people who are a menace to society but are still shocked by the actions of the outlaws.

One of the things that makes this book so compelling to read is that it's not a thrill-a-minute pulp story. The act of tracking down the killers is something that takes Wade a long time, and throughout the journey, he reflects back on his past. It is through these flashbacks that readers discover how deep his friendship with Emmett was and how much Wade is sacrificing in the name of revenge. This isn't to say that the book is devoid of action either, as Wade and his posse end up in quite a few life-or-death situations. The author has done a great job with the supporting cast, and after spending so much time in the saddle and around campfires with them, it's impossible not to like them. Of course, this makes the scenes where they are in mortal danger even tenser.

All things considered, <u>Wade Garrison's Promise</u> is a great read and has more depth than what the Western genre typically has to offer. It's not just the story of a man on a journey of vengeance but also explores the toll that it takes on him both mentally and physically. The Wade Garrison, towards the end of the story, is not the same naive young man who promised to avenge his friend at the start. It is this character growth that ensures that Wade grows on readers and will make them want to know what it is that drives him in further books.

All Rights Reserved

Copyright @ 2010 by Richard Greene

No part of this book may be reproduced or transmitted in any form or by any means, electronic or mechanical, including photocopying records or any information storage and retrieval system, without permission in writing from the author.

ISBN: 978-1-4349-9820-0

The author makes no claims to be an authority of the American Indian, particularly the Arapahoe Tribes of Colorado. This story is a work of fiction. Names, characters, places, and incidents are the products of the author's imagination or are used fictitiously and are not to be construed as real or accurate. Any resemblance to actual events, locale organizations, or persons living or dead is entirely coincidental.

Richard and his Lhasa Apso Jackson

About the Author

Richard Greene was born in Denver, Colorado, in 1939 and grew up in a small two-bedroom house in Englewood, a suburb of Denver. In 1954 his parents divorced, and his father moved to Houston, Texas. Soon after, Richard dropped out of ninth grade and worked various jobs, including sacking groceries at a local supermarket and as an electrician's apprentice for a neighbor. He spent his summers with his dad, who owned 'The Texan' bar on the outskirts of Houston, Texas, where he got an education in life, unlike his friends back in Englewood, Colorado. In August 1956, Richard enlisted in the United States Navy at seventeen. After boot camp and Yeoman School in March 1957, he was transferred to the USS Belle Grove LSD-2 (Landing Ship Dock), serving in the South Pacific, taking part in the atomic testing at Eniwetok and Bikini Atolls in 1958.

Honorably discharged in 1960, he worked at Samsonite Luggage for a short spell and then went to work for Burlington Truck Lines as a billing clerk. The trucking industry fascinated Richard, so he attended Denver Traffic School to learn the trucking industry's ins and outs. He worked as a dock supervisor for United Buckingham in Denver and a sales representative for Californian Motor Express in Fresno, California, and Los Angeles. Moving back to Denver, he went to work as Claims

6

Prevention Manager for Consolidated Freightways, which included investigating road accidents of CF trucks within 100 miles of Denver. After a year with Consolidated, he transferred from Denver to the General Claims Department in Portland, Oregon. In 1973 Richard left the Claims Department to become a supervisor in the Collection Department for Consolidated, where he remained until his retirement in December 1995 as Manager of Collections.

Still residing in Portland, Oregon, Richard, and his wife Cathy spend much of their time with their children and grandchildren. Richard's other interests are golf, long walks, reading, and oil painting.

I welcome all comments, good or bad. They both help me become a better writer, so please, visit my web page www.richardjgreene.net and leave your comments on my message board with your email address.

Facebook at https://www.facebook.com/richardgreene.7393

Twitter at https://twitter.com/@dickiejoe, All of my books are available on Amazon as ebooks or paperback.

Wade Garrison's Promise

Preface

As a young man, Wade Garrison was a simple fellow who came west
chasing the stories he had read about in cheap Western novels while
growing up on a farm in South Carolina. He was not a violent man, and
like most men of humble beginnings, he held his name and promises in
high regard.

Watching the pine coffin containing his friend Emmett Spears'
lifeless body lowered into the dark grave, Wade made a silent promise of
revenge. It was a promise that would take him far from the girl he loved
and the Circle T Ranch in eastern Colorado.

However, as young Wade Garrison trailed the four men responsible for his friend's death, he would soon find himself unprepared for the death and violence he would find. He was unaware that he would lose himself in the process of fulfilling his promise to avenge Emmett Spears.

One

July 12, 1872

Dawn on the Plains of Colorado

The cry of a solitary coyote broke the silence of a quiet dawn on the Colorado Plains. Wade Garrison lay under his blanket, his head on his saddle, watching the night fight with the dim light of dawn. The early morning colors of pink, reddish-orange, and purple filled the light blue sky above the horizon. While waiting for the sun to come up, his mind wandered back to early morning chores, his family, and his home in South Carolina. Six years of his life have passed since he left his home that day in 1866. He could feel the sun's warmth as it rose above the horizon and thought of his mother smiling though her eyes welled with tears. His ten-year-old sister held their mother's hand as tears made their way down her wet cheeks finding the crevices of her mouth.

Sitting in a wagon a few feet from the depot platform, his grandfather stared at the hills in the distance beyond town, refusing to say goodbye. The old man was stubborn and angry with young Wade for leaving home for the foolishness of the West he had read in the dime novels he used to hide under his mattress. His grandfather had lost his

11

only son to the war a few years earlier, and now his only grandson was leaving on a foolish quest. Dealing with another loss was just too difficult for the old man.

"All aboard!" yelled the conductor.

Wade hugged his mother, promised he'd write, then hugged his ten-year-old sister, telling her to be good. He glanced at his grandfather, who sat stubbornly in the wagon, hoping the old man would turn and smile or at least wave. Disappointed and sad for his grandfather, Wade climbed up the steps into the rail car and found a seat next to an open window. He leaned out the open window and looked down at his mother standing on the platform with red, welling eyes that she wiped with her hanky. The train lurched forward and began moving slowly out of the depot while his mother walked along the platform, telling him to be careful and write when he could. Reaching the end of the depot platform, she stopped as the train picked up speed for that West in the dime novels.

The sun was well above the eastern hills, and the day had come to life, filled with the sounds of birds and a nearby stream. Wade tossed back the blanket, sat up, stretched, and stood in time to see the lonely coyote disappear over a ridge. He wondered at the coyote's destination as he walked to his hobbled horses, feeding off prairie grass a few feet away. As Wade approached, the packhorse raised its head and looked at him with big dark eyes. He petted its nose before bending down to check the rope around its front legs, then turned to the sorrel mare. She looked up from the grass, shook her head gently, and snorted as if saying good morning. Satisfied both were alright, he built a fire, cut up the last slab of bacon, and thought he would buy more at the next town.

After eating, he loaded the packhorse with what supplies he had left, bridled, and saddled the mare. He rolled up his slicker and blanket, tied them behind the saddle, and made sure the fire was out by shoveling dirt over it with his boot. He took one last look around the campsite, then climbed into the saddle. He rode west toward the mountains looming in the distance and the small town of Sisters. At twenty-two, Wade Garrison was a lean, good-looking man who stood five feet ten inches tall with blue eyes, a friendly smile of even white teeth, and a square jaw. Days in the sun had left his face tanned and filled with tiny squint lines at the edges of his eyes and upper cheeks. He had light brown hair that could use a cut and his face a razor.

The town of Sisters was not unlike other small towns of eastern Colorado or New Mexico. Its main street of wagon ruts hitching rails and an occasional barking dog cut a straight line between hotels, several stores, restaurants, two saloons, a bank, and a sheriff's office. The second street of businesses cutting the town in half led north toward Colorado Springs and south toward Pueblo. The town had taken the name "Sisters" from two girls whose family's wagon had the misfortune of breaking down while on their way to California in 1840. Before they could repair their wagon, a small war party of Arapahoe Indians happened upon them, killing the entire family. A few years later, someone discovered silver in the hills, and this small town sprang up and took the name "Sisters" in their remembrance. The silver strike played out quickly, but ranchers and farmers had settled on the eastern plains, and the town remained.

The dusty street was busy with midday traffic of shoppers and storekeepers sweeping the morning dust from the boardwalks and children playing in the dusty street. The aroma from a nearby café found Wade, and his belly moaned for something to eat. Riding past the café toward the sheriff's office, he imagined a plate of beef and beans or maybe a hot tortilla. He pulled up in front of the Sheriff's Office, climbed down, tied his horses securely to the hitching rail, walked up the steps to the boardwalk, and stepped inside.

A lean man in his forties sat behind the desk, cleaning a Winchester rifle. The man looked up, took a drink of coffee from a tin cup, and waited for Wade to make the trip across the room. "Something I can do for you, young man?"

Wade gestured to one of two straight-back chairs in front of the sheriff's desk. "Mind if I sit?"

"Help yerself," he said while leaning forward and holding out an open hand. "Seth Bowlen."

Wade shook the hand, noticing the scar cutting through the right eyebrow running the length of his cheek and the cloudy blue eye. "Wade Garrison."

"Nice to know you, Mr. Garrison. Coffee?"

Wade nodded. "Thanks." Sitting down, he took off his hat and set it in the other chair.

Sheriff Bowlen stood, turned to a big coffee pot sitting on a pot-bellied stove behind him, and poured two cups while apologizing for its strength and bitterness. Sheriff Bowlen was easygoing, lean, and wiry in his early forties. The handlebar mustache was the same black and gray as his thick hair, and bushy eyebrows covered his upper lip. Years on the trail left his face leathery and lined, but he was still a good-looking man. He had been a lawman most of his adult life in Kansas, then New Mexico and Arizona, and now, here in Sisters. Sheriff Seth Bowlen grinned dryly as he sat down in his creaky chair and gestured to his right eye. "Souvenir from a drunken asshole in Kansas a few years back."

Wade sipped the bitter brew, wondering if the sheriff could see out of the eye, but he wasn't about to ask. He looked down into the coffee understanding the sheriff's apology about it being strong and bitter. When he looked up, the sheriff was smiling.

"Warned you about the coffee, young man." The Sheriff opened a drawer, pulled out a small whiskey bottle, poured a fair amount into his coffee, and held up the bottle in an offering.

Wade shook his head, thinking it a bit early, and politely refused.

Bowlen corked the bottle, put it back in the drawer, closed it, and looked at Wade over the rim of his cup as he took a drink. He sat back, held the cup with both hands in his lap, and looked at Wade. "I'm sure you didn't stop by for my coffee. What's on your mind, Mister Garrison?"

Wade took a small sip of coffee. "Been trailing four men but lost them in the rocky flats a few miles southeast of here."

The sheriff was familiar with the area, knowing it made tracking difficult at best. "You a lawman, Mr. Garrison?"

Wade raised his brow as he shook his head. "No, sir, I'm not."

Bowlen looked interested. "Mind telling me why you're tracking these fellas?"

"Killed a friend of mine up in Harper a few days back."

Bowlen pursed his lips in thought. "They know you're trailing them?"

Wade shook his head. "No reason for them to know, I guess." Then he explained that his friend, Emmett Spears, had been shot five times in the Blue-Sky Saloon in the town of Harper.

The sheriff sipped his whiskey coffee, leaned forward, and rested his elbows on his desk. "Seems a mite overkill. What the hell did this friend of yours do to deserve getting shot that many times?"

14

"Being foolish mostly," he said softly. "Seems Emmett stood up to these four because they were picking on the town fool."

"Not a very good reason to shoot a man five times." Then Bowlen asked, "You there when it happened?"

Wade shook his head. "I was riding line at the Circle T northeast of Harper."

The sheriff contemplated this young man sitting before him for a few moments. "So, you work for Toliver Grimes?"

Wade looked surprised. "Emmett and I both did. You know Mr. Grimes?"

"I've had the pleasure of spending time with him over the years. You say you and this Emmett fella both worked for the Circle T?"

"That's right."

Bowlen thought about that for a moment. "Are you still employed by the Circle T?"

Wade frowned, wondering what difference that made. "Suppose not, at least not until I find these men."

Bowlen's expression turned serious. "And when you find these four men, you plan to use that gun strapped to your side?"

Wade looked down at the forty-four Colt pistol in his holster.

"Keep it holstered while you're in my town," warned the sheriff.

"I ain't looking for any trouble, Sheriff."

Bowlen smiled. "That's good to know, but someone like you always makes me a little nervous. I don't want any killing in my town." He leaned back in his chair. "How do you know the four men you're trailing are the same ones who did the shooting?"

"There were a couple of boys from the Circle T in the bar that gave a description to the sheriff of Harper." Wade shrugged, looking disappointed. "But he's getting on in years, and luckily for him, not much happens in Harper." Wade looked thoughtful. "I guess he ain't one to go trailing after some drifters across the plains or into the mountains."

Bowlen sipped his coffee and then shrugged. "Can't blame old Harry much for that. His jurisdiction ends with the town line."

Again, Wade looked surprised and wondered if Seth Bowlen knew everyone. "You know Sheriff Harry Block?"

Seth shook his head. "Like most of us, old Harry has seen better days." He paused in memory, then asked, "What do these fellas look like?"

Wade sipped his coffee, turned to the window, and looked at the building across the street. "They're all about the same height, around five-eight, medium build. One had blonde curly hair, one black hair, another had red hair with freckles, and the fourth was a big man said to have been a black half-breed."

Bowlen looked curious. "A black half-breed Indian?"

Wade shrugged. "That's what they said."

"Hmmm," said the sheriff thoughtfully as he slowly shook his head. "Ain't no one like them passed through Sisters." Then he leaned forward with narrowed eyes. "And if they should while you're here, I don't want any killing." He stared at Wade. "You come and get me."

"I'm not a gunman, Sheriff," Wade softly said as he set his half cup of coffee on the desk. "Thanks for the coffee." Then he stood. "That café down the street have good food?"

"Food's good," said Bowlen as he leaned forward. "Maybe you ain't no gunman, Mr. Garrison, but any time a man like you comes into my town tracking someone, a killing usually follows." He leaned back in his chair and smiled sarcastically. "I'm a mite curious. If you ain't a lawman or a gunman like you claim, then just what the hell you plan on doing when you do catch up with these men?"

Wade shrugged. "Haven't quite figured that one out yet."

Seth stared at him for a long moment thinking he was a fool. "You seem like a nice young man Mr. Garrison, so I'm gonna give you some free advice. Go back to the Circle T. You're not prepared for what you're about to find trailing these four men."

Wade considered that. "Maybe so, but Emmett was my best friend."

"Well, Son, sometimes it's best to let things be as they are, especially if you ain't prepared for the consequences."

Wade looked down at the floor and then at Bowlen. "Maybe you're right, Sheriff. I don't know one way or the other, but this is something I have to do."

Bowlen stared at him while wishing he could convince the young man to return to the Circle T. "Graves are full of people with that philosophy Son." He paused, knowing he was in a useless argument. "How long do you plan on staying in Sisters?"

"Not long." Wade turned and walked to the door, opened it, and turned. "I'd like to spend the night and get supplies in the morning if that'd be alright."

Bowlen put his cup on the desk, smiled, and stood. "Yer welcome here as long as you stay out of trouble, Mr. Garrison." He scowled. "You get into trouble in my town, then you and I will have a little problem." He nodded at Wade's gun. "Keep that gun holstered."

"Like I done told you, Sheriff, I ain't no gunman." Wade turned and walked out into the late afternoon sun. Closing the door behind him, he decided he would eat after boarding his horses and found a room at the hotel.

Sheriff Bowlen picked up his cup, walked to the window, sipped his whiskey coffee, and watched the young man untie his horses and walk across the street to the café. He considered the young man for a few more moments, deciding he'd be buried someplace far from the Circle T. Then, he returned to the chore of cleaning his Winchester.

Wade opened his eyes from a restful sleep to the sounds of roosters and looked out the window at the new morning. He got up, dressed, and headed for the café and breakfast, after which he stopped by the general store and bought a small slab of bacon and a few supplies. He walked toward the livery and was not surprised to see the sheriff leaning with his back against one of the big open doors.

"Leaving?" asked Sheriff Bowlen.

"Soon as I saddle up." Wade set the supplies on the livery's dirt floor, picked up the saddle blanket, and put it on the mare, followed by the saddle. He turned and smiled at the sheriff. "Come to say goodbye?"

Bowlen smiled. "Something like that." Then he stepped up to the stall and eyed the mare, thinking she was a fine piece of horseflesh. Noticing the long rifle resting against the side of the stall, he said, "Don't see many Sharps these days."

Wade glanced at it. "S'pose not." Then, without looking up, he lifted the stirrup, placed it on the saddle horn, and tightened the cinch.

Seth Bowlen watched in silence, sizing up the young man for a few moments, then leaned against the stall post and watched Wade load his supplies.

Finished with the packhorse, Wade picked up the Sharps, put it in the sheath at the front of his saddle, grabbed the lead rope to the packhorse, the mare's reins, and walked past Bowlen into the warm morning sun.

The sheriff followed. "I never used one myself. I knew a few who did, but I don't believe I could ever get used to two triggers on one gun."

Wade fussed with the packhorse's halter. "It's easy once you get used to it. After setting the first trigger, the second doesn't need much of a pull. There's less of a jerking motion, and that adds to the accuracy."

17

Bowlen glanced at the gun. "Sort of like a hair trigger."

"Guess so," Wade replied with a thoughtful look.

Bowlen walked to the packhorse, pulled on one of the straps that held the supplies and looked at Wade. "Come to any conclusion as to what you might do if you catch up with these four men?"

Wade shrugged and put one hand on the saddle horn and his left foot in the stirrup. Pausing, he looked at Seth and smiled as he lied. "See if I can get someone to arrest them, I guess." Then he climbed into the saddle, sitting tall as he wrapped the lead rope of his packhorse around his saddle horn. He looked down at Bowlen and grinned. "As I said, Sheriff, I ain't no gunman."

Bowlen smiled sarcastically. "It'd be better if you were, Mr. Garrison." Then he gave him a quick nod. "Good luck to ya."

Wade knew that what the sheriff said about being better off if he was a gunman was true. He turned his mare and rode out of town, hoping to pick up the trail of the four men who had killed Emmett.

Riding southwest in the stillness of the prairie, he thought about what Sheriff Bowlen had said and of Emmett lying in the cold ground. It was quiet; the only sounds were the horse's hooves on the hard red Colorado soil. For some reason, he remembered Emmett's laugh and smiled at how his friend got angry when the other hands of the Circle T teased him. The thing about young Emmett was that he was likable and naturally brought about the teasing. Wade thought it would be nice if he or Old Man Grimes could write to Emmett's family, telling them what happened to their son. But Mr. Grimes said he never knew where Emmett had come from, and the only thing Wade knew was that he was from somewhere in Ohio.

The hours passed without any sign of the four men or their tracks, so Wade stopped, climbed down, and looked south and west into the foothills. Wondering which direction the four men would have ridden, he decided to take a chance and ride west and then followed the foothills for no other reason than he figured there was water there. Wade climbed down, poured some water into his hat from a water bag, let the horses drink, then climbed back into his saddle and rode west toward the Colorado Foothills. Coming to a small stream, he climbed down and walked along the bank, searching both sides of the small stream for the turned hoof and the horseshoe with the imperfection.

An hour passed before finding the horse's tracks he sought in the muddy bank. He knelt, reached out, and gently touched the track with the imperfection in the hoof that resembled a crooked river or a snake. Excited by his find, he followed the tracks on foot for a while, then climbed back onto his horse and followed them along the stream.

After several hours he stopped by the stream to let the horses drink while he sat in the saddle with one leg curled around the saddle horn and wondered about the four men's destination. While the horses drank, he looked across the lonely prairie that started at the foothills at the base of the tall Rocky Mountains, then disappeared into the eastern horizon. Curious about how far he had come, he turned and looked behind him to the north, where the prairie met the foothills, and then to the south, saw the same scenery of prairie, foothills, and tall mountains. Thirsty, he got down, knelt next to the stream, cupped his hands, filled them with the cold clear water, and drank. He stood and wiped his wet hands on his pants as his eyes followed the stream that disappeared around a bend. Feeling tired and hungry and thinking the horses were tired, he led them to the shade of cottonwood and aspen trees and made camp for the night.

Making a fire pit with rocks, he built a fire and filled a small coffee pot with water from the creek. He carefully poured the coffee grounds, placed the small pot on one of the flat rocks close to the fire, sat back, and waited for the water to boil. As he waited, he mentally counted the money he had spent and hoped what Mr. Grimes had given him would last at least two months. He remembered how upset Mr. Grimes had been at the news of Emmett's death. It was plain the old man liked the boy, and it seemed Mr. Grimes always watched Emmett with a prideful look and smile. Some said Emmett reminded the old man of his son, who died from a fever at fifteen. His death had so upset Mrs. Elsie Grimes that she put on a new dress, walked out to the small graveyard under an oak tree, where her son lay buried, and put a forty-four pistol to her head. It was soon after that they say that Old Man Grimes became a recluse who stayed in the big house most of the time and let the foreman run things.

The wranglers said that when young Emmett showed up looking for work in sixty-eight, a year before Wade appeared on the scene, Mr. Grimes quickly became his old self, and the place became a happy ranch again. All though the old man watched over Emmett like a father, he did so without showing favoritism over the other hands. While everyone noticed his feelings for the boy, no one seemed to mind because it brought the old man out of the house.

Wade picked up a small piece of wood and tossed it into the fire, and as he stared into it, he remembered the day of Emmett's funeral.

July 7, 1872

Emmett Spears was laid to rest in the same small cemetery surrounded by a white picket fence under a tall oak tree, where Mrs. Grimes and their son are buried. Afterward, Mr. Grimes took Wade into the big house to his study. Wade could barely make out the books in the bookcase in the corner next to the window and the paintings on the far wall in the dark, chilly room. Mr. Grimes sat in the leather chair behind the big desk in silence, staring down at his folded hands. The window behind him silhouetted his big frame, and although Wade could not see his face in the bright light, he knew it held hate and sorrow. Tolliver Grimes was a big man who stood just over six feet on a big frame of well over two hundred fifty pounds. The years had left their marks of lines and small scars on an otherwise handsome face, framed by a white beard and full head of white hair. The old man's voice was full of hate as he pointed to a leather wallet filled with money lying on the corner of his desk.

"There's enough to last a month or two if you're careful," he said. Then he stood, walked around the desk, and put one hand on Wade's shoulder. "I know he was your friend, Son, but are you sure about this?"

"I'm sure," said Wade looking sad yet determined.

Grimes frowned. "I wish I could go with you, Son. Sheriff Block in Harper's too old and won't leave the confines of the town." He took his hand from Wade's shoulder and sat on the edge of his desk. "I wouldn't trust anyone else with this money. I'm afraid most of these boys would buy whiskey or give it to a couple of whores."

"Too many of us," said Wade softly, "would just get in the way of what I have to do."

Grimes nodded. "I suppose that's true." Then he stood from the edge of the desk, walked to the corner behind it, and reached for something. When he turned, he held his Sharps rifle with a thirty-four-inch barrel, double-set triggers in one hand, and a bandolier filled with shells. "Take this with you. These shells are my own fifty caliber load with a hundred and ten grains of black powder. On a good day, this old gal has a range close to a thousand yards."

Wade took the Sharps feeling its weight.

Grimes smiled proudly. "Weighs thirteen pounds. And she's accurate as all hell, but you know that already."

Wade smiled. "Yes, sir, I do." Then he cradled the rifle in the elbow of his left arm, took the bandolier, picked up the wallet of money from the desk, and shoved it under his belt.

The old man turned and walked around his desk to the window and looked out at the short white picket fence where his son, wife, older brother, and Emmett lay buried. The room was quiet as Wade watched the old man knowing he missed Emmett almost as much as he did. Then Mr. Grimes softly said, "Be careful."

"I don't know how long I'll be."

The old man stared out the window at the picket fence, grave markers, oak tree, and the endless prairie. "Your job will be waiting no matter how long it takes. Just find the bastards."

Wade stared at the back of the old man for a moment, then turned and walked out of the study with no idea what he would do when he found these men. He stepped out of the front door, closed it behind him, walked down the porch steps, and thought Harper would be a good place to start.

Stepping inside the bunkhouse, Wade paused to look at Emmett's empty bunk next to his before he gathered a few things from his footlocker. Closing the top of his wooden locker and feeling his friend's loss, he stood.

Jessup Haggerty walked from between his and Johnny Pardee's bunks. In his late twenties, Haggerty was a big man who stood over six feet, weighing well over two hundred pounds, with cold dark eyes, black curly hair, and a clean-shaven square jaw. "So, you're really going?" he asked.

Wade stopped, looked at Jessup, nodded, and started toward the door.

Johnny Pardee was lying on his bunk, and as he stood, he asked, "You want one of us to come along?" Johnny Pardee was a lean man of five foot eight in his late twenties. His black hair was combed straight back, and his handsome face bore the scars of a hard life. His ankles still bore the scars of a chain gang in Louisiana.

Wade looked at the two men who had always taken pleasure in teasing Emmett and knew it was always in fun. He knew they liked Emmett and felt terrible about his death. "This is something I have to do alone. I promised Emmett."

Haggerty looked worried as he placed his arm on the top edge of his bunk. "These guys aren't like most cowhands, Wade. They're killers, and they'll do the same to you they did to Emmett." He paused a moment with a sad look. "We liked Emmett too, Wade. Sure, we teased him all the time, but that's because we liked the little shit." He looked at Wade. "You sure you don't want one of us to come along?"

Wade looked appreciative. "Thanks, but this is something I have to do myself. Besides, I don't think Mr. Grimes would like us much, leaving him shorthanded and all."

Haggerty frowned. "Guess you're right but let me give you a piece of advice. You can't meet these bastards on equal footing. They'll kill you in an instant."

"That's right," said Pardee. "Staying alive is something I learned the hard way. Do whatever it takes for you to stay alive and them dead. Shoot them in the back if you have to. They'd sure as hell do it to you." He paused. "When killing's involved, there ain't no fairness. Just staying alive to get the job done is what you need to do."

Wade wondered if he had the guts to kill the four men as he stared at Pardee. He nodded his understanding and walked out of the bunkhouse, across the yard and into the barn.

Another hand named Stu had just finished saddling Wade's mare. "Mr. Grimes told me to saddle your horse." Then he nodded to another stall. "Had me load up that packhorse yonder with supplies."

Wade glanced out the barn's big open doors at the big house and knew that Mr. Grimes wanted these men dead as much as he did.

"Want me to come with ya?" asked Stu. "I liked Emmett a lot, not as you did, but I sure liked him."

Stu Parks was a skinny young man of six feet with a tan face, blonde hair, blue eyes, and crooked teeth. Wade was unsure how old he was, possibly in his late teens or early twenties, but neither was Stu. Like Wade, he had left his home in Georgia soon after the war, moved from place to place, and finally ended up at the Circle T. Then Wade thought of Jessup and Johnny Pardee. If anyone were to come with him, he would want one of them, thinking Stu would just be in the way. "No, Stu, I don't think Old Man Grimes can spare you."

"Then why's he letting you go?"

Wade wanted to keep his and Mr. Grimes's business to himself, so he shrugged. "I figure it's because Emmett and I were best friends." Not *wanting to discuss the matter any further, he offered a hand. "Other than that, Stu, I've no idea."*

Stu shook Wade's hand, told him to be careful, wished him luck, and held the mare steady while Wade climbed up.

As Wade settled into the saddle, Stu handed him the lead rope of the packhorse. He wrapped it around his saddle horn and looked down at Stu. "Guess I'll be seeing you, Stu." Then he nudged the mare and rode out of the barn toward the town of Harper, thinking he would start with Old George at the livery.

Harper, Colorado

Wade rode up to the livery corral, climbed down, went inside to look for the old man everyone fondly called Old George, and found him as he cleaned one of the stalls. "George," called Wade.

The old man stopped what he was doing, turned, leaned the pitchfork against the railing, and pulled a dirty rag out of his rear pocket. He wiped the sweat from his face looking sad. "Sorry about yer friend Emmett." He put the rag back into his pocket while looking at Wade's horse and packhorse tied up to the corral out the big open doors. "Looks like you're really going after them fellers."

Wade nodded. "I am."

George looked sad. "Those fellers had no call to shoot your friend."

"What can you tell me about them."

"Well," began the old man. "One had blonde hair rode a sorrel with a mark of imperfection in one shoe that brought to mind a crooked river or snake. The big man with black hair rode a spotted gray with a slightly turned left front leg. They'll be easy tracking."

"What about the other two?"

George thought for a minute. "The redhead rode a black and the half-breed a spotted black-and-white." George walked a few steps toward the open doors. "They headed south." He turned back to Wade. "My guess is they's headed to New Mexico or Arizona." George paused as he looked up into a cloudless blue sky. "It's been a few days, but we've had no rain or wind, so their trail should still be there."

Wade held out an open hand.

George took it and shook it firmly. "Best of luck to ya, Mr. Garrison."

Wade thanked him, walked out of the livery, and started to climb into the saddle when he heard a woman call his name. He turned and saw Sarah Talbert standing on the steps to Mason's General Store while her mother sat in the wagon next to her father, Mr. Talbert. Wade led the horses across the street, hoping they would not try and talk him out of going because his mind was made up. "Howdy, Mrs. Talbert." Then he looked at Mr. Talbert. "Afternoon, Sir."

"Good afternoon, Wade." Mr. Talbert offered his hand. "Sorry to hear about your friend Emmett. He was a nice lad."

Wade shook Mr. Talbert's hand firmly. "Appreciate you saying so, Mr. Talbert. Emmett was a good hand, an honest man, and a damn good friend."

"I'm sure he was all that Wade," replied Mr. Talbert in a soft voice. Then he climbed down and turned to help Mrs. Talbert from the wagon.

After Mrs. Talbert stepped onto the dirt street, she put one hand on Wade's forearm, squeezed it gently, and said how sorry she was about Emmett's death. "He used to make me laugh," she said sadly.

Wade forced a smile. "Me too, Mrs. Talbert."

She turned, walked up the steps to the boardwalk, paused, and looked at her daughter. "We'll go on inside, Sarah. I'm sure the two of you have some talking to do."

Wade tied the horses to the hitching rail, walked up the steps, stopped at the second step, and looked into Sarah's brown eyes. "Morning, Sarah."

"We heard you were going after those terrible men who shot Emmett," said Sarah while trying to hide her fears.

Wade could sense the fear in her voice.

"I wish you wouldn't go."

He turned and looked up the busy, dusty dirt street. "Something I have to do, Sarah." He turned and looked into her big brown eyes. "Don't expect you to understand, but I made Emmett a promise over his grave."

Her voice quivered. "I understand that Emmett's dead, and you might be next if you go after these men over some stupid promise." She put her hand on his forearm and looked into his blue eyes. "I'm asking you not to go, Wade. Let the law handle these men."

He looked into her brown, welling eyes as a single tear made its way down her cheek, dropping onto her blue dress. "I have to go, Sarah. There ain't no explaining it. I have to."

"No, you don't, Wade," she pleaded and then, with anger in her voice, said, "You're just stubborn and foolish, and you getting killed won't bring Emmett back."

He looked into her watery brown eyes as she pleaded with him not to go. Then he took her in his arms, kissed her, and as he held her, he softly said, "I'll be back." Then he turned, walked down the steps to the dirt street, untied the horses, and climbed into the saddle. He wrapped the lead rope of the packhorse around his saddle horn as he looked down into Sarah's pleading eyes. He smiled, pulled the brim of his hat down, and turned the mare south, leading the packhorse down the street. Though he wanted to, he never looked back for fear that if he did, he wouldn't go.

Sarah stood on the boardwalk steps, watched for a few moments, then wiped the tears away and hurried into the store.

The sound of the water in the pot boiling brought him back from his memories of Emmett, Sarah, and the Circle T. He slid the pot away from the fire to let the grounds settle, and after a few minutes, he picked up his tin cup and filled it with hot, black coffee. He leaned back against his saddle, took a sip, and thought it tasted good, even if it was a little strong. He stared into the fire and thought of Sarah standing on the boardwalk the day he left with tears in her eyes. He could smell her perfume from memory and her softness when he held her.

Wade Garrison was not a violent man by nature. The only things he ever shot his forty-four Colt and thirty caliber Hawkins rifle at were rocks, fence posts, and a tree now and again. The only serious shooting he ever did was with Mr. Grimes's fifty-caliber Sharps rifle, winning the Harper shooting contest two years running. The only thing he ever killed was a coyote once, and he came to regret that.

While sipping his coffee, he glanced at his holstered pistol that sat atop his saddle next to the Sharps rifle still in its sheath. He thoughtfully contemplated his revenge for the killing of Emmett Spears, not sure he could do what he had vowed. With doubt creeping over him, he thought of the others back at the ranch. Jessup Haggerty, for one, was a big, mean man who talked of killing men during the war. Then he thought of Johnny Pardee from New Orleans, still bearing the scars of a chain gang, or Dobbs from Montana, who loved to get drunk and fight on Saturday nights.

Hell, he thought to himself, any of these men would probably kill without hesitation, but Emmett had been his best friend, and it was up to him to seek justice for Emmett. He drank his coffee as his thoughts

26

returned to Sarah Talbert standing on the boardwalk in front of the store and pleaded with him not to go.

Wade could still hear her words about this being a stupid promise, knowing she did not understand and probably never would. Mr. Grimes understood the hate he held inside for these men, which showed plainly on his face in the library the day Wade left. Sarah would never understand, and Wade knew that Emmett would be sitting by this fire if it were himself they had buried. Pushing such things out of his mind, he checked on the horses and then fixed something to eat.

His tin dish cup and small frying pan cleaned and put away, he lay down, wrapped himself in his blanket, rested his head on his saddle, and stared into the fire. He thought of Sheriff Bowlen's advice about going back to the Circle T and letting the law handle the killing of his friend. It was sound advice, but he knew the law would not seek revenge for Emmett the way he would. He closed his eyes, waited for sleep, and knew Sheriff Bowlen's advice, while being good advice, was the advice he could not follow.

Two

Wade opened his eyes, pushed his black hat back that covered his face, and sat up, feeling stiff from sleeping on the hard ground. He tossed his blanket off, got up, stretched the stiffness from his body, and built a small fire. Seeing there was still a half-pot of coffee inside the coffee pot and not being a wasteful person, Wade set it next to the fire. While the coffee warmed, he cut a few strips of bacon, wishing he had a couple of eggs and a biscuit to go with it.

Breakfast eaten, he sat back and enjoyed a cup of coffee while his mind turned to Emmett and the deep loss he still felt. He hated the men that killed his friend and wanted to see them dead, yet he wondered if he had the nerve to kill them. He recalled Sheriff Seth Bowlen's last words when he told the sheriff that he was no gunfighter, saying: *It'd be better if you were.* Wade knew that was true and wished he were braver or meaner because no matter how much he hated these men, he didn't know if he had what it would take to kill them. He tossed what coffee was in his cup onto the small fire, stood, pushed dirt over it with his boot, and packed up the packhorse. After he saddled his mare and climbed onto the saddle, he rode along the stream, following the trail of the men he hunted.

It was quiet and peaceful as he followed the tracks along the stream into the foothills toward the tall Rocky Mountains. The morning sun felt warm, yet the mountain air was crisp and clean. A slight breeze played in the trees as sparrows darted here and there, chirping their morning songs mixed with the horse's hooves on the bank of the stream. He pulled up next to a pine tree to let the horses drink when he was startled by a large crow springing from a nearby limb, calling out its warning. His hand quickly found the butt of his pistol, then, feeling a little foolish at being frightened by a bird, he watched the crow disappear up the canyon. But he also knew that he was on the trail of four men that would kill him for no reason other than pure enjoyment. Becoming more vigilant after the crow incident, he nudged his mare deeper into the forest.

The tracks he followed left the muddy stream bank and disappeared into the underbrush. Fearful he might ride into a trap, he pulled the mare up, placed his hand on the butt of his pistol, and glanced around into the soft, dim light of the trees. The soft breeze made its way through the branches of the fir trees, and an occasional bird sang out. Other than that, it was quiet. He got down and searched for the tracks he had been following. Several minutes passed when he stepped out of the trees onto a narrow trail. Wondering its destination as it disappeared into the trees further up, he turned and looked back along the trail to an opening in the trees that gave a beautiful view of rolling hills and the vast Colorado Plains.

After a few moments of enjoying the scenery, he looked down at several tracks in the dirt and wondered how often the trail was used and by who. He bent over and started looking for the turned hoof and the imperfection in the horseshoe. It took several minutes before he found what he was looking for, then he climbed up on the mare and looked around. Nudging the mare into a walk, he tugged at the packhorse and followed the tracks along the narrow winding trail into the canyon of pine and aspen trees.

An hour passed, and suddenly the tracks left the narrow trail and disappeared into the tree's thick underbrush and dark shadows. Wade climbed down, studied the tracks that led into the forest, and wondered if they knew he was following them. Feeling uneasy, he put his right hand on the butt of his pistol and glanced around the thick forest. The eerie stillness held the slight breeze passing through the trees and a few birds chirping. A lonely crow that he couldn't see cawed out, and a curious red squirrel stopped in the middle of the trail, stood on its hind legs looking at him, and then disappeared up the tree. The mare snorted, breaking the silence, then shook her head, rattling her reins. Wade spoke softly to the horse and rubbed her neck as he looked up and down the narrow trail, fearful that the four men may be hiding in the shadows. Cautiously he led his mare and packhorse into the thick underbrush and followed the four men's horse tracks that left broken branches of shrubbery and trampled grass. As Wade walked deeper into the forest, he soon lost the tracks in the mixture of grass, pine needles, and pinecones. He stopped, tied the mare and packhorse to a tree, drew his pistol, and began to look for the tracks.

He had walked but a few yards when he came to a clearing with a small cabin about a hundred yards to his right. Stepping behind a large tree, he watched a thin line of smoke float lazily from its chimney and wondered if the cabin belonged to the men he had been tracking. He stared at the cabin for several moments, glanced around, and then stepped away from the tree and carefully made his way toward the cabin, using trees and bushes for cover. A few yards from the cabin, he stopped behind a large fir tree and watched for some sign of life. There was a small empty stable big enough for two horses a few yards from the cabin. Looking back at the cabin door, he thought, if the owners were gone, why would they leave a fire burning? Filled with curiosity about the cabin, the four men, and their horses that were nowhere in sight, he made his way to another tree where he could see the front of the cabin, the door, and another window. The door was slightly ajar, and two shutters of a nearby window moved slightly in the soft breeze. It was quiet but for the slight breeze and an occasional crow or sparrow. It was too quiet, he thought, and why was the door slightly open? He looked back over his shoulder at his horses, and after a few moments of arguing with himself about leaving, he turned and looked at the cabin, wondering what he would find inside.

He looked at the forty-four Colt he held in his right hand, then at the cabin's open door, knowing people do not just get up and leave their homes with a burning fire and the door open. Not unless they were in one hell of a hurry. The shutter moved slightly from the small breeze, taking his eyes away from the door, and when he looked back at the door, a small yellow dog stood in the doorway whining as if hurt. The dog looked in his direction, backed up two steps, barked at him, and then disappeared into the house.

Sensing something was wrong inside the cabin, Wade waited several moments to see if anyone would come out to see why the dog barked. When no one did, he decided to take a chance and investigate. He moved cautiously from tree to tree and soon stood beside the cabin next to the small, covered porch. The little yellow dog came out of the house, looked up at him, whimpered, and went back inside with its tail between its legs.

Carefully, Wade stepped onto the porch with his back against the wall and moved to the open door. The dog came out of the cabin again, looked up at Wade, and whined. Wade noticed blood on its face and chest, fearing something terrible waited for him. As the dog disappeared inside, Wade cocked the hammer of his pistol, moved the door open with the barrel of his gun, and looked inside. In the dim light of the cabin, he saw the dark image of the dog sitting next to what appeared to be a small body. He stepped inside and quickly moved into the shadows with his back against the inner wall. A small fire in the fireplace filled the room with a dim orange light covering the body of a small boy of seven or eight years lying on his stomach, his face in a pool of blood the dog was lapping up.

Wade wanted to yell at the dog to stop but feared someone might be waiting in the shadows with a gun. Glancing around the room, he wondered who would harm a child, and then noticing a partially open door, he pushed the dog away from the blood with his boot, stepped over it, and slowly walked across the room of creaking boards. Pausing next to the door that was slightly ajar, Wade glanced back at the dog licking the boy's face. Wishing it would stop, he pushed the door open with the barrel of his pistol and looked inside. Shutters covered the only window, and although the room was dim, he could see it was a mess. The chest of drawers was lying on its back, its empty drawers on the floor, and clothing was everywhere. Surprised at seeing a woman's nude body lying on the bed, he softly whispered to himself, *"What the hell happened here?"* He never saw the man sitting in a chair at the foot of the bed until he stepped into the room. Startled, Wade turned his pistol toward the man. "Mister?" he softly said. The man never moved, and then Wade saw his head was tilted back, arms and feet tied to the chair.

He wanted to get some light in the room, so he walked to the window, pushed the shutters open to let more light in, and then returned to the bed where the nude woman lay with her wrists and ankles tied to the bed's four bedposts. Leaning closer to the woman, Wade looked at her bruised and bloody face. Feeling sorry for her, he reached out and touched the side of her neck for a pulse. Not finding one, Wade noticed the bruises on her neck and imagined the terror she must have suffered. Wondering if the four men he was after could have done this, he stepped back, knowing that whoever it was, made the husband watch. The man had been severely beaten, and his throat cut so severely that it almost decapitated him. Feeling the need to get out of the cabin, he hurried out of the room, picked up the dog, carried him outside, and closed the door.

He put the dog down, rushed to the edge of the porch, leaned against a porch post, and vomited while the little dog clawed at the cabin door, wanting to get back inside. Wade had never seen a dead person before, let alone three, and wanted to run to his horse and ride back to the Circle T. Looking west at the sun heading for the horizon and knowing it would be dark soon, he looked at the door, thinking he needed to bury this family. Standing, he spat the foul taste of vomit from his mouth, stepped off the porch, and headed for his horses.

Wade put the horses in the small stable, unsaddled the mare, unpacked the packhorse, and gave them what little hay there was. He stepped out of the small stable, looked down at the tracks of several horses, knelt, and found the turned front hoof and flaw in another shoe. Wade stood and followed them a short distance to where they disappeared up the canyon. Wondering if they did this or found the same thing he did, he returned to the cabin's grisly scene. After several minutes of rummaging around, he found a narrow rope, picked up the dog, and tied him to a tree. While the dog barked, whined, and tugged at the rope, Wade went back inside and covered the three bodies with blankets. Feeling nauseous again, he hurried outside and stood at the edge of the porch, fighting the urge to throw up.

Moments passed before he turned and looked at the cabin door in memory of what was inside. Hearing the dog whine, Wade watched it pull at the rope, feeling sorry for him. He did not want to go back inside for a while, so he gathered some firewood from the pile next to the house, and while the little yellow dog whined and growled, he built a fire. Having no appetite, he made a pot of coffee, poured a cup, and sat back against a tree, exhausted. The small yellow dog settled down, laid close to Wade with its head on its paws, and stared at the cabin door, whimpering. Feeling sorry for the little dog, Wade petted it while he drank his coffee and softly said, "Sorry, little fella, but you can't go back in there."

Not hungry, Wade unwrapped the last of the bacon, smelled it to make sure it was still good, and fed it to the dog before digging two graves with a shovel he found in the stable. After digging two graves, Wade returned to the cabin and wrapped the small boy in the blanket he had laid over him earlier. He went into the bedroom, closed the lifeless eyes of the woman, and wrapped her in a blanket. As he lifted her, he thought she wasn't a very big woman, carried her outside, and gently placed her body in one of the two graves. Wade returned to the cabin for the boy, put him in the grave next to his mother then returned to the cabin for the husband.

After spreading a blanket on the floor, he took out his hunting knife, knelt next to the chair, and cut the ropes from the man's hands and feet. Then, as he gently laid him upon the blanket, he looked into the bloody, lifeless eyes with the same eerie-clouded color as his wife's. It was then that he saw that somebody had cut his eyelids off. He had heard stories of Indians doing that to captives when they tied them to anthills in the hot sun and knew that whoever did this wanted to make sure the man watched his wife being raped, beaten, and strangled. Wade felt sorry for the man as he wrapped him in the blanket, carried him outside, and placed him in the second grave. After filling both graves with dirt, he said a small prayer and went back inside. He stood in the dim light for several minutes, looking at the overturned furniture, broken dishes, and clothing strewn all over the floor. The fire had long since died, and the room was getting chilly. Wade turned away from the scene, walked outside, closed the door, and after making sure it was secure, he wondered what difference it made.

Standing on the porch, he saw that the sun was behind the mountains now, and it would be dark and chilly soon. Looking at the little dog tied to the tree staring back at him, he felt sorry for the little mutt. Stepping off the porch, he walked to the tree, sat down, leaned back against his saddle, and petted the dog. Noticing the night had swallowed up the cabin, he drank his coffee and thought about the family he had buried. Feeling the weight of the day, he placed some wood on the fire, lay down, covered up with his blanket, and closed his eyes. As tired as he was, Wade could not find the sleep he so desperately wanted and needed. The fire was a comfort, as was the little yellow dog that lay beside him, but this was a terrible place, and he wanted the night to pass quickly so he could feel the warm sun of a new day.

The graves he had dug, and the wooden crosses he had crudely made were barely visible in the dim light of the campfire, giving them a ghostly appearance. The little yellow dog whined for the boy and looked at where Wade had buried him, and he felt sorry for the little dog. He petted him and decided he would take the dog with him in the morning, hoping he could find someone in a town who would give him a good home.

Wade opened his eyes, raised his head, looked for the dog, and saw him lying on the grave of the boy and the boy's mother. The rope he had used to tie the dog to the tree was now a little shorter, evidence of the dog's determination and chewing ability. The dog raised his head, looked at Wade, whimpered, and laid his head back down on his front paws, looking sad with the rest of the chewed rope still around his neck. Wade thought about coffee and breakfast but decided he wanted to get away from this terrible place, so he saddled his mare, packed up the packhorse, and picked up the dog. While it barked and nipped at him, he held it tight and climbed into the saddle. Once settled, he grabbed the dog by the nape of the neck and looked into its dark, sad eyes. "Listen, little fella. I can't just leave you here. Some hungry bobcat or wolf would have you for their dinner, or you'd starve to death."

The dog barked and whined for a moment, but then, as if he knew, he put his head on Wade's arm, whimpered, and relaxed. Wade looked down at him and wondered if dogs cried. Then he nudged the mare into a walk, and without looking back, they rode the trail that led up the canyon.

Three

Roscoe's Creek

The town of Roscoe's Creek took its name after Roscoe Givvens, the man who built a small cabin and settled along the creek after finding a small amount of gold back in 1852. The town lay in a small valley between the mountains and snowed in most of the winter. People rushed in, dug mines, panned for gold in the creek, and the town sprung up. Eventually, the gold played out, some folks left broke and poor, while others stayed in small shacks on either side of town and managed a modest living. Some turned to farming small plots of land and sold their seasonal crops to the stores, while others still searched for the mother lode they believed was still there.

If the weather permitted, the stage line went through twice a week, bringing mail and an occasional customer for the restaurants or the hotels. As Wade rode up the narrow dirt street, he aroused the curiosity of several people who followed from a safe distance. He thought they were simply curious at first, but as the following grew, he noticed they looked angry. He stopped in front of a sign over the boardwalk that read "Sheriff." Climbing down, he glanced around at the angry faces and wondered what had their dander up. Holding the small dog in his left arm, he tied the horses to the hitching rail and walked up the steps to the boardwalk while his right hand moved to the butt of his gun. He paused at the sheriff's office door, glanced around at the angry faces, opened the door, and stepped inside.

A man sat behind a small desk looking close to fifty and overweight. His brown hair was thinning and showed a lot of gray, as did his handlebar mustache. The man's expression was curious as he pointed to the dog. "Nice little dog you have there."

Wade heard the door open behind him, turned, and saw several men step inside, looking upset over something. He turned and looked at the sheriff. "Picked him up a few miles from here."

The men stood by the door, talking to one another in voices too low for Wade to understand the words clearly, but he knew they were talking about him. The sheriff told them to keep their mouths shut or go back outside, and then he asked Wade what his name was.

Wade glanced at the men who stood just inside the door and then at the sheriff. "Name's Wade Garrison."

The sheriff nodded to one of the three chairs in front of his desk. "Have a seat, Mr. Garrison. I'm Sheriff Frank Wells, and I'm just a little curious about that little dog you're holding."

Wade sat down, took off his hat, glanced at the men by the door, then set his hat on the edge of the sheriff's desk. While the men behind him whispered to one another, he told the sheriff about following four men who had killed his friend Emmett Spears in Harper. He lost their trail in the rocky flats near the town of Sisters, where he spent the night but picked them up again the next day. Then he lost them for a while when they left a narrow trail in the mountains. He paused, turned to look at the men who were now quiet, and then looked at the sheriff. "I followed the tracks through the trees to a cabin." He paused, looked down at the dog, and recalled what he found inside. "Someone had killed the entire family."

That brought a flood of angry, low whispers from the men behind him. Then one of them asked, "What're we gonna do about this, Frank?"

"Keep quiet!" yelled the sheriff.

Wade felt a little nervous about the men standing behind him, so he stood closer to the window where he had a clear view of them and pushed his black duster back away from his pistol.

"Quiet down," yelled Wells. Then he looked from the men to Wade. "What happened?"

Wade glanced at the men. "I don't know what happened. I found the boy on the floor. Someone had cut his throat, and this little dog was licking the blood from his face." He heard angry whispers from the men at the door and turned to the sheriff. "The woman had been beaten and more than likely raped and then strangled."

Sheriff Frank Wells looked disgusted and sad. "What about Charles Barton?"

Wade told him how he found him, covered them in blankets, and buried them in a small clearing not far from the cabin.

Wells stared down at his desk, and then he looked at Wade. "You think these four men you're trailing are the ones who did this to the Bartons?"

Wade shrugged. "Can't say for sure, but I believe so. Their tracks led away from the cabin."

The men who stood near the door got noisy.

"Shut up!" yelled Wells.

"Someone's got to pay!" yelled one of the men.

The sheriff scowled at the man he called Gil, told him to take it easy, and then looked at Wade. "What makes you think these four you're trailing killed the Barton family?"

A voice in the crowd said, "He's making the damn story up, Sheriff."

"That's right," yelled another man.

Sheriff Wells looked at the two men. "I said shut up. All of you."

Wade looked at the angry faces and was suddenly afraid he was about to be arrested for the killings. "As I done told the sheriff, these four killed a friend of mine. I tracked them from Harper, and their tracks were at the cabin."

"He's lying to you, Frank." A voice yelled.

Wells looked angry. "I told you, boys, to shut up. If you can't do that, get your asses out of my office." He stood with a mean look. "I mean it now, damn it."

Wade looked at Sheriff Wells. "Look, Sheriff, I've been following these men for three days after leaving Sisters. I work for Tolliver Grimes at the Circle T east of Harper. I tracked these men to Sisters, where I talked to Sheriff Seth Bowlen to see if he'd seen them hanging around and then spent the night." He paused. "If I had killed this family, do you think I'd ride in here carrying this little dog and then come in here and tell you about the killings?" The room filled with inaudible words again as Wade turned and glanced at each man's face while his hand moved to the butt of his pistol.

The sheriff took notice of that, told everyone to be quiet, and looked at Wade. "That might be so young, fella, but Charles Barton and his family were nice people, and we don't want you riding out of town until we've had a chance to find out just who you are."

"You think I killed them folks?" asked Wade while he wondered how in the hell he was going to get out of this mess.

The room went silent as the sheriff stood and walked from behind the desk, drew his gun, and asked Wade to remove his hand from the butt of his pistol. "No, son, I don't, but I need to send someone back to the cabin and then Sisters to verify your story before this group of fine upstanding citizens hangs you."

"Shit, Sheriff," Wade said with an angry look. "By then, those four will be long gone. We need to get on their trail before it gets cold."

"I'll just take that gun, young fella," said the sheriff.

Wade took his hand away and let the sheriff take his pistol from its holster, wishing he had stayed away from the town of Roscoe's Creek.

The sheriff looked at the others. "Any of you brave boys up for riding out after these four?"

Gil was the only one that said he was up to it.

The sheriff smiled with a slight chuckle as he looked at the rest. "Didn't think as much." He turned to Wade. "What you say is probably the truth, but as you can see, this brave group at the door ain't exactly excited about trailing four men when they have you." The sheriff returned to his desk, put Wade's gun in a drawer, and sat down in his creaky chair. "You can stay here in my jail until we get word as to whether or not you're who you say you are, and if the story of what happened back in Harper checks out, you'll be on your way."

Wade looked at the sheriff. "Until then, I'm under arrest for something I never did?"

Wells smiled. "Let's say you're a guest of Roscoe's Creek for a few days. We'll take your horses to the livery, put them away with some fresh hay, and you can bed down here." He grinned as he gestured with both hands. "Food's free, and it ain't half bad."

"Wonderful," said Wade with an unhappy look as he turned to the group of men at the door and realized he had no real chance to get out of the building anyway. Doing the only thing he could, Wade sat down in the chair with the little yellow dog on his lap and looked back at the others. "Not that I distrust anyone in this room, Sheriff, but I'd like my stuff brought in here if you don't mind."

Sheriff Wells chuckled and then told everyone except Gil and another man to get out. After the others left, he asked the two to take care

38

of the horses after they brought Wade's belongings inside. Wells leaned forward and spoke in a low voice. "I'm doing this for your own good, Son. Charles and his family were fine people and well-liked around here, especially by Gil. When word gets out about that family, I don't want some idiot who doesn't know the whole story to take a shot at you." He looked out the window. "It won't take long to verify your story. Then no one will be confused and start taking potshots at you." He opened the top drawer, took out a ring of keys, walked to the nearest cell, unlocked the door, opened it, and grinned. "You can stay in this one."

Wade smiled. "Dog needs to take a shit, Sheriff."

Wells looked at the dog. "Forgot about him," he said thoughtfully. "Go on and take him outside. After he does his business, he can spend the night with you. We'll figure out what to do with him in the morning."

Wade and the dog walked toward the door just as Gil came in carrying Wade's saddle and rifle. He looked at Wade with a questioning expression, then at Sheriff Wells.

"Dog's gotta shit," said Wells.

Gil looked at the dog, then at Wade, and then at Sheriff Wells. "Man's got a Sharps."

"That so?" said the sheriff looking interested. "You plan on doing some long-distance shooting, Mr. Garrison?" Before Wade could answer, Sheriff Wells said, "I'll just take care of that until you leave." After looking it over and making sure it was unloaded, he placed it in the corner behind his desk and turned to Gil. "You up for a ride?"

Gil shrugged, looking uncertain. "Spect so, want me to ride over to Sisters?"

"That'd be the idea after you check out Barton's cabin. When can you leave?"

"Right now, I reckon. That is right after I take care of this here fella's stock, saddle my horse, and tell the missus where it is I'm off to."

"Let Harry finish up," said Wells. "Give Sheriff Bowlen my regards. I'll expect you back in a couple of days."

A couple of days thought a disappointed Wade.

Gil nodded, gave Wade a quick disapproving look, and headed for the door. Wade, the dog, and the sheriff followed him outside so the dog could do his business.

Wade walked back inside the jailhouse, settled into his cell, and wished he had ridden past Roscoe's Creek.

As the little dog got comfortable on the foot of the cot, Wells closed the door but left it unlocked. "I don't think you're the type to try and run off, Mr. Garrison." Then he grinned. "I'd only have to come after you, and that'd piss me off."

Four

The day slowly passed without incident while Wade and Sheriff Wells played checkers, drank coffee, and talked. During the evening of the second day, while they played their fifth game of checkers, Wade asked Sheriff Wells how he ended up in Roscoe's Creek.

Wells was not pleased with the question, especially about 'ending up,' because that sounded like the end of the line. And maybe that's what it was for the sheriff, who didn't want to admit it. The Sheriff overcame his resentment and told Wade that he was born in West Virginia and left home at fifteen. Eventually, he became interested in the law, and while passing through Omaha a year or two later, he got his first job as a part-time deputy. Sheriff Wells grinned and said the rest of his time was spent shoveling the shit out of horse stalls at the livery and cleaning up after drunks at the saloons and whorehouses. "I didn't mind that so much," he said with a grin. "Them whores were always nice to me."

He continued his story of spending a couple of years in Omaha, a small town in Kansas, where he became a full-time deputy and later as a sheriff in a small town in Texas along the Red River. From there, he moved west to New Mexico, hiring on as a scout for the Army tracking Indians with an old tracker named James Cross, who taught Wells everything there was to know about tracking. "Cross was captured by some Comanche's tortured and killed." He paused in memory. "After a few years of scouting for the Army, I quit and passed through here a few years back. I was tired and broke, and they needed a sheriff, so I took the job and stayed on." He looked at Wade. "Roscoe's a quiet little place. Not much happens around here." He paused for a moment. "Oh, we get a drunk or a jealous husband chasing his wife's lover now and again, but

41

other than that, it's a pretty quiet little place." He drew a deep breath, let out a long soft sigh, and smiled. "Most men like me end up in a place like Roscoe's Creek."

Wade smiled. "Sounds like there could be worse places." Wade took a liking to Sheriff Frank Wells, and the feeling was mutual.

"I'm tired, Son," uttered Wells. "So, if you don't mind us not playing another game of checkers, I think I'll turn in."

"Alright by me, Sheriff," said Wade. "I'm tired of losing anyway."

Wells laughed, stood from his chair, walked around this desk to the front door, locked it, and pulled the shades down over the windows. After saying goodnight, he walked into a room in the rear of the jail and went to bed. Wade walked into his cell, closed the door, sat on the bed, and thought about Sheriff Wells' stories. The little dog jumped on the foot of the bed, curled into a ball, and closed his eyes. Wade smiled, glad he brought the dog with him, closed his eyes, and thought of Sarah Talbert.

Wade passed the time in his cell sitting on his cot petting the little dog when Gil walked in the door, followed by Sheriff Seth Bowlen from Sisters. Sheriff Wells got up from his desk and hurried to greet Bowlen as if they were old friends. As they shook hands and said hello, Bowlen said they'd have been here sooner, but he had to take care of a few things in Sisters, and then they stopped at the cabin. Seeing Wade, he walked across the room to the cell and grinned. "I see you're enjoying the hospitality of Roscoe's Creek."

Wade's expression was despair as he stood and walked to the unlocked but closed cell door.

Seth's smile left his face. "A few days after you left, a family a few miles northeast of Sisters were murdered much the way the family Gil here said you found a few days back." He looked at Frank Wells. "Seems these boys Wade here's been trailing are mucho mean, my friend."

Wade thought of Sarah and the Talbert's. "Do you know the name of the family?"

"Rumwell, I believe," replied Bowlen while opening the cell door. He looked past him to the saddle and other things heaped in the corner of the cell. "Gather your belongings, Son. We've got some riding to do."

"We?" asked Wade, looking surprised.

"That's right, Mr. Garrison," said Seth. "I aim to get these four before they kill anyone else." Then he glanced around the cell. "I don't see that Sharps of yours."

Sheriff Wells gestured to the corner behind his desk. "I've been keeping it safe for Mr. Garrison. Along with that nice forty-four Colt he's carrying."

Bowlen turned, saw the big gun against the wall in the corner, and looked at Wade. "Well, go get it." Then he looked at Sheriff Frank Wells. "You coming?"

"Wish I could, Seth, but I'd just slow you boys up."

"Nonsense," replied Bowlen. "We're tracking these fellas, not racing with them. Besides, I don't know anyone who can track any better'n you." He looked at Wade with a grin. "Frank here spent a lot of years tracking Indians for the Army."

"He told me while beating me at checkers." Wade was not sure he wanted a bunch of people riding with him.

Sheriff Wells looked embarrassed as he grinned. "I tracked Indians before I knew better. Besides, a hell of a lot of them got away."

"You're too sensitive, Frank," said Bowlen. "You gonna tag along or not?"

Wells scratched his head as he looked around the office and then grinned. "Shit, there ain't much going on here anyway. You may as well help catch these bastards. I'll have to tell the mayor so's he can tell old Tom Hughes to take care of things while I'm gone."

Gil Robinson had the look of a small boy about to be left behind. "Mind if I tag along, Frank?"

Wade felt frustrated, thinking, '*Another one.*'

"It's alright with me," said Frank. "But this ain't my party. It'd be up to Seth there." He turned to Bowlen. "Gil's a pretty fair tracker himself, and with two of us looking, we might find their tracks a mite faster."

Bowlen thought about that. "An extra gun would come in handy. Get yer stuff. We'll meet up at the livery."

Gil grinned like a fool as he hurried to the door, where he stopped and turned. "Frank, my horse is plum tuckered after that trip to Sisters and back. Mind if I grab a fresh mount at the livery?"

Wells thought for a moment. "Tell Pete to let you have a horse, and I'll see the mayor pays him out of the town funds."

Gil grinned and said he would take his horse home, tell his wife where they were off to, gather his belongings, and meet them at the livery.

Wade asked what they should do about the little yellow dog. Gil looked at the dog lying in the cell on the end of the bed. "I'll take him to my place." Then he walked into the cell. "My Annie and little Annabelle can take care of him until we get back."

As Gil walked past with the dog, Frank looked at Bowlen. "You need another mount?"

Seth shook his head. "Mine's fine. We're tracking these boys, and I don't plan on running my horse into the ground in the process."

Wade looked from Wells to Bowlen. "I trailed them four heading south until I reached Roscoe's Creek.

Frank looked at Wade. "You telling me they rode past this town?"

"About a half-mile close," said Wade.

The four men rode out of Roscoe's Creek, believing the four men they were tracking were probably heading into New Mexico or Arizona, and rode southwest. After Wade explained the marks on one horse's shoe and how the other had a turned hoof to Frank Wells and Gil Robinson, they rode on ahead, riding in crisscross patterns looking for the tracks while Bowlen and Wade handled the two packhorses. It was slow going and took most of the day before Wells finally found the tracks, whistled as he waved, pointed southwest, indicating their direction, and then waited.

After Wade caught up with Wells, he dismounted and knelt to one knee. "Same tracks, alright." He pointed to one of the horse tracks. "There's the mark on the left side of the shoe."

Wells looked riled. "You think I picked up someone else's trail?"

Wade looked regretful, stood, and looked at Frank. "Thought no such thing, Sheriff. I just wanted to see for myself. I've been after these men for a while."

Seth grinned. "Don't be so damn thin-skinned, Frank."

Sheriff Wells grinned, looking apologetic. "Sorry if I misunderstood. It looks like they changed direction, and maybe they are heading over Raton Pass."

"Alright," said Bowlen, "you boys have a trail to follow. Let's get after them."

They rode until it was too dark to see the tracks and made camp along the Arkansas River. While Gil tended to the horses, Wade relieved the packhorses of their burden for the night and tethered them. Bowlen and Frank Wells gathered firewood for the night, and then they all settled in for beans and coffee. Wade sat in silence, glanced at the others, and considered the men in whose company he now traveled. He already knew Seth Bowlen's reputation and heard Frank Wells' story, so he asked Gil Robinson how he came to be in Roscoe's Creek.

Gil Robinson was a fifty-year-old man with a robust chest and big hairy arms. Like Wells and Seth Bowlen, his face was tanned and leathery. His once curly brown hair had turned a little gray, the same as the beard on his face. He had a friendly smile of yellow teeth, and dark eyes under bushy eyebrows. Wade recalled their first meeting in Roscoe's Creek, not liking the man very much. But now, as they traveled together, he liked what he saw. Gil settled back against his saddle and told of fighting for the Union during the war, then scouting for the Army back in sixty-six and sixty-seven. He smiled at Wade. "That is until I met a young, widowed schoolteacher with a small daughter in Canon City." He went on to tell that the Army had stopped for supplies, and Gil fell in love, quit the Army, stayed on in Canon City, and took a job in a store so he could get to know the schoolteacher. He grinned at Wade and said it was something he hated, but it kept him close to the widow Annie. "One thing led to another," he said. "Before I knew it, we were married and moved to Roscoe's Creek, where Annie began teaching school while I did odd jobs." He also panned for gold and silver, finding enough that made his time looking profitable.

During a moment of silence, Bowlen put his head on his saddle. "Interesting story Gil and I appreciate hearing it, but we've a hard ride ahead of us tomorrow, so best we all get some sleep."

Five

By daylight the next morning, Wade and the others had eaten breakfast, broke camp, and were on the trail of the killers. That trail led them into a dry creek bed that curved in and out of the foothills at the base of the Rocky Mountains. Sheriff Wells rode point with his eyes focused on the tracks in the sandy creek bed where it emptied into the vast Colorado plains. He paused to take in its greatness and beauty, then rode up a small hill for a better view before riding back down the hill into the dry creek bed. Dismounting, he waved and waited for the others, and as they rode up, he nodded toward the hill and pointed. "Farmhouse just over that hill."

The others quickly dismounted, left their horses in the creek bed, and followed Wells up the small hill. They stopped just below the top, knelt, and looked at the farmhouse barn and corral about four hundred yards in the distance.

Frank took his long glass out of his saddlebags, ran up the hill, put it to his eye, and looked at the house. "Looks deserted."

Bowlen pointed toward the corral. "How about the corral?"

"Don't see anything moving down there."

Wade became worried and thought of the cabin. "Same as the Barton place."

Bowlen stood. "Whatever happened here is over." He turned and hurried down the hill to his horse, drew his pistol, and walked back up the hill leading his horse. "Let's see what the hell's happened down there."

Wade and the others got their horses drew their guns, and as they walked toward the peaceful setting and in range of rifle fire, they kept their eyes on the farmhouse windows and barn. After a few minutes, they stood at the steps of the front porch staring at the front door and windows. Their horses became impatient smelling water in the trough next to a hand pump, so Wade led his horse and packhorse to the trough so they could drink.

Seth Bowlen told Gil to mind the horses, stepped onto the porch, and called out. "Hello in the house! I'm Sheriff Seth Bowlen from Sisters!" Getting no response, Seth walked to the window and looked inside, but the curtain was drawn.

Wade stepped onto the porch, thought of what they may find inside, and waited to see what Seth would do.

Bowlen stepped away from the window to the door and yelled, "We're coming in! Don't go doing anything foolish! We don't want to hurt anyone, and we sure as hell don't want to get ourselves shot!" He stood with his back against the wall, gave Wade a look, lifted the latch, and gently pushed the door open to the sound of creaking hinges. With his back against the wall, he cautiously stuck his head around the doorjamb and peered into the dimly lit room. He stepped inside, and as his eyes adjusted to the dim light of the room, he saw a closed door across the room and stairs that led to the second floor. Wade stepped inside to the sound of crunching, broken glass under his feet and stood next to Seth.

Sheriff Wells stepped on the broken glass as he rushed past Seth and stood next to Wade.

Wade looked down at the floor, saw several small broken glass figurines, and thought of the Barton's.

Bowlen gestured to the windows. "Open them curtains and let some light in."

Wells pulled the curtains back, letting the room fill with light.

"Place looks like a tornado had blown through," said Seth. He glanced around the room that was in disarray as he walked across the floor and opened the closed door. The kitchen was in the same mess as the other room, with breakfast dishes, coffee cups, saucers, and food lying on the floor. A single coffee cup lay overturned on the table, contents in a puddle on the floor.

Wells was standing next to Seth. "I count five plates." He walked to the table and touched some of the food. "Cold."

Wade moved to the iron stove and held his hand above it. "Same here." He looked at Seth. "Place has been like this a while."

Seth nodded, walked back into the living room, stood at the base of the staircase, and looked up at the second floor, afraid of what they may find. As he put his right foot on the first step, it creaked, causing him to pause and look at Wells. "Check on Gil." Then he looked at Wade. "Let's you and me see what's up these stairs."

Wade remembered what he had found at the Barton place and wasn't too happy about going upstairs. He followed Seth to the top, where he stood in the quiet hall and looked at the closed doors of three rooms. Seth gestured down the hall with his gun, walked past Wade, and stood next to the door with his back against the wall. Looking at Wade as Seth turned the doorknob, pushed the door open, peered inside, and whispered, "Oh my word." He stepped into the room, stood in the doorway, and softly uttered, "Good Jesus."

Wade looked past Seth into the room, and as he stepped around him, he saw a man he presumed to be the husband on his knees, tied to the end of the bed facing his dead wife. His face was bloody, and Wade knew someone had cut off his eyelids. The front of his gray shirt was covered in dried blood from the cut along his throat. On the bed lay a woman with her face bruised and bloody. Wade presumed she had been raped the same as the Barton woman and fought the need to vomit as he had at the cabin.

Bowlen walked over to the bed and touched her neck with two fingers checking for a pulse. Finding none, he looked at Wade and shook his head.

Seth took a long look at the couple and then at the clothes strewn on the floor, along with empty drawers.

Wade turned away. "I'll check the other rooms." Then he stepped into the hall.

Not wanting to remain in the room, Seth turned from the gruesome scene, followed Wade, and closed the door.

Wade put his hand on the doorknob of the second room, turned the knob, slowly opened the door, and looked inside. He could tell the room belonged to a boy and was in total disarray like the other rooms. Relieved at not finding a body, he turned and walked out of the room.

Bowlen reached the third door across the hall and waited for Wade. Seth reached for the knob, cautiously opened the door, and stepped inside, finding the room like the others. The mattress was propped against the wall, and girl's clothing was scattered everywhere. There was so much of it they almost didn't see the young boy lying on the floor. Seth walked over, knelt, and moved the clothing covering most of the boy's body. "He's been shot in the chest."

Wade leaned against the door jamb, feeling sorry for the boy. Then he turned to Seth. "Wonder where the girls are?"

Seth stood and pointed to the boy. "He's got a hunting knife in his hand." He glanced around the room. "From the looks of things, I'd say this boy tried to protect his sister."

"Seth," said Wade. "It looks to me like there may have been two girls."

"What makes you think so?"

Wade bent down, picked up two pieces of clothing, and held them up for Seth to see. "Different sizes."

"Shit," said Bowlen as he looked down at the boy, then turned and hurried out of the room.

Wade looked at the boy, dropped the clothing, and followed Seth down the stairs. Stopping at the bottom, he asked, "Where are you going?"

Seth never answered for fear of what he may find inside the barn.

Frank Wells walked out of the kitchen, stood next to Wade, and watched Seth. "What the hell's going on?"

Wade quickly explained what they had found upstairs and the missing girls.

Seth stood at the front door and hollered outside for Gil to check the barn.

A few minutes later, Gil stepped out of the barn and hollered, "Someone had shot and killed two mules."

"Nothing else?" yelled Bowlen as he leaned against the door jamb and felt relieved.

Gil looked puzzled as he walked toward the front porch and shook his head no.

Seth told him what they found upstairs, then said, "They've taken the two young girls." He stood away from the door jamb, stepped back into the house, and kicked a chair that lay on its side across the room in anger. "My guess is they'll try and sell them in Mexico or to some Indians along the way."

Gil stepped inside, looking worried. "How old you think the little girls are?"

"Not sure," said Bowlen. "But from the clothes we found, they can't be very old. Five or six, maybe seven."

Wade looked at Seth with an angry and determined face. "Well, we best get after them."

Seth walked to the door, placed his left hand high on the door jamb, and looked across the yard at a small group of cottonwood trees. After several moments he turned with a sad look. "We've got to bury

49

them, poor folks, upstairs." He looked at Wells. "Wade and me will stay and do the burying. You and Gil take the packhorses and keep after these bastards. We'll catch up as soon as we can."

"Wells looked at Gil. "Let's go."

As the two walked past Bowlen, he grabbed Frank by the arm. "If you find them, you wait for us, you hear me? Wait for Wade and me. These are some mean bastards."

"Alright, Seth." Sheriff Wells walked across the porch, stepped off, took the lead rope to Wade's packhorse, mounted his horse, and waited for Gil. As soon as Robinson secured the second packhorse and climbed onto his horse, the two men rode south. Bowlen walked to the edge of the porch and watched Wells and Gil as they rode past the barn into the flatlands, chased by a small cloud of dust. A few minutes passed before he turned and told Wade to see if he could find a couple of shovels in the barn. "You start digging the graves while I take care of things upstairs." Then he walked back across the porch and went inside.

Wade headed for the barn, filled with the fear of finding more families before they could stop these crazy bastards.

Bowlen wrapped the bodies in blankets and went outside to help Wade dig the three graves, and when they finished, they carried the bodies outside, placed them in the graves, and covered them with dirt. Seth said a short prayer put on his hat, picked up a shovel and headed for the barn.

"Where you off to?"

"To bury the mules."

"What for?" asked Wade, wanting to get after Wells and Gil.

Seth tossed his hands in the air and kept walking.

Wade stared after him for a few moments wondering why and then he went inside, found some twine, gathered some branches, sat down in the dirt, and started making crude crosses. While inside the barn, Seth dug a hole big enough for the two mules. Wade had just finished with the crude crosses when Seth stepped out of the barn, telling him to bring the horse.

Without saying a word, Seth took the rope off his horse, wrapped it around one of the mule's legs, the other around his saddle horn, then climbed in the saddle and dragged the mule into the hole. After both mules were in the hole and covered with dirt, Wade wiped the sweat from his forehead and looked at Seth. "Why take the time to bury the mules?"

"Something I had to do," he said. "Can't explain it none." Then he walked to his horse, climbed in the saddle, and looked at Wade. "Let's go." He turned his horse and rode in the direction Frank and Gil had ridden.

Wade stared after him for a curious moment, climbed onto his mare, took one last look at the house, the barn, and the graves, turned his mare, and followed.

They rode at a slow pace in silence for several minutes when Sheriff Seth Bowlen suddenly took off his badge, turned in the saddle, and put it in his saddlebags.

Curious about that, Wade asked him why.

"I'm just a city sheriff, Wade, and I ain't got no jurisdiction out here. I'm the same as you, Frank Wells, and Gil."

Worried, Wade asked, "Since we ain't the law no more, what're we gonna do when we catch up to these guys?"

"Kill them," replied Bowlen coldly. Then he spurred his horse into a trot and followed the trail left by Wells and Robinson.

Wade stared after Bowlen thinking it was a strange thing for a lawman to say but felt good about him saying it. He nudged his mare and rode after Seth.

Six

It was too dark to follow the trail left by the murdering kidnappers, so Frank Wells and Gil Robinson stopped to make camp near a rock formation of pine trees and sagebrush. Gil started to unload the packhorses when he saw a faint light he thought might be a campfire about a half-mile to the south. "What's that?"

Wells was also looking at it. "Looks like a campfire."

"Reckon it's them?"

"Possible," Wells said thoughtfully. He turned and looked in the direction Seth and Wade would be riding. "Wonder what's keeping them two?"

Gil glanced back toward the north, turned, and stared at the light as he stepped closer to Frank. "What do you wanna do?"

"We can't build us a fire. They'd know we were following and more'n likely skedaddle south."

Gil glanced back along their trail covered in darkness and then at the campfire in the distance. "We could wait for Seth and Wade or sneak up a little closer and see if it's them."

"My thoughts exactly," said Wells. "But be damn quiet about it."

They climbed back onto their horses and rode slowly toward the light, and as they got closer, they saw three fires instead of one.

"That's peculiar," said Wells as they stopped. He reached behind him, took his long glass out of his saddlebag, pulled it apart, and looked at the campsite. "There's more than just four men in that camp."

Gil became worried. "Think them bastards met up with some other no goods?" He looked back over his shoulder. "Wish Seth and Wade would hurry along."

Wells was still looking through the long glass wishing for the same thing.

Gil Robinson didn't think he had heard him, so he repeated. "Wish Seth and Wade would hurry along."

Frank took the looking glass from his eye. "So do I. Them's Indians in that camp. Arapahoe, most likely."

Gil looked worried. "Do you think they got the four we're after and them children held captive?"

Wells looked back into the darkness, wondering about Seth and Wade. "Just our damn luck." He looked back at the campfires, climbed down from his horse, and pushed the long glass together. He stuck it in his belt and looked up at Gil. "Stay here. I'm gonna try and get a little closer." He told Gil to mind the horses, stay alert, and be quiet. "If the four we're trailing ain't with them Indians, they're most likely holed up out here someplace."

Gil thought on that, climbed down, gathered the reins, and lead ropes to the horses. "Don't be too long." He glanced around into the darkness and whispered. "Don't get caught."

Wells looked up at the starry sky, thankful there was no moon. After he got his bearings from the stars in relation to the campfire so he wouldn't get lost coming back, he said, "I ain't planning on getting that close." Then he turned and started walking. "I'll be back soon."

Gil watched Frank disappear into the darkness as he pulled the horses around him, knelt, drew his gun, and peered into the night from under the horse's bellies. As the minutes passed, he thought of what Frank had said about the others hiding somewhere and sorely wished Frank would hurry or that Seth and Wade would ride up. Then Gil wondered how he would know if it was Seth and Wade or they him and feared he might get shot by accident. Hoping Frank won't be long, he wished he were home with Annie in their warm, soft bed.

Frank had been gone for almost an hour while Robinson searched the darkness between him and the campfires, wondering where he was. He didn't hear any yelling or excitement coming from the camp, which gave him hope that the Indians hadn't taken Wells. Hearing something, he peered into the darkness, hoping it was Frank and not an Indian or them four they were after.

"Don't shoot Gil. It's me," whispered Frank.

"Come on in," whispered Gil.

"Don't shoot," whispered Wells.

"Stop yer fretting, Frank. You already said it was you."

"Yeah," replied Wells stepping out of the darkness. "But I know how fidgety you are at times."

Gil grinned. "Well, you'd be fidgety too if you were left here all alone."

"Try going out there a few hundred yards and see how good that feels." chuckled Wells.

"Any sign of the four we're after or them little gals?"

"Nah," said Frank. "Only them Arapahoes."

Gil looked in their direction. "What the hell are they doing so far south?"

Wells grinned. "Wanna go ask them?"

"I'm not that curious. How many you figure are out there?"

"A dozen or so, I reckon. More than enough to be trouble." Then Wells walked to his horse. "Let's loosen the cinches of the saddles but leave them on."

"How about the packhorses?"

"They're more than likely pretty tired," said Frank. "We passed a small hill earlier. You stay with the horses, and I'll go back and see if I can find it."

"Hurry," said Gil.

Frank disappeared into the darkness and returned within a few minutes. "There's a small hill not far from here with some trees and rocks for cover."

Frank led Gil and the horses to the hill, where they unpacked the packhorses, loosened the girths on their saddles, hobbled the horses, and made camp without a fire. They rested against the supplies keeping a sharp eye on the Indian camp, figuring Seth and Wade had stopped for the night.

Gil woke just before dawn and nudged Frank. "Time to get up."

Wells sat up and glanced around, looking like he'd had a tough night. He tossed off his blanket, crawled up the small hill, looked toward the Indian camp, and thought that either their fires had gone out during the night, or they had already broken camp and moved out.

The sun would be up soon, and in that pale light just before dawn, Gil crawled up the small hill and lay down next to Frank. "See anything?"

Without looking away from the long glass and the Arapahoe camp, Wells said, "Not much, but it appears they're still there. I can see their ponies and several of them heathens moving about."

Robinson looked behind them, seeing two riders in the distance. Hoping it was Sheriff Bowlen and Wade Garrison, he poked Wells and pointed at the riders. "Company."

Wells looked through his long glass again at the Indians, pushed it closed, and turned to watch the two riders.

As Wade and Bowlen approached, Frank ran toward them, keeping the hill between him and the Indians waving his hat and gesturing for them to get down. Understanding his meaning, Bowlen told Wade to dismount and walk their horses. When they reached Wells, he told them about the Arapahoe.

Wade was disappointed as they followed Frank back to the camp wishing they had found the four men and the two little girls.

After tying their horses to a bush, they crawled up the small hill and joined Gil, who was keeping an eye on the Arapahoe camp.

Bowlen asked for Frank's long glass, pulled it apart, and looked at the Indians. "Seems somethings got them riled up a bit Frank." He handed the long glass back to Wells. "Must have seen Wade and me coming before we got behind the hill." He looked back toward the Arapahoe. "Poor luck, I suppose." Then he looked around at the trees and rocks, contemplating how they would defend this place.

Frank looked through the glass. "Yep," he said. "Five are riding this way." Then taking the glass from his eye, he chuckled. "They probably figure it's just the two of you and no sense letting the others in on the party."

Wade found little humor in that as he hurried to his horse for his Sharps and bandolier of cartridges, hoping he didn't get killed and scalped before fulfilling his promise to Emmett.

Wells hollered, "Hold on; I think that's Dark Cloud out in front riding his big gray."

"Dark Cloud?" repeated Wade as he walked back to the hill and lay next to Frank.

"Wells was looking through the long glass. "Yep," he said. "It's him. He won't be any trouble." He pushed his long glass together and looked at Wade. "A trapper I once knew had lived with the Arapahoe years back, and he told the story that the Indian's mother and father getting caught in the open during a bad storm with hail, lightning, and thunder while she gave birth. His father thought it was a bad sign believing the young brave would always have a hard life. As he held him up to show the great creator, he named him Dark Cloud and asked the creator to guide him through life."

Gil grinned. "Old Dark Cloud does a pretty fair job of living up to his name."

Frank looked sad. "Hadn't seen him around for a while. I heard a while back that he was over on the western slope."

As the five Indians approached, Frank Wells stood, and upon seeing him, the Indians pulled up their ponies and waited. Wells made a sign of friendship, telling the others to stand up, hoping their numbers would make a difference. He held his rifle in the air and then slowly cradled it in the crook of the elbow and forearm of his left arm across his body. Then he waved a greeting with his right hand, told the others to wait where they were, and walked down the hill toward the Arapahoe.

The Indian Dark Cloud waited until Frank was within a few yards, said something to the others, then swung his right leg over the head of his gray horse and slid off. He made a gesture of friendship and then cradled his rifle in his left elbow as Frank had. They shook hands heartily, squatted, and Frank did most of the talking. He was too far away for Wade and the others to hear what he was saying. Dark Cloud nodded twice in agreement, pointed toward the southwest, then back at his camp. Wells did some more talking, and as the two stood, the Indian held up one hand, showing two fingers.

Frank said something and hurried back to the others while the Indians waited. He climbed the hill sat down, glanced back at the Indians, and looked at the others. "Says they saw the four men we're after heading toward the southwest. Said they had two young girls with them."

Wade stared at the Indians. "What are they waiting for?"

Wells turned and glanced back at them. "Promised him some grub. Dark Cloud said they hadn't had much to eat. Their guns are empty, and their lances make poor weapons against the quick rabbits. I told him we'd let them have a little of our stuff." He turned and motioned for Dark Cloud to come into the camp. "They asked for some ammo, but I told him we hadn't any to spare." Then Wells told Gil to help him with some of their supplies and explained they could replace them at the next town.

Having never been this close to an Indian, Wade watched the Indian dressed in rawhide leggings, a red loincloth, and a faded dark blue sleeveless army shirt that fit snugly over his broad shoulders and muscular dark arms. His long black hair with a touch of grey was in two braids hanging down either side of his head past his shoulders.

Wells gave the food they could spare to the Indian who, after taking it, shook Frank's hand, looked at the others, turned and walked down the hill toward his gray horse. He said something to the other Indians, swung onto his big gray with the food, and rode toward their camp.

"I've known that Indian for a long time," said Frank Wells. "And I've never known him to be troublesome."

Gil looked concerned. "Did he say how them gals were, Frank?"

"Said they looked afraid."

They gathered their belongings and rode southwest with Frank and Gil in front, riding in the familiar crisscross patterns in search of the tracks they had lost in the dark. It took a while, but now that Frank and Gil had found the tracks, the party rode a little faster, worried about the young girls. They rode all day, stopping now and then to rest the horses, and now that it was getting dark, they made camp along a small stream. They ate a little supper and then sat on the hard ground with their backs against their saddles, drinking coffee in thoughtful silence.

Gil glanced at the others and started to say something but decided to let it go and just looked at the flames of the fire, knowing no one was in the mood to talk.

Wells tossed a piece of wood onto the fire and looked at Seth. "Noticed earlier you don't have your badge on Seth. Any particular reason?"

Bowlen looked away from the fire at Frank. "Our authority ended when we left town. We're no different than Gil or Wade there or anyone else."

Frank thought about that a moment, took off his badge, and put it in his saddlebag. "Guess you're right. We are a little bit out of our jurisdiction." Then he looked into the darkness. "Wonder what the closest town is?"

"Sangre, maybe El Nacho," replied Gil lazily.

"Sangre probably," said Seth, then he looked at Frank. "Doubt, El Nacho. I believe it's a little farther south. Why are you asking?"

Frank looked at Seth. "We need to replace what we gave them Indians. And I'm just thinking them killers will need supplies before long."

Gil adjusted himself against his saddle. "Pretty sure them boys will stay away from any towns. Four men and two little gals will bring attention to them. I'm of the mind they'll be sticking close to the foothills."

"They could head up into the mountains," offered Wade.

Gil looked at him. "The mountains will be tough going with them little gals."

Wade took a deep breath and let out a long sigh. "I sure as hell hope they're alright."

Bowlen looked at him thoughtfully. "Best not think on the little ones too much." Then he looked into the fire. "We best get some sleep. I want to be on their trail by the time the sun comes up."

Seven

By noon the following day, the group had crossed the Cucharas River, was now at the base of Cucharas Mountain, and followed the killer's trail that had turned southeast. Gil had ridden ahead doing the tracking and disappeared behind one of the many foothills that separated the Rocky Mountains from the Colorado plains. As the others rounded a hill, they saw Gil had dismounted and was on one knee, looking at the ground. Thinking he may have lost their trail, they rode a little faster, and as they pulled their horses up, he pointed down the stream and then up toward the top of the foothills. "Looks like they split up."

Seth looked at the tracks for a moment. "Wonder what they're up to."

Frank had been looking at the tracks. "Looks like four horses headed directly south. The lone rider's heading straight west."

Just then, something hit the packhorse Frank Wells was pulling, followed by thunder echoing through the hills. The animal fell, kicking and screaming as it tried to get up while the men scattered, dodging bullets hitting trees and rocks. Finding shelter in a group of trees, they quickly dismounted while Seth asked if anyone was hit. Each said no as they drew their pistols and knelt next to a tree or boulder.

Frank looked at the packhorse lying motionless on the ground and cursed his stupidity for not realizing why the four had split up. He looked at Wade. "Sorry about your horse. I must be get'n too old for this shit," he said in anger. "Should've seen what was coming."

"It was my fault." Offered Gil looking apologetic. "I was the one out in front and saw the tracks. Had more than enough time to make out what they were doing b'fore you three came riding up."

59

"What's done is done," said an irritated Bowlen. "They know they're being followed now, and that may be a good thing for them little gals."

Wade looked at Seth. "Why's that?"

Frank quickly answered. "They'll have to keep moving."

Without telling the others, Wade pulled the Sharps from the scabbard on his horse and then made his way through the trees to the other side of the small clearing.

Bowlen was the first to notice he was gone, and as he looked around, he saw Wade off to the right sneaking through the aspen trees. "What the hell does he think he's gonna do?"

Wells watched Wade as he moved through the trees. "Kill the bastard, I hope."

"If he doesn't get himself shot in the process," offered Gil.

"Dumb shit," said Bowlen angrily.

Gil looked at Seth. "We going after him?"

"We wait," replied Bowlen. "Maybe the dumb shit will get lucky."

Ten minutes of silence passed, and the three were getting a little edgy and worried about Wade. Gil suggested they split up and head out to find the young fool, but Frank and Seth disagreed, so they waited. Ten more minutes passed when Wade appeared at the top of a hill two hundred yards away, yelled, and waved his arms. They climbed on their horses and rode up the hill with the second packhorse and Wade's mount in tow. Bowlen quickly asked if he was some kind of an idiot or just plain naïve.

Wade grinned. "Both, probably. Doesn't matter now. The bastard's gone." He held a couple of spent cartridges in his hand for the others to see. "Sharps. Not a very good shot." Then he looked at the others. "At this distance, he could've got at least two, maybe all four of us." Wade pointed toward the south. "His tracks lead along the hills toward the arroyo, probably on his way to meet up with the others."

"Not for long," said Seth with an angry look. "Mount up. We're heading after them."

Gil looked at the dead horse and their supplies. "What about the stuff on the packhorse?"

Seth lifted the stirrup of his saddle to check its cinch while looking at the second packhorse. "That horse has too much already. Get what's important, split it four ways, and we'll each carry a little."

Wade tossed the empty cartridges to Gil, climbed on his horse, and rode toward the dead packhorse, thinking Mr. Grimes may be a little pissed at losing a fine horse.

Gil tossed the cartridges to the ground, mounted his horse, and followed Wade and Frank to get the supplies. Seth looked at the cartridges thinking he and the others had been lucky. He turned toward the south, where Wade said the ambusher went, climbed up on his horse, and rode to the dead packhorse. After splitting the supplies up four ways, they rode into the arroyo and headed south. It was getting late when they made camp took care of the horses, built a small fire, and after eating, Gil doused the fire before it got dark.

It was early morning and still dark when Gil Robinson woke up, tossed the blanket off quietly, got up, and walked into the trees for privacy near a small cliff. As he looked into the night, he saw what appeared to be the glow of a campfire in the distance, hurried back to camp, woke the others, and led them back to where he saw the campfire. "Think it's them?" he asked of no one in particular as all four looked at the faint glow in the distance.

"Dumb shits if it is," said Frank.

"Maybe they want us to see it," offered Seth thoughtfully.

Wade figured it the same as Seth. "They could be trying to get us to ride into a trap."

Bowlen nodded in agreement. "Could be. They know we're after them."

Robinson looked despondent. "Let's hope they don't kill them little gals and make a run for the border."

"Not to worry, Gil," said Seth. "Them little gals are as good as gold across the border, especially if they ain't been violated. They won't harm them none."

"Will Mexicans buy little white girls?" asked Wade.

Seth looked at him. "More than likely, they'll sell them to the Apaches."

"That could be an empty camp," said Frank thoughtfully.

"What's an empty camp?" asked Wade.

"Back in the day," began Wells. "Indians used to do that, making the Army split their forces. That way, they'd have a smaller force to deal with."

"And it worked," said Gil. "Until the Army got wise."

61

Seth turned away and headed back to camp, talking over his shoulder. "Well, we ain't got no choice in the matter. Let's break camp and get mounted up."

The others followed and listened as Seth told them they would check the camp, and if it was empty, they could at least pick up their trail again when the sun came up. Then he looked to the east. "Figure we got about two hours b'fore sunrise."

They made their way along the ridges of the foothills keeping close to a creek bed and trees for cover. By the time the sun was up, they were standing next to the smoldering fire.

Gil kicked at the smoldering ashes. "Bastards never even spent the night."

Frank Wells knelt to one knee and carefully looked at the footprints. "If they had, there'd be a lot more footprints." He looked at Gil. "They didn't stay long."

Wade was on one knee a few yards away, studying the ground, then he stood and pointed to the south. "Looks like four horses headed south."

Gil looked at the others as he pointed. "There's four heading in that direction." He looked at Seth. "Question is, which tracks belong to the little gals?"

Wells looked angry. "These boys sure know how to lay down some confusing tracks. These three here appear to be carrying light loads like the little gals." Then he pointed to the others. "Those four look normal, but one mount looks light." He scratched his chin. "That could be the gals on one horse."

"Could be," agreed Gil looking uncertain. "Could be either."

"Damn it," said Seth angrily. "We best make damn sure which has the little girls because they're in for one hell of a life if we don't make the right choice here."

Silence fell on the group as they studied the tracks that led south and west. It was plain that no one wanted to make the decision that could be the end of finding the little girls and the four rapists and murderers.

Seth tied his horse to a nearby tree and started gathering wood. "I'm hungry and need my coffee. We'll have breakfast and then head out." He looked at Frank and Gil. "You two follow those four to the south. Wade and I will trail the others to the west."

"If these are the decoys, we'll catch up as soon as we can," said Frank. Then he and Gil unloaded enough supplies for coffee and breakfast.

By early afternoon Frank, Gil, and a single unsaddled horse caught up with Wade and Seth. Gil told of finding two of the three horses drinking from a small creek about two miles from the decoy camp. Both had the same brand as the two dead mules back at the farm, and one had gone lame with a split hoof.

"Gil there had to shoot him," said Wells. "We brought the other one to help with the rest of the supplies we took off the dead packhorse. After finding the trail of the other rider, we followed his tracks, figuring he'd be heading back to the others." He paused and pointed to the ridge above them. "The tracks led us to that ridge up there, and that's when we saw the two of you."

Wade looked up at the ridge feeling a bit uncomfortable. "You sure he ain't still up there?"

"Trail looked a few hours old," said Gil. "He's more'n likely passed this way b'fore you two got here." Then he grinned. "Besides, if anyone were up there, most or all of us would be dead by now."

Wade found no humor in Gil's remarks. He glanced around for better cover as he remembered the last time Gil miscalculated the men they were trailing. Looking up at the ridge, he said, "Well, maybe so, but I don't like it none. We'll move on down the slope and rest the horses a half-hour or so, then get back after them."

They found a small stream amid the tall pine and aspen trees, giving them excellent cover from the ridge above. They climbed down, letting the animals have a good drink, and then hobbled them in the shade where they could feed on the weeds and grass. Gil and Wells sat on the ground with their backs against a dead tree, while Wade sat against a rock near his mare. Seth looked toward the west, thinking about the little girls and their family.

Gil suddenly sat up and then pointed toward two small mountains. "If memory serves me correctly, ain't Gus's trading post about ten or so miles up that small canyon yonder?"

Frank Wells looked and nodded in agreement. "Yep. Big Gus Parker's place."

"Thought so," replied Gil.

Frank looked at Wade and then at Seth, still staring toward the west. "Seems these four will be needing supplies by now." Wells paused for a response, and when none came, he said, "They've made no stops to supply up that we can see since they killed those poor people and took them little girls."

Bowlen turned to Frank. "Maybe. If they plan on making a run for Mexico, they need to stop somewhere. Gus's place is the closest, and there ain't a lot of people hanging around to ask questions." Seth stood. "Mount up, boys. The horses have rested enough."

They reached Gus Parker's Trading Post on the Big Stony River in the first range of mountains about two hours before dusk. Seeing four horses tied to the hitching rail out front, they left the trail taking cover in the fir and aspen trees several yards from the log building and dismounted.

Wade pulled his Sharps from its scabbard while the others drew their pistols and knelt beside a tree where they had a clear view of the horses and door of the trading post. Only three horses had saddles; the other was a packhorse.

Gil looked at the others. "I wonder where them little gals are?"

"These ain't the ones we're after," said Wade. "We're trailing a sorrel, black, spotted gray, and a black-and-white spotted."

"Shit!" said Bowlen. "They were either here and left, or we guessed wrong. Let's get inside and see if Gus knows anything."

Shots suddenly rang out inside the trading post. Wade and the others backed into the cover of the trees as the door opened, and three men hurried out of the door and ran for their horses, chased by a big man firing his pistol. The three men returned fire, and the big man went down. Seth Bowlen took quick aim and dropped the last man. The other two turned as they ran and fired back, hitting the trees, causing the horses to rear up. Wade turned to check on the horses while Frank and Gil shot at the two men hitting a packhorse instead. The two men returned fire as they untied their mounts, swung onto their saddles, and galloped toward the top of the hill. Wade ran into the open, knelt while pulling the hammer back, aimed, and fired. The Sharps kicked against his shoulder as the fifty-caliber shell exploded, and without looking to see if he hit his target, reloaded, aimed at the last rider, pulled the first trigger, and then the second. The Sharps kicked, and he saw the second man hunch forward and after a few yards, tumble from his saddle. Both riderless horses ran up the trail for several yards and stopped.

"Holy shit," said Seth looking surprised. "That last one was near three hundred yards."

Wade's hands were shaking, and his heart pounded against his chest as he recalled Seth's words about not being prepared for what he may find. "Staring at the two men, he said, "I never killed anyone before."

Remembering his first kill, Gil put his hand on Wade's shoulder. "Don't take it too hard. If anyone deserved getting shot, I'd say it be these fellas. It appears they were trying to rob old Gus."

Concerned over Big Gus, Frank Wells rushed to the man and turned him over. Seeing the hole in his shoulder, he asked if he was okay.

"Do I look okay" replied Gus in an angry voice and then, seeing who it was, grinned. "What the hell are you doing here?" Gus was a big man, standing six feet, weighing well over two hundred pounds, with black hair and a beard.

"Let's get you inside, Gus," said Frank as he helped him to his feet.

Gus cussed the men who shot him. "I knew them bastards was trouble the moment they walked in the place."

Wells helped him up the steps of the trading post and inside while Wade and Seth brought up the horses. Wade looked down at the wounded packhorse, kicking and screaming, trying to get up. Feeling sorry for the animal, he reached for his pistol, but Seth drew his gun and shot the animal in the head.

Thankful for that, Wade tied the horses to the hitching rail and headed for the door.

Gil rode up the trail to check on the two men Wade had shot and gather their horses.

Wade followed Seth into the trading post, where he and Seth looked into another room, seeing Frank tending to the big man lying on a messy bed. Seth found an old chair and sat down while Wade stood at the door and watched.

Gus raised his head and hollered at Wade. "Check on Rooster."

Wade glanced around. "I don't see no rooster."

Seth stood, saw someone's feet sticking out from behind a counter, walked over, and looked down at Rooster, shot in the left eye. "Damn" is all he could say.

"How's Rooster?" yelled Big Gus from the other room.

"Rooster's gone, Gus," replied Seth sadly. "Rooster's gone."

Curious about who Rooster was, Wade walked across the room and looked down at the man's bloody face. "Who was Rooster?"

"What's that about old Ben Rooster?" asked Gil as he walked inside carrying the guns of the three dead men.

"Rooster done got himself killed," replied Frank from the room where he tended Gus.

"That you, Gil?" called out Big Gus.

"It's me, Gus," replied Gil as he followed Seth into the room. Standing beside Gus's bed, he watched Frank tend to the big man's wound. Leaning closer for a better look, he asked, "You doing alright?"

Thinking it was a stupid question, Gus looked up. "Do I look alright?" Then he groaned in pain as he tried to make himself comfortable.

"Who were those boys?" asked Gil.

Gus watched Frank mess with his gunshot. "Be damned if I know. They come in here and bought a couple of drinks." Then he looked up at Robinson. "They didn't think I was watching, but I was. I'm always watching everyone." He winced in pain and looked up at Frank, tending his wound. "Take it easy." Then he looked at Gil. "I saw one put something in his shirt, and I told him to put it back, but the asshole pulled his gun. Old Rooster came out of the storeroom, and the bastard shot him." Gus looked mad. "Rooster never had a chance." His face turned to sadness as he winced in pain, telling Frank to be careful.

Irritated by Gus's complaining, Frank turned to him. "You can do it yer self if you've the mind to."

Big Gus grunted and then looked at Seth. "How do Seth? Been a while."

Seth nodded. "It has at that. Sorry, it's under such circumstances."

Gus looked at Wade leaning against the door jamb, and then he looked at Seth. "I turned, dove for the door to this room, grabbed my pistol, and started shooting. I chased them outside, and you boys know what happened after that." He winced as Frank touched his wound and then looked at Seth. "You still sheriff'n?"

"Over in Sisters."

Big Gus winced and looked up at Frank. "Careful there, Frank."

"Quit being such a candy ass," replied Wells.

Gus looked worried. "How's it looking?"

"Yer lucky it was a small caliber," said Frank, and then he nodded toward Wade. "Instead of his Sharps."

Big Gus looked at the slender young man. "Thought I heard a cannon go off while I was lying on the ground dying."

"You weren't dying," chuckled Frank.

Gus looked up. "Well, it felt like it." He looked at Wade. "Case you hadn't figured it out, I'm Big Gus Parker, and who might you be?"

Seth glanced back at Wade. "That's Wade Garrison. He took two down as they rode off up the trail. It must have been five hundred yards."

Wade looked at Seth. "Thought you said three hundred."

Seth grinned. "Appears I was wrong the first time." Then he sat down on an old chair that moaned from his weight and placed his hat on a small table. "I took out one trying to get on his horse." Then he grinned. "Frank and Gil there shot a horse thinking it was another robber."

That brought laughter from Gus and Wade, but Frank and Gil didn't think Seth was all that funny.

Big Gus looked down at his bleeding shoulder and the knife Frank held in his hand, ready to dig the bullet out. "I could use a damn drink b'fore you start cutting on me with that little knife of yours."

Wells grinned as he pulled it away. "Reckon, I could use one myself. Where is it?"

Without looking away from his bleeding shoulder, he nodded to the store beyond his bedroom door. "Under the counter. Glasses are in the cabinet behind the bar. The least I can do is give you boys a drink for saving me and my place."

Gil said he'd get it and hurried out of the room, returning shortly with a bottle of whiskey and five glasses, looking for someplace to sit it all down.

Big Gus grinned. "Don't get much company back here."

Gil gave each a glass and poured five drinks which the four gulped down as if they were in a hurry. Grinning, he quickly poured them another.

"I said a drink, asshole," said Big Gus.

Frank chuckled. "Consider the second payment for my doctoring."

Gus grunted with a frown, downed his drink, and watched as Frank took the whiskey bottle and poured a little over the knife blade. Frank handed the bottle to Big Gus, who took several good drinks, handed the bottle to Gil, and looked at Frank. "Get after it."

Frank took a leather strap hanging on the wall, shoved it into Gus's mouth, and told him to bite down. As he started digging for the bullet, the other three stepped closer to watch. He stopped and looked at them. "You boys are in my light. Mind going into the other room?"

Disappointed, they walked into the store, and while Wade and Seth sat down on the crude homemade furniture, Gil got another bottle of whiskey and poured each a drink. He started to take a drink when he looked at Rooster lying on the floor, downed his drink, stood, and asked Seth to help him take poor old Rooster outside so they could bury him.

By the time Frank got the bullet out, Big Gus had passed out. Frank cleaned the wound and bandaged it, stood back to admire his work while thinking the big man was somewhat puny when it came to pain. Then he washed his hands, cleaned his knife, walked to the open front door while drying his hands on a towel, and watched Wade, Gil, and Seth dig a grave for Ben Rooster. Feeling bad about Rooster, he turned and went back into the bedroom to check on Gus, and seeing he was doing alright, sat down in the chair next to the bed, leaned back, and closed his eyes.

With Rooster and the dead horse buried, the others walked into the trading post waking Frank from his short nap. He checked on Gus again, then joined them in the store for another drink of Gus's whiskey. After they talked for a spell, Gil cooked dinner.

Frank filled his plate and sat down when Big Gus woke up and hollered for Frank. Wells let out a sigh, set his plate down, went into the next room, and asked Gus if he was hungry. The big man shook his head no and asked for a drink of whiskey instead. Frank yelled for Robinson to bring Big Gus a stiff one.

Gil poured whiskey into a tall glass, took it into Gus, and watched the big man down it faster than Gil had poured it. After handing the glass back to Gil, Gus laid his head on the pillow and quickly went back to sleep.

Frank and Gil walked out of Gus's bedroom, finding Seth busy making a fire in the big stone fireplace, saying it would take the chill out of the air. Still holding the near-empty bottle, Gil settled back against the woodpile, looked at Wade, and offered him a drink.

Wade said no thanks, then sat on a stool in front of the big stone fireplace. Watching the flames dance above the logs, he wished they would get after the four men and the little girls.

Seth gave Wade a curious look wanting to know more about the foolish young man. "Where's your family?"

As the others listened, Wade told of his home back in South Carolina, his pa getting killed in the big war, and his leaving home. "I get letters now and again from ma or my sis." Sadly, he told of his grandpa passing two years ago and wished he had made a trip back before the old man died.

"It's a sad thing when members of the same family are at odds with one another," offered Gil Robinson.

Wade looked at Seth Bowlen. "Hope you don't mind me ask'n Seth, but can you see anything out of that eye?"

Frank quickly said, "I remember the night when that young fella cut you."

Seth smiled. "Well, I'd like to forget it."

Wells chuckled as he looked at Wade. "Seth, there was sheriff'n in a little town in the Kansas Panhandle. I had trailed a no-good cattle thief across the Red River to---" He paused and looked at Seth. "What was that little town?"

"Culpepper," replied Bowlen harshly.

"Yeah," said Frank. "Culpepper Kansas. I was a sheriff in a little town called Broken Wheel, Texas. It wasn't much of a town but big enough to need a sheriff, and it had its share of shit going on back then. Anyways, I had caught the little bastard and stopped in Culpepper to get some sleep and put my prisoner in jail for the night. I didn't know Seth then, but he took my prisoner and locked him up while I stopped for a drink at the saloon before getting a room. I hadn't been there more than a few minutes when a fight broke out over some gal, cards, or something. I don't rightly recall."

Seth never looked up from the flames of the fire and listened as Frank told the story.

"Any how's," said Wells. "When Seth there came in to break it up, this kid pulled a knife and laid Seth's forehead and cheek clean open. Bled like a pig."

"Enough of the storytelling Frank," said Seth. "That was a long time ago."

"What happened to the kid?" asked Wade.

Frank leaned forward and rested his arms on his knees. "Seth wrestled the knife out of the foolish boy's hand and then proceeded to kick the shit out of them, threw him in jail, and then went to see the doc."

Seth looked at Wells with a wry smile. "You could've helped me out a bit Frank."

"Damn," laughed Frank. "I wasn't about to interfere. I was afraid you might've shot me in the process."

Bowlen grinned. "Process hell more'n likely in the ass." That brought laughter to the room, and as the laughter faded, he looked at Wade. "I can see some out of it, but everything's a mite cloudy. I saw an eye doc once. He had a name for it that I don't recall but said it'd get worse over time."

Wade looked curious. "So that was the first time the two of you met?"

Frank nodded. "It was, and when I went to pick up my prisoner the next day, I was surprised to see the kid that cut Seth was still breathing. I figured he'd taken the kid out back and put one between his eyes for almost putting his eye out. But the boy was alive. Seth's face was half bandaged, and he was in a shitty mood nursing a bottle of whiskey that we shared until late afternoon."

Seth stared into the fire as it consumed the logs and said, "We ran into one another a couple of times over the years in New Mexico and Arizona." He smiled as he glanced at Frank. "We were deputies for an insane sheriff named Charles Danner in a little border town called Rio Delanco for a while, then went our different ways."

"Where's Rio Delanco?" asked Wade.

Seth looked at him. "Sits on the west side of the Rio Grande about ten miles north of El Paso."

Frank chuckled. "You're right about Sheriff Danner. He was one insane son-of-a-bitch."

Seth and Frank smiled at one another as if they shared a secret.

"Yes, sir," said Wells looking at the fire in memory. "He was one crazy bastard."

"Why's that?" asked Wade.

Gil took a drink of whiskey from a new bottle he had taken from under the counter and sat down on the floor, resting against the woodpile that was a little smaller now.

Seth reached for the bottle, took a quick drink, and looked at Wade. "Sheriff Danner wasn't a man holding a lot of patience when it came to sheriff'n. He was a big man over six feet, had big hairy arms and big hands." He looked at Gil Robinson. "A lot like Gil there, but Danner was bigger yet." Seth's expression turned sad as he looked into the fire. "He had a wife and daughter taken by some renegades." Seth looked away from the fire at Wade. "Danner spent almost twenty years looking for them."

"I felt sorry for Danner," said Wells in a sad tone. "I always figured that maybe he'd spent too much time alone searching for his wife and daughter." He spits into the fire. "Never did find them."

Seth sighed. "One night Charles Danner locked himself in one of the cells, drank a bottle of whiskey, put his forty-four Colt in his mouth, and pulled the trigger."

"Made a hell of a mess," said Frank with a frown. "Blood and brains all over the ceiling. Some of it dripping on the floor. Old Danner shit and pissed his pants about the same time the bullet splattered his brains all over the place." He paused with a sad look. "We had a hell of a time getting the keys out of the cell so's we could get him out and buried. The next day Seth and I went our separate ways only to end up just a few miles apart here in Colorado."

Seth grinned as he looked at Frank. "I hated leaving that young deputy Billy French with that mess."

Frank laughed. "Served the dumb shit right for thinking he knew more than we did."

Seth stopped grinning as he looked at Frank Wells. "And now both of us are at the end of the trail, as they say, both having seen better days while French is a United States Marshal."

Frank nodded, then took a hefty drink. "Nothing lasts forever."

Seth raised his brow, nodded, and grinned. "Now that's a damn fact, my friend. Best we all get some sleep. We've got a big day ahead of us."

Eight

The sound of voices woke Wade from a restless sleep that had held the images of his friend Emmett the Barton family, and the others they had buried. He closed his eyes, listening to the soft words wishing he hadn't drunk so much of Gus's whiskey last night. Getting up, he walked outside, feeling the crisp morning air. A soft breeze made its way up the canyon mixing with the sounds of the flowing water of the unseen Big Stoney River. Crows cawed, and birds sang their early morning greetings mixed with the words and voices of his companions as they sat around the porch drinking coffee and talking.

Seeing Wade, Gil smiled. "Have a seat, and I'll get you a cup of coffee." Then he stood and went inside.

Wade's head was pounding as he sat on a cut stump that served as a chair next to Frank Wells, sitting on the porch floor with his back against the log building. Seth and Big Gus sat on a crudely built bench that Gus had made. Surprised at seeing Big Gus up and around, he asked how he was feeling.

Gus touched his shoulder gently with one hand and said he was sore, but he was sure he would live thanks to Frank's doctoring.

Wells grinned proudly and took a drink of coffee.

Gil came out of the trading post with a cup of coffee and handed it to Wade.

Wade took the chipped cup, thinking it smelled a little strong but thanked him anyway.

Gil sat on another stump, took a sip of coffee, and continued his story. "Like I was gonna say before Wade came out, back in the day when

72

the Army was chasing Indians in these parts, white folks weren't safe anywhere's."

Wade took a drink of the strong bitter coffee, thinking it was awful. "Don't seem things have changed all that much," he said, looking at Gil. "Folks still aren't all that safe." He tossed the rest of his coffee over the edge of the porch.

Gil looked puzzled. "Too strong?"

Wade set the empty cup on the porch next to him and nodded. "A little." Then he looked at the others. "We've been burying more'n our fair share of bodies, and if we don't get going, we'll be burying a few more. Maybe even them little gals."

Silence hung heavy in the air for several moments while everyone considered what Wade had said. Seth, along with Gil and Frank, resented Wade's insinuations. "You're the last one to get up," said Seth.

Wade realized that was true and felt he spoke out of turn. "I apologize for speaking out of turn."

Seth knew the boy was merely hungover and in a bad mood. "I know you're in a hurry. Hell, we all are. We'll get on our way in a bit. Gus here's allowing us to fix us some breakfast b'fore we leave, and we were waiting for you to wake up." Then he smiled. "Ah hell, as if the rest of us never spoke out of turn." Then he chuckled.

The others accepted his apology with a nod while understanding his impatience, and nothing more was spoken on the subject.

Seth drank the last of his coffee and looked at Wade. "Gus here told us that a few hours b'fore them other fellas stopped by yesterday, another man with a packhorse showed up and bought supplies."

"That's right," said Gus as he pointed up the trail with his good arm. "I watched the man ride up that trail yonder where a couple of riders were waiting just beyond them aspens at the crest of the hill."

Wade looked up the trail and imagined the riders. "What'd he look like?"

Gus pursed his lips in thought. "Red hair, freckles, stood about five feet eight or nine, hard to tell fer sure. He was slouching a bit like he didn't want to look at me. That got my curiosity up, so's I came outside to see which way he went, and that's when I seen them other fellas."

"Didn't see anything of two little girls, did ya?" asked Wade.

"Gil there already asked," said Gus. "And as I told him, I didn't see any little girls. But that doesn't mean they weren't up the trail a ways keeping out of sight. Two little gals with four men would've looked a mite odd to me, so my guess is they were further up the trail."

Wade stood and started down the steps.

"Where you going?" asked Bowlen.

"Check their tracks to see if'n they're the ones we're after."

Bowlen gestured to Wells. "Frank already took care of that while you were sleeping. They're the same ones, alright."

Wade looked at Frank. "You sure?"

Frank looked irritated. "I've been tracking longer'n you been riding, Son. I'm sure they're the men we're after."

The sheepish look returned to Wade's unshaven face. "Didn't mean no disrespect."

Wells nodded, accepting Wade's apology, sipped his coffee, and looked at the sun as it slowly rose above the trees across the clearing. "Here it comes."

The others looked up, feeling its warmth on their faces.

Seth turned to Wade, walking up the porch steps. "Don't fret yerself. We'll be getting after them just as soon as we eat and load the supplies Gus let us have on account."

Frank laughed. "On account of Gus here feels obliged for us saving his sorry ass from them no-goods."

Gus grinned as he looked at Wells. "You mean that dangerous no-good packhorse you and Gil shot and killed."

Everyone laughed except Frank and Gil.

Seth stood. "We best go inside, eat some breakfast, and be on our way." Then he looked at Gil and Wade, told them to saddle the mounts and load up the packhorses while Gus prepared breakfast. Then he turned to Gus. "If you don't mind, we'll take one of them bigger horses belonging to the men we killed yesterday as a packhorse." Seth was thinking about splitting the supplies among three horses to lighten their loads so they could travel a little faster.

Gus shrugged. "Take whichever ones you want."

Seth looked at Gil. "Pick a good one. As soon as we eat, we'll be on our way."

After a few minutes on the trail, Frank and Gil thought the tracking was too easy. "It's as if these fellas want us to follow," said Gil.

Wells had a worried look as he stopped his horse and glanced around, searching the dark shadows beyond the trees and rocks, half

74

expecting to see the men they were chasing. "Gives me the willies," he said. "Makes me think back on scouting for the Army, but I'm of the mind that these fellas are a tad bit sneakier than any Indians I ever tracked."

Gil's eyes also searched the shadows, his hand on the butt of his pistol, ready to turn his horse and ride if they rode into a trap. The others were not far behind, bringing up the three slower packhorses, so Frank and Gil pulled up and waited.

Wade approached the two men, pulled up, and asked, "Lose their trail?"

Gil was busy watching the shadows beyond the tree line and never heard the question.

Frank looked from the shadows to the horse tracks that headed up the canyon and then at Wade. "Trail's a mite too easy to follow for some no goods trying to hide from those chasing them."

Bowlen looked down at the tracks and let his eyes follow them up the trail, then glanced to the right and then to the left. "I don't like it none. These fellas are either stupid or smart, and I don't particularly want to learn which. They already took a couple of shots at us." He looked at Frank, then at Gil. "Either of you know how far this trail goes up this canyon and where it comes out?"

Gil looked at Frank. "Don't this trail follow the canyon around that small mountain called Henry's Peak, maybe two, maybe three miles further up?"

Frank nodded. "It forks at the base of a waterfall and a big pool. One trail heads west to the town of Cedars. The other heads east through the foothills and winds up back in the plains." He looked at Gil. "I seem to remember one forking at some point, one trail heading south and the other southwest."

"That's right," said Gil. "Trappers used it a lot back in the day b'fore this place got all trapped out." He turned and spit.

Frank looked thoughtful. "Been a while. Four, five years, maybe six since I came this way."

Seth looked at Frank and Gil. "Any chance they'd head to Cedars?"

"I doubt they would, Seth," said Frank. "I think they'll stay away from populated areas as long as they have them two little gals." He paused. "And now they have the supplies they got from Gus."

"If they's going to Mexico," said Gil, "they'll take the trail back to the plains, head for Raton, and then beat it south to the border."

Frank looked up the canyon thoughtfully, then turned in his saddle and looked across a small ravine with a creek that fed into the Big Stoney further down the canyon. "We can bypass this trail," he said thoughtfully. "There's an old mountain trail a bit further up that ridge there. It comes out near Stewart's Revenge. From there, it's a short piece to where that trail meets the one coming out of the foothills, and the fork Gil was talking about." He looked at the others. "Maybe these here boys we're after ain't familiar with that old trail. If not, we could get ahead of them."

Wade looked curious. "What sort of town is Stewart's Revenge?"

"It ain't a town," said Frank. "It's a place."

Wade started to ask what sort of place, but Frank nudged his horse and headed off the trail. Gil took the third horse from Seth, and then they followed Frank. Wade stared after them for a few moments thinking about Stewart's Revenge. He spurred his horse, tugged at the lead rope of his packhorse, and followed the others down a small embankment. Once across a narrow, rocky stream, they rode up a steep embankment of trees and thick underbrush.

The going was slow, and at times the terrain was so steep they had to stop, dismount, and lead the horses up the mountain. It was not a very large mountain, and they were thankful for that, but the going was still treacherous and tiring. Three hours later, they were on the small narrow trail finding it overgrown from lack of use, and to their relief, Frank could not see any familiar tracks. As they rode in a single file, Wade knew they were easy targets. The four men spoke very little, keeping a sharp eye on the trees, rocks, and underbrush for an ambush as they followed the narrow trail that snaked along the side of the mountain. After a while, the trail stopped climbing and began a slight descent, and as they rounded a bend, Wade could see the foothills and eastern plains disappear into the distant horizon. The narrow trail curved and emptied into several acres of grass and wild purple flowers.

Frank stopped, and the others pulled up in front of a large rock formation that stood two stories high, three in some places.

Wade thought it looked like a giant had placed rocks and boulders of all sizes, some as big as wagons, on top of one another. It reminded him of a rock formation near the Circle T. Only this one was much larger. It was a magnificent sight covering several acres, with the narrow trail disappearing into an opening between the giant boulders.

"Kyle Stewart's Revenge," said Gil Robinson softly, almost religiously, while staring at the formation.

"That's right," said Frank.

"Who was Kyle Stewart?" asked Wade.

Frank glanced at Wade and then looked at the rocks. "Old Man Stewart and some thirty others took revenge on some Indians for killing his wife, two boys, and little girl back in fifty-eight. Stewart and his men happened upon this place and killed every buck, young child, and squaw. The story is, they just went crazy with the killing and even killed the Indian ponies."

Wells nudged his horse along the trail that led into the rock formation, and one by one, the others followed through the canyon of boulders. Wade was the last to follow, tugging at his packhorse, worrying about the possibility of one of the giant boulders crashing down on them. It was eerily quiet. The sound of the horse's shoes on the rocky trail echoed off the boulder walls, sounding more like twenty horses instead of seven. Wade looked up at the large boulders above him, fearful of ambush. Then the trail emptied into an open grassy area of two or three acres.

Frank pulled up his mount and looked around. "This is where Stewart and the others took their revenge. We'll rest the horses for a while. They've had a tough time of it."

"Shouldn't we push on?" asked Wade feeling fearful that they would lose their trail.

"No need," replied Gil. "If those men come the way we think they will, this trail put us a little ahead of them, and the horses could use a rest, some water, and food. Same as us."

Wade considered that. "What if they don't come the way you think they will?"

Frank looked at Wade. "Then I guess we go find them."

Seth grinned at Frank's humor. "Looks like the grass is good. We'll hobble them over there in the shade."

That said, they dismounted, unsaddled their horses, unloaded the packhorses, and poured water from their canteens into their hats for the animals to drink. Afterward, they hobbled the horses where they had plenty of green grass to feed on, and then the men settled down to take a much-needed rest themselves.

Wade's curiosity about this place of violence would not let him rest, so while the others sat back against their saddles eating deer jerky and beans, he got up and explored a little. As he studied the high walls, he imagined the Indians down here being shot by Stewart's men from the rocks above and thought it must have been a terrible slaughter. Wade envisioned the shouting, screaming, and sounds of guns from the men above and the Indians down here. He did not know Frank was next to him until he spoke.

"A lot of killing happened here that day," Wells said softly. "If you look around some, I imagine you can still find a skull or bone that the wolves and mountain lions didn't drag off."

"Place is quiet," said Wade. "Almost ghost-like."

"Yeah, it has that way about it. These were peaceful Navajos, and none had taken part in the killing of Stewart's family."

Wade's expression was both surprise and disbelief.

Frank scowled as he looked up at the rocks. "About a week or so later, the Army cornered an Apache raiding party near Wilson's River, capturing about thirty bucks. That was when Kyle Stewart learned the awful truth of this place." Wells paused to spit. "The Army found some things that belonged to Stewart's little girl, a doll or something. I don't rightly recall what it was." He paused with uncertainty on his face. "But they found some other stuff that belonged to another family who lived on a farm hit after Stewart's place. It was the Apache who raided his place and not these Navajos."

"Good Lord," replied Wade softly.

Wells looked up at the rocks. "After they gave whatever it was to Kyle Stewart, he returned to his place, set his stock free, and set fire to the house. Then the story goes that he sat in the living room and let the place burn down around him. Reckon he couldn't live with what he and the others had done."

"What became of the other men who rode with Stewart?"

"A few of them packed up and left the area. Some stayed and lived with what they had done."

"Whatever happened to the Stewart place?"

Frank thought about that for a moment. "Far as I know, no one has ever settled on Stewart's place. By now, the winds have spread the last of him and the ashes of the house over the Colorado plains." Frank patted Wade on the back. "Best eat and get some rest. Got a feeling we'll all need it b'fore long."

Nine

The trail from Stewart's Revenge snaked along the foothills to the flatlands and finally to the fork in the trail Gil had described. He and Wade were on foot leading the horses, searching for the familiar tracks, while Frank and Seth looked on the trail that headed southwest. After several minutes of looking, all four rode back to the fork.

Seth looked at the others. "Looks like they haven't come out of the hills yet."

Frank Wells rested his hands on his saddle horn, fearful they may have headed west to the little town of Cedar after all.

Wade looked southeast. "Raton Pass is in that direction. The other trail heads southwest disappearing back into the foothills. Either way is a possibility for a run to Mexico." He looked at the others. "I'm for splitting up."

"Just what did you have in mind?" asked Seth thinking the same thing but wanting to see what young Wade had on his mind.

Wade glanced from one to the other. "We know they haven't passed this way and didn't take the same trail as us. Gil said earlier that we'd probably get here sooner, and it looks like that's just what happened. I say two of us ride back along this trail, the one they'd be riding if they come this way, keeping to the trees and out of sight. If they find they've left the trail and headed in another direction, one follows, and one comes back for the others and the packhorses."

They thought over Wade's plan for a moment, and then Seth, curious to see what Wade had in mind, asked, "Who goes and who stays?"

"Well," said Wade. "Guess that'd be up to you."

Frank Wells looked at Seth. "Sounds like a reasonable plan."

79

Gil nodded his agreement. "It's better than if all of us waited here. Got nothing to lose but time."

"Alright," said Seth. "Frank and I will take the second trail. You two stay put." He looked around, then pointed to a ridge of pine and aspen about four hundred yards to the north, giving plenty of cover and a good view of the terrain. "You two take the packhorses up that ridge yonder and wait. If we ain't back by sundown, you boys stay put and don't build any fires."

"And if you ain't back by sunup?" asked Gil.

Frank looked at Gil. "One or both of us will be back by then." He reached into his saddlebag, took out the long glass, and gave it to Gil. "If not," he said, "you'll know what to do."

As Seth and Frank rode west, staying in the trees away from the trail, Gil softly said, "Sure hope we didn't screw this thing up." Then he looked at Wade. Let's get these horses up that ridge."

Wade felt disappointed and fearful they'd lost the four men. "Hell, we're no closer to these guys than we were two days ago."

Gil could not disagree and saw no sense in saying anything further on the subject. They rode up the ridge and found a good spot behind some rocks in the shade of several aspen trees. They left the horses saddled but loosened their cinches, took the supplies off the three packhorses, hobbled them, and gave them water. They settled in for what they feared would be a long wait behind the rocks looking down at the valley floor where the trails meet and then separate heading in different directions.

Wade looked at Gil. "What did Frank mean that you'd know what to do if they weren't back by sunup?"

"We go looking for them."

Wade looked confused. "Wouldn't we do that anyway?"

Gil chuckled. "Frank likes to hear himself talk. It makes him feel important."

Wade grinned as he thought about that for a moment. "How long have you known Frank?"

Gil thought for a moment. "Not sure, but a while, I reckon. We first met when we both scouted for the Army several years back. I lost track of him when I stopped scout'n and got hitched." He glanced at Wade, looking apologetic. "Sorry, my Annie hates that. She prefers married. Anyway, one day, I was walking down the street of Roscoe's Creek and saw Frank riding into town. He looked tired and hungry, and his horse didn't look much better, so I invited him to dinner. The town just lost its sheriff to a fever, so he stayed on, becoming sheriff, and here we are trailing some no goods with you and Seth Bowlen."

The hours slowly passed, and the sun spread its orange glow over the red soil as it dipped below the mountains to the west. Long shadows stretched across the red soil with patches of brown and yellow grasses with purple flowers. It was a beautiful sight, with the familiar red soil and rock formations turning orange-red while the white bark of the aspen trees turned the same color as the setting sun. Noticing that Gil had dozed off, Wade wondered how he could sleep at such a time. Turning from Gil to the Colorado plains, he saw riders come out of the trees along the trail Seth and Frank had taken earlier that day.

Excited, Wade reached over and shook Gil. "Riders."

Gil sat up, took the long glass out of his coat pocket, pulled it apart, and looked at the riders. Several seconds passed before he looked at Wade. "It's them. The girls are on the third horse." He put the long glass back to his eye. "Looks like that half-breed you told us about is bringing up the rear."

Wade watched the riders. "Can you see if the little girls are alright?"

"Appears they are," said Gil while he looked through the long glass. Then he turned and smiled at Wade. "They's alive."

Wade felt happy and hopeful that his task might soon be over. He asked for the glass and looked through it at the men who killed Emmett and the others for the first time. The two girls were on a horse between the three men and the half-breed. "I can shoot the horse the girls are riding."

Gil considered that. "These bastards might just shoot the girls and leave them."

Wade didn't like that possibility as he watched the group ride slowly toward the crossing of the two trails. "Maybe we should try and get a little closer?"

"Yeah," agreed Gil. "Let's see if we can do that without being seen."

Wade checked the hobbled legs of the packhorses while Gil tightened both cinches on their saddles, then both swung up onto their horses and rode down the ridge staying in the trees. Wade pulled up in the trees and looked at Gil. "I wonder where Seth and Frank are?" Gil was about to say something when the four men and two little girls took off at a gallop. Gil raised his arm and pointed. "There's Seth and Frank now, riding out of the trees about two hundred yards behind the four men."

The half-breed stopped, turned his horse, pulled his Winchester from its scabbard, and fired, hitting Frank's mount tossing him as it fell. Seth turned his horse just in time, missing Frank, then fought to control the animal as it bucked and turned in small circles. Seth got control of the horse, pulled up, and looked at Wells to make sure he was alright. Frank waved as he slowly got up, yelling at him to get the girls. Seth pulled his Winchester from its sheath and spurred his horse into a gallop. He wrapped the reins of his horse around the horn of his saddle, stood in the stirrups, aimed, and fired, missing his target.

"Let's go!" yelled Gil. "We can cut them off." Spurring his horse into a gallop to cut the four men off.

Wade pulled his Sharps from its scabbard, put a shell in the chamber, spurred his mare, and followed Gil down the slope.

Seth saw Wade and Gil ride out of the trees and knew what they were trying to do, stood in the stirrups, and fired at the half-breed.

The man in the lead turned and seeing Gil and Wade ride out of the trees, took aim with his rifle and fired. The bullet hit the dirt in front of Gil's horse, causing it to jump and jerk to the right, almost throwing Gil. Wade had to turn his mare to the left to miss Gil, but the horses still bumped, and Gil's horse almost went down. Getting control of his horse, he spurred it into a gallop and followed Wade.

The third man holding the reins of the horse the girls were on tossed them into the air, hoping they would go after the girls. The four turned their horses galloping south and away from the two girls.

Seth rode at a gallop, stood in the stirrups, aimed at the last man, and fired his Winchester, missing his target. Concerned about the girls, he shoved his Winchester back in its sheath, turned his horse, and rode after them.

Wade and Gil kept up their pursuit of the four men. The lead rider pulled up, took aim at Wade with his Sharps, and fired. He missed Wade but hit Gil, who was right behind him, in the shoulder. Wade turned in time to see Gil and his horse go down. Concerned about Gil, Wade pulled up, stood in the stirrups, and aimed at the closest rider. With the mare having done this before, she stood still while Wade pulled the two triggers feeling the kick of the exploding cartridge. Moments later, the rider he aimed at jerked to one side but did not go down, and by the time he reloaded, they disappeared over the hill.

Wade cursed the lousy luck, but knowing he hit his mark, he turned the mare and hollered at Gil, sitting on the ground holding his left shoulder. "You alright?"

Gil looked unhappy as he waved for him to go on.

Wade turned in the saddle and looked to the south seeing Seth had the two girls. Relieved that they were safe, he told Gil to sit tight while he rounded up his horse and checked on Frank. When he got to Frank, he was standing on the trail next to his dead horse that took a bullet in the head meant for Frank.

Frank looked up at Wade. "You hit anyone?"

Wade nodded. "I think so. They were pretty far out, but it appeared the half-breed on the spotted horse jerked a bit as if shot, but I ain't sure."

Frank pulled the saddle off his dead horse, tossed it on the horse behind Gil's saddle, took the reins, climbed up, and rode to Gil and asked if he was okay.

"Been shot worse than this," replied Gil. "I'll live, I reckon."

Seth and the little girls, looking terrified, rode up and stopped a few feet away.

Wade looked at them as they cried, asked if they were alright, and when neither answered, he looked at Seth and asked if they were hurt.

"They're more'n likely terrified," Seth said. "I tried telling them they were safe, but I think they're just too scared right now."

While Frank looked at Gil's shoulder, Seth looked at the ridge and then asked Gil if he could ride. Gil said he could, so Seth told him to mount up behind Wade, and they headed toward the ridge.

When they reached camp, Wade put a blanket on the ground for the girls, and as they sat down, they embraced one another. Neither spoke as they watched the men build a fire to fix supper.

Ten

The first thing Wade did when he woke up was to check on the two little girls huddled up to one another. Relieved they were still sleeping, he looked toward the eastern horizon where the sun was about to come up. The cry of a coyote somewhere in the distance broke the stillness of a chilly morning. Wade looked at Gill Robertson, who appeared to be resting comfortably after being shot in the shoulder. He pushed his blanket back, stood, and stretched his stiff back. Seeing that Seth and Frank were still sleeping, he looked down at the ashes of last night's fire and decided to gather some wood while the others slept and build a fire.

Wade got the fire going, then filled the coffee pot with water from one of the canteens, added the coffee grounds, and sat back, taking pleasure from the warmth of the fire. Watching the flames dance above the burning wood, he thought about his shot yesterday at the half-breed, hoping he had wounded him. Wade looked at the others as they slept, was thankful for their company, and knew he had a better chance of catching the four men with their help, and wondered what they would do with the two girls and Gil. He was certain Gil could not continue, and then there was Frank's horse.

Frank's snoring interrupted Wade's worries over continuing after the four men.

Seth raised his head, looked at Frank from under his hat, sat up, took off his hat, and scratched his head vigorously, looking sleepy. He put the hat back on and looked at Wade. "Thought them little gals were gonna cry forever."

Wade looked at the two lumps under the blanket. "Took them a while, that's for sure. I was glad they finally cried themselves to sleep." Then he looked at Bowlen. "Coffee?"

Seth nodded yes, threw back his blanket, moved closer to the fire, and warmed his hands while Wade poured him a cup of coffee. Holding the tin cup, he warmed his hands, then took a drink and looked at the girls. "Them two's lives have surely changed."

Wade looked at them, thinking that was true enough, recalling his pain when learning his pa had been killed during the Civil War. He felt empathy for the two little girls losing both parents and older brother to such terrible men and wondered if they would ever be alright.

Gil moaned, opened his eyes, and asked for some water.

Wade picked up the canteen, gave him a drink then asked if he was hungry.

Gil gently his head, then closed his eyes.

The talking woke Frank. "You should eat something, Gil," he said, sitting up on one elbow, his hair a mess.

Wade checked Gil for a fever. Finding none, he looked at Seth and then Frank. "No fever."

"Good," Smiled Frank tossing his blanket back. He moved next to the fire warming his hands while watching Wade pour a cup of coffee. Taking the cup, he thanked him, took a sip, looked at the girls, and softly said, "Wonder what'll come of them two now that their family's dead?"

Seth looked at the girls feeling sorry for them. "Maybe they got some relatives they can stay with."

Wade said he hoped someone would take them in. Then he stood and said he was going to check on the horses. As he walked away, Frank asked him to bring some beans and jerky back from their supplies for breakfast. Their talking must have awakened the two girls because they both sat up, looking sleepy-eyed as each yawned.

Frank smiled at them. "Morning, ladies."

Seth smiled. "Sleep well?"

They huddled together with arms around one another, looking afraid.

Seth smiled again. "Nothing to be afraid of, girls. Those men can't harm you now."

The older one looked at Seth. "Can we go home?"

Frank smiled. "Why don't you two girls come over by the fire where it's warmer?"

They looked at one another, then hesitantly moved next to the fire, where the older girl put her arm around her younger sister as if protecting her.

Seth felt sorry for them. "We never got much of a chance to talk last night, but it seems like I remember one of you had the name, Jessica."

The oldest looked at him. "That's my name."

"Oh yes," smiled Seth. "I remember now." Then he looked at the younger girl. "And what do we call you?"

"Clementine," she replied shyly. "My name's Clementine."

Jessica's eyes glanced from one of the men to the other. "We're Jessica and Clementine Osborn."

Wade returned with the beans and jerky, said hello to the girls, knelt next to the fire, and started fixing breakfast.

Clementine looked at him. "Is that what we're having for breakfast?"

Figuring he would have a hard time with breakfast, he smiled at her. "It is if you're hungry." He paused with a smile. "Are you hungry?"

They looked at one another, nodded their heads, then Clementine asked, "Can we have pancakes and honey?"

Wade looked regretful. "Sorry, but we don't have either."

"That's okay," said Jessica looking disappointed. "The other men didn't have any either."

Wade felt terrible for the two girls having to eat such things as beans and jerky for breakfast. It was alright for grown men but not for little girls such as these, and he recalled times back home when he and his sister raided the honey jar.

Jessica and Clementine watched the men closely for several minutes, both fearful of who they were. Jessica's face was dirty, her brown hair tangled and wild-looking, her big brown eyes still puffy and red from crying.

Frank smiled at Jessica. "You say your last name is Osborn?"

"So is mine," offered Clementine.

Frank grinned. "Well, it's a downright honor to know you two. I'm Sheriff Frank Wells from Roscoe's Creek. Do either of you know where that is?"

Feeling a little better knowing he was a Sheriff, they shook their heads saying, "No."

Wells nodded at Seth. "That fella, there is Sheriff Seth Bowlen from the town of Sisters." Then he gestured to Wade, seeing a bit of ash on his face. "That young fella with the dirty face is Wade Garrison."

Happy to be with two sheriffs, the girls giggled softly at Wade.

He made an ugly face and quickly wiped the ash away with both hands.

"You're funny," giggled Clementine.

Then Frank pointed to Gil. "That one there's Gil Robinson, and he's from Roscoe's Creek, same as me."

"Is he hurt bad?" asked Jessica, looking worried.

"Not so much," replied Frank, but he was still worried about infection but never mentioned that to the girls. "He hasn't any fever, so I think he'll be alright."

Jessica looked into the fire with a sad expression as her eyes began to well with tears. "Those men hurt our ma and pa and Mitch."

"We know, darl'n," said Seth looking sad. "That's why we came after you. Was Mitch your brother?"

Clementine looked at Seth. Her face was dirty, her blonde hair was a mess, and her blue-gray eyes were full of tears. "Mitch tried to protect us from those bad men." Then Clementine put her head against Jessica's chest. "They shot him," she said, then they both began to cry.

The men watched them for a moment feeling bad and unable to offer any words of comfort the two would understand. Not knowing what else to do, Wade picked up a tin plate, spooned some beans, and handed it to Jessica. "You need to eat."

She wiped her eyes, took the plate, looked at the beans, and then at Wade. "Thank you."

Frank smiled and asked Wade if he was going to give her a spoon or fork or if he was going to let her lap it up like a dog, and that made her and Clementine giggle. Wade grinned and gave her a spoon, dished up a second plate for Clementine, asking if she wanted a spoon or fork or if she preferred to eat like a dog.

"A spoon," she said with a giggle.

Wade handed her a spoon then he and the others watched as the two began to eat. Then he dished up a tin plate of beans, picked up his coffee cup, sat back, and took a drink while watching Jessica. "How old are you?"

She said she was eight and her sister was six, then she looked sad and said that Mitch was thirteen. Then as tears filled her eyes said, "That is, he used to be."

"I'm sorry at what happened to your family," Wade said, then motioned to the others. "We all are."

"Are you taking us home?" asked Jessica.

Gil had been awake listening. "Afraid not, girls. You see, there's no one at your place who can take care of you now. Do you have any relatives or friends who live close by?"

"We came from Indiana by wagon last year," said Jessica. She looked at her sister. "We have a gramps back there but no grams on account she's dead."

Clementine spoke up. "We have an uncle."

"Uncle Pete," said Jessica. "His name is Uncle Pete, but pa says he's about as bright as the moonless night."

While the girls ate, Wade, Seth, and Frank moved closer to Gil so they could talk without the girls hearing. After much deliberation, they agreed that Gil would head back to Roscoe's Creek with the two girls in the morning if he felt up to it. Gil was sure his Annie would welcome them into their family and that his daughter Annabelle would love to have two little sisters. He smiled, saying that was something she often talked about. Gil suggested that if he were up to the task by tomorrow, Frank would take his younger, faster horse while he rode one of the packhorses. Feeling tired, Gil closed his eyes and drifted off to sleep.

Wade said he would saddle up and track the four men for a few miles before the wind blew their tracks away after breakfast.

Seth did not like the idea all that much but agreed. "You be careful," he told Wade looking concerned.

"I'm gonna track them just far enough to make sure they don't double back toward the mountains or the town of Cedars."

Frank turned to ask Gil where the long glass was, but he was sleeping comfortably, so he gently went through Gil's coat pockets, pulled it out, and handed it to Wade. "Keep a sharp eye on the hills ahead of you."

Seth told Wade to take it slow and listen to his instincts.

Wade nodded his understanding, took the long glass, and shoved it into his saddlebags. After saddling the mare, he told the others he would be back in a few hours. Then he rode down the slope toward the fork in the trail.

Wade found the tracks of the four men right off and followed them southeast, figuring they were heading toward Raton Pass into New Mexico Territory. He had followed their trail for about eight miles and was thinking of turning back when he found a dead campfire figuring the four men had stopped for the night. Getting down from the mare, Wade knelt to one knee and touched the ashes. Finding them cold, he stood seeing a bloody rag that someone had tossed into the bushes a few feet away, walked over, and picked it up.

Knowing he had hit the half-breed, he threw the rag down, and while looking at the tracks, he saw that one rider broke off and headed east while the other three rode south toward Raton Pass. Figuring it was the half-breed, he took the long glass from his saddlebags and searched the hills to the south and the plains to the east. Seeing no signs of them in either direction, he pushed the long glass together, put it in his saddlebag, and looked down at the tracks of the single rider heading east. Thinking he was hurt and heading for the nearest town, Wade took off his hat and held it above his head while looking up at the clear blue sky, figuring it was close to midday. Looking in the direction the lone rider had gone, he knew he should go back for Seth and Frank. He climbed back onto his horse, looked back in the direction of Seth and Frank Wells, and headed east at a gallop, following the single rider.

The trail led Wade to Sierra Mesa's small Anglo, Mexican town on the Purgatoire River in southern Colorado. Pulling up several hundred yards from the edge of town, he took out the long glass and looked up the single street of adobe and wooden buildings. Looking further up the main street, he saw the spotted horse tied to a hitching rail. He pushed the long glass together and, as he put it in his saddlebags, wished Seth and Frank were with him. After making sure his Colt revolver was loaded, he nudged his mare toward Sierra Mesa.

It was not a very big town, maybe a dozen buildings and a few adobe huts with thatched roofs and a spattering of trees behind the buildings on either side. The sun was hot, and a slight breeze sent small swirling dust devils along the dusty, empty street in front of him. A Mexican man came out of a door, stood at the edge of the narrow boardwalk, waited for him to pass, then crossed the street toward the cantina. Two white women walked out of a store on the other side of the street carrying packages and hurried along the boardwalk, disappearing into a boarding house.

With his hand on the butt of his pistol, he continued up the street past three horses tied to the hitching rail at the Cantina as laughter and music spilled out the swinging doors. Glancing from one building to the other and the alleyways between, he rode at a walk toward the black and white spotted horse, ignoring the mixture of whites and Mexicans walking along the boardwalks or crossing the street. He rode past the spotted horse tied at the rail and saw the small sign 'Doctor-Doctora' suspended above the boardwalk. Wade continued up the street, stopping at the hitching rail in front of a Café, dismounted, and loosely tied the mare to the hitching rail. He glanced up and down the street as he stepped onto the boardwalk just as a heavyset Mexican woman wearing bright-colored clothes walked out of the Café. She paused to look at him, then tossed water from a bucket into the street. After giving him a closer look, she turned and walked back inside.

Before the door closed, Wade caught the smell of cooking inside the café. He paused in the shade of the building, took off his hat, wiped the sweat from his forehead with the sleeve of his shirt then put his hat back on. Stepping away from the building, he started walking toward the spotted horse. The door of the Doctor's Office suddenly opened, and the half-breed stepped out onto the boardwalk. His arm was in a sling, and the shoulder of his shirt was bloody. Wade turned and looked at the half-breed's image in the big window as he climbed onto his horse and rode across the street to the cantina, where he climbed down and went inside.

Wade stared at the swinging doors to the cantina, imagining the half-breed inside drinking whiskey or tequila. Then he opened the door to the Doctor's Office and stepped inside. A thin Mexican man turned from the cabinet where he had just put something and smiled. "Hello, señor. I am Doctor Ortega. May I be of some service?"

Wade shook his head, and asked if there was a sheriff in town.

"No, señor," said Doctor Ortega looking concerned. "The sheriff died from a snake bite several days ago, and no one has taken his place." He paused, looking at Wade. "Señor, is there something I can do for you?"

Wade gestured toward the door. "The man who was just here, is he badly hurt?"

The doctor gave Wade a curious look. "If I may ask, señor, are you a friend of his?"

Wade nodded that he was. "How badly is he hurt?"

The doctor looked puzzled. "The bullet did some damage to the muscle but missed the bone. I told him to take it easy for a few days."

Wade thanked him, turned, and walked out the door, and when he looked across the street at the cantina, the spotted horse was gone. Afraid the half-breed would get away, Wade hurried to his horse and rode south out of town, hoping he could overtake the half-breed.

About a mile southwest of Sierra Mesa, the trail Wade followed left the stage trail and headed south across the plains toward Raton Pass. Wade stopped to study the tracks for a moment thinking the half-breed was on his way to join the others and considered giving up the chase and go back for Seth and Frank. He glanced west, thinking Seth would be pissed, but he spurred his mare and followed the lone rider anyway. Minutes later, Wade rode to the top of a hill, stopped, took the long glass out of his saddlebag, stood in the stirrups, and looked across the vast Colorado plains. It took a minute, but he saw the half-breed riding at a walk heading south. Wade lowered the long glass and saw a wide gully to his left framed by cottonwoods snaking its way south. He put the long glass back in his saddlebags, nudged the mare, and rode into the gully.

He looked up at the sun, thinking it was hot and the mare was probably hot and tired. He rode along the gully for several minutes, pulled up, took the long glass out, and searched for the half-breed. Seeing he had ridden past the half-breed who was about a quarter mile behind him now, riding at a leisurely pace.

Dismounting, he loosened the saddle cinch and poured some water from his canteen into his hat, and while the mare drank from the hat, he drank from the canteen. When the horse finished, Wade put his hat on and hung the canteen's strap over his saddle horn. He looked at the half-breed again through the long glass, figuring he had about fifteen minutes. Wade put the glass away and pulled the Sharps out from its scabbard. Then he took a cartridge from the bandoleer, shoved it into the Sharps breech, sat down in the shade, and placed the gun against the tree. He leaned back against the cottonwood, thinking it was getting hotter, and watched the mare nibble on a small clump of grass. Smiling, he thought of the first time he saw her and the day he met Emmett Spears.

1868

It was the end of July 1868 when Wade jumped down from a wagon, he had hitched a ride from town to the gate of the Circle T ranch. Thanking the man, he pulled his carpetbag from the back, turned, and walked through the open gate and past the barn toward the house. Seeing a man with gray hair sitting in a chair on the porch, peeling an apple with a knife, he stopped a few feet from the porch's steps.

"Can I help you, son?" asked the man.

Wade stepped a little closer. "I'm looking for Mr. Grimes."

"You've found him. Now, what do you want with him?"

"A job."

Mr. Grimes shoved a piece of apple into his mouth and chewed while staring at the young man he had watched climb down from a wagon and walk through the gate. "You have a horse?"

"No, sir."

"A man ain't much good without a horse on a ranch."

"No, sir, I guess not. But I'm a good worker and mind my own business."

Thinking those were good attributes, Mr. Grimes stared at him. "Where's home?"

"South Carolina."

The old man grinned. "Came west looking for adventure, I take it."

Wade looked defeated. "Ain't found much of anything but cold nights and hunger, and I'd be grateful for a job of any kind."

"You might try one of the smaller places."

Wade thought about that. "Small place is a small job for small wages, Mr. Grimes. I didn't come all this way to be a small person."

Tolliver Grimes liked the answer, invited the young man onto the porch, and then told him to sit on one of the wooden chairs. After a few minutes of talking, he liked the boy, and although he wasn't shorthanded, he gave Wade a job as a ranch hand and drover.

Wade looked worried. "But I ain't got a horse."

Tolliver stood, waited for Wade to stand, and the two shook hands. "Let's see about a place to sleep and a horse. I'll take the price of the horse, saddle, and such out of your wages a small amount at a time if that meets your approval."

Wade grinned as he agreed and followed Mr. Grimes off the porch of the big house and across the yard toward the barn and corral. As they walked, Mr. Grimes talked about some of the ins and outs of the ranch business. The two stopped by the corral, where Mr. Grimes paused to lean on the top rail, his left foot resting on the bottom railing while he admired a young colt. As a young man rode toward them, Mr. Grimes stood away from the corral and waved him over. The rider dismounted, Mr. Grimes patted him on the shoulder and turned to Wade. "This here's Emmett Spears." Then he turned to Emmett. "This young fella is Wade Garrison from South Carolina, and I just hired him on as a drover."

The two shook hands, then Mr. Grimes told Emmett to help Wade pick out a good horse and saddle. "After you've done that, take Mr. Garrison to the bunkhouse and find him a place to live." Mr. Grimes turned back to Wade and shook his hand once again. "Hope you like it here, Mr. Garrison." Then he turned and walked toward the main house.

Emmett Spears was a tall, slim young man of about twenty. He took off his gray, well-worn hat to knock the dust of a hard day's work from his pants and faded red shirt. The empty hand attempted to comb back his unruly dark red hair that hadn't seen a barber in weeks. A thin straight nose sat between deep-set friendly green eyes above cheeks that housed a scattering of freckles. The boyish young face bore the lines that were the trophies of working in the sun. After he dusted himself off, he smiled with uneven white teeth. "Let's head over to the other side of the barn. These studs are used for breeding only." Then he asked, "So you're from South Carolina?"

"That's right."

"What the hell you doing way out here?"

Wade grinned, thinking of what Mr. Grimes had asked. "Got tired of working the farm, I guess and wanted to see something else."

Emmett shrugged, looking sad. "I left my home back in Ohio for much the same reasons. When did you leave home?"

Wade thought about that for a moment. "A couple of years ago."

"Where ya been all this time?"

Wade shrugged. "Working here and there. Most of my time was in Denver, cleaning barrooms and such, and then I worked on a couple of small farms. That wasn't quite the way I had it planned when I left home."

Emmett laughed. "It never is, I guess."

Reaching the corral on the other side of the barn, Emmett stopped at the fence, placed one foot on the bottom rail, and leaned on the top railing with his arms looking at the horses. Wade did the same, enjoying the scene of several fine looking animals, and after a minute, Emmett told *him to pick one. Wade was a good judge of horseflesh and immediately took a liking to a big black standing next to the fence.*

"How about the black one over there?"

Emmett looked at the horse thoughtfully. "He's not for riding."

"Why not?"

"Belonged to Charles Grimes, the old man's dead son. Mr. Grimes won't let anyone ride him. He comes out here just about every day, feeds him an apple or some oats, and talks to him. No one knows what he says, but afterward, he goes up to that big house and gets drunk." He went on to tell how the boy had died.

Wade looked toward the house. "Sounds kinda sad."

"Guess it is," said Emmett thoughtfully, then he told of how Mrs. Grimes had up and killed herself one night. After a few moments of silence, he pointed to another horse. "Now that sorrel over there, the one with the white stockings on her legs, is one I like."

"She is pretty," agreed Wade. "And big for a mare."

"She's fast, too," chuckled Emmett.

"Well, I think I've found my horse," grinned Wade.

Emmett slapped him on the back. "Let's go into the tack room and get a saddle and bridle, then we'll see about a bunk." The bunk turned out to be next to Emmett's, and after that day, the two were inseparable.

Wade cleared his mind of the past and got to his knees on the gully bank to see over the top. Looking through the telescope for the half-breed, he found that he had ridden past him and was about three hundred yards to the south. Thinking of yesterday's near miss, he returned to the gully, picked up his Sharps leaning against the tree, swung up on the mare, and rode out of the gully. After a few moments, when Wade figured he had a good shot, he pulled up, raised the Sharps' sight, put the gun to his shoulder, took aim through the small peep sight at the solitary rider, and gently pulled the first trigger. Pulling the second trigger, the calm, quiet air filled with the Sharps explosion as it recoiled against his shoulder. The rider jerked to the right and then fell. The riderless horse jumped and kicked its hind legs as it bolted for a short distance, then stopped. Wade ejected the shell, put in another, and rode toward the riderless horse.

When he got to the half-breed, Wade put the Sharps away while watching the wounded man crawl toward a large rock. He dismounted, bent down, took the half-breed's pistol from its holster, and tossed it several feet. Wanting to look the man that killed Emmett in the face, Wade turned him over. His dark-complexioned face twisted from pain as blood seeped from the corners of his mouth. He managed to push himself up a little, looked up at Wade, and coughed up a little blood. "Who the hell are you?"

Wade knelt and looked into his dark eyes. "I'm the man that killed you for killing my friend Emmett Spears and the families you and your friends terrorized before you murdered them."

The breed coughed up blood. "Who the hell is Emmett Spears?"

Wade looked at the large bloody hole in the man's chest. "You ain't got much time."

The half-breed looked down at his chest, knowing that was true. "Guess not." He frowned at Wade. "Who was this Emmett fella?"

"Emmett Spears was the man you boys shot five times back in Harper. He never even had a gun."

The half-breed's eyes looked tired as he slowly blinked. His chin and cheeks were bloody from coughing up blood. "Oh yeah. But I wasn't there," he said in a whisper, and then he coughed. "I was upstairs doing a whore."

Feeling disappointed about Emmett and angry about the families, Wade leaned a little closer to the half-breed's ear. "That may be so, but I'm sending you to hell for the others you've killed and those two little girls you took."

Wade was not sure the half-breed heard what he told him because he had stopped breathing. Looking into his lifeless eyes, Wade regretted his death because he wanted him to suffer a little more before making his journey to hell. Standing, he stepped back and looked into the face of the third man he had killed in as many days and felt no remorse. Hearing the sorrel mare whinny, he turned and looked at her, then walked toward the black and white spotted horse standing several yards away. Speaking softly to it so it wouldn't bolt, it stared at him as he slowly reached for the reins, and after taking them, he rubbed the horse's forehead, turned, and led it back to where his mare waited.

Wade tied the half-breed's horse to the horn of his saddle and thought about placing rocks over the body but quickly decided not to, saying, "Let the vultures, coyotes, and ants finish you." Unbuckling the breed's holster, he pulled it out from under him, picked up the pistol he had tossed away, and shoved it into the holster. After he draped them over the half-breed's saddle horn, he took a last look at what he had done, climbed into his saddle, turned the mare, and rode away.

Eleven

The sun was just above the Rocky Mountains in the west when Wade and the spotted horse he had in tow rode past the fork in the trail he had crossed earlier in the day. A lone rider rode down the slope to the red dirt plains and galloped toward him, chased by a small cloud of red dust. Wade pulled up and waited, knowing it was Seth Bowlen and that he probably wasn't happy.

Seth looked angry as he pulled up. "Where the hell have you been?" He waited for an answer, then said, "We been sitting up there not knowing whether to leave Gil and the little gals and come after you or wait."

Wade glanced at the ridge where Gil, Frank, and the girls were. "Sorry," he said, sounding tired.

Seth looked at the horse in tow. "Ain't that the half-breed's horse?"

"Yeah, I'll explain when we get to camp. I don't particularly want to have to tell it twice." Wade nudged the mare into a walk and then into a gallop toward the knoll and camp.

Still angry, Seth spurred his horse and followed.

"Where the hell you been?" asked Frank as Wade rode into camp, noticing the extra horse he knew belonged to the half-breed.

"Isn't that the half-breed's horse?" asked Gil Robinson.

Thinking that was obvious, Wade tied the mare and the half-breed's horse to the branch of a tree, walked past Gil toward the fire, and smiled at the girls. He knelt, picked up a tin cup, and filled it with hot coffee. Taking a drink, he looked at Wells. "Haven't had anything to eat all day."

Frank glanced at Seth tying his horse to a branch of another tree, knowing he was angry, and turned to Wade. "We were about to eat when Seth saw you." Frank paused to look at Seth and then at Wade taking a drink of coffee. "Seth's been fretting all day."

Wade sat in silence, staring into the fire as he took a drink of coffee.

Seth shrugged softly. "You had us worried, is all."

The three thought Wade was acting a little peculiar as Frank dished up a tin plate of food, handed it to Wade, and asked about the half-breed.

"He's dead," said Wade softly, then dished up a fork of food, shoved it into his mouth, and ate in silence, thinking about the day.

Frank and Seth looked at one another and decided to let Wade eat, so they sat down, dished up their food, and waited for him to tell them about the half-greed.

Wade ate the plate of food but ignored the jerky that Frank offered, and now he sat back and drank the strong coffee. After some minutes of silence, he drank the last of his coffee, placed the empty cup next to the rocks surrounding the fire, and told them of the killing.

Seth grinned, "Tell me you didn't say any words over that scum."

Wade looked up. "Only that I was sending him to hell." He nodded at the spotted horse and said Frank could have it so Gil could ride his horse. Feeling tired, Wade got up and unsaddled both horses, and when he finished, he laid down with his head on his saddle, pulled his blanket around him, and quickly went to sleep.

Seth knew the killing of the half-breed, or any man, no matter how much you hate them, can weigh heavy on one's shoulders. He poured another cup of coffee, and for the rest of the night, no one spoke of the half-breed. The girls soon became tired and went to sleep, and since Gil was wounded, Seth and Frank took turns at watch. In the stillness of the night, Seth stared into the fire, filled with concerns over the consequences that had walked into young Wade Garrison's life. He looked at the young man who slept peacefully and knew he would return to Harper, a different man.

Wade was the first to rise early the next morning, feeling energetic and unusually happy. The sun was not yet above the eastern hills, and the morning air held a slight chill. While the others slept, he quietly gathered wood, built a fire, poured the last of the water from one of the water bags into the pot for coffee, and thought of the stream a mile or so up the canyon. Yesterday's killing visited him only briefly, and then he put it away and thought of Sarah Talbert. He wanted to see her again, smell her hair and perfume mixed with the other smells of cooking and washing. He wanted to hold her, hear her soft laugh, and see the softness in her eyes. He wanted to make love to her and wished he had before he left.

August 1868

It was Saturday afternoon and Wade's first payday at the Circle T Ranch. He and Emmett Spears were in Mason's General Store in the town of Harper. Wade had just purchased a new black Texas flat hat that he had always wanted and was looking back at Emmett as he walked out the door instead of where he was going and ran into a woman. Looking embarrassed, he stepped back and quickly took off his new hat. "Pardon me, ma'am."

The woman gave him a stern look. "Quite alright, young man." She brushed off the front of her dress and smiled at him. "Might be better if you walked out of the door looking forward instead of at what's behind you."

Wade's face flushed. "Yes ma'am." Then he noticed a girl near his age standing beside an older man behind the woman.

She smiled, but the man wore a frown as he said, "That's good advice, young fella. That way, you won't trample the womenfolk."

Wade stared at the young girl. "Yes sir." Then he looked at the woman. "I certainly am sorry and do apologize if I hurt you any."

She had a forgiving smile. "I'm not hurt." She turned to the young girl. "Come, dear."

Wade stepped aside, looking a little sheepish.

The young girl smiled.

Wade felt his face flush.

The woman looked at her daughter, then at Wade with a disapproving look. "Come along, Sarah. We've some shopping to do."

As the girl and her father walked past, Wade took another step backward, bumping into another woman. He turned and apologized.

Getting a stern look from the woman who scolded, "Watch where you're going, young man."

Wade apologized for a second time. "Yes ma'am, and I'm mighty sorry." Stepping outside, he walked along the boardwalk, searching for the young girl through the store window. Seeing her holding a bolt of cloth while talking to her mother, he stopped suddenly, causing Emmett to bump into him.

Emmett started to say something when he saw what Wade was looking at and smiled, thinking his friend was smitten.

The young girl looked up from the bolt of cloth, turned and smiled at him over her shoulder, then looked away just as the older man stepped between them with a scowl on his face. Wade nodded and smiled, trying to look friendly, but the man turned away.

"Who was that?" asked Wade as he and Emmett turned to walk along the boardwalk.

Emmett glanced over his shoulder. "That was Mr. Jasper Talbert. He owns the Double J a few miles northeast of town."

Wade looked at Emmett in disbelief. "Not him. Her."

"Oh, that was his wife, Janice Talbert. In case you can't figure it out, Jasper and Janice own the Double J Ranch."

Wade was frustrated. "No, you fool. The girl."

Emmett glanced back toward the store. "That was Sarah Talbert." Then he slowly shook his head. "She sure is a pretty thing." He turned and looked back at the store once again. "One of the prettiest girls around, Harper, I reckon." Then he put one hand on Wade's shoulder and gently shoved him toward their horses. "C'mon, let's go have a beer before we head back to the Circle T."

As they walked toward their horses, Wade turned and looked back, seeing Sarah Talbert at the window. Wade smiled and walked into the porch post.

Sarah Talbert turned away quickly, knowing the young man would be embarrassed.

While Emmett laughed, Wade quickly looked at Sarah, seeing she was looking the other way, thankful she did not see his clumsiness. Embarrassed, he hurried down the steps to his horse, wishing Emmett would shut up.

While they sipped on their beers, Emmett talked of things Wade paid little or no attention to. His mind was full of Sarah Talbert. The picture of her standing on the boardwalk smiling at him was all he could think about, wishing he hadn't been so clumsy. While Emmett continued to talk, Wade stared into his warm beer, the foam now gone and the beer quickly becoming flat.

Sarah Talbert was a pretty girl of sixteen, stood just over five feet, thin, small-breasted with long light-brown hair, which she often wore in a ponytail that bounced and swayed from side to side as she walked. Her slightly freckled oval face looked friendly, as did her big brown eyes.

Emmett's voice suddenly interrupted Wade's thoughts of Sarah Talbert. "You hearing anything I'm saying?"

Wade blinked and looked at him. "Sure."

Emmett laughed. "Like hell. You have been thinking about Sarah Talbert."

Wade felt his face flush. "So?"

"So, nothing," grinned Emmett. "A lot of fellas have tried courting Miss Sarah, including yours truly, but something's always gotten in their way."

Wade looked at him with a puzzled face.

Emmett chuckled. "Mr. Talbert."

Wade smiled at the humor, and nothing more was said on the subject. He knew a poor cowhand like him had little or no chance at all with a rancher's daughter.

Back on the Knoll

The others disturbed Wade's thoughts of Sarah Talbert as they began to wake and move around the camp. Seth stood, stretched, and complained that he was getting too old for this and would be glad when it was over. Frank nodded in agreement, and then seeing Gil sit up, he checked his wound and felt his forehead to see if he had any fever. Finding none, he returned to his bedroll. Jessica and Clementine had moved next to the fire and huddled under their blanket for warmth. Wade poured four cups of coffee, apologizing to the girls that he did not have something warm for them to drink, and asked if they were hungry. They nodded, and Clementine asked him if they had anything besides beans. Before he could answer, Frank asked them if they liked rabbit. Their eyes filled with excitement, saying they did. Frank grinned as he stood, reached for his rifle, and said he was going to shoot a rabbit for breakfast.

While Frank was gone, Jessica looked at Wade. "What's gonna happen to Clementine and me now?"

While Wade considered the question, Gil looked at the two girls and smiled as he told them about his wife being a schoolteacher in Roscoe's Creek, their daughter Annabelle, and this cute little yellow dog that Wade had found. He looked down at the ground for a moment and then at the girls. "We would like you to come live with us."

They looked at one another with fear on their faces as their eyes welled.

Wade smiled. "You have no place else to go, and Gil has a nice house. With his wife being a schoolteacher, she can teach you all sorts of things."

"I don't know," said Jessica as she wiped her face.

"Just try it," offered Wade. "If you don't like it, we'll find someplace else."

The girls looked at one another for several moments, and then Clementine put her head on her sister's shoulder and cried. Jessica put her arms around her sister and looked at Gil with red, teary eyes. "Guess we got no other place to go for right now." Then she asked about their clothes and other things. Gil thought about that for only a moment and told them that after they were safe at his home in Roscoe's Creek, he would go back to the farm and get their clothes and other things. Clementine asked if they could go with him, but Gil told them it would be better if they stayed in Roscoe's Creek with his missus. Hearing a shot, they knew Frank had bagged a rabbit.

A breakfast of beans and rabbit seemed to satisfy the girls, and to the men's delight and relief, Clementine ate a second helping. While the men finished their coffee, they talked about Gil taking one packhorse with enough supplies to get them back to Roscoe's Creek. Wade, Seth, and Frank would head into the nearest town with the other two packhorses, pick up a few supplies, and continue their pursuit.

Gil's strength had come back, and while his shoulder was still sore, he managed to get around quite well, so the others were not too worried about him making the trip back to Roscoe's Creek. He told them that he would ride along the front range of foothills heading north instead of winding back the way they had come. He felt the trail along the foothills would be easier going for the girls, and there was the possibility of staying at a farmhouse or two along the way. Hopefully, that would give the girls a warm place to sleep and a good home-cooked meal. After the supplies were loaded onto Gil's packhorse and the horses saddled, Wade helped the girls onto their horse. He smiled as he told them everything was going to be alright. Jessica smiled and asked why he was not coming with them. Wade told her that he and the others had to continue after the bad men, but

101

he promised that he would look in on them when they got back to Roscoe's Creek. That seemed to please them.

Gil turned to Frank with an outstretched hand that Frank shook firmly, telling him to mind the young girls so they did not get hurt. Gil smiled, said he'd take good care of the girls, and told Frank to watch the skyline. Then Gil turned and shook Seth's hand, then Wade's. Looking regretful that he couldn't go along, he gave a quick nod and said goodbye. Frank helped him climb onto his horse and tied the lead rope of his packhorse to his saddle horn. Gil nudged the horse down the slope onto the Colorado plains, then he and the girls headed north toward Roscoe's Creek.

Twelve

Sierra Mesa was a busier place when Wade, Seth, and Frank rode up the dusty street than when Wade visited the town the day before. A mixture of Mexicans and whites crowded the dirt street and boardwalks. Two white men stood from their chairs outside the sheriff's office and watched them as they slowly rode by. Wade noticed neither wore a badge recalling the doctor telling him that the sheriff had died from a snakebite. Still, he wondered who they were.

Seth smiled and tipped his hat as he rode by. They gave him a friendly wave and returned to their chairs.

The three made their way through the people crossing the street and pulled up in front of Taggert's General Store. They dismounted, tied the horses to the railing, then walked up the steps across the boardwalk and into the store of stuffy smells, greeted by a thin matronly woman behind a counter.

After they exchanged hellos, Frank told her they needed some supplies when she turned to a door that led to a back room and yelled, "Mark, we got customers out here!" Moments later, a short heavyset balding man appeared in the doorway. Smiling, he moved next to his taller wife and asked what they needed. Seth looked around while he told of their needs as another woman walked into the store. The thin matronly woman, the storekeeper, smiled at the woman, waved, and walked from behind the counter while the heavyset man turned to Seth with a businesslike expression. "You were saying."

They were loading their supplies onto the packhorses when someone called out, "Señor!"

Wade turned, seeing Doctor Ortega standing on the boardwalk. Feeling uneasy, Wade glanced at Seth and Frank, then looked at the doctor, said hello, and waited while the doctor walked down the boardwalk steps.

The man smiled at Wade and said it was a pleasure to see him again. "Did you catch up with that man who was injured yesterday?"

Wade's heart jumped, thinking he should have told Seth and Frank. "No, he headed south, and I had to get back to our camp some miles west of here."

Seth and Frank looked on in silence, curious about the question since Wade had not told them about Sierra Mesa and the doctor, only killing the half-breed.

"I see," said Ortega with a worried look. "I was curious as to how he was getting along after so much loss of blood."

Wade pictured the half-breed lying on the ground with a big hole in his chest as he looked at the Doctor. "Sorry, I can't be of any help Doc." Looking a bit uncomfortable, he glanced at the spotted horse Frank was riding and hoped the doctor hadn't noticed the half-breed had been riding it.

The doctor turned to the others. "Good morning, gentlemen. My name is Juan Ortega, and I am the doctor of Sierra Mesa."

Seth and Frank sensed Wade's nervousness, said hello to Ortega, and mounted their horses. "We best be on our way," said Seth.

Wade shook the doctor's hand, said goodbye, and climbed into the saddle.

As they rode down the dusty street, Frank looked at the sign Cantina across the street. "Don't know about you boys, but I could use a hot meal and a drink."

Seth looked at the livery up the street. "I'm sure these horses could use a good meal of oats while we eat. You two go on inside, and I'll take the horses to the livery and join you after I get the stock settled."

Wanting to get on with the hunt and out of Siera Mesa, Wade looked at Seth, "We ain't staying long, are we?"

"A couple of hours, maybe," said Seth. "These horses haven't had much to eat except prairie grass, and they need a good meal of oats and hay." He looked at Wade. "We'll get after these boys soon enough."

Wade knew Seth was right but wanted to get on with it. He and Frank dismounted, dusted themselves off walked up the steps and through

104

the swinging doors of the Cantina. Several tables filled the room, and a long bar took up most of the wall. Letting their eyes adjust to the dim light, they picked an empty table next to the wall and ordered two beers. They had just ordered their second beer when Seth pushed through the swinging doors and joined them at the small table. He plopped down in the chair and, seeing a waitress, motioned her over. As the waitress left to get their food and a beer for Seth, he looked at Wade. "What's with that Mexican doctor?"

Wade started to answer just as the fat Mexican woman brought their food. He waited for her to put it on the table and then told them the story of following the half-breed into Sierra Mesa. Of talking to the doctor and then following the half-breed south, and they knew the rest.

Frank glanced around, leaned forward, and spoke in a low voice. "If they find out you killed that half-breed, we'd have a lot of explaining to do, especially since you shot him in the back with that Sharps of yours."

"Better'n he deserved," responded Seth quietly as he looked around.

"I ain't arguing that," said Wells. "But a town full of strangers not knowing what the hell's going on might take exception to that." He looked at Wade. "Don't get me wrong. What you did was the right thing. I don't like sitting in jail while we explain ourselves."

"Well," Wade said in a voice above a whisper. "There ain't no sheriff because he died from a snakebite a few days back, and the town doesn't have a replacement yet."

"Guess that is a bit of luck," said Frank with a chuckle, and then his expression turned remorseful. "For us, not the sheriff."

They finished eating, walked to the livery, got their horses, bought a couple of oats, and headed out of town. It was not long before the hot summer breeze rushed the smell of the rotting body of the half-breed at them. They lifted their handkerchiefs over their noses and cut a wide path around the vultures feeding on the half-breed's body. Seth and Frank turned to the racket occasionally, but Wade rode on with his eyes focused on the mountains in the distance, thinking of Raton Pass.

By late afternoon they had followed the Santa Fe Trail to the base of Raton Pass. Knowing their horses were tired and needed a night's rest and food, Frank Wells turned off the trail. He stopped near a grove of aspen trees and a small stream and turned to the others. "This'll do fine for the night.

The trees, shrubs, and rocks will give good cover, and the small stream has plenty of water for the horses and our coffee."

No one told the other what to do after they dismounted. Each man just took it upon himself to take care of what was necessary. It was Frank's turn to cook, so he took what he needed out of the satchels he had taken off the packhorses. Seth unsaddled his horse and then began to rub him down with a cloth he had picked up at the livery in Sierra Mesa. As he rubbed his horse down, he offered Frank unwanted cooking advice.

Wade gently rubbed his sorrel with the soft cloth and smiled at the two men and their bickering. The sorrel and the other horses were busy eating their oats, and the mare seemed to enjoy the attention.

Once Frank had dinner ready, the three ate while making small talk about the day's events and the possibilities of where the three men they were trailing might be heading. Frank said that he believed they were heading for the small town of Raton, where they would likely wait for the breed to catch up. Wade asked what sort of place Raton was.

Seth grinned. "It ain't much. The place started as a watering hole with a trading post. I heard there's a cantina or two there now." He shrugged. "But I ain't sure."

Frank thought on that for a moment. "If there ain't a cantina or saloon, these three won't wait long."

Seth agreed. "No more'n a day, then they'll head south to Santa Fe. After that, it's anybody's guess."

"Sure, do hope we catch them before that," said Wade thinking he would like to get back to Harper and Sarah Talbert.

Frank looked uncertain. "They might even head south to El Paso to cross the river into Juarez."

After dinner, Wade went about the task of rubbing down the mare and packhorses while Frank and Seth found the need to lay by the fire and reminisce about old times. Wade wanted to get on with the task of the men they hunted, but he was tired and knew the stock needed a good night's rest, water, and food. Finishing the last horse, he patted the sorrel on the neck and headed for the campfire. It was a quiet night filled with an occasional coyote or owl, the fire's popping, and the muffled voices of Seth and Frank talking about old times. He poured a cup of coffee, sat on the hard ground, leaned back against his saddle, and took a sip while listening to Seth and Frank talk of old times. Their words became soft and distant and soon disappeared from Wade's mind as his memory took him back to Sarah Talbert.

September 1869

It was Friday night, and Wade lay in his bunk reading a book he had borrowed from Mr. Grimes. Emmett had been playing cards with some of the other hands but grew tired of the game and losing, so he returned to his bunk. "What's the name of the book?"

Wade stopped reading and looked at his friend, a little confused by the question since the name was on the cover.

Wade looked at the cover of the book. "It's called Moby Dick, *and it's a story about a white whale."*

Emmett chuckled. "Why would anyone write a whole book about a whale? Ain't that a big fish?"

Wade realized that Emmett probably could not read and sat up on one elbow. "It's a story about whale hunters and this crazy Captain Ahab chasing this big white whale called Moby Dick. They chased it all over the ocean, trying to kill it."

Emmett considered that briefly, then lay back on his pillow and stared at the bottom of the bunk above him. "Wish I could read."

"You can't read any?" asked Wade, realizing he had been right.

Emmett looked embarrassed. "Nah, I never got much schooling. My ma taught me my numbers a bit, and I can sign my name." Then filled with excitement, he looked at Wade. "Got a pencil?"

Wade said he did, got out of bed, knelt on the floor, and pulled a wooden footlocker out from under his bunk. He opened it, took out some paper and a pencil, then sat down on his bunk and wondered what he wanted them for if he couldn't read nor write.

Emmett quickly sat up, took the paper and pencil, and scribbled his name.

Wade read the scribbled letters. "Emit Spears." Then he smiled at Emmett. "That's good."

Emmett nodded with a prideful smile, lay back down, and looked up at the bottom of the bunk above him. "Yep, sure would be nice to be able to read a book like that."

107

Wade looked at Emmitt. "My ma taught me how to read while I was little. "When I was in Mr. Grimes' house one day, I saw all these books of his, and I told him about how I used to read about the west b'fore I up and left home. Mr. Grimes said if I ever wanted to borrow a book, just ask. He lent me this here book to read, saying it was a really good story." Then his eyes lit up. "If you like, I could read it aloud. That way, we'd both know the story."

Emmett thought on that for a moment, then turned with a big grin on his face looking interested, then he glanced at the other men playing cards or checkers a few feet away. Looking embarrassed, he leaned toward Wade and whispered, "I'd like that, but could we do it when we're out with the cows during the day?"

Wade looked at the others, understanding his feelings. "S'posen we could." Then he closed the book and tucked it under his pillow. "We'll start from the beginning tomorrow."

Emmett grinned, looking pleased, laid his head back on his pillow, and quickly fell asleep.

Wade was always curious how anyone could fall asleep so darn fast. He wanted to finish the book, but he had promised Emmett. Even if he hadn't used the words, it was still a promise, and he was brought up to always honor one's promise, spoken or not.

The next morning came early at the Circle T Ranch. The sun had begun its climb over the eastern hills, greeted by the clang of the breakfast bell mixed with the roosters' crows and barking dogs. Wade pushed back his blanket and, feeling the early September chill, wished someone had built a fire in the pot-bellied stove a few feet away.

Looking half-asleep, Emmett sat up and stared out the window at the barn and corral, wishing he could crawl back under the covers. He turned from the window, looked at Wade's head sticking from under his covers, and told him it was time to get up. Getting out of bed, he grabbed his pants from a peg on the wall next to his bunk and headed for the outhouse dressed in his faded red underwear.

Wade tossed his covers back, greeted by the same chilly morning that greeted Emmett. He put his feet on the cold wooden floor, stood, took his pants off the peg, and slipped into them. Pulling his suspenders up, he followed Emmett and the others out back to take his turn.

Wade and Emmett hurried to the mess and took seats at one of the three long crowded tables for a meal of eggs, potatoes, and meat. No one spoke during meals except to ask someone to pass a plate of food because if they dallied, they would be hurried outside by Mr. Grimes to start work before they finished their meal. The Old man wasn't one to let a few minutes pass without making something of them.

Breakfast was about over when, like the rooster crowing on time, Mr. Grimes walked through the door and yelled. "Ain't paying you boys to waste the day eating! Now finish up and get the hell out of here." The sound of silverware on plates suddenly got faster and louder.

It was Saturday, and the men only had to work until noon, but Mr. Grimes wanted his money's worth, and besides, rousting his men gave him pleasure. He studied the men as they shoveled food into their mouths as fast as they could and, with an ornery grin, said, "I volunteered two of you boys to help with the barn raising at the McSweeny place this afternoon." He paused to let them look around at each other, wondering who the unlucky bastards were. Barn raising was hard work, not like shoveling shit in the barn, riding in search of strays, or a dozen other jobs where one could goof off a little. Nope, barn raising was hard work, and sometimes with hammers and planks of wood falling, it could be downright dangerous.

"Emmett," Mr. Grimes called out, "I think it's about time you and Wade lent a hand."

Emmett looked at Wade with a fretful expression while the others laughed with relief, teasing them. Mr. Grimes couldn't help but find humor in the teasing as he stepped outside and closed the door leaving the men to have their fun with Emmett and Wade.

It was Wade and Emmett's turn to clean the stalls, a job Emmett hated. While shoveling horseshit into a pile and putting down clean hay, Wade asked Emmett if he had been to many barn raisings.

Emmett was upset about going. "They ain't much fun." Then he complained that it was Saturday, and they should have the afternoon off.

Wade considered that for a minute. "Won't we get extra pay for this?"

"I s'pose," replied Emmett as he shoved his pitchfork into the dirty hay and tossed it into the center of the barn. "Thing is, I'm hoping we could get started on that book."

"There'll be time for that, Emmett, but for now, we best get done so's we can head over to the McSweeny place. Mr. Grimes told us to be there b'fore noon."

"I guess," said Emmett with slumped shoulders.

Arriving at the McSweeny ranch a little after eleven in the morning saw several men already hard at work on the barn. One side of the barn and a partial rear wall was all that was up, but there was plenty of yelling, sawing, and hammering going on.

Emmett's expression told of his displeasure with the barn's progress. "Gonna be a while, I guess. It looks like they're working a mite slow."

As they climbed down from their saddles, Wade grinned, hoping to lift Emmett's spirits. "Maybe we can hurry them up a bit."

Emmett looked distraught. "Won't do no good. By the time we get done, it'll be dark and too late to ride into town."

"There's tomorrow."

Emmett turned to tie his horse up with the others. "Tomorrow's Sunday. Ain't much going on in town on Sunday. Besides, as slow as these guys are, we'll probably still be here."

Wade looked around at the men working and hoped Emmett was wrong. He tied his sorrel up next to Emmett's black horse and started to follow him across the barnyard. Glancing around, Wade almost bumped into Emmett, who had suddenly stopped.

"Well, now," said Emmett. "Look who's here helping the woman folk."

It took Wade a moment, but then he saw Sarah Talbert and her mother busy preparing the food for lunch on some long tables. His heart skipped a beat at the possibility of talking to her. However, his hopes for that talk quickly disappeared.

Emmett poked him with his elbow. "There's Mr. Talbert." Then he elbowed Wade and laughed. "Looks like you and Miss Sarah are gonna have to wait to get acquainted."

Wade didn't see the humor as he watched Mr. Talbert talk with another man near the partially built barn. Mr. McSweeny saw the two and rushed over, offering his gratitude for the help. He grabbed their arms and escorted them to the partially completed barn, telling Mr. Talbert that he had two more men to help, then turned and left.

Mr. Talbert told Emmett to help with the raising of the next wall.

With an unhappy look, Emmett turned and walked away.

Mr. Talbert turned to Wade with a stern look remembering him from the general store.

Wade held out his hand, but Mr. Talbert either ignored it or did not see his outstretched hand while looking around at the men working. Wade let his hand drop, wiped it on his pants then put both hands in his front pockets. "Ain't never built a barn before."

Mr. Talbert turned to him with a disappointed look. "Well," he said thoughtfully. "Can't get any work done with your hands hidden in your pockets."

Wade felt embarrassed and quickly took his hands out."

Then he surprised Wade with a wry smile. "Maybe carry some lumber for a spell until you get the hang of things."

Wade grinned back, hoping he was making some headway with Mr. Talbert. "Yes sir." He turned and headed for the men doing the sawing, and as he carried the lumber back and forth, he wondered if Emmett was going to stay mad all day. The minutes passed, and as he carried lumber from one pile to another for cutting, he would try to sneak a look at young Miss Talbert. She was much too busy to notice him, and Wade surely wanted her to see him. He had stopped again to look at Sarah Talbert when the men doing the sawing yelled for more lumber. Wondering if they knew who he was looking at, he felt embarrassed and hurried with the piece of lumber, put it down, and turned to get another when he noticed Mr. Talbert was watching him. They looked at one another briefly, and then Wade picked up a couple of good-size pieces of wood and started toward the men doing the sawing.

Someone yelled, "Come and get it!"

The men working on the barn dropped their tools, letting them crash on the ground below, climbed down, and headed for the row of tables filled with food. Understanding what Emmett meant about being a dangerous place, he watched the men who had been doing the sawing run past and nearly knocked him down. Wade heard Emmett call out and then saw him wave while he ran toward the tables filled with food in what reminded Wade of a stampede. He hurried to get in line, thinking this would be a good time to talk to Miss Sarah Talbert.

The line had quickly grown, with Emmett already in line and talking to Sarah Talbert when Wade got there. He watched as Emmett smiled at her and said something that caused her to smile as she put some food on his plate and then smiled at the man next in line. All of this was

111

giving Wade a slight case of jealousy as the line slowly moved toward her. The minutes passed almost as slowly as the line was moving, but he was finally at the table, where he picked up a plate and fork. As the line slowly progressed toward her, he kept looking at her, hoping she would look his way, but that was not to be his good fortune.

The only one who looked at him was Mr. Talbert, sitting on a stump a few feet away, holding his plate in one hand, his fork in the other, eating. Wade smiled and nodded, but Mr. Talbert shoved the fork of food into his mouth, glanced at his daughter, and then at Wade. Feeling a bit awkward, he turned his attention to the food on the table, trying not to look at Sarah or her father. However, that was far too difficult. After looking at her, he shifted his gaze to her father, staring at him.

Finally, the line had slowly moved, and he found himself standing in front of her, and the thought of her father watching no longer mattered. At least not for the moment. She smiled as she looked down at his empty plate. "Heaven's sake," she said. "You done passed up most of the food." She took his plate, walked back along the table, and filled it with food.

He tried to follow, but he ran into the men in line behind him, and when he finally made it to the other end of the table, she had turned the other way. He hurried back along the line at the complaints of the other men to where she stood with his plate filled with food.

She was frowning. "Thought you left."

"No, ma'am," he said as he looked back along the line at the other men. "Just got a little crowded." He glanced at Mr. Talbert to see if he was still watching, and Wade was not disappointed.

She smiled and handed him the plate. "I'm Sarah Talbert."

"Yes ma'am, I know." Wade felt his face flush and almost spilled the plate of food while taking off his hat. "Name's Wade, Miss Sarah, Wade Garrison."

As the men behind him told him to keep moving, Wade looked at them and wished they would go away. He looked at Sarah, smiled, walked away, and wished he was the last in line so they could have talked a little more. Then he looked at her father, who was still staring at him, turned, and hurried to where Emmett was sitting.

Emmett had been watching the whole thing and felt sorry for his friend. "Miss Sarah Talbert sure is a pretty little thing."

Wade sat down on the ground next to Emmett, glanced up at him, and then at Sarah. The only thing he was thankful for was that he was out of Mr. Talbert's line of vision.

Emmett knew that his friend had a crush on her. And since he could never get anywhere with her, he hoped Wade could, but thinking of Mr. Talbert, Emmett had his doubts.

Seth's voice asking Wade if he wanted another coffee brought him back from memory and the thoughts of Emmett and Sarah Talbert. He leaned forward with his empty cup and watched as Seth poured the last of the pot into it. He thanked him, settled back against his saddle, and took a sip. "How long until we get to Raton?"

Frank stared into the fire and pondered the question. "Well," he finally said. "Ten, maybe fifteen miles, and we have to go over Raton Pass." Wells looked up from the fire. "S'pect if we get an early start, we should get through the pass and be there by late afternoon."

Seth looked south toward the mountains. "Let's hope we don't get one of those summer storms before we get to the other side."

Frank Wells nodded. "I've seen it rain so hard in the mountains once it let loose boulders the size of wagons that came crashing down the mountain. We were knee-deep in mud and water."

Wade imagined the scene hoping the weather would be hot and dry and the sky blue.

Thirteen

As Frank had predicted, it was late afternoon when the three men reached the ridge overlooking the watering hole now called Raton. Wade was still complaining about paying twenty-five cents per horse to use Uncle Dick Wootton's Road over Raton Pass. Both Seth and Frank had explained several times that Dick Wootton and his Indian workers had blasted the rocks away, built the bridges, and shoveled the dirt to make the road, and the fee was reasonable. However, their words fell on deaf ears, and they were tired of explaining and ignored his most recent protest. Tired of hearing about the twenty-five cents, Frank pulled up and dismounted, said they needed to rest the horses a spell before they headed down the steep grade.

Wade dismounted and asked Wells if he could borrow the looking glass.

Frank took it out of his saddlebags, and as he handed it to him, he looked toward the southwest and the thunderhead slowly moving north along the mountain range. The July sun was warm, but the thunderheads might bring the chance of a summer storm of rain, lightning, and, more than likely, hail. "Looks like we could still get caught in a bad storm."

Seth looked at the mountain range to the south at the big white and gray thunderheads. "Looks like it." Then he turned and looked down at the town of Raton far below them. "If them three aren't down there, it might be a good idea to wait this storm out b'fore heading out after them. I sure as hell don't want to try and swim out of a flash flood."

Wade half listened as he looked through the long glass, more interested in Raton's watering hole, which means "small rat" or "mouse" in Spanish. Hoping the place was not crawling with them, he pushed the long glass together and handed it to Frank.

Seth gestured to the town. "Place has grown some since the last time I was here."

Frank agreed. "Seems they've been a mite busy. Let's get down there and see if Wade's friends are still hanging around."

Wade did not appreciate the term friends, but he knew Frank was trying to be funny. They climbed onto their horses and headed down the trail to the old watering hole that is now the small bustling town of Raton.

Riding down the dirt street, they looked at every horse tied to the hitching rails, searching for the three horses belonging to the men they hunted. After riding the length of the dusty street, they stopped at the edge of town and looked back along the street in silence, clearly disappointed. Raton had grown from the original watering hole to several buildings, including the old trading post, two Mexican cantinas, three cafés, a saloon named "The Watering Hole," and a two-story hotel. Several men were busy constructing three new buildings, and a scattering of small shacks dotted the hillside.

Wade rested his forearms on his saddle horn and looked up the street. "We either missed them, or they never waited for the half-breed." Then he looked at the half-breed's horse Frank rode and thought of the horrible smell of the half-breed that was food for the vultures and crows.

"Well," said Seth thoughtfully. "Let's split up. I'll mind the packhorses. Wade, you ride up to the end of the street and check the old trading post. Frank, you check the two cantinas on the left, and I'll stay here with the horses and keep a sharp eye out." He looked at Wade and then Frank. "If anyone finds them, no one does anything until he gets the others."

Fifteen minutes later, Wade tied his horse in front of a crudely built building of logs and mud. A rough-looking sign that read "Raton Trading Post" in white paint sat above the large solid front door propped open by a boot-sized rock. Two glassless windows were on either side of the door, but both had solid wood shutters propped up by long skinny sticks. He started up the steps to the porch and thought about the Sharps in the scabbard on his saddle. Imagining the look on Mr. Grimes' face while he tried to explain that someone in New Mexico owned it. Retrieving it from its scabbard, he cradled it in his left arm. He walked up the steps to the trading post and through the open doorway, where he paused to let his eyes adjust to the dim light.

A tall, lanky man with black hair and a beard wearing a dirty apron over his dark shirt and pants stood behind the counter, talking to three men. The lanky man continued talking to the others while looking at Wade and the Sharps.

Wade wanted to get a better look at the three men, so he casually walked around the store to a place where he could see their faces.

The man behind the counter curiously watched Wade while listening to what one of the men was saying.

Wade noticed the man watching him, so he paused now and again to look at this and that as if interested in buying something. When he was sure these men were not the three men he was after, he walked outside. Shoving the Sharps back into the scabbard, Wade looked toward town and wondered how Frank was making out. Untying the mare, he started walking toward town to look for Frank and Seth, hoping they had better luck.

While he walked down the dirt street in the heat of the late afternoon sun with the mare in tow, he searched the boardwalks, porches to the stores, and dusty street for the three men. Seeing the half-breed's horse tied up to the hitching rail in front of a cantina but no Frank, he glanced around for Seth. Not seeing him, he walked to the hitching rail, tied his horse next to Franks, retrieved the Sharps, and stepped onto the boardwalk with it cradled in his left arm. Pausing on the boardwalk, Wade glanced up and down the street and busy boardwalk, wondering where Seth was with the packhorses. Thinking Raton was a busy place, he pushed through the swinging doors and stepped inside.

Frank sat alone at a table near the front window, sipping a cloudy liquid from a mug.

Wade walked past several tables, sat down, and looked at the drink.

Seeing the puzzled look on Wade's face, Frank said, "Mescal."

A thin Mexican waiter asked Wade what he wanted. He asked for a beer, but the waiter said they did not have any and offered him a glass of mescal. Wade looked at the glass in front of Frank and asked if he could get a shot of whiskey.

"Mescal," replied the waiter. "If the señor wants whiskey, then the señor should go to the trading post."

Wade shrugged and said he would take mescal, and as the waiter walked away, he looked the place over. Thinking it was a little dirty, unlike the Blue Sky Saloon back in Harper, he waited for his drink.

Frank took a quick sip, made a sour face, and asked if he had run into any of his friends.

Knowing who Frank referred to, Wade shook his head no. When the waiter arrived with his mescal, Wade paid him and took a quick sip, understanding Frank's expression when he took a drink. "I wonder where Seth is."

Wells looked out the cantina window and wondered the same thing. "Maybe we should go looking for him b'fore he gets himself lost or in trouble."

"Good idea," replied Wade as he pushed the mescal away and stood. He watched Frank gulp down both drinks and wondered how he could stomach the stuff.

They stepped out of the cantina onto the busy boardwalk, saw Seth walking up the street leading the horses, and waited.

Seeing them, Seth walked a little faster. "See anything?"

Both shook their heads no.

Seth looked disappointed. "Damn. It looks like these bastards didn't wait for the half-breed like we'd hoped."

"Maybe we ought to ask around," suggested Frank. "Maybe someone saw them."

Wade agreed, and Seth told them to get their horses and follow him up the street to the trading post. "We'll ask there."

"I was just there," said Wade.

Frank looked at him. "Did you ask about your friends?"

Feeling a little foolish, Wade said no.

"Well, let's go ask." Seth turned and started walking toward the trading post.

Wade followed the two up the street, and after tying their horses to the hitching rail, Wade got his Sharps and followed the others inside. The three men Wade had seen earlier were gone, but the lanky, bearded man was still behind the counter, busy at something.

"How you doing, asshole?" asked Seth with a grin.

"Well, I'll be a---" said the lanky man letting the sentence trail off as he hurried around the counter. "Seth Bowlen," he said, offering an outstretched hand. "You son-of-a-bitch." As they shook hands, he saw Frank standing behind Seth. "Hello, Frank, you ugly old bastard."

Frank grinned. "I thought someone would have killed you by now." After they shook hands, Frank turned to Wade. "This here's Wade Garrison. Wade, Bill Shanky."

He firmly took Wade's hand and shook it. "Seen you in here earlier looking around and thought you might be casing the place." Shanky turned to Seth and asked what they were doing in Raton.

"Passing through," replied Seth. "You work here?"

Bill Shanky glanced around proudly. "Hell no. I own this place going on to two years now."

Seth glanced around. "That a fact? That calls for a drink." He looked at Shanky. "On you."

Bill laughed, turned, and walked around the counter, talking over his shoulder. "I see you ain't changed much, Bowlen."

They followed Bill to the counter and watched as he bent down. When he stood, he was holding a bottle of whiskey in one hand and a small shot glass on each of his four fingers in the other hand.

Frank leaned against the countertop on one elbow. "Mite empty in here. Business must be a little slow, or maybe the people of Raton hate you."

Bill frowned. "Gets a little slow at times," he said as he poured the drinks. "I heard about the city of Raton a couple of years ago from some fellas passing through Santa Fe." The drinks poured, he pushed them across the counter, lifted his glass gulped it down, and watched the others drink. "They said that a man by the name of Dick Wootton and some Indians had built a road across the pass, and people were moving back and forth almost daily."

"He charges twenty-five cents a horse," complained Wade.

Seth and Frank gave him a quick look wishing he'd forget about the money.

Shanky poured four more drinks, put the bottle down, took a sip, and continued. "So, I sold my place in Santa Fe." He looked at Wade. "I had a saloon and store there."

"More like a garbage heap with walls," grinned Bowlen.

Shanky found no humor in that as he looked at Wade. "It was a nice place."

Wade smiled as he listened to Shanky talk about selling his saloon and store in Santa Fe and bought this trading post.

"Some days," said Shanky, "it is a mite slow as you can see, but other days when the wagons make it over the pass or a group are heading north, it gets mighty profitable." He leaned forward. "I own a livery out back and have a blacksmith for shoeing and mending wagon wheels." Then he grinned. "Yessir boys, gonna make myself even richer." He started to pour four more drinks, but Seth put one finger under the bottle's neck, lifted it, and smiled. We haven't eaten yet, and it's too early to get drunk."

"You boys must be getting old," chuckled Shanky as he put the cork in the bottle while asking where they were headed.

They told him about Wade's friend Emmett, the Barton and Osborn families, and the two little girls. Then they told him about Gil Robinson getting shot and taking the two little girls back to his wife and daughter in Roscoe's Creek. Then Seth told Shanky they had trailed the three to Raton, purposely leaving out the part about the half-breed, seeing no reason to make Wade uncomfortable. Shanky asked what the three men looked like.

After Wade described them, Bill's face lit up. "Why I believe them three fellas were in here yesterday or the day b'fore. I ain't sure which, but they was sure enough in here."

Wade glanced at Seth and Frank with hope as he looked at Shanky. "Did you see which way they headed?"

Shanky pursed his lips and shook his head. "Afraid I didn't, but one of their horses needed shoeing." He pointed over his shoulder toward the livery out back. "My hired hand, Curley, might know."

Wade turned and headed for the door talking over his shoulder. "I'll check with this Curley fella."

Seth followed Wade outside, and while Wade rushed around the corner of the building, Seth thought he was a little too impatient. Stepping off the trading post porch, Seth looked up into a dark gray sky and figured they were in for a good storm. Looking to the southwest, he could barely make out the mountains drenched by the summer rain, and lightning flashes warning of the violent storm approaching Raton.

Wade walked around the corner of the trading post, looking excited. "Curley said he shod the gray."

"The one with the turned hoof?" asked Seth.

Wade nodded s, and then he looked up to see what Seth was looking at and said, "Clouds are getting pretty dark. Think maybe we ought to spend the night?"

Bowlen nodded. "We can get an early start in the morning." He looked disappointed. "Storm's gonna wash their tracks."

"I know," replied Wade sounding frustrated.

Frank walked outside, stood at the end of the porch, and looked skyward. "Looks pretty bad. Maybe we ought to wait it out."

"We were just discussing that very thing," replied Seth. "Looks like we're gonna lose their tracks."

"Can't do nothing about that now," replied Wells. "Old Mother Nature's gonna have herself a good cry in a bit."

Seth looked up once again. "Well," he said thoughtfully. "Let's hope she ain't too unhappy. We best get the horses inside the livery."

They untied their horses and headed around the corner of the trading post, and as they walked into the livery, a thin man in his late sixties or early seventies greeted them with a friendly smile of missing teeth. He introduced himself as Curley to Seth and Frank and watched as the three men unsaddled their horses and unloaded the two packhorses.

Curley grinned at them. "Don't you boys go worry'n none about these here horses or your belongings." Curley pointed to a door at the back of the livery. "I sleep in that little room yonder. I lock this place uptight, and I'm a light sleeper." Then he smiled. "Have been since the war."

After they put their belongings in the corner near Curley's room and made sure their horses were secure in their stalls, they thanked him and walked toward the big open doors.

Curley called out to Wade. "Hey, young fella."

Wade turned and started walking toward the old man while Seth and Frank headed toward the trading post. Curley looked at the other two as they walked toward the trading post and lowered his voice. "Them fellas you were ask'n about earlier. They friends of yours?"

Wade shook his head. "No, why you asking?"

Curley looked unsure. "Well, I heard them arguing about waiting for someone. The big man whose horse I shod wanted to wait, but the one with blonde hair was afraid the men trailing them would catch up." He looked at Wade questioningly. "The way I see it, you and the others must be the ones trailing these three. I heard something about another man taking too much time. The big man said he could catch up with them in Santa Fe."

Wade looked at the road that disappeared up the slope and through the trees. "Was that yesterday?"

"Day before." Curley's expression changed from friendly to angry as he turned his head and spit tobacco juice onto the livery dirt floor. His gray curly hair bulged from under an old confederate hat, and his thin, tanned clean-shaven face wore the lines of hard times.

Wade noticed he had a black eye. "Who blackened your eye?"

"I've seen all sorts in my time," Curley said. "The big one riding the gray gave it to me." He turned and spat again. "Bastard said I was taking too long shoeing his horse, and when I told him he could do it himself, he up and slapped me, then told me to shut up and get his horse shod. I turned away, and the one with blonde hair kicked me in the ass, which hurt like hell, telling me to get on with it. I was mad as hell but too old to do anything."

Wade felt sorry for the old man as he looked at the bruised skin around the red bloodshot left eye. "We've been trailing them for several days."

Curley looked at Wade. "I don't know what they did, but I wish much luck to you and yer friends in catch'n them."

"I have a feeling we'll need that luck, Curley." Wade turned and walked to the trading post wishing he had been there to help Curley. When he walked into the trading post, Seth, Frank, and Bill Shanky were at a small table talking. The soft rumble of thunder from the approaching storm made its way across the room, causing them to stop talking and look toward the open doorway as if they expected the thunder to walk through it.

Wade asked about a hotel, thinking of a soft bed and clean sheets.

Thunder rolled overhead like a hundred drums. Shanky looked up at the ceiling for a few moments, then turned to Wade. "Stay in the hotel across from the café down the street."

"Expensive?" asked Frank.

Shanky shrugged. "Don't know, but if you've a mind for a bath, there's a bathhouse run by a Chinese family named Kim next to the hotel. A hot tub of clean water will cost you twenty cents." Then his face filled with a grin. "Even get your back washed by one of Kim's daughters if'n you like."

Wade was not too keen on the idea of a woman bathing him, but Seth chuckled and slapped Wells on the back. "How about it, Frank? Wanna get that little guy of yours washed by a China gal?"

Shanky laughed. Wade chuckled, but Frank only smiled and looked a little embarrassed. "I can do my own cleaning, thank you, but a bath does sound kinda good." He sniffed his clothes. "It's been a while."

Another rumble of thunder passed overhead. Seth stood and looked through the open doorway at the dirt street outside the trading post seeing it was getting dark but not from the sun going down. He lifted his head, sniffing at the air. "Smells like rain." Then he turned to the others.

"Don't know about you boys, but a good hot meal, shave, and a hot bath sound mighty inviting."

Frank agreed as he stood and said they best get to it before it rains. They said goodbye to Shanky and walked through the open doorway into the dim light that warned of the coming storm. Thunder rolled overhead, and Wade looked up at the dark menacing clouds, glad they were not out in the open. They hurried down the busy street past Mexicans and whites, who rushed to get somewhere before it started to rain. They hurried along the boardwalk to the restaurant across from the hotel, stepped inside, sat next to the window, and ordered dinner and coffee.

While they waited for their coffee, the rain pelted the window lightly at first, then so heavy they could scarcely see the hotel across the street. Lightning flashed, followed immediately by the loud, sharp crackle of thunder that shook the building. Frank thought of confederate canons as he watched the rain quickly fill the wagon ruts and hollows of the street, turning the once dry hard ground into mud. Pebble-size hail began to fall with the rain leaving the street looking like a light snow had fallen. As the minutes passed, the sound of hail on the roof and outside the window softened, the hail stopped, and the heavy rain turned to a light shower.

Moments later, the clouds separated, and the late afternoon sun broke through. The rain stopped, and it was quiet once again. The three men sat in their chairs looking through the windowpanes at the street of mud and hail, awestruck by the power of the storm that now headed over Raton Pass into southern Colorado. The waiter placed their food on the table, disturbing their thoughts of the storm.

The air still held the fresh smell of the summer storm as the three walked out of the restaurant. Knowing the storm was dumping its mixture of rain and hail on the town of Sierra Mesa, Wade thought of the half-breed lying in the mud and hail. The setting sun colored the storefronts across the street, and the landscape east of town a reddish-orange as the three made their way across the muddy street. They walked up the steps to the hotel's porch, stomped their feet, took off their hats, and entered the small lobby.

A man in his mid-thirties looked up from the book he was reading. He smiled as he brushed the front of his black suit. "Good evening, gentlemen. That was some storm we had."

"That it was," replied Seth as he glanced around the lobby and held up three fingers. "Need three rooms."

"Of course," said the hotel clerk. He pushed the register and inkwell with a pen toward the counter's edge. "If you would just sign the register."

Seth placed his hat and coat he had taken off on the counter, signed the register, and then waited for Frank and Wade to sign.

The clerk turned the register around and read their names. "Welcome, Mr. Bowlen, Mr. Wells, and Mr. Garrison." Then he turned, took three keys from the small hooks on the wall behind him, and handed one to each.

Seth took his key and asked if he knew anything about the bathhouse next door.

The clerk smiled with a prideful look. "I use it myself once a week."

Frank and Seth looked at one another as neither had ever bathed once a week, and if they had, they would not be bragging about it.

The clerk pointed to a door near the bottom of the stairs. "After you gentlemen get settled in your rooms, come down the stairs and walk through that door to Mr. Kim's Bathhouse."

The three stared at the door for a moment, thanked him, and then headed for the steep staircase that led to the second floor. Frank stopped partway up the stairs, turned, and asked if they could get a shave next door.

The clerk looked up and rubbed his chin as he smiled. "Mrs. Kim gives the closest shave in Raton."

Frank's expression was uncertain as he looked at Seth on the steps above him, then at Wade on the step below. They continued up the stairs, where Frank stopped at the top, looked around, and lowered his voice. "Either of you ever been shaved by a woman, let alone a Chinese woman?"

Wade smiled at the expression on Frank's face. "I have. And by a Chinese woman a couple of times."

"Where?" asked Seth looking surprised.

"Denver," replied Wade being sure to leave out that Sarah Talbert had once given him a shave with her father's razor.

Frank looked hesitant. "I ain't sure I want some woman fussing around my neck with a razor."

Seth glanced back down the stairs and along the hall as he leaned closer to Frank and lowered his voice. "You ain't poked this, Mrs. Kim, have you, Frank?"

"Hell no," replied Wells with a surprised look. "Why, you know I been with you since we got here."

123

Seth patted Frank on the shoulder. "Then you ain't got nuth'n to worry about because she ain't pissed at you yet." Then he laughed and playfully pushed Frank down the hall.

Wade chuckled as he followed them down the hall, looking for their rooms. As Seth and Frank entered their rooms, Wade unlocked his door and stepped inside a small room with a single bed and a nightstand with a kerosene lamp. A small potbellied stove and a box of kindling sat in the corner next to the window. He walked to the window and looked down at the street, still covered with hail and muddy from the rain. Lightning in the distance, followed by soft rumbles of thunder, warned of another storm. As he watched the flashes in the distance, he thought of the day that he and Sarah got caught in a sudden downpour a few miles from her father's ranch.

A knock came at the door, followed by Seth's voice. "You ready to meet Mrs. Kim?" asked Seth in a humorous voice.

Wade grinned, turned from the window, and opened the door.

Their guns, coats, and hats put away, the three men went downstairs and stood by the door to the bathhouse, neither sure of what they would find on the other side.

Frank turned to the clerk in the white shirt behind the counter. "I guess we're ready."

The clerk smiled, set his book down, and walked from behind the counter. "I'm sure you gentlemen will enjoy this. I certainly do." He opened the door, stepped inside, and held the door open. "This way, gentlemen." As the three stepped inside the bathhouse, the clerk called out. "Mr. Kim, customers are waiting."

An elderly Chinese man they presumed to be Mr. Kim, dressed in a black silk shirt and pants, both of which seemed a little large and short around the ankles and forearms, hurried from behind a black curtain. He wore a small round black hat on the top of his head, and his long hair was in a braid that hung past his waist. An elderly Chinese woman wearing identical clothes as Mr. Kim hurried from behind the same curtained door and smiled as she bowed. The clerk assured the three men they were in good hands and smiled at Mr. Kim, who smiled back as he bowed. As the clerk left, Mr. Kim bowed and smiled as he pointed to another doorway. "Please."

The three looked at one another, unsure of what to do next.

Mr. Kim sensed their apprehension, smiled, gently took Frank's arm by the elbow, and stepped toward the door where Mrs. Kim waited.

She smiled, bowed, and opened the door to a room that contained several metal tubs. They glanced at one another as they followed Mr. Kim through the door, and as Wade was about to go in, he turned to an opened doorway of another room where several young Chinese girls were busy washing laundry. One said something to the others, and the room filled with laughter. Mrs. Kim yelled at them in Chinese. They covered their mouths and giggled. Mrs. Kim hurried to the open door, said something the girls found funny, and closed the door. Wade followed Mr. Kim and the others through the doorway, curious about what she said that was so funny.

The bathing room had one long narrow window that was too high to see out, and if not for the fire in the large stone fireplace in the corner, the room would be dim. Mr. Kim lit a kerosene lamp, then another, and another while Wade glanced around the room of five metal tubs, small plain wooden tables, and benches next to each tub.

Mr. Kim told the three men to take off their clothes but leave on their underwear and have a seat in the chairs by their tubs.

Thinking that was strange, the three took off their pants and shirts, leaving their underwear on, sat down on the chair by their tubs, and waited. Mr. Kim hurried to the back door, opened it, and yelled something in Chinese that got a response from another man outside.

Mrs. Kim came in carrying several small towels, a shaving mug, and a straight razor setting them on the table next to Wade. Seth and Frank watched with interest as she wrapped one of the small towels around Wade's neck, picked up the mug and small brush. While she whisked the brush around the mug, making lather, she examined Wade's neck and face. Sitting back, she smiled. "Nice face." Then she applied the lather to his face and neck, picked up the straight razor, and carefully shaved his face and neck under the scrutiny of Seth and Frank.

Wade turned, rubbed his hand over his face, nodded, and smiled at Seth and Frank when she finished. "Not one nick."

Mrs. Kim shaved Frank and Seth while three Chinese men made several trips carrying two buckets of hot steaming water pouring them into the tubs. When the tubs were filled, the three men shaved, and with Mrs. Kim gone, they were ready for their greatly anticipated baths. Wade walked to one tub, looked down at the clear, steaming water, put one finger in, grinned at the others, and took off his long red underwear. Surprised by Mrs. Kim entering the room before Wade could get into the tub. He grabbed his pants and held them in front of him, looking embarrassed.

125

Without so much as a look at him, Mrs. Kim placed a bar of soap and a small scrub brush on each of the tiny tables next to the tubs. Then she backed out of the room and bowed as she closed the door.

Wade stared at the door for several moments anticipating her return and laid his pants on the bench along with his long white underwear. He got into the tub before Mrs. Kim returned and slowly lowered himself into the hot water. Feeling relaxed, he turned to Seth and Frank. "You fellas better get in before Mrs. Kim comes back."

They looked at the door, undressed, and climbed into their waiting tubs of hot water. Seth laughed and splashed at Frank, who turned away from the splashing, cursing Seth, and when he turned, Seth had disappeared. Seconds later, he popped up, spewing water from his mouth at Frank. Wells found no humor in the deed and cursed Seth a second time. Wade laughed and tossed his wet washcloth at Seth, hitting him in the face. With a surprised look, Seth grabbed the wet cloth and threw it back at Wade, hitting the side of the tub. Frank decided to get into the water fight, and the washcloths flew.

The commotion brought Mrs. Kim running into the room, yelling in Chinese. They stopped and looked at her like children did when their mother scolded her. She walked toward them, chattering in Chinese, pointing at the water and wet washcloths on the floor. She stood in silence in the center of the room looking at them, then bent down and picked up their clothes to their loud protests, which she ignored while giving each garment a thorough examination.

Having heard the commotion, Mr. Kim entered the room and assured the men that his wife was only taking their clothes to wash them. Mrs. Kim looked at her husband and said something in Chinese before backing out of the room with their clothes. Mr. Kim picked up their boots and said his daughters would clean them and have them placed outside their rooms by morning, along with their clean clothes.

Frank looked worried. "How the hell we gonna get upstairs if we ain't got no clothes?"

Seth and Wade looked at Mr. Kim, waiting for an answer, but Mr. Kim smiled, bowed, and backed out of the room amid loud protests. Minutes later, he reappeared with three large towels and robes. "Wear these, please."

Not liking the idea, they argued with Mr. Kim about their clothes and wore the robes in public.

Having heard the noise and suspecting the problem, the clerk from the hotel appeared in the doorway where he and Mr. Kim talked for a moment, and then the clerk turned to the three men. "Everything is alright, gentlemen. Your clothes and boots will be cleaned and left outside your door in the morning."

"They just leave our stuff in the hall?" questioned Seth.

The clerk smiled and nodded. "Yes. You will hear a knock on the door in the morning. That knock will be your clothes arriving."

They thought about that for a moment, then Frank asked, "We have to wear nothing, but them robes up to our rooms?"

The clerk smiled. "Everyone does. I assure you it's perfectly alright." Then he said something to Mr. Kim and left.

As Mr. Kim closed the door, Frank looked at Seth with a puzzled look. "How much you think all this is gonna cost?"

Seth smiled. "I've no idea, but since we ain't got no clothes, I'm just happy we ate first." Then he laughed as he laid back, slid down until his head disappeared underwater, then sat up and shook his head much the way a dog would when wet.

Frank laughed and yelled something that sounded like a rebel yell and did the same thing. Wade smiled at the two, thinking they were nothing more than a couple of kids.

Fourteen

Wade knelt and filled the pot-bellied stove with kindling and wood, put a match to it, and waited until the fire was going before he closed the small iron door of the stove. He stood, pulled at the tied belt of the heavy robe Mr. Kim had given him, walked to the window, and looked out into the night. Lights from the buildings below cast their orange and yellow light across the boardwalks onto the muddy puddles reflecting the soft glow of the windows. Lightning flashed several times in the distance, and he wondered if they would get another rain before morning.

He turned from the window to the bed, sat down, and reached for his pocket watch on the table. Seeing it was eight o'clock, he envisioned the others back at the Circle T playing cards or checkers. He thought of Emmett sitting against the wall on his bunk, legs outstretched in front of him, listening as Wade read the story of the White Whale. Emmett had long lost his concerns over the others, knowing whether he could read or write because he knew that most of them signed with a mark each month for their pay while he could at least sign his name.

The joy Wade found in remembering Emmett suddenly turned to sadness, then anger, and that into hatred. He watched the sky outside the window light up with flashes of lightning too far away to hear the thunder and thought of how much he missed his friend. He stood, took off his robe, wished he still had his underwear on, blew out the lamp, and slipped his naked body between the cool sheets. The flames inside the stove flickered between the tiny cracks and vent of the door, and he thought of the pot-bellied stove of the bunkhouse at the Circle T. Thunder rolled across the room, rain lightly pelted the window, and he thought of the storm three years ago.

August 1869

Wade and Emmett were supposed to collect strays one afternoon north of the Circle T, but instead of looking for strays, Wade read Moby Dick aloud. Emmett had his right leg draped over his saddle horn, listening as Wade read the last chapter about Ishmael, the sailor Captain Ahab, and the other men of the whaler Pequod.

"Best put the book away," said Emmett in a disappointed voice. "Here comes a rider."

Wade looked up at the lone rider and knew at once it was Sarah Talbert. Becoming flustered, he dropped the book, and as Emmett laughed at him, he climbed down to get it.

Emmett shook his head. "How many times do you have to see Miss Sarah b'fore you stop acting the fool?"

Wade picked up the book and looked toward Sarah and then Emmett. "Can't rightly say, Emmett. Maybe I never will."

Emmett looked at Sarah as she rode toward them and lowered his voice. "Well, I sure hope it's soon cuz this is getting embarrassing."

"Why are you getting embarrassed?" asked Wade. "It's me that's turning red from embarrassment."

Emmett grinned. "I know that, but you're my best friend, and I worry about you." He looked at Sarah riding toward them. "But I can't blame you none Wade. Guess I'd get flustered too if'n she liked me as she does you."

Wade smiled as he climbed back onto his horse. "Well, don't go worrying about Miss Sarah and me."

"Who said anything about Miss Sarah?" chuckled Emmett. "It ain't her that does the blushing."

Before Wade could think of anything to say, Sarah pulled her horse to a stop.

"Hello, Wade," she said with a friendly smile.

Wade felt his face flush. "Hello, Sarah."

She looked at Emmett with a smile not quite as big as the one she had for Wade. "Afternoon, Emmett."

He nodded and smiled as he touched the brim of his hat. "Miss Sarah."

She smiled at Wade again. *"Mind if I ride along for a spell?"*

Emmett chuckled. *"That's like ask'n---"*

Wade quickly interrupted. *"You know we won't."* Then he gave Emmett a look.

Emmett smiled at Wade, slowed up his horse, and rode behind them. Emmett had once sought Miss Sarah's attention, but he was glad that his best friend and Sarah were friends, and he held no jealousy in the matter. The truth was that Emmett had found favor from the daughter of a nearby farmer named Hattie Dougherty. He spent most of his time away from the Circle T at the Dougherty farm these days. He enjoyed helping Mr. Dougherty with one thing or another to gain favor with the man and be near Hattie at the same time. Of course, his help was invariably rewarded by a home-cooked dinner which allowed him to sit across the table from Hattie, exchanging smiles under the watchful but approving eyes of Mr. and Mrs. Dougherty. Emmett grew tired of riding behind the two and decided to leave them alone. *"I think I see a couple of strays over yonder,"* he said while pointing to a small grove of cottonwood trees about a quarter mile to the south.

Wade and Sarah pulled up, turned, and looked in the direction he pointed. *"Where?"* asked Wade.

Sarah put her hand over her eyes, shading them from the sun. *"I don't see anything."*

"Well," replied Emmett, *"they're there alright."* He turned his horse and headed toward the cottonwoods yelling over his shoulder, *"You two go on. I'll take care of the strays."*

Wade watched him ride away, feeling glad he was gone, yet sorry. Then he turned to Sarah. *"I'll see you get home."*

"But what about the strays?" she asked while looking at the dusty trail left by Emmett.

Wade turned and looked. *"I reckon Emmett can manage a couple of strays."* Then he looked at her and smiled. *"Besides, I don't think your ma and pa would ever forgive me if I were to leave you alone and your horse were to throw you."*

She blushed. *"I've been riding since I could walk, so I think I know how to stay on a horse."*

He thought about that for a moment. *"That may be, but a rattler could up and scare your horse, causing her to throw you."*

"Well," she said thoughtfully, *"I suppose it could."* Then she smiled. *"Maybe it would be best if you rode with me for a spell."*

130

Wade grinned and took one last look at Emmett as he rode away while he and Sarah rode northwest toward her father's ranch.

They had ridden about a half-mile when Wade thought it was getting a little dark and looked up at the dark gray clouds. "Looks like we could get rained on."

He pulled up and looked for somewhere to sit out a bad storm. Lightning flashed to the southwest, followed by low rumbling thunder, and from experience, he knew that hail and heavy rain often accompanied thunderstorms. Sarah saw the worried look on Wade's face and, becoming concerned herself, asked if everything was okay.

"I don't like the looks of those clouds coming in." Then he looked in the direction Emmett had ridden. "Hope Emmett's okay."

Sarah looked up at the dark clouds. "I'm sure he is."

Wade stood tall in the stirrups and looked to the west. "There's a formation of rocks and boulders west of here and an old shack."

She looked in the direction he was looking. "I passed them earlier."

A bright flash lit up the sky, followed by a loud crack of thunder, frightening their horses that rose on hind legs, bucked, and started to bolt. Wade got control of the mare, and as it began to rain, he helped Sarah with her horse. "C'mon," he yelled, "let's get to those rocks before it gets any worse."

They turned the horses due west and rode at a gallop through the heavy rain of lightning and thunder. A few minutes later, Wade saw the rock formation thinking the shack in the middle of the rocks would give shelter and safety from the storm. They could barely see across the prairie through the dark metallic curtain of heavy rain. The prairie was dark and looked more like late evening than early afternoon.

Lightning lit up the prairie, followed by thunder, scaring Sarah's horse that bolted to the right and away from the flash and Wade. The thunder was deafening as it rolled and rumbled across the prairie. Wade spurred his mare after Sarah turned her horse toward the rocks, and within minutes they were at the old shack. He jumped down, took the reins of Sarah's horse to hold it steady while she jumped down, and ran for the shack. Fearful the horses would run away, he led them inside the small shack leaving it a little crowded. Lightning flashed, filling the shack with blinding white light as thunder rolled through the shack. Sarah saw Wade *was having difficulty controlling the horses and grabbed the reins to her horse, and together they could hold them steady.*

Part of the roof leaked, but that was no surprise to Wade as he looked at Sarah's wet hair and face. The door flew open, letting the wind blow the rain inside, scaring the horses that neighed, kicked, pulled at their reins, and reared up, hitting their heads against the leaking roof. Wade gave his mare's reins to Sarah, pushed the door closed, and held it shut.

As suddenly as the storm had begun, it was over, and the silence of the shack filled with the horse's heavy breathing. Distant thunder to the north of them was not quite as loud, telling Wade the storm was over. He slowly pushed the door open, looked outside, then turned to Sarah and asked if she was okay.

Sarah laughed, knowing her hair was a mess and her clothes were wet. "I think so."

Wade looked at the mare's wide eyes that still held the fear of the thunder and lightning. He reached out, touched the mare's neck, and spoke softly. "It's over girl." Then he turned to Sarah. "You sure you're okay?"

Soaked and chilly, Sarah nodded and smiled, glad it was over.

He led his mare outside, then Sarah and her horse followed. Stopping after a few yards in the warm sunlight, they looked up at the blue sky and scattered clouds to the west and southwest while the dark gray clouds of lightning had moved north.

Sarah laughed. "You're soaked."

Wade chuckled, looked at her hatless head of wet hair, and laughed. "Sorry, you lost your hat."

She looked at her wet clothing and felt a chill that caused her to shiver.

"Better get you home. You'll catch a cold."

She shivered and nodded. "Guess we better."

He took her arm to help her onto her horse, but she paused and looked up into his blue eyes and then at his lips. He leaned his head down and gently kissed her. She responded by putting her arms around his neck, and then he put his arms around her waist, holding her tight against him. Thunder in the distance reminded them that her family was indeed worried.

The Hotel Room in Raton

Wade opened his eyes and looked around the small cold hotel room and the pot-bellied stove, whose belly was cold and empty. It was getting light outside, and he could see the tips of the tall mountains to the west that were the first to greet the morning sun from the east. A knock on the door made him turn, remembering his clothing. He tossed the sheet and blanket back, put his feet on the cold hardwood floor, covered himself with the robe, and walked to the door. He listened for a moment, then opened it just a crack and looked into the hall. Not seeing anyone, he opened the door a little more and saw his boots and clothing stacked neatly in front of his door. As he reached down to get them, he looked up and down the hall, seeing Seth and Frank's clothing neatly placed outside their doors. He picked up his clothes, shut the door, and put his clothes on the bed. After examining his boots that looked like new, he set them on the floor and dressed.

He walked to the window and looked at the tall snow-capped peaks in the distance, covered in sunshine that would soon touch the valley floor. Looking at the street below, he recognized the waiter from the night before walking along the boardwalk. The man stopped at the door, unlocked it, and went inside. Moments later, the restaurant filled with soft orange light, and Wade was suddenly hungry. Curious about Seth and Frank, he went to the door, opened it, and looked into the hallway seeing their clothes were gone. Hoping no one had stolen them, he closed the door picturing the two men arguing with Mr. and Mrs. Kim. Contemplating a fire in the stove to take the chill off, a knock came at the door.

Seth spoke in a whisper through the door. "You in there, boy?"

Wade opened the door. "Morn'n."

Seth nodded toward Frank's door. "Let's see if Frank's up and go have some breakfast." He grinned. "Then get back to trailing them, friends of yours."

Wade found no humor in that.

The three men walked up the street of Raton to Bill Shanky's trading post, where Wade gave Seth money for supplies. While he tended to that task, Frank and Wade went out back to saddle the horses and get the packhorses ready.

Curly was already awake, holding a tin cup of coffee as he greeted them with a familiar toothless grin. He set his coffee cup on an old barrel and helped Wade with his mount and the packhorses.

133

Wade and Frank were walking out of the livery leading their horses just as Seth and Bill Shanky came around the corner carrying the supplies Seth bought. After stowing everything on the packhorses, they shook Shanky's hand and then Curley's. Nothing further to say, they climbed up onto their horses and nudged them into a walk heading south toward Santa Fe.

Wade settled in his saddle and then turned to look back at Curley standing alone near the open doors of the livery, watching as they rode away. Wade felt bad for the way the men treated the old man and waved goodbye. Curley grinned and waved back, then turned and went inside, unaware of Wade's silent promise to him.

Fifteen

Wade rode behind Seth and Frank, thinking about old Curley and the three men mistreating him. The more he thought about it, the more he realized that it should not have surprised him. Not after what he had seen these men do to the Barton and Miller families. Wade pushed the images of old Curley and the others from his mind and thought about the trail ahead of them. Wondering where it would take them, he was beginning to have misgivings about their success in catching these terrible men. He glanced around at the New Mexico Territory, thinking it was not much different from southern Colorado. He looked at the backs of Seth and Frank, riding up ahead, and was glad they were with him. Wade could track reasonably well, but he was not the tracker Frank Wells was nor the gunman they were. And he knew that when it came down to the killing, he would need their help.

Seth turned in the saddle and looked at Wade. "You getting antisocial on us?"

"Just think'n some."

Frank grinned as he looked over his shoulder. "About that little gal back in Harper?"

Embarrassed, Wade ignored Frank. "How far to Santa Fe?"

"Close to seventy miles," said Wells. "Give or take a few." He looked over his shoulder. "Come up and ride with us so I don't have to yell all the time and get a kink in my already sore neck."

Wade smiled, nudged the mare, tugged at the lead rope to his packhorse, and rode next to Seth. "That's a far piece. I'm not sure these fellas will hang around for very long."

135

Seth nodded in agreement. "You may be right about that, but as you just said, Santa Fe's a far piece from Raton and the evil these boys have left along the way. Chances are they might feel safe enough to linger a bit with a whore or two."

Wade considered that thinking they could rape any woman they wanted for free. "I hope you're right."

"The thing with men like this," said Frank, "is that they don't think about getting caught, just about doing the deed."

Seth nodded in agreement. "Frank and I've both brought a few men to justice on account of that reasoning alone. Sometimes the bastards make it easy for you."

Wade hoped that was the case with these men.

After being on the trail for more than five hours, they were tired, and the horses needed rest and water. Reaching the top of a hill that overlooked a small valley of rolling hills nestled between the mountains, Seth pointed to a small river and trees that looked like a good spot. "Down there. We'll let the stock rest a spell while we have us some coffee and something to eat."

"Sounds good," agreed Frank. "Maybe even a nap."

Wade was not keen on stopping, but he knew his mare and packhorse were tired and needed water, food, and rest.

They rode down the hill to the stream, where it made a slight bend by several cottonwoods. After they stopped, Wade unsaddled his mare, led her to the river, and watched her drink. Seth and Frank did the same before they unpacked the horses and let them drink. There was plenty of good grass, so they hobbled the horses and let them graze, saving the oats for another time. Frank filled the dented gray coffee pot with water while Seth gathered wood for a fire. Wade knelt by the packs searching for the coffee and some beef jerky. Finding both, he gave Frank the small burlap bag of coffee and watched as he quickly poured an unmeasured amount into the pot. He sat down, leaned back against his saddle, and bit off a piece of jerky. Seth sat a few feet away, resting against his saddle, looked at Wade eating, and asked for the jerky. Wade tossed it to him, sat back, and enjoyed his lunch, waiting for the coffee to boil.

It was a peaceful setting. A slight breeze rustled the leaves of the cottonwoods, grasshoppers buzzed, birds sang, and the shallow stream was silent. Wade took a sip of coffee, wishing Frank had gone a little easy on the grounds, and looked across the river at the opposite bank of bushes, various size rocks, and cottonwood trees. They sat in silence, enjoying the quiet afternoon, their coffee and jerky, with each lost in their thoughts. Now and then, one turned to check on the stock making a meal of the tall grass.

Frank opened his eyes and realized he had fallen asleep, then looked at Seth against the tree with his hat pulled over his eyes. Wade was lying down with his head on his saddle. Noticing the fire was about out, he put some wood on it, picked up the pot of coffee, raised the lid, and saw there was enough coffee for a cup each. He set it next to the fire to warm up when it went eerily silent. He looked around when a voice called out, "Just stay where you are, boys. Keep yer hands away from them sidearms, and no one will get hurt!"

Startled, Seth sat up, waking from a sound sleep. And as they raised their hands, several armed men walked out of the cottonwood trees on the other side of the stream.

"Don't make any sudden moves," said one as they stepped into the shallow stream.

"What's going on?" asked Frank as he started to get up.

The voices woke Wade up, and while half asleep, he wondered who they were and what they wanted.

"Just sit down," replied the man wearing a sheriff's badge. "I'll do the asking."

The three watched the men as they walked out of the river onto the sandy bank.

The man with the badge pointed his rifle at Seth. "Keep yer hands away from that pistol, mister."

Seth raised his hands a little further above his head. "Ain't looking for no trouble." He counted eleven men as they encircled them.

"Get their guns," said the sheriff.

Two men stepped forward. The older one took Seth's and Frank's guns, while the younger took Wade's pistol and rifle that lay against his saddle.

"Lookie here, Pa," the younger man said to the sheriff while he held up the rifle.

The sheriff narrowed his eyes and looked at the Sharps. "Bring that over here, Son."

"Mind if I ask what the hell's going on here?" asked Seth.

The man ignored Seth while he examined the Sharps. "Ain't seen one of these in a while." He looked at Wade. "Any good with this?"

Wade glanced at the other men. "Fair."

The sheriff looked at him. "I bet you're more than fair."

Wade glanced at Seth, then Frank wondering what was going on while the sheriff turned his attention to the Sharps.

Seth was getting edgy. "I asked what the hell is going on."

A big man of about fifty with graying brown hair in need of a shave stepped forward and put the muzzle of his rifle against the scar on Seth's face. "We're asking the questions." Then the man put his right foot on Seth's chest and pushed him back against the tree. Frank and Wade started to get up, but two men stepped closer, shoving their guns into their faces. "Easy," said one.

The sheriff reached out and put a hand on the big man's chest. "Take it easy, Henry." Then he told the others to calm down and back off.

The sheriff was a short, heavyset man with long black graying hair that looked dirty. Wade estimated his age to be close to fifty, and like the others, he needed a shave. The one who called him pa appeared to be close to twenty or maybe a little younger. He was thin and about the same height as Wade, with dirty black hair and beard. The other men were a mixture of tall, short, slender, and heavyset of different ages, looking no different from any you would find working on a ranch or farm.

Frank tried a different approach and looked at the short heavyset man. "We'd sure like to know what you fellas want."

The heavyset man grinned. "I'm sure you would, mister."

Frank looked up at him as one of the other men, a short skinny man looking like a farmer, stepped toward the sheriff. He held a rope, and all three knew it was not for cattle. "Let's get this over with, Ben," he said with a mean and hateful look.

"Take it easy, Ward," replied Ben. He looked at the others. "Let's not get hasty here." Then he looked at Seth. "Name's Ben Cole. I'm the sheriff of a little town a few miles west of here called Fallon."

Seth looked relieved. "I'm Seth---"

Cole interrupted. "We'll get to all that in a minute, but right now, we're gonna tie you boys up. That way, you won't try nuth'n, and these boys here won't shoot any of you needlessly." He stepped back while several of the men began tying their wrists.

Wade tried to get up, but the younger man who had taken his pistol and Sharps hit him over the head with his pistol.

Wade collapsed, and Seth and Frank argued that hitting Wade was unnecessary.

The sheriff quickly bent down and checked Wade. "He's alright, just dazed a little." He looked at the man that hit Wade and lowered his voice. "Damn it, Son, that'll be enough."

Wade opened his blurry eyes finding his hands tied behind his back. He shook his head to clear it but quickly stopped because that made it hurt all the more. He glanced around at the others, then looked up at the smirk on the young man's face and silently vowed he'd get even.

Sheriff Cole stepped closer to Wade and examined the wound on his head. "Sometimes my son here gets a little overenthusiastic, you might say. You okay, Son?"

Wade looked at the sheriff. "I think so, and I ain't your son."

"Figure of speech," said the Sheriff.

"Alright," said Frank. "You have us tied up, so we can't run away. You've taken our guns, and still, no one has told us what the hell's going on here."

Sheriff Cole got angry. "In time, I told you." Then he turned and told two men to go back across the river and get their horses.

Bobby saw the jerky sitting next to Frank, bent down, and picked it up.

Frank looked up. "It's plain your mother never taught you any manners."

Bobby grinned as he bit off a piece.

"Put it back, Bobby," said the sheriff in a disappointed tone, and then he turned to the others. "I don't want anyone getting overanxious here. I want to get these three back to Fallon in one piece so's they can stand trial, and the whole town can witness their hanging."

The three looked at one another, and then Seth looked at Sheriff Cole. "Stand trial for what?"

One of the men shoved Seth back against the tree with his boot. "Let's just get it over with, Ben."

Sheriff Cole looked at him. "I told you to take it easy, Roger, and I weren't joking none about that." He turned, facing the others. "Don't push me on this. We're taking these three back to Fallon to wait for the U.S. Marshal from Santa Fe, and then they'll stand trial." He paused. "I'll shoot anyone that gets in the way of that."

"Stand trial for what?" asked Wade with a puzzled look.

Bobby leaned down. "Fer murder, that's what fer."

Seth looked surprised. "Who the hell are we supposed to have killed?"

The man named Henry gave Seth a mean dirty look. "As if you don't know, you bastard."

Frank looked at Wade, then Seth, and then at the others. "Hold on boys. You've made a grave mistake here---"

One of the other men interrupted Frank. "You were told to shut up!" interrupted one of the other men.

Sheriff Ben Cole turned and stepped between his men Wade and the others. "Everyone settle down." Then he turned to Bobby and another man telling them to untie the three, and when they took the ropes off their wrists, he told them to saddle their horses and pack up. Ben Cole and the others watched as Wade, Seth, and Frank broke camp, loaded the packhorses, and saddled their mounts. After they were in their saddles, their hands were tied to the saddle horn of their saddles.

Bobby Cole rode next to Wade, grinning from ear to ear. "Nice little filly you got there. After we hang you, fellas, I'm gonna enjoy ride'n her and shoot'n that big Sharps." Then he chuckled, spurred his horse, and rode toward the front of the column next to his pa, Sheriff Cole.

Wade stared at Bobby, wishing his hands weren't tied. As he watched them, he wondered who they were supposed to have murdered and how in the hell they were going to get out of this mess.

Sixteen

It was late afternoon when the posse and their prisoners rode down the hill toward Fallon, New Mexico. Wade's head pounded from the bump on his head, and he wished they would hurry and get to the jail so he could lie down. Fallon sat at one end of a green, peaceful valley of rolling hills between the mountains. The dirt road they were on ran straight through town, turned north across a wide stream where some children played, then disappeared between the hills. Houses of different sizes dotted the hillsides north and south of town, and a small school and white church nestled in some cottonwoods near the river. The town looked like a peaceful place. As they rode up the main street of Fallon, busy with wagons, riders, and pedestrians, Wade noticed people were stopping to stare and talk in whispers. It was not long before the good people of Fallon began to line up the street and boardwalk, watching as the men rode past. One man yelled at the sheriff and asked if these were the men, while others talked of hanging to save the town the expense of a trial.

Wade and the others worried they might not reach the safety of the jail. One man ran up to Frank and cursed as he grabbed his leg to pull him from his horse. The sheriff pulled his gun and fired a shot into the air, and as it became quiet, he told everyone to keep back, or he'd shoot the first man that tried to harm his prisoners.

Bobby hollered, "We got them!"

Their silence turned to fist-waving shouts of profanities and calling out for a quick hanging.

Sheriff Cole gave his son a dirty look. "Bobby, keep your damn mouth shut."

Wade hoped they could make it to the jailhouse and wondered if Sheriff Cole could keep an angry mob from hanging them for something they didn't do. The angry townspeople followed the riders up the street, yelling for the sheriff to turn them over. Keeping his gun in view to deter any violence, he promised to shoot the first man who tried to take one of his prisoners. When they reached the jail, the sheriff untied them, helped the three men off their horses, and hurried them inside. He put Wade into one cell, Frank, and Seth in another, and locked the cell doors.

Sheriff Cole took a shotgun from the rack behind his desk, checked to make sure it was loaded, and with a determined look, stepped outside to confront the angry, noisy crowd. He stood at the edge of the boardwalk in front of the jail, held the shotgun, barrel down in one hand, raised his other, and asked for silence. "You may as well all go on home. I'm not about to turn these men over for a lynching. I'm sending for the U.S. Marshal at Santa Fe, and he should be here sometime tomorrow. Now, I promise each and every one of you that if these men are lynched before their trial, I'll have the United States Marshal arrest every damn one of you for murder."

Someone yelled out, "Why are you protecting them, Ben? Let's hang them now!"

Angry voices agreed.

Ben Cole looked at the man. "Because we ain't a bunch of killers, that's why." Then he pointed at the jailhouse behind him. "We're gonna let the law handle these three, and if found guilty, they'll hang."

A middle-aged woman of fifty stepped forward. "And suppose they aren't found guilty? What then?"

Inaudible words of anger rose from the crowd, heads nodded, and clenched fists waved.

Ben Cole raised the shotgun, pointed the barrel at the crowd so everyone could see he meant business, and asked for silence. As the people of Fallon quieted, he looked at the middle-aged woman. "I doubt that'll happen because the people of this here town will be the jury."

Seth, Frank, and Wade looked at one another, not liking the odds. Wade grabbed the bars to his cell, thinking of Sarah. "We don't stand a chance."

The crowd settled down and began talking among themselves, apparently satisfied with that line of reasoning. Cole let them talk with one another for a few moments before telling them to go home and let the law settle this. As the crowd slowly disbursed, he turned to two men from his posse and told them to unpack the three's belongings, take them inside, and take their stock up to the livery. Sheriff Cole took one last look at the crowd making sure they were leaving before he, Bobby, and the big man named Henry went inside.

Seth looked at the Sheriff. "Smart what you told those folks. Now, do you mind telling us who we supposedly killed?"

Bobby looked at them. "You know damn well who they were."

"Shut up, Bobby," said an angry Cole. Then he looked at Seth. "For killing a family east of here."

Wade got up from his cot. "What, family?"

Bobby hurried to the cell door and looked at Wade. "Don't act so innocent. That Sharps of yours blew the chest out of young Willie Jackson yesterday."

"Couldn't have," replied Wade. "All three of us were in Raton yesterday."

"Likely story," said Henry looking skeptical.

"Wade's right," said Seth. "And if you send someone over there, several people can vouch for that."

Sheriff Cole thought about that for just a moment. "Oh, I could send Paul here up to Raton, but that won't prove nuth'n. Even if they said you boys were there. You could still have done the killing."

"How?" asked Frank.

Wade turned and kicked the bunk sitting against the back wall of his cell, then held his throbbing head, wishing he hadn't done that. Looking in pain, he sat down, resting his head in his hands.

Frank continued their case. "What happened to this family?"

"They's tortured and murdered," said Sheriff Cole.

"How were they murdered?" asked Seth.

Sheriff Cole turned away. "I'm tired, and plum talked out." He turned and walked to the gun rack behind his desk, put the shotgun away, and picked up the coffee pot from the pot-bellied stove beneath the gun rack. He shook it, then turned to Bobby and told him to get some water and make a fresh pot of coffee.

Seth let out a long sigh. "Sheriff, my name's Seth Bowlen. I'm the sheriff of Sisters up in Colorado."

Ben Cole turned, looking surprised as well as interested as he sat down.

Bowlen gestured to Frank. "This here's Frank Wells, the sheriff of Roscoe's Creek up in Colorado."

Bobby pointed to Wade. "And where's he supposed to be sheriff'n?"

Irritated at his son Cole said, "Let the man finish Bobby."

Seth glanced at Bobby wanting to punch the little shit but kept talking to the elder Cole. "He ain't a sheriff. He works for Tolliver Grimes, owner of the Circle T near Harper, Colorado."

Ben Cole digested that quickly and asked if they had any way to prove they were who they claimed to be.

Seth nodded at their saddlebags sitting in the corner. "Our badges are in our saddlebags behind you."

Cole told Bobby to check it out.

Everyone waited while Bobby hurried across the room and started digging through the saddlebags. Seconds later, he stood and held up two badges as he walked toward the sheriff.

Sheriff Ben Cole took them, examined them closely, and looked at Seth. "What are two lawmen and a cowpuncher with a Sharps rifle doing in New Mexico?"

Seth told them about the killing of Wade's friend in Harper, Colorado, by three men leaving out the half-breed, then of the killing of the Barton and Osborn families and the abduction of the two Miller girls.

"And just where are these little girls now?" asked Ben Cole.

Seth explained about Gil Robinson getting shot and taking the two girls back to Roscoe's Creek while the three of them trailed the killers to Raton.

Bobby Cole chuckled, looking doubtful. "You don't believe them do ya, Pa?"

Sheriff Cole smiled. "If all that's true, Mr. Bowlen, and if that's your real name, then why hide your badges? If I were trail'n some no goods, I'd keep my badge on where people could see it."

Bobby turned to his pa. "They could've stolen them badges, Pa."

"That's a fact Son," agreed Cole. "They sure could have."

Seth's knuckles turned white from gripping the bars. "Since we were out of our jurisdiction and in another state, we thought it best if we took them off." He let go of the bars, looked at Frank, and then back at the sheriff with frustration. "Didn't occur to us that a group of idiots would accuse us of being the ones we been chasing."

Anger filled the sheriff's face.

Wade gripped the bars and looked through them at the sheriff. "Check out our story."

"Time enough for that during your trial," said Cole looking tired. "Right now, it's getting near supper time, and I'm hungry." He turned to Bobby. "Son, I want you to go home and ask yer ma to fix us something to eat." He looked at the three prisoners. "Tell her we've three guests."

"We ain't gonna feed these killers, are we, Pa?"

"Son," the sheriff said softly. "We ain't cruel people, and these three are more than likely hungry, same as me."

"If it were up to me, they'd go hungry," said Deputy Paul.

Henry glared at Seth. "I agree with Paul."

Cole had lost his patience. "But it ain't up to you boys now, is it? And I ain't asking your missus to do the cooking now, am I?"

Paul looked apologetic. "Sorry, Sheriff. Want me to spend the night?"

"Be a good idea, but you best go home and eat, get some rest, and come back around ten tonight." He looked at Henry. "Can you spend the night?"

Henry nodded. "I'll have to let my missus know."

Cole nodded. "Ok, go tell your missus and get back here. We'll all four sleep here tonight." He glanced at Seth and the others. "If some of them law-abiding citizens have one too many, they may get it in their heads to try their hands at a lynching." He turned and looked at his prisoners. "I don't want these boys getting hung before the Marshal gets here."

"Alright then," said Paul. "I'll head home and be back around ten."

Sheriff Cole followed Paul and Henry to the door and locked it after they stepped outside. Hearing the coffee boil, he rushed across the room and moved the pot to the side of the stove. He looked at his prisoners and asked if they wanted coffee. They all said yes, so he filled three metal cups with coffee, handed each a cup through the bars, sat down at his desk, and took a drink of coffee.

Wade sat on his cot with his back against the wall staring at the far wall through the bars holding his coffee with both hands wishing they had not stopped. A few moments passed, and then he stood, walked to the edge of his cell, and looked at Sheriff Cole through the bars. "Sheriff," he said softly. "I know you don't want to talk about this, but how did this family die?"

"You're right about that boy," said a tired, annoyed Cole. "I don't want to talk about it. Now drink your damn coffee and let me enjoy mine."

Frustrated, Wade turned and sat back down on his cot against the wall, wondering if he would ever see Sarah again.

Frank stood, walked to the bars that separated the two cells, and looked at Wade. "Now I know how you felt back in Roscoe's Creek when you carried that little yellow dog into my jail."

"I'd rather be back in Roscoe Creek's jail, that's for sure." Wade looked at Sheriff Cole and raised his voice. "At least the sheriff there had some damn sense about him."

Frank and Seth chuckled, but Sheriff Cole ignored him and continued drinking his coffee, hoping they didn't have any visitors during the night.

The silence was interrupted by pounding on the front door. Cole jumped up, hurried across the room, unlocked the door, and opened it. A middle-aged woman walked in carrying a tray of food covered with a white dishtowel, followed by Bobby Cole with another tray. After Mrs. Cole set her tray on the sheriff's desk, she looked at her husband with an unhappy look, turned, and left in a hurry. Bobby set his tray down, watched his mother hurry out the door, then turned to his pa. "I think ma's a little mad."

The sheriff knew his wife was more than a little mad over him asking her to feed these three men. He lifted the towels off the trays, bent down, and smelled the food. "You boys are in luck. We got cornbread, beans, and bacon."

Being hungry, Wade sat up and watched as the sheriff picked up two plates, handed them to Bobby, then picked up a third and walked over to the cells. They bent down, placed the plates on the floor then slid them through a slot under the bars meant for feeding.

"Enjoy the food, boys," said Cole as he and Bobby returned to the desk and dinner.

Wade dug right in as if he had not eaten in days.

Seth and Frank watched him for a moment, and then Frank winked at Seth while asking if he thought the sheriff's missus might have poisoned their food.

Wade stopped eating and looked at the food, wondering the same thing. Having lost his appetite, he put his plate on the floor and sat on his cot with his back against the wall, wishing he was back at the Circle T.

Sheriff Cole laughed right along with Frank and Seth, and then Frank told Wade they were only funning him.

Wade ignored them and stared at the ceiling remembering the day Mr. Talbert rode up to the big house of the Circle T and asked Mr. Grimes if he could have a word with Wade.

June 1870

Wade and Emmett Spears had just ridden into the barn and started unsaddling their horses when young Stu Parks walked in. "Wade," he said. "Mr. Grimes wants you up at the main house."

Wade's expression was curious as he glanced at Emmett, then Stu. "What for?"

Stu shrugged with a puzzled look. "Don't rightly know. He just told me to tell you to get up to the house as soon as you rode in." He looked through the open barn doors toward the big house. "Mr. Talbert rode in a while back, and they've both been inside ever since."

Wade glanced at Emmett with a worrisome face.

Emmett shrugged as he stepped next to the door and looked toward the big house in thoughtful silence while Stu headed for the bunkhouse.

Wade stepped away from his mare and stood next to Emmett. He took off his hat and rubbed the back of his neck, thinking this wasn't good. Without taking his eyes off the house, he asked Emmett if he would finish the mare for him.

Emmett said he'd be glad to, and then he put one hand on Wade's shoulder, stared at the big house, and lowered his voice. "Think maybe Sarah's with child?"

"No," answered Wade in a stern voice showing his anger. Giving Emmett a dirty look, he walked out of the barn toward the big house. "Damn it, Emmett. We ain't done nothing."

Emmett grinned, knowing that was true, and called after him. "Been nice knowing you, Wade. I'll see to it that Mr. Grimes writes your ma."

Wade turned and looked over his shoulder and saw no humor in his current situation, wishing Emmett would be a little more supportive. He stared at the big house as he walked toward it, wondering what Mr. Grimes wanted. Wade glanced back at Emmett, seeing he had already walked back into the barn. He walked up the porch steps, stood staring at the door, knocked, and waited. The Indian squaw Mr. Grimes had named Bertha and had been with the Grimes family for several years opened the door and glared at Wade. She was short and heavyset, her black hair worn in a long braid that hung down her back. She wore a faded red dress and a yellow shirt.

"Mr. Grimes wants to see me."

She gave him a disapproving look, and then backed away from the door so he could enter. After he was inside, Bertha closed the door, gave him a silent look, walked across the room, and disappeared into Mr. Grimes' study.

Wade stared at the door she had walked through and wondered why she never smiled or talked, thinking it must be an Indian thing. He stood in the middle of the living room for several minutes, looking around the room of paintings and fine furniture.

The door finally opened, and a somber-looking Mr. Grimes motioned with one hand. "Wade, come in here."

Wade could feel his face flush, and his palms began to sweat.

Mr. Talbert sat in a chair by the bookcase with his hat in his lap, looking serious like he did when he and Emmett helped build the McSweeney barn.

Afraid to say anything to Mr. Talbert, Wade looked at Mr. Grimes and waited to see what he wanted.

Tolliver closed the door and pointed to one of three wooden straight-back chairs. "Have a seat Wade." He smiled as he gestured to Mr. Talbert. "I'm sure you know Mr. Talbert."

"Yes, sir," replied Wade as he looked at Mr. Talbert, wiped his hand on his pants, extended it, and said hello.

Mr. Talbert leaned forward in his chair and firmly shook Wade's hand without a greeting.

Wade looked at Mr. Talbert's expressionless face wondering why he wanted to see him.

"Have a seat Wade," said Tolliver Grimes, then he turned to Mr. Talbert. "I'll leave you and Wade alone for a spell Jasper. I'll be on the front porch." Then without looking at Wade, he stepped out of the room and closed the door behind him.

The room filled with a heavy silence as Jasper Talbert stood and walked to the wall of books, eyed them for a moment, then sat on the edge of the desk and looked at Wade, seeing a mixture of fear and curiosity on the boy's face. "I'm sure you're curious about this, so I'll get straight to it."

Wade's heart was beating so hard that he feared Mr. Talbert might hear it.

"The thing of it is," continued Talbert, "I know that you and my Sarah have been seeing each other whenever she can get away."

Wade's mouth opened slightly, but nothing came out.

Mr. Talbert waited for him to speak, and when he didn't, he said, "I might be old, Mr. Garrison, but I'm not blind."

"Yes, sir."

Talbert smiled. "I think you mean 'no sir.'"

"Yes, sir. I mean no, sir."

Jasper Talbert grinned as he stood and sat in the chair next to Wade. "Don't worry, boy. I don't aim to shoot you."

Wade stared into Jasper's brown eyes, feeling somewhat relieved.

"That is unless there is a reason for me to shoot you." He stared at Wade for a moment. "Is there a reason that I should shoot you?"

Wade felt his face flush. "No, sir."

Jasper smiled. "Glad to hear that. I'd hate like hell to mess up Tolliver's library."

Wade found no humor in that as he stared at Mr. Talbert, wondering why he rode all the way from the double J to see him.

Jasper Talbert laughed. "It was a joke, boy, relax. I'm not here to run you off or shoot you. The fact is, my Sarah made me promise to go easy on you, and that's just what I'm doing." He grinned at Wade. "Leastwise, that's what I'm trying to do."

Wade wondered what it would be like if he wasn't going easy on him, forced a smile, and tried to think of something to say, but his mind was blank.

Jasper stood, walked back to the edge of the desk, turned, looked down at him, and wondered what it was Sarah saw in this young man. "I've known about you and my Sarah ever since that rainstorm last year."

Wade thought about that day and their first kiss and stopped thinking about it in case Mr. Talbert could read his mind. Then he told himself people can't read other's minds but thought about his mare just in case.

Mr. Talbert had a serious look. "We had quite a talk about you yesterday, my Sarah and me. Her mother found a letter you had written expressing some mighty deep feelings. So, my missus and I had a long talk with Sarah."

Wade wanted to jump up and run out of the room.

"I never read the letter myself," said Jasper. "I don't believe in prying, but my missus ain't of the same mind, so she pries when it suits her. Especially when it comes to Sarah, so she read the letter and the others you've written."

Wade was embarrassed and could feel his face flush while his heart pounded against his chest. He looked up at Mr. Talbert with a pleading face. "Sir, I hope you're not asking me to stay away from Miss Sarah."

"Funny that you should bring that up. I talked to Sarah about that very thing, and she refused to stop seeing you." He paused and shifted his weight, looking uncomfortable. "She refused, and I have to tell you that was the first time Sarah ever refused something I asked her to do."

The room filled with a heavy silence as Mr. Talbert stood, picked up his hat and looked at him with a stern look. "We'll be expecting you for dinner this Sunday, Mr. Garrison." He paused. "Try not to be late. My missus would be a bit unhappy if you are." Then he put on his hat and walked out of the library.

Wade sat there by himself, staring at the closed door, going over what Mr. Talbert said about Sunday dinner. Listening to Talbert's footsteps grow fainter on the other side of the door, he wiped the sweat from his forehead. Moments later, he heard Mr. Talbert and Mr. Grimes's voices but couldn't understand what they were saying, and then he heard laughter.

Minutes later, the door opened, and Mr. Grimes walked in. "I guess you'll be wanting an advance to buy a present."

Wade looked confused. "Sir?"

"I understand from Mr. Talbert that you've been invited for supper next Sunday?"

Wade nodded. "Well, yes, sir, I have, but—"

"But nothing, boy," interrupted Mr. Grimes. "You can't accept a meal from Janice Talbert without taking her a little gift of some sort." He looked at Wade. "Now, do you have any money?"

Wade was confused, and his face showed it. "A little. I was saving up for a Sharps rifle like yours."

Mr. Grimes chuckled as he turned to sit down behind his big desk. "Well," he said. "That Sharps may have to wait for a spell." Then he grinned. "You've got to start saving for other things." He laughed, being pleased with himself. "Now go on, get the hell out of here."

Wade stood, slowly walked to the door, opened it, and turned to Mr. Grimes. "What sort of gift?"

Tolliver thought for a moment. "A new vase or something made of glass would be nice."

Wade considered that as he turned and walked out of the study, across the living room, and wondered what Mr. Grimes meant by "other things." As he opened the front door, muffled laughter came from behind the closed door of the study.

The Jailhouse in Fallon

Wade opened his eyes and looked up at the small, barred window near the cell ceiling. It was chilly, and the one blanket allowed by the town of Fallon was not enough to keep out the morning chill. He sat up, wrapped the old blanket around him, stood at the end of his bunk on his tiptoes, and tried to see out the cell window. The only thing he could see were the tops of some trees and the morning sky turning from black to the lighter blue that comes with the first light of dawn. He heard the movement, turned, and saw Frank relieving himself in the bucket left by Sheriff Cole for just that purpose. Feeling the urge himself, he looked around and saw the bucket he had kicked out of frustration the night before lying on its side under his cot. Wade tossed the blanket onto his cot, knelt, and retrieved the bucket. When he finished, he looked around, wondering what to do with it.

Wells was watching him and grinned. "I always enjoyed this part of the morning back in Roscoe's Creek."

Wade smiled wryly. "S'pect you did, Frank, but how's it feel now?"

Without answering, Frank turned and nudged Seth with the toe of his boot. "Time to get up."

"What for?" replied Seth sleepily. "We ain't going nowhere."

"Time to get hung," replied Frank amusingly.

Wade didn't think that was funny as he walked to the bars of his cell and saw someone asleep on the floor in the corner near the door. Curious about the others, he saw someone on a cot in the far corner by the desk. Another lay on the floor next to the desk, and another's legs sticking out from behind the desk. He figured the one in the cot was the sheriff and, hoping they'd be up soon, sat on his cot with his back against the brick wall. As he sat in silence, he worried about getting hung and never seeing Sarah or the Circle T hands again.

It wasn't long before Sheriff Ben Cole stirred, and minutes later, he built a fire in the potbellied stove in the corner behind his desk. When he had the fire going, he walked over to his son, asleep on the floor next to the desk with Wade's Sharps next to him. "Time to get up, Son." Then he walked past the cells, eyed his prisoners, and nudged the person who slept on the floor. "Time to get up, Paul." As Paul set up looking sleepy, the sheriff told him to go home and eat breakfast but be back by noon. Sheriff Cole then woke up Henry telling him the same thing.

Paul pushed his covers back slowly, got up, stretched, glanced at the prisoners as he walked to the door, took the board away, opened the door, and walked out.

Sheriff Cole waited for Henry to leave, then bolted the door and walked to the cells. "You boys ready for some coffee?"

They all said they were while Frank slid the bucket toward Seth with his foot. "Your turn."

Mrs. Cole delivered a breakfast of scrambled eggs and potatoes with the same absence of pleasantries as yesterday. As the sheriff slid the plates under the cell doors, Wade looked at him hesitantly, then at Seth and Frank, who ate with great enthusiasm. Deciding the food had to be okay since they all survived yesterday's meal, he picked up the plate, sat on his bunk, and began to eat.

After breakfast, Cole and his son Bobby let the three out of their cells to empty their buckets and visit a nearby outhouse, and now they sat on their cots, wondering about their future.

Seth stood, walked to the bars, and looked at the two Coles playing checkers. "I'd still like to know how that family was killed."

The sheriff looked up. "I don't want to talk about that right now, Mr. Bowlen. You'll find all about the charges of murder at your trial."

"We get to talk to a lawyer?" asked Frank.

Sheriff Cole looked at him thoughtfully. "Have to send for one from Santa Fe, I suppose." Then he chuckled. "We only got one, and he'll be prosecuting you boys in front of a Territorial Judge."

Bowlen felt the urge to kick the shit out of both men, but he was behind bars, and they had the key. Instead, he sat down on his cot and looked at the others in disgust. Neither Seth nor Frank had ever witnessed such a combination of stupidity and stubbornness before, and they had known many a lawman in their day. Seth thought that even as crazy as old Danner was, he would tell a man the nature of his crime.

It was late afternoon when the door opened, and two men wearing the dust of the trail on their hats, boots, and long tan dusters walked in. Both were big men, one a few years younger than Seth, the other about Wade's age. They glanced at the three men as they walked past the cells toward the sheriff and his son, who were playing checkers. Wade got up from his cot and walked to the bars for a better look.

"Sheriff Ben Cole?" asked the older man with brown eyes, light brown hair, a handlebar mustache, and a square jaw.

Sheriff Cole stood. "That'd be me," he said with a smile. "This here's my Deputy, Bobby Cole."

The older man extended his right hand. "I'm U.S. Marshal Billy French, and this here's my deputy Todd Jewett."

Todd Jewett was a young man, clean-shaven with black hair, brown eyes, and had a way about him that told others he was a serious man.

Sheriff Ben Cole and Deputy Bobby Cole shook their hands, and Sheriff Cole pointed to the three men. "There they are," he said proudly.

French looked at the three men. "We got here as fast as we could. Where'd you catch these three bad hombres?"

Sheriff Cole glanced at the three men. "We caught up with them yesterday camped along the river, eight or so miles from here."

"That so?" said French as he turned and walked to the bars with a grin. "So, you two have turned to killing women and children in your old age?" He extended his hand through the bars. "How are you doing Seth? Good to see you, Frank."

After they shook hands, Seth nodded to the sheriff. "When the sheriff there said he had sent for the U.S. Marshal in Santa Fe, Frank and I were hoping it'd be you."

Surprised by what was happening, Sheriff Ben Cole glanced at his son Bobby and then looked at the Marshal. "You know these men?"

French turned and grinned. "I do, and neither of these two ever killed anyone unless they deserved killing." Then he glanced at Wade. "Can't rightly vouch for that one, though."

That wasn't much of a comfort to Wade.

Wearing a happy grin, Seth gestured at Wade. "That young fella's Wade Garrison from up around the town of Harper, Colorado." Then he looked at Marshal French. "The three of us, plus a friend of Frank's named Gil Robinson, trailed four men who killed a couple of families up our way and stole two young girls. We got the girls back, and Wade killed one of the bastards in the process."

French glanced around. "Where is this Gil fellah?"

"Gil got shot in the shoulder," said Seth, "so he took the girls and headed home to Roscoe's Creek."

Marshal French nodded as he considered all that, then looked at Ben Cole. "May as well open up, Sheriff. These three aren't the same ones who did the killing."

Deputy Bobby Cole's face showed his disappointment. "And what makes you so sure about that?" Then he looked at Wade. "That one there was carrying a Sharps, and one of the Jackson boys had a hole blown in his chest that I could put my fist through." Then he looked at the sheriff. "Pa said it was a Hawkins or a Sharps buffalo gun."

Wade gripped the bars in anger. "One of the men we been after is carrying a thirty caliber Sharps. Mine's a fifty caliber." Then he looked at Bobby. "You seem to have taken an unhealthy liken to that Sharps of mine."

"Don't make no difference," replied Bobby ignoring Wade while looking at his pa. "I still think they're the bunch we been after."

"Put a lid on it, Bobby," said Ben. Then he looked apologetically at Billy French and the others. "The Jackson boy and Bobby here were best friends."

French looked at Bobby with sympathy. "Sorry about that, but these men are innocent of killing your friend or anyone, and right now, I'm asking they be set free."

With a disappointed look, Bobby looked at French. "They still could have killed my friend and his family." He pointed to Wade. "And I bet he's the one that did the raping."

Wade gripped the bars a little tighter, wishing he was out of the cell so he could kick the shit out of Bobby.

Marshal French looked like he was at the end of his patience with the fool as he stepped away from the bars toward Bobby and raised his voice. "Because we had another killing down near Santa Fe!"

"When?" asked Wade.

"Yesterday," replied French over his shoulder while he stared at Bobby. Then he gave the sheriff a stern look. "Now, let these three men out."

154

Cole looked apologetic as he walked behind his desk, took the keys from a hook, unlocked the cell doors, and stepped back. Wade pushed his cell door open and stepped out, glaring at Deputy Bobby Cole.

As Frank and Seth stepped out, Seth grinned at Sheriff Cole. "Mind if we have our guns and badges back, Sheriff?"

Billy French looked at Ben Cole. "You took their badges?"

"They weren't wearing them," replied the sheriff. "They had them hidden in their saddlebags."

Seth looked at Marshal French. "Out of our jurisdiction and out of state." Then he looked at the sheriff. "Never figured on getting arrested."

"Makes sense," said French with a laugh. "You tell that to the sheriff?"

"We did," replied Frank looking irritated. "But they were more interested in arresting us, and all but the sheriff there were in the mood for hanging."

French looked at the sheriff. "You're damn lucky nothing happened to these men, or you and your deputy and whoever else were with you would be in my jail in Santa Fe." Then he turned to Seth. "You know what these fellas look like?"

Seth shook his head. "Ain't neither of us ever seen them, but Wade there got their descriptions from them that saw them kill his friend in a saloon up in Harper."

Wade gave the same description he had given to Seth and Frank. Then he told him about the unusual markings on the shoe of one horse and the slightly turned right foot of another.

French frowned thoughtfully and said they were the same as those found at the farm near Santa Fe. He looked at Ben Cole. "How about the tracks at the Jacksons' place?"

"The same," said Sheriff Ben Cole.

The Marshal asked, "You check the marks of these fellas' horses?"

Sheriff Ben Cole looked at Bobby and then shook his head no.

Billy French looked disappointed. "Seems that'd be on my list of things to do right off."

Ben Cole looked rueful. "We'd have gotten around to it."

"After you hung us?" asked Wade sarcastically.

Both Ben and Bobby Cole gave Wade a dirty look.

Billy French told Cole to give them back their guns, and while Wade examined his, he half-listened to the other's talk about getting out of this town and riding into Santa Fe after Billy and Todd had breakfast.

155

Word had spread about the U.S. Marshal being in town, and a small crowd of angry townspeople had gathered outside the jail. Sheriff Cole stepped outside to the edge of the boardwalk and explained that the men they had been holding were not the same ones who did the killing. It took a few minutes of explaining, but after he told them of another killing near Santa Fe, the crowd dispersed.

Wade and the others gathered their belongings and headed for the door. Wade walked past Bobby and Ben Cole as if they weren't there while Seth, more understanding of the sheriff's position, smiled, extended his hand, and thanked the sheriff for his hospitality.

Frank Wells grinned and held out an outstretched hand, saying he could not remember a more memorable evening.

Sheriff Cole grinned, shook their hands, and said he was glad it turned out the way it did.

Marshal French looked at the clock on the wall above the sheriff's desk and then out the window. "Be dark in a couple of hours." Then he turned to Seth and the others. "We'll leave after breakfast in the morning." Billy shook Cole's hand, opened the door, and stepped onto the boardwalk. After the others were on the boardwalk next to him, he gestured to the hotel up the street. "You boy's go on to the hotel and get a room while Todd and I take our stock to the livery."

Wanting to get out of Fallon, Wade quickly ate his breakfast, excused himself, and headed for the livery to saddle his horse.

Billy watched Wade walk out of the café. "Seth, that friend of yours seems in a bit of a hurry."

Seth watched Wade disappear past the window, take a bite of food, and swallow. "Boys on his way to a place called Revenge."

French took a drink of coffee and nodded. "That's a mistake he'll have to learn on his own. Same as you and I." He looked at the clock above the door, wiped his mouth with the cloth napkin, and stood. "You boy's head on down to the livery." He smiled. "Breakfast is on me."

Seth walked into the livery as Wade tightened the cinch on his saddle, thinking of what Billy had said in the café. "In a bit of a hurry?"

Wade slipped the bridle over his mare's head. "The sooner I get out of this town, the better I'll feel."

Frank chuckled. "Don't take it personal, Son."

Having just walked into the livery and hearing what Wade said, Billy French and Todd Jewett grinned as they passed Wade's stall on the way to their horses.

Wade stopped what he was doing and looked at Frank. "I take almost getting hung and my belongings owned by that little idiot very personal."

With their horses saddled and the supplies loaded, they walked out of the livery leading their horses into the dirt street. They climbed up and rode them past the jailhouse, where Bobby Cole sat on a chair. He stood, walked to the edge of the porch, grinned at Wade, and spit into the street.

Wade pulled up, got off his horse, walked up the steps, and punched Bobby in the face, knocking him backward across the boardwalk into the chair he had been sitting in. Sheriff Cole came running out of the jail just as Bobby got up, his mouth and chin covered in blood from a broken nose. Bobby shook his head and wiped his nose with his right hand as he looked at Wade. "I'll kill you for that."

Sheriff Cole stepped between them and looked at his son. "You ain't killing anyone, damn it. Now you're my son, and I love you dearly, but I can't say you ain't been asking for that."

"Get out of the way Pa!"

Sheriff Cole looked at his son. "Let it go, Son, or I'll put your ass in a cell." Then he looked at Wade. "Sorry about the misunderstanding and the manners of my only son. I'd appreciate you leaving before he does something stupid and regretful."

Wade gave the sheriff a quick nod and, without looking at Bobby, walked down the steps, climbed onto his horse, and rode toward the edge of town.

Seventeen

During the ride from Fallon to Santa Fe, Billy, Seth, and Frank occupied their time talking about times past and the people they had known when they were deputies in Rio Blanco. Their stories of Sheriff Danner brought laughter to Deputy Marshal Todd Jewett.

Wade wanted to be alone, so he only half-listened as he rode a few yards behind them. His thoughts were of Emmett Sarah and even Bobby Cole, and for some reason, he felt a sense of regret for having hit Cole without warning, even if he had been a thorn in his ass. Three weeks ago, Wade would have climbed up onto his mare and rode out of town. But the Wade Garrison of today was a troubled young man filled with hate and anger.

Laughter from up ahead disturbed his thoughts of Bobby Cole, and as he watched the men ahead of him, he wondered how they had learned to cope with the death, hate, and anger he now felt. He looked at Seth smiling while he talked about Sheriff Danner, wondering how he had come to deal with the death and violence he had known over the years. He wasn't born that way.

Seth turned his head and glanced over his shoulder at Wade, sensing something had him by the neck and would not let go. He pulled at the reins of his horse to slow him, so Wade could catch up. "You have the face of trouble about you, Wade."

Wade frowned and looked at the hillsides instead of Seth. "Guess I do."

"You regretting that business with the Cole boy?"

"Guess you could say that. Shouldn't have just walked up and hit him."

"Why?"

That surprised Wade. "Just shouldn't have."

Seth drew in a breath and sighed thoughtfully. "Funny thing about battles in war and fistfights in a bar or on a boardwalk. It's the outcome that counts, especially in our business. I have seen a man give another a chance once and got the shit kicked out of him. The man who did the kicking was the one that deserved it, and you can bet your young ass he never regretted it. But the other fella sure as hell did."

Wade thought about the surprised look on Bobby Cole's face when he got up as Sheriff Cole stepped between them.

Seth looked at the backs of the others riding ahead of them. "I've seen many a good men die, giving the other man a fair chance when it's them who needed the edge." Bowlen took a deep breath and let it out slowly. "I have been a deputy or sheriff most of my adult life, Son, and I mean to tell you that just because a man is decent and fair-minded don't mean he needs to be that way when it comes to a fight." Seth pointed to his bad eye. "That's a lesson I learned the hard way a long time ago. In our business, it's better for the towns and decent folk in them if it's the other man that doesn't walk away."

"Maybe," replied Wade with a doubtful look.

Seth looked at him, thinking of himself at a younger age. "A lawman needs fear on his side. Without it, he's a step away from being dead. Men need to know that you give no quarter and don't expect none." His eyes narrowed. "Then they'll fear you, boy, and that's your edge. If they fear you, they'll hesitate." He looked at Wade, patted him on the shoulder, and smiled. "You'd make a pretty fair lawman Son. You have the sense of it, the desire for it, and even the ability, but you have that one flaw that kills most lawmen."

Wade looked at him.

"A sense of fair play."

"I don't see no harm in fair play," argued Wade.

"Maybe. That is if you're playing horseshoes, checkers, and other childish games." He paused in memory for a moment. "My pa was a blacksmith in a little town in Missouri named Turner Creek, where I grew

159

up. There was a man whom I idolized by the name of Wes Connors. He was the sheriff and a fairer man you've never met. I spent a lot of time cleaning the jail and other odd jobs just to be near the man." Seth paused and smiled in memory. "Followed Wes around like a little puppy, to my pa's displeasure. One day two men rode into town, got drunk, and began bullying the townspeople and bothering decent women as they walked along the boardwalks. Sheriff Connors told the two men they could ride out of town, or he'd arrest them. They smiled at Wes, causing him to relax a bit, and then they pulled their guns and shot him twice in the belly. Before the town knew what happened, the two men rode out and were never seen nor heard of again." Seth grimaced in memory as he looked at the far-off hills. "Took Sheriff Wes Connors a long time to die from being gut shot. I sat outside his office on the boardwalk with my head buried in my forearms, crying while listening to him screaming in pain before it went quiet. I didn't know my pa was sitting beside me on the boardwalk until I heard the door to the sheriff's office open. When I raised my head, the doc came out, looked at my pa, and then me. The doc just looked sad as he turned his head and walked away."

"He the reason you became a sheriff?" asked Wade.

Seth nodded. "Years later, I told my parents I was leaving to be a sheriff somewhere's. My pa sat me down and asked if I remembered Sheriff Wes Connors. I thought it was a strange question at the time but said I did. Pa put his hand on my shoulder and said Wes was a good God-fearing man and a fair man, but being fair is what killed Wes Connors, not those two men. They were just the instrument. I thought on that for several years, not fully understanding what he meant until that night in Culpepper when I damn near lost my eye. It'd been better if I had drawn my gun. The fool drunk would have dropped the knife. I'd have a good eye, and I wouldn't have beaten the poor son-of-a-bitch half to death in anger."

They rode in silence while Wade thought about that.

"Being fair and being stupid are close to the same thing." Seth grinned. "Those who live the longest act first apologize later. I'm not telling you what you did back in Fallon is acceptable because I'm not sure the Cole boy would have thrown the first punch. But I am telling you that in our business, being fair is the same as being dead." He looked at Wade and nodded. "You can take that to the bank Son." Then he nudged his horse into a gallop and joined Frank and the others letting Wade consider what he had told him.

160

The afternoon sun was low in the western sky when the five men rode up the main street of Santa Fe toward the Marshal's office, attracting a following of townspeople with mean looks while pointing at them. A man ran up and asked Billy French if they were the men who killed the Mitchel family. French explained they were friends of his from Colorado, and they were after the same men. When they reached the hitching rail in front of the Marshal's office, a short, bald, and heavyset man walked out of the Marshal's office with a shotgun resting on his right shoulder. Looking the others over, he asked, "Who you got there?"

"Friends of mine," replied French as he took off his hat and slapped the dust from his pants. "Need you to take these men and their stock up to the livery along with mine and Todd's if you wouldn't mind, Chris." He turned to the others and told them to come by for some coffee after they had taken care of their stock, then he and Deputy Jewett went inside.

The heavyset man turned first to Wade and held out his hand. "Deputy Chris Rollins."

Wade and the others shook his hand, introduced themselves, and followed him up the street to the livery.

Billy French sat behind a large wooden desk with his feet on top, a coffee cup cradled in his hands when Wade and the others walked in. Deputy Jewett was sitting in one of three chairs holding a coffee cup in his hands, his feet on the same desk. Marshal French nodded at two empty chairs and looked at Jewett. "Get them some coffee, will ya, Todd?"

Deputy Jewett took his feet from the desk, set his cup down, stood, and got their coffee. Seth and Frank took their coffee and sat in two of the three chairs, while Wade took his and sat on a small bench next to the four empty cells. Deputy Chris Rollins walked into one of the cells, picked up an empty bucket, turned it upside down, and sat down a few feet from Wade while Jewett returned to his chair,

Wade sipped his coffee, thinking it tasted good.

Seth looked at Billy. "You make the coffee?"

French nodded.

"Figures," said Seth complaining it was too strong and bitter.

Billy French grinned, ignored the remark, drank his coffee, and asked Deputy Rollins if there was any trouble while he and Jewett were gone.

Rollins shook his head. "Nah, it was pretty quiet. Can't vouch for the Mexican side of town."

French looked at Frank and then Seth. "How far do you boys plan on trailing these three?"

Seth glanced at Wade. "Till it's over."

Wade nodded, pleased with Seth's answer.

French made a face. "I sure as hell hope that won't be very long." Then he smiled at Billy. "You coming with us?"

He looked down at his cup thoughtfully. "Don't look like I got any choice in the matter."

"We need to rest our horses," said Seth.

Marshal French stood. "Well, I ain't leaving until morning."

"Want me to come along?" asked Deputy Rollins.

Billy shook his head no. "I need you to stay here with Chris. This may take a few days."

It was plain Rollins didn't like the idea of being left behind, but he nodded his head, accepting the plan. "Want me to spend the night here?"

"Be a good idea. I'll come by the first thing." Then he drank the last of his coffee and put the cup on his desk. "You boys are welcome to spend the night. Be cheaper than any of the hotels in town." He chuckled. "You're used to it anyway."

Wade glanced at the cells, remembered Roscoe's Creek and Fallon, and thought he had spent a lot of time in jails lately.

"Where you off to?" asked Seth.

Billy stopped at the door and turned with a small smile. "Home. I ain't seen my missus since we rode into town, and I'm certain she's wondering what's keeping me."

"Missus?" asked Seth with a surprised look.

Billy French grinned. "Been married these past fifteen years."

"To the same woman?" asked Frank.

French smiled at Frank, opened the door, said he would be back in the morning, stepped out, and closed it behind him.

Seth looked at Deputy Jewett. "He really married?"

Jewett nodded his head. "Right, nice lady."

Wade looked at the closed door, thought of Sarah, and remembered the first time he took her. The smell of her perfumed hair still lingered in his memory, as did the softness of her skin and the tenderness of their lovemaking. He recalled being surprised at the strength in her small arms when she held him that afternoon on the blanket in the rocks beside the old shack where they would meet in secret. Then his thoughts turned to Hattie Dougherty and her grief over the death of Emmett two weeks before they were to be married. Wade remembered how she cried at the funeral and told him she was carrying Emmett's child. These men not only robbed him of a best friend and Hattie of a husband but his child a father. Filled with a hate that he could not hide, he stood and walked outside into the late afternoon sun that was about to dip below the mountains to the west. He watched it for several moments, then stepped off the boardwalk and walked up the dusty street toward the livery.

It was quiet inside when he walked through a small doorway near the back of the stable. The light inside was dim, and he could barely make out the mare in the stall several feet away, recalling the day Emmett pointed to her. He suddenly felt sad and angry. He missed his friend as he walked into the mare's stall and softly spoke so she would recognize his voice in the dim light. She turned her head, looked at him with her big black eyes, and neighed softly.

He gently rubbed the mare's neck and felt the need to return to South Carolina and his mother. He recalled the time he sat on the porch next to her rocking chair, filled with despair over something he no longer remembered, while she gently stroked the top of his head. His mother usually had the answers; if she didn't, she understood in a way no one else could. He wished he could talk to her and tell her that he felt something of himself slipping away from all the death, cruelty, and hate that had become part of his life. The mare gently nudged him, and he looked into her dark eyes with tears in his, lowered his head, and leaned against her neck.

"You alright, Mister?"

Embarrassed, he turned to a boy standing several feet away next to the side door. "I'm fine," he said as he quickly brushed the tears from his face with one hand and, in a voice that tried to sound happy, said, "Just checking on my horse."

The boy walked across the livery and looked at the mare. "She's a fine one and big. I bet she can run."

He looked at the freckled face of the young boy about nine or ten, thought of Emmett Spears, smiled, and patted the mare. "That she can."

The boy stepped closer and held out his hand. "Name's Jimmy Rogers."

He shook the boy's hand. "Wade Garrison."

"You one of the men following them that killed the Mitchel family?"

163

"How'd you know about that?"

"Heard some men talking." Then he looked around the barn to see if anyone was listening and stepped closer. "I saw them. The ones who did the killing."

Wade knelt and put his hands on the boy's shoulders. "When?"

"Day or so ago, I reckon."

"Where?"

Jimmy pointed at the far wall. "West of town. I think they're head'n south."

"You tell the marshal?"

The boy shook his head no. "They said the men who did the killing were over in Fallon, so's I never saw any reason to." He glanced around with a worried look. "Now I'm too scared to say, 'cause everyone will get mad at me."

Wade knew that might be true. "Well, we won't tell anyone. But you have to take me to the spot where you saw them. Is it far?"

The boy shook his head and pointed to the side door. "Just out that door through some trees by a small stream. I's hiding when they stopped to water their horses."

Wade was glad they did not see the boy, for they surely would have killed him. He stood and gently turned the boy by the shoulders, told him to show him this place, and within minutes, the two stood at the stream. Darkness was at hand as Wade slowly walked while looking down at the ground, searching for the familiar tracks. Finding them, he knelt and stared at them for several moments, then stood and followed them while the boy watched. He stopped and looked in the direction the men rode. "What's in that direction?"

"Not much," replied Jimmy.

"Any farms or ranches?"

Jimmy thought for a moment and shrugged. "Not sure, but there's a town called Pine Springs, but I ain't sure how far."

"You ever been there?"

Jimmy nodded. "Lots of times with my pa." Then he turned and pointed back toward Santa Fe. "Just outside of town, the road forks. Take the west fork, and it'll take you to Pine Springs."

"Pine Springs," repeated Wade thoughtfully while looking to the south. Then he turned, knelt, and gently put his hand on the boy's arms. "You don't need to tell anyone else about this, Jimmy. They may get mad, as you said." Then he stood. "We better get back."

164

"What're you gonna do, Mister?"

"Gonna get the others and head into Pine Springs. Come on, let's get back." They walked along the creek until they got to the edge of Santa Fe, where Wade told the boy to go home, and then he hurried back to the Marshal's Office.

Wade hurried up the two steps, ran across the boardwalk, opened the door to the jail, and stepped inside. Deputy Chris Rollins lifted his head from the desk, looking sleepy and bewildered, and asked if everything was alright.

Wade ignored the question as he looked into the empty cells and then at Rollins. "Where are the others?"

Rollins glanced at the cells and shrugged. "I don't know. They just up and left a while back."

"You ever been to Pine Springs?" asked Wade.

Thinking that was a curious question, Rollins nodded. "A time or two."

"How far is it?"

Curious why Wade was asking all the questions, Deputy Rollins said, "Fifteen miles, more or less. I'm not exactly sure. Why are you asking?"

Without answering, Wade turned and walked outside, standing at the edge of the boardwalk. He glanced up and down the street, wondering where Seth and Frank could be. Stepping off the boardwalk, he headed toward the nearest saloon. Not finding them, Wade went to the next saloon, getting the same results, and then the next. He stood on the busy boardwalk outside the last saloon, looked up and down the street, and wondered where Frank and Seth could have gotten. The music from the saloon behind him mixed with the words and laughter of people walking by. Anger and frustration held him as he stepped from the boardwalk into the street, filled with desperation thinking this was their first real break since Raton.

Hearing his name, he turned and saw Deputy Jewett dodge horses and a wagon walking across the street.

"Mr. Garrison," smiled Jewett. "Out enjoying our Santa Fe nightlife?"

Wade shook his head. "I'm looking for Seth and Frank."

Jewett thought a moment and then nodded down the street. "I saw them earlier. I think they headed toward the Mexican side of town." Then his expression turned curious. "Something wrong?"

"Maybe." Wade glanced in the direction of Jewett's nod, thanked him, and started walking.

Todd Jewett watched Wade as he hurried toward the Mexican part of Santa Fe, wondering what he meant by maybe. Left with that mystery, he turned and walked up the street.

Wade walked across the bridge spanning a small stream into the Mexican side of town. The piano music of Santa Fe behind him gave way to the Mexican guitar music from the cantina up ahead, where he hoped to find Seth and Frank. Wade stepped from the street onto the busy boardwalk and looked over the swinging doors. Pushing the doors open, he stepped inside the noisy, smoke-filled room and walked to an empty spot at the bar. Before ordering, he saw Frank sitting at a table with a young señorita smiling as she poured two drinks from a bottle.

Frank saw Wade standing at the bar and, thinking he looked lonely, motioned him over.

Wade made the short trip and stood next to Frank. "We need to talk."

Frank grinned and introduced him to the girl. "Sit and have a drink."

Wade looked at the girl as he pulled a chair from the table and sat down. Thinking she was pretty, he looked at Frank. "Where's Seth?"

Frank grinned, turned his head, and looked at the second-floor balcony. "Busy." Then he looked at Wade and laughed as he pulled the girl onto his lap. "And I'm about to get busy." Then he smiled and nodded at a couple of girls who sat at a nearby table smiling. "Why don't you and one of the little gals get busy?"

Wade looked at the two girls and thought one was very pretty and the other homely. He looked at Wells. "We need to get to the town of Pine Springs."

Frank looked at Wade with a puzzled look. "And why is that?"

A girl screamed, the small Mexican band at the back of the room stopped playing, and the place suddenly got quiet. The girl said something in Mexican that Wade did not understand, slapped one of the men at the table, then turned and walked toward the stairs. The man laughed and said something to the others that brought laughter to the table. With that, the band continued their song.

166

Wade scooted his chair closer to Frank, leaned toward him, and told him about the tracks and the town of Pine Springs.

Frank looked at him. "You sure about that?"

Wade quickly nodded. "We need to get to Pine Springs."

Frank thought on that for a moment while he sipped his drink. "It's late, and I ain't one for hightailing it out of town after these three without any sleep."

"Sleep or no, we need to get after them."

Frank took another drink, glanced at the girl, put his glass on the table, and leaned toward him. "Look, Son, I'm too damn old to light out in the middle of the night, and so's Seth. We aren't moving from here until tomorrow morning, and neither are you. Besides, our horses are dead tired and need food and rest."

Wade was anxious and disappointed. "We're close to them, Frank."

"I realize that," he said, sounding irritated. "But they could be gone from that town by now, or they could stay there with a couple of whores. Makes no difference right now because either way, they'll be there tomorrow, or they won't."

Wade sat back and looked at the girl on Frank's lap, whispering something in his ear. He looked around the cantina and finally at the second floor balcony, feeling disappointed.

Frank leaned forward and put one hand on his shoulder. "Look, Son. Seth and I have been chasing no goods for a long time, and one thing's for sure when you're tired, you make mistakes, and mistakes get you killed. If we rode through the night and found them in the morning after having no sleep, they'd kill us all."

Wade sighed and nodded, knowing Frank was right. "Reckon, you're right."

Frank pushed the bottle toward him. "Now, have a drink."

He looked at the bottle, stood, and said that he was going back to the Marshal's Office.

"That's sensible," said Frank. Then he reached for the girl, pulled her onto his lap, and looked up at Wade. "Don't go getting any ideas about going it alone. You'd get yourself killed and never see that Sarah of yours again."

Wade turned and walked toward the door.

Frank watched him until he disappeared through the swinging doors and hoped he would not do something stupid like he did when they were ambushed back on the trail. Wells turned and looked at the Mexican girl, gave her a hug, smiled, and poured another drink.

Outside, Wade sat on the steps amid the noisy crowd and considered what Frank said about being tired and getting killed. The night was warm, the sky black and full of stars, and he remembered sitting on the bunkhouse porch with Emmett looking up into the same black sky of stars, wondering what they were. Emmett was sure they were the windows of heaven where angels looked down, as told to him by his mother when he was a child. Wade knew better, but he let Emmett believe what his mother had told him.

Wade sat there for several minutes thinking of Sarah, wishing he could hold her in his arms and feel her warm body against his. Someone walking down the steps of the boardwalk bumped into him, interrupting his daydreams of Sarah. Glancing over his shoulder at the swinging doors of the cantina, he thought about Seth upstairs with a whore, and Frank smiling at the young señorita, knowing they would be upstairs before long. He stood, kicked at the dirt, walked up the street, across the bridge, and headed for the Marshal's office.

Jewett and Rollins were playing checkers and drinking coffee when Wade walked in. Todd Jewett looked up and asked if he had found Seth and Frank.

Wade told him about the whores over in Mexican Town and then about the tracks he had found, leaving out the part about the boy. Jewett glanced up from the checkerboard, looked interested, and asked if he was sure about the tracks.

Wade said he had been following the same tracks since Harper. "I'm sure."

Jewett picked up his cup and looked at Wade over the rim as he took a drink. Setting the cup down, he asked, "You ain't thinking about heading off to Pine Springs alone, are you?"

Wade shook his head. "Frank said to wait until the morning after we've all had a night's rest. So, I guess that's what I'll do."

Relieved, Jewett moved a checker.

Wade walked into a cell, lay back on the cot, and stared at the ceiling listening to Jewett and Rollins.

Rollins studied the board, thinking of what Wade had told them. "Think we should tell Marshal French?"

168

Jewett stared at the checkerboard while considering his next move. "I guess we should."

"You sure you want to disturb Billy this time of night?" asked Deputy Rollins. "He might be a little pissed."

Jewett's expression was thoughtful. "Rather have him pissed about telling him than pissed about not telling him."

Rollins looked at Jewett. "French may want to ride out tonight."

Wade sat up on his elbows, filled with hope, and decided to get up and wait for Billy's response.

"Well, that'd be the marshal's choice," replied Todd. "And it's a choice he needs to make." Then he stood and looked down at the board. "We'll finish this later." He walked toward the door while Rollins carefully picked up the checkerboard and placed it on top of a shelf, turned, and asked Wade if he wanted a cup of coffee.

Thirty minutes later, the door opened, and Todd Jewett stepped inside, closed the door, and walked toward Wade and Rollins. "Billy says we leave in the morning.

Wade got up, walked into his cell, lay down on the cot without taking off his boots, and covered up with his one blanket.

Early the next morning, Billy French walked into the Marshal's office and, seeing Deputy Rollins making coffee, said, "Better hurry with that, Chris. We'll be leaving soon."

Awoken by Billy's voice, Wade opened his eyes, sat up on one elbow, and watched French walk into Frank's cell. He put his boot against Frank's cot and shook it. Frank opened his eyes and slowly sat up on his cot, listening to Billy tell Rollins to get Jewett. "On your way back, stop by the livery and tell Buck we'll be by to get our horses in about an hour." He looked at Wade and then Frank as he walked out of their cell. "Coffee's ready."

Feeling a little hungover, Frank put his bare feet on the cold floor, closed his eyes for a few moments, then put on his socks and boots.

"Where's Seth?" asked Billy.

Wells slowly stood, scratched the top of his head, and yawned. "Probably still with that little whore over in Mexican Town."

Billy turned to the big window. "Well, you better go wake him."

Frank frowned at the idea. "I don't think Seth would take kindly to being disturbed so early."

Billy grinned. "I'm sure that's true. But you need to go find him, and you need to do it now."

Frank sat on the edge of his cot, looking tired. "Can I piss first, Marshal?"

French ignored Frank and looked at Wade, sitting in one of the chairs next to his desk, and asked about the tracks.

While Frank went outside to find the outhouse, Wade got up and poured a cup of coffee while telling the marshal about the boy showing him where he saw the three men. Marshal French asked the boy's name, but Wade said he never asked. French thought on that for a moment and started to say something when the door opened.

Returning from the outhouse, Frank stood in the doorway and looked at Wade. "I'm going after Seth. Wanna come along?"

Wade slowly shook his head, having no desire to see Seth in a foul mood. "Not particularly."

Frank looked disappointed. "Didn't think as much." Then he closed the door.

Wade turned to Billy and asked, "We going to Pine Springs?"

He nodded. "You say you found them tracks along a stream west of town?"

Wade nodded toward the livery. "Not far from the livery."

Marshal French looked worried. "A couple of small farms lay between here and Pine Springs."

Wade worried about the families as he took a drink of hot coffee.

Todd Jewett walked in, and before he could close the door, French said, "Go wake up Old Man Dempsey and ask him to get over here right away."

"It's a little early," replied Jewett as he looked at the clock in the corner by the door.

Marshal Billy French was in a hurry to get after these men and check on the farmers. He glanced at the clock and then looked at his deputy. "I don't give a shit. Wake up the old bastard and tell him to get his ass down here."

"Yes, sir," replied Jewett as he turned and hurried out the door.

Deputy Rollins walked in, having stopped at the livery. "Buck's up and said he'd be waiting."

French looked at Chris Rollins. "Jewett's going with us, Chris."

Rollins looked disappointed. "Sorta figured as much."

"I know you'd like to come along," said Billy. "But I need you here in Santa Fe. Someone has got to keep a lid on this town."

Chris nodded in disappointment. "Yes sir."

Billy stood to pour some coffee into his cup while asking Chris if he wanted a cup. Chris forced a grin. "Sure do." He sat down, watched as French poured the coffee, and told him that he figured Dempsey could lend him a hand while they were gone.

Chris made a gesture with open hands. "Howard Dempsey was a sheriff at one time, so I think the two of us can sit on things till you and Todd get back."

"Well," said Marshal French, "you'll be in charge, but try to rely on old Dempsey's experience."

Chris's eyes lit up. "Don't worry none about us, Billy. We'll do just fine."

"I'm counting on that, Chris." He took a drink of coffee. "I'll tell Dempsey you're in charge."

Wade had been sitting in a chair with his cup of coffee, watching and listening to French and Chris. Wade admired Marshal French for the way he did not take away Deputy Rollins' pride. Wade took a drink of coffee, looked at the door, and thought it seemed a long time had passed since Frank left to find Seth. He imagined the scene when the door opened, and the two walked in with Seth, looking unhappy.

Billy looked at Bowlen. "You look like hell, Seth."

"I feel like hell," he replied with a tired, hungover look. "Any coffee?"

Rollins stood, checked the pot, and said no, but he would make a pot while they waited on the others.

Seth looked tired as he sat down, closed his eyes, and waited for Rollins to make a fresh pot of coffee.

Bowlen had just finished his second cup of coffee when Deputy Jewett walked in, followed by a heavyset, older man.

Dempsey glanced at the others and then looked at French. "Got here as fast as I could, Billy."

The Marshal introduced Dempsey and gave Rollins instructions on what to do until he and Jewett returned. Then he made it clear that Deputy Rollins had the last say about things.

Dempsey nodded his understanding and smiled at Deputy Rollins.

French looked at the others. "Let's get some breakfast."

171

Just after seven A.M., the five men walked out of the café and returned to the Marshal's office. Inside, Billy took a Winchester rifle from the gun rack on the wall next to his desk and tossed it to Todd Jewett. Then he took a twelve-gauge from the same shelf, made sure it was loaded, then shoved a box of shells into his coat pocket.

Seth grinned as he looked at the twelve-gauge. "There's only three of them, Billy."

Frank chuckled, but Billy ignored the comment and headed for the door.

Wade grinned at Seth, then he and the others followed Billy out the door and up the street to the livery.

A big heavyset man walked out of the open doors and eyed each man as they walked into his livery. He was naturally curious about where they were going at such an early hour but never asked.

Horses saddled, the five men climbed up and rode out of the livery with two packhorses in tow. No one spoke as they rode down the main street of Santa Fe, across the bridge into Mexican Town, turning south toward Pine Springs.

Eighteen

It was midmorning when the five men stopped at the top of a small hill overlooking a farmhouse, barn, corral, and chicken coop a quarter mile from the stage road that led back to Santa Fe. Frank Wells took out his long glass, as did Marshal Billy French, and both men looked at the scene below.

"Looks quiet," said French.

"Uh-huh," replied Wells as he continued to look at the house.

Wade thought of the peaceful settings at the cabin and the Miller farm, imagining what awaited them inside this house.

Frank saw someone step outside. "It's a woman."

Marshal French watched as she walked to the end of the porch and raised her hand, shielding the sun from her eyes as she looked in their direction. "Looks like whoever it is has seen us."

French lowered the long glass and looked at Frank Wells. "Looks determined."

"Don't they all?" replied Frank with humor as he watched her.

"Let's get down there," said Billy. He stuffed his glass into his saddlebags, spurred his horse to a walk, and headed down the hill.

While the others followed, Frank stared at the figure on the porch a moment longer, put his glass away, and followed.

The woman stood on the edge of the porch with one hand over her eyes, watching the five men as they slowly rode down the hill. Curious who they were, she disappeared inside and reappeared moments later, holding a double-barrel shotgun across her faded brown dress.

Seeing the gun, Frank leaned in his saddle toward Wade. "Never did trust a female with a gun."

Wade half-smiled, finding humor in Frank while feeling relieved she was alive.

She was a woman of forty, big-boned and shapely. Her dark brown hair was cut short, needing little attention. Her eyes were brown, her lips full, and her complexion dark from the sun. As the five men rode closer, she raised the gun, pointed it at them, and said, "Best stop right there."

Marshal French pulled up, raised his right hand for the others to stop, settled in his saddle, and tried to look friendly. "Morning, ma'am." He took off his hat and pulled his tan duster to one side showing her his badge. "I'm United States, Marshal Billy French, from Santa Fe. This here's my Deputy Todd Jewett, and these others are friends of mine."

She looked at the badge, then at French and the others, as she lowered the shotgun and smiled. As she stepped off the porch, she said, "My man ain't around right now, and a woman alone with children can't be too careful these days."

"That's true enough," said French. "Mind if we get down?"

She smiled. "Please do. My name's Sally Arden. My man Joseph and our son Chad are out looking for our goats that somehow got out last night."

Wade looked at the others, and all were of the same mind that it might have been a ruse to get the men away.

Mrs. Arden pointed toward the house. "Have some fresh coffee inside if y'all have a mind for some, or maybe some fresh buttermilk." Then she looked back at the house. "That is if'n my youngest ain't drank it all while I was out here worrying about the five of you."

Seth took off his hat and smiled. "Sorry, Mrs. Arden. We didn't mean to scare you and the children."

"Seeing five men is scary anytime, Mr.---" She let the sentence die.

"Bowlen, ma'am," he replied. "Name's Seth Bowlen. I'm the sheriff of a little town in Colorado called Sisters."

"Colorado?" she said with a southern drawl with a surprised yet curious look.

"Yes ma'am." Seth pointed to Frank. "That there's Sheriff Frank Wells, from Roscoe's Creek, Colorado, and the young fella there is Wade Garrison from Harper, Colorado."

"You a sheriff, Mr. Garrison?" she asked.

Wade thought of Sheriff Cole asking the same question, smiled, and shook his head. "No, ma'am, a cowhand for the Circle T Ranch a few miles northeast of the town of Harper."

She glanced from one to the other. "Never heard of either."

"Mind if we water our stock?" asked French.

Wondering what the men from Colorado were doing with the Marshal from Santa Fe, she quickly eyed them and pointed to a trough by the corral. "Help yerself." Then she turned, walked across the front porch toward the house, and talked over her shoulder. "When y'all finish watering them horses, come inside, and you can explain why the law from Colorado is riding with the law from New Mexico onto our place."

Seth called after her. "That son of yours and your husband, are they riding or walking?"

"Walking," she said as she reached for the knob of the door. She stopped and turned. "Why are you asking?"

"Just curious, Mrs. Arden," replied Seth.

She gave Seth a long curious look before she went inside, leaving them to water their horses at the trough.

While the mare drank, Wade stepped closer to Billy as he glanced over his shoulder at the house. "Think them goats got out by accident?"

"Can't rightly say," replied Billy French in a low voice. "But I doubt it, and I don't like it none."

Wells looked back at the farmhouse and then around the place and spoke in a whisper. "It could be an old Indian trick to get the man away from the house so they could easily kill him."

Wade suddenly felt worrisome as he glanced back at the house and then looked at Seth. "Maybe we should go looking?"

"Good idea," replied Seth, then he looked at French. "Wade and I are gonna look around a bit."

Marshal French gave them a quick nod, turned, and looked back at the house. "The rest of us will go on inside and keep the missus busy." Then he looked at Wade and Seth. "Watch yourselves."

Seth and Wade climbed onto their horses and rode along the corral, looking for the turned hoof and flawed horseshoe tracks while following the boot prints in the dirt of the husband and son.

Marshal Billy French and the others tied their horses to the corral, walked to the house, stomped the dirt from their boots, took off their hats, and went inside.

Mrs. Arden was kneeling on the floor, pulling a clean dress over the head of a young girl of four or five. "Child won't stay clean for more than a minute." When she finished, she stood and patted the girl, looking prideful. "This here's Nancy."

The men smiled at the girl and said hello.

Nancy frowned as she moved behind her mother and stared at them from around Mrs. Arden's dress.

"She ain't used to strangers," apologized Mrs. Arden, then she told the girl to go to her room, saying, "I'll be along directly."

After the girl disappeared through a doorway, Mrs. Arden asked where the others were. French explained they had ridden out to find her husband and help with the goats.

She thought about that for a moment and suddenly became worried. "What's the law from Colorado doing with a U.S. Marshal from Santa Fe? Are my man and son in danger?"

Marshal French could see the worry in her eyes. "The truth is, Sheriff Bowlen, Frank Wells, and Mr. Garrison have been trailing some killers from Colorado, and their trail led here."

"Killers?" she asked with a frightened look.

"Yes ma'am," replied Frank. "They killed three families up in Colorado and a couple of families near Santa Fe. Maybe more, we're not sure."

"Land sakes," replied Mrs. Arden. Then she turned and looked out the window toward the hills where her husband and son had gone. "My man and oldest boy, Chad, are out looking for the goats, and neither has a gun."

"I'm sure they're fine," offered French trying to sound reassuring.

Mrs. Arden never looked at him as she walked to the kitchen door, opened it, and stood in the open doorway, staring past the barn. With fear in her voice, she said, "My two younger boys went fishing along the river beyond the barn."

Marshal French looked at Todd Jewett and gestured toward the door without saying anything.

Todd understood, nodded, and walked to the open doorway where she stood. "Excuse me, ma'am. I'll get my horse and fetch your boys home."

She looked up at him with a mixture of fear and gratitude. "Thank you. There's a river beyond the barn and a big oak tree. That's where you should find them."

"Yes ma'am," said Todd.

Mrs. Arden watched as he hurried across the yard to the horses, swung up into the saddle, rode at a gallop past her, and disappeared behind the barn.

Billy French was standing next to her. "I'm certain they're fine."

She turned with fear in her welling eyes, brushed away her tears, and half-smiled. "Land sake, look how I'm acting when nothing's happened yet."

Frank Wells wanted to get her mind off her family for a few moments. "You said you had some fresh coffee, Mrs. Arden?"

She wiped the tears from her eyes with her apron. "Heavens to Betsy, I don't know what's come over me, forgetting my guests like I had no manners."

Frank smiled at her. "I take it you folks are from the south?"

Smiling, she said, "My southern accent give me away?"

Wells grinned. "Yes ma'am. Mind me asking where you're from?"

"Anniston, Alabama."

"Well," said Frank. "I wouldn't know where that is, but it's Anniston, Alabama's loss."

Her face flushed as she smiled. "Why, thank you, what a nice thing to say." She started toward the stove. "I'll get y'all that coffee now."

French stood in the kitchen doorway, looking in the direction Seth and Wade had ridden, hoping they would find her husband and son alive. Hearing the sounds of cups and saucers behind him, he turned, thinking that she was a brave woman, and he hoped she was as strong as she was brave. Then he turned to the hills beyond the barn, hoping Todd would find her two boys.

Seth and Wade followed the boot prints of Mr. Arden, the boy, and those of the goats into a small gully, only to lose them in the dry creek bed of rocks and small boulders. They climbed down from their horses, tied them to a berry bush, and started searching on foot for the tracks among the shrubs on the bank of the dry creek bed. Wade found the tracks once again, and they followed them up the steep bank out of the gully.

Seth stopped, knelt to one knee, drew his pistol, glanced around as he stood in a low crouch, and started to walk slowly.

Wade drew his pistol and followed Seth quietly through the thick underbrush and cedar trees.

Seth stopped several steps later, knelt to one knee, and whispered, "I think we found them," he said, gesturing to a young boy and an older man with a bloody shirt.

Bowlen glanced around, then stepped toward the two. "It's alright, Mr. Arden; we're friends."

The man looked at Seth with fear on his face. "How'd you know who I am?"

Seth holstered his gun, moved next to Mr. Arden, and looked at the blood-soaked shirt. "Let's have a look at that wound. Your missus told us about the goats getting loose. She's a mite worried about the two of you." Seth looked at the wound. "Did you see who did this to you, Mr. Arden?"

"Got a glimpse," he said, pointing toward the low ridge fifty yards up the hill. "I heard the goat crying, and as I stepped out of them bushes, I looked up and saw three men up there on that ridge, felt the bullet go in, saw the puff of smoke, and heard the gunshot." He paused. "Had enough sense in me to push Chad away."

Seth glanced up at the ridge about a hundred yards away and went back to examining the injury. "Looks like the bullet went clean through." He turned and looked at Wade. "We need to get Mr. Arden back to the farmhouse."

"I'll be alright," he said. "Got shot worse than this at Vicksburg during the war." He looked up at the ridge. "Why would anyone be shooting at my boy and me?"

Seth considered that as he looked up at the ridge. "You're lucky they didn't stick around to finish the two of you off."

"Probably would have," said Mr. Arden as he pointed past Seth. "If it weren't for that, there Indian."

Seth and Wade turned, seeing Dark Cloud sitting cross-legged on a large rock next to a raspberry bush, his rifle lying across his lap.

Seth grinned. "We know that Indian."

"He with y'all?" asked Mr. Arden.

Bowlen shook his head no. "Surprised he's this far south."

Arden looked from Wade to Seth. "And who might you two fellers be?"

"My name is Seth Bowlen, and this is Wade Garrison." Then he asked, "Can you stand?"

"I think so," said Mr. Arden.

Seth helped Mr. Arden to his feet, and as they walked to the horses, he told him who the three men were. "We've been trailing them

178

for more than three weeks. The Marshal and his deputy from Santa Fe are at your place right now." Seth looked at Wade. "Where's that Indian?"

Wade looked around. "Don't know, but I'm sure he's around somewhere."

Reaching the horses, Seth helped Mr. Arden onto his horse and handed him the reins.

Arden looked at Seth. "So, you know that Indian?"

"No one ever knows an Indian," replied Seth as he wondered what the Indian was doing in New Mexico. "But I've talked to him some over the years."

Joseph Arden looked down at Seth. "Well, his yelling in Indian ran them others off. Probably thought there was a passel of them." Then he glanced around, looking for the Indian. "Wish he'd taken a shot at them with that rifle he's holding onto."

Seth thought on that a moment and remembered the Indian asked for some cartridges up in Colorado. "He may be out of bullets."

Wade held the reins to his mare while the boy climbed up. He was small-boned with blonde hair and blue eyes like his father. And like his father, he had a worried look on his face.

Seth smiled. "Your pa's gonna be alright, boy."

They led their horses, carrying Mr. Arden and Chad back along the riverbed to where they had entered it earlier. As they climbed up the far bank, they saw Dark Cloud sitting on his gray a few yards in the shade of the trees.

"Kinda spooky," said Wade above a whisper, so the Indian never heard.

The Indian nudged his gray out of the shade, stopped, and pointed south. "Other white men gone now."

"How do you know the other white men have left?" asked Wade.

Dark Cloud looked at Wade and thought that was a foolish question, so he never answered. He held his rifle in the crook of one arm, nudged his big gray, and rode past them and up the bank.

Seth looked at Wade. "Never doubt what an Indian tells you. It's often the truth."

Deputy Todd Jewett rode at a gallop in the direction of the river, fearful that he might find the boys dead. Minutes later, he reached the top of the hill overlooking the river that was not much more than a large creek winding its way south between a mixture of fir trees, cottonwoods, and boulders. He pulled up and looked down at the oak tree on the other side of the river where the two boys should be. Worried that something had happened to them, Todd gently spurred his horse down the hill keeping an eye out for the boys. Reaching the river's edge, he let his horse have a drink while he turned in his saddle, looking first in one direction and then the other. Contemplating whether to go upstream or down, Todd quickly decided to go for the latter. He guided his horse along the sandy bank while scouting both sides of the stream for some sign of the boys.

Worried that the men they were chasing might be nearby, he drew his pistol and cocked it as he nudged his horse up a small embankment and then downstream. Coming upon a slight bend in the river, he stopped in the stillness of the gurgling stream and looked upstream and downstream. Worried that he was going in the wrong direction, he noticed another wider bend of the river several yards downstream. Knowing that the best place to fish is where the water slows, Todd nudged his horse toward the next bend. A few minutes later, he saw the two boys sitting on the riverbank in the warm sun, their poles propped up against big rocks, fishing lines in the river's slow current.

The boys heard Todd's horse neigh, turned, and watched as the rider came closer.

When Todd was close enough to talk without yelling, he asked, "You two, the Arden boys?"

Fearful, they stood, and the taller one said, "I'm Benjamin Arden."

Todd Jewett grinned and looked at the younger. "And who might you be?"

"Whose ask'n?" said the boy with a defiant look.

Todd found humor in the young boy and smiled. "Name's Todd Jewett, Deputy Marshal from Santa Fe. Your ma sent me to fetch the two of you home."

"We ain't done nuth'n," said the smaller boy looking worried.

Jewett smiled. "No, you boys ain't done nothing, and you're in no trouble that I'm aware of."

"Then why'd ma send a Deputy Marshal after us?" asked Benjamin.

Jewett looked around, feeling uncomfortable out here in the open.

The boys saw the gun he was holding. "You gonna shoot us if we don't come?" asked Richard Arden, the younger boy.

Jewett looked at the boy, then at his gun, and grinned. He did not want to alarm the boys, so he put it away and lied. "I'm afraid a bear might be lurking around."

The boys looked around, and Benjamin said, "I don't think we have any bears around anymore."

"Glad to hear it," said Todd. "Now, how about you boys gather your stuff and climb up here so's I can take you to your ma."

They did as they were told and climbed up behind Todd.

After the boys were safe at home Marshal Billy French, Frank Wells, and Todd Jewett sat on the porch and wondered what kept Seth and Wade.

French stood and looked past the corral. "Someone's com'n."

"Looks like Seth and Wade walking," said Jewett. "That must be Mr. Arden and his son they have with them. Then, seeing the Indian, Todd said, "There's an Indian with them."

Marshal French turned his head and yelled to Mrs. Arden. "Ma'am, looks like Seth and Wade found your husband and son."

Frank stood. "That Indian looks like Dark Cloud. What the hell's he doing in New Mexico?"

"You know the Indian?" asked French.

Wells stared at the Indian. "I've had a few dealings with him now and again."

Mrs. Arden hurried out the kitchen door and ran across the small porch. Seeing the blood on her husband's shirt as Seth helped him down from the horse, she ran to him. "My God, Joseph, what happened? Are you okay?"

Joseph Arden told her he had been shot but assured her it was not serious.

"Shot?" She said with a worried look, then looked at her son to see if he was hurt.

"I'm okay Ma, really, I am."

She looked at her husband. "By who? And for heaven's sake, why would anyone shoot at y'all?"

He wanted to get inside and lie down. "We'll talk later, Sally, but right now, I'm tired and hurting some."

She looked worried. "Let's get you into the house so I can have a look at it." She turned to her son, hugged him, then thanked Seth and Wade for going after them. Then she turned, took her husband's arm, and started toward the house.

French looked at Todd. "Give Mrs. Arden a hand."

"No need," she said as they walked toward the house.

Frank Wells stepped from the porch, walked to Seth, and nodded at Dark Cloud, who sat his big gray next to a cottonwood tree beyond the goat pen. "Where'd you find him?"

Seth glanced at the Indian. "He was with Mr. Arden and the boy. Mr. Arden says they'd probably be dead if it weren't for him. Said he yelled something in Indian, and the three fellas took off. You might see what he has to say before he disappears again."

Frank Wells thought that was a good idea and started toward the Indian, waving a greeting.

Dark Cloud dismounted and walked toward Frank, returning the friendly gesture.

Seth watched them for a moment, turned, and followed the others inside, leaving Frank and the Indian to talk.

Mrs. Arden walked into the kitchen from the bedroom, filled a pot with water, set it on the stove, and stoked it with wood.

Seth knew she was worried, so he told her that he had patched up many gunshot wounds like her husband's, and if she'd like, he'd help her.

She smiled while fighting back the tears and nodded, saying she would appreciate it. Then showed Seth into the bedroom where Mr. Arden was resting and returned to the kitchen for the hot water.

When Mr. Arden's wound was bandaged, and he rested comfortably, Sally Arden and Seth walked out of the bedroom, surprised to see Billy at the stove fixing dinner. While Seth headed for the back door to wash up, she put on a clean apron and helped Billy with dinner.

Frank walked in the door and, finding the kitchen table set asked Mrs. Arden if she could spare a little food for the Indian.

She looked out the window at him, looking lonely in the shade under the oak tree. A smile lit up her face saying there was plenty to go around, and if not, she would cook up a few more eggs. "Ask him to come in," she told Frank.

That surprised Frank and the others. "You sure about that, ma'am?"

She turned with a frown and nodded toward the door. "Go on now. That man out there saved my husband and son, and I'll not have him eat outside like a heathen." Then she smiled. "Though one he may be. Please do as I ask and invite him inside."

Frank Wells raised his brow, gave a bewildered look, went outside, and asked Dark Cloud to come in and eat.

The Indian shook his head no and then pointed to the sky. "It's a good day, warm and quiet." Then he looked toward the house. "Too many tongues inside. Quieter out here."

Frank glanced back at the house. "Well, I can't disagree with that," he said and pictured everyone sitting around the table talking at once. He went inside and told Mrs. Arden that the Indian preferred to stay outside under the blue sky.

She looked disappointed. "I suppose he can eat where he wants."

"Now, don't take it personally, Mrs. Arden," said Frank. "I think he feels a little odd being the only Indian and all."

Mrs. Arden smiled. "You may be right, Mr. Wells. But please go on and fix him a plate of food and take it to him."

Frank did as she asked.

Dark Cloud was grateful and thanked him as he took the plate of food and began eating with his fingers instead of the fork Frank had brought.

Wells returned to the house, set the fork on the table, sat down, and told the story of how the Indian happened to be around when Mr. Arden was shot. "Dark Cloud," Frank began, "said that he and that band of Arapahoes we ran into a while back happened upon Gil and them two little girls. He said Gil was with fever, so he stayed with him for one day and a night while the rest of the Indians rode west into the mountains to meet up with his brother. Gil told him what had happened and about us heading over Raton, so after Gil and them girls headed north towards Roscoe's Creek, Dark Cloud headed south." Frank looked at Wade. "Said he found the black Indian dead a few miles north of the pass. Said there wasn't much left, not even enough to smell."

Wade never looked up from his plate.

Frank continued. "He says he was riding west of Raton when he came across the three men. He backed his gray into the trees so they couldn't see him, and after they rode by, he followed them."

Mrs. Arden brought a chair from the other room, sat down, and looked at him. "Go on, Mr. Wells."

He smiled at her. "This next part ain't so nice, Mrs. Arden, and I apologize for having to tell it. So, it might be best if you went in with your husband and children."

She looked up with a small smile. "I appreciate y'all's concerns, Mr. Wells, but I ain't no city girl or a child. Since we left Alabama, I've seen most things people do to one another, so you go on with your story. I aim to hear the whole of it." She glanced around the table. "If y'all don't mind. That way, when I say my prayers tonight, I can thank the Good Lord for sending the five of you and that Indian sitting outside to save us from those terrible men."

Frank smiled at her and thought she had a lot of sand. "Yessum." Then he looked down at his hands and continued his story. "The Indian followed them to that homestead where they killed the family that dumb sheriff blamed us for. He said he couldn't do anything but sit up in the hills and listen to the screaming. Says he feels bad about not doing anything to stop them, but he had no bullets for his gun." Wells paused and looked at the window, and while he couldn't see him, he imagined the Indian sitting under the tree eating. "I ain't sure, but I think he's afraid we may blame him for not helping that family."

"No one feels that way," said Marshal Billy French.

The others nodded in agreement.

Frank looked out the open doorway at the Indian sitting against the tree, staring toward the house, and wondered what was on his mind.

Billy French gulped his coffee, then stood and looked at Sally Arden. "Thanks for everything, Mrs. Arden, but the time has come for us to leave."

As she stood, the others pushed their chairs away from the table and stood. Each thanked her for the meal as they followed the marshal outside, where they checked the packhorses and tightened their saddle cinches.

Mrs. Arden stepped onto the porch and watched while saying a quick, silent prayer for the men and the Indian that came calling this day.

Frank Wells took the stirrup from the saddle horn after he tightened the cinch and looked at her standing on the porch. He patted the black and white horse on the rump, walked over to her, and smiled. "Thanks again for everything, Mrs. Arden. I hope Mr. Arden heals real soon."

"Thank you, Mr. Wells, and I hope y'all catch these men before they bring harm to anyone else."

He nodded. "Yessum, so do I."

She looked at the Indian sitting against the tree and asked, "The Indian going with you?"

Frank turned. "He sorta goes where he wants, but he's welcome to come along and knows it."

"Well," she said as she extended a hand, which he took gently. "All y'all' are always welcome here."

"Why, thank you, ma'am," Frank said, smiling. "And again, thanks for your hospitality." He turned and walked to his horse while the others waited. He started to climb up but turned his head and looked at the Indian. "You coming?"

Dark Cloud stood and drank the last of the water. Holding the glass up for Mrs. Arden to see, he gently placed it next to his empty plate by the tree and climbed onto the back of the big gray. The five men tipped their hats to Mrs. Arden and turned their horses south toward Pine Springs. As Dark Cloud rode his gray past, Mrs. Arden, at a walk, they briefly looked at one another, then he nudged the horse and followed the others a short distance behind them.

Frank Wells slowed his horse and as the Indian caught up, handed him a half-box of cartridges. Dark Cloud looked at the box and then at Wells and smiled.

Nineteen

The sun was bright orange, setting low in the sky just above the mountains as the men rode toward Pine Springs.

Wade enjoyed the end of the day, thinking how soft everything looked painted orange, and recalled evenings with Sarah after Sunday dinner. He turned in his saddle, looked back along the trail, and then at the hills in the distance. "Where's that Indian of yours, Frank?"

Wells smiled. "I'm sure he's around someplace."

Deputy Jewett turned in his saddle and glanced around, looking a little apprehensive. "It's a mite spooky having an Indian lurking about."

Wells chuckled. "Might be, I s'pose, but he is a fine Arapahoe."

Jewett looked at Wells. "How long have you known that Indian?"

Frank thought about that for a moment. "Ten, twelve years, maybe longer." Frank glanced around, wondering where the Indian was. "Some years back, me and Gil Robinson helped him bury his wife and child. Both died from smallpox, the white man's disease." Frank frowned with a sad look. "Damned near wiped out half the village in just a few days. Soon after, he headed into the mountains, and we never laid eyes on him for several years. Then either Gill or I would run into him from time to time. We'd sit and talk, maybe do some trading, and then he'd up and disappear for weeks, even months at a time."

"Maybe he's already in Pine Springs," offered Wade with a chuckle.

"I doubt that," said Billy. "Indians stay clear of the white man's towns."

Seth frowned. "Can't say I blame them all that much."

They rounded a bend seeing Pine Springs in the distance.

The sun was about to disappear behind the mountains, with just a slender tip fighting to stay a little longer. The five men made their way up the wagon-rutted dirt street in silence, passing in and out of the long evening shadows. They looked over every horse tied to the hitching rails for the sorrel, black and spotted gray.

Seth Bowlen looked around. "Busy little place."

Marshal Billy French glanced at each of the riders passing by. "We'll keep riding up the street and look for the horses you boys been following before we stop and visit Sheriff Russell Boedecker."

"Why not check the town out ourselves?" asked Wade.

French looked at him. "If it were my town that some lawmen rode into, I'd expect them to stop by, say hello and state their business. And that's just what I aim to do."

Seth looked at Billy. "What sort of man is this Boedecker?"

"Russell's been around a while," said French. "Getting on in years, you might say."

Seth grinned. "You mean like Frank there?"

Frank Wells found little humor in that, but Wade and Todd sure did.

Billy French grinned as he looked at Wells. "A might older, I'd say."

As they rode along the crowded street, music poured from the open doorways of the three saloons mixing with the sounds of horses, wagons, and pedestrians busy with early evening shoppers.

They pulled up in front of a building with a sign reading "Sheriff," climbed down, tied their horses to the hitching rail, and stepped inside. An older man was sitting in a wooden chair with his feet on an old maple desk that looked older than the man. His head was laid back, with his face pointing toward the ceiling. His mouth was open, and he was snoring.

French shut the door somewhat hard.

The old man jumped up from his chair, nearly falling over. Looking half asleep and a little embarrassed, he smiled as he looked at a grinning Billy French. "You scared the living shit out of me."

Marshal French grinned. "Sorry, Russell."

Russell Boedecker had been sheriff of Pine Springs most of his life. Grinning as he looked at Billy with tired red eyes, he stood to shake his hand. His once thick black hair was now white as the winter snow, the same as the handlebar mustache and bushy eyebrows. His tanned face was wrinkled and leathery, his teeth stained from coffee and tobacco juice. His

187

slightly bent frame that was once straight showed the years of hard times. The once lean muscular body now carried the belly of an older man with stooped shoulders. He glanced past French at the others. "You here on business?"

"Fraid so, Russell," replied French.

Boedecker looked at the others. "Figured you were. That a posse behind you?"

French turned and looked at the others, then at Sheriff Boedecker. "It is."

The sheriff studied the others carefully. "Mind telling me who it is you're after?"

"Some bad hombres. Mind if we sit a spell while I explain?"

Sheriff Boedecker gestured to the two chairs in front of his desk. "Two of you can," he said with a grin. "The others can either lean against the wall or sit on the floor." Enjoying his own humor, he sat down in his creaky chair.

French looked around, sat on the edge of the old maple desk, and waited while Todd, Seth, and Frank Wells sat down. Wade looked around, stood by the stove, and leaned against the wall.

Boedecker looked at Wade and pointed to a cell. "There's a stool in that first cell." Then he smiled at Billy. "Not used to so much company at the same time."

Wade decided to stand.

After everyone seemed comfortable, Boedecker looked at Marshal French. "Alright, Billy. Who you boys hunting?"

Billy got up from the edge of the desk, walked to the pot-bellied stove in the corner, and lifted the coffee pot lid. With a disappointed look, he returned to the edge of the desk and told Boedecker who they were after and why. Then Billy asked Wade to describe them for the sheriff. After Wade gave the sheriff their description, Billy asked if he had seen any strangers in town who might fit those descriptions.

Boedecker thought for a few moments, then shook his head no French. "Can't say I have Billy." Then he looked at the others and shrugged while clearing his throat. "There's always a few strangers in town, and unless they cause trouble, I let them be." He looked at French. "Truth is, I ain't been feeling all that good of late, so I haven't been out of my office for a couple of days."

Billy smiled as he looked into the old man's tired eyes, knowing he was getting too old to be a sheriff. Knowing that would be him in a few short years, he said, "Well, I hope you feel better soon. Mind if we have a quick look around?"

Sheriff Boedecker's eyes narrowed. "Not as long as I go along. This here is still my town Billy, even if you are a United States Marshal."

"Wouldn't have it any other way, Russell. Like you said, it's your town."

"Just so we both know that." Boedecker stood, took a gun and holster from a peg behind his desk, buckled it on, and grinned at Billy. "Let's have that little look around." He walked past everyone to the door, opened it, and stepped out onto the boardwalk. After the others stepped outside, the sheriff shut the door, walked to the edge of the boardwalk, and thoughtfully glanced up and down the street.

"What are you thinking?" asked Billy as the six looked up and down the street.

The sheriff cleared his throat and looked in one direction and then the other. "Saloons or whorehouse?" he asked of no one in particular.

"Let's give the saloons a try first," said Seth, then he grinned. "No sense in preventing the good citizens of Pine Springs from enjoying a poke unless we have to."

The others chuckled and followed Sheriff Boedecker into the rutted dirt street toward the first of three saloons. Stepping onto the boardwalk, they stood in front of the big window and looked inside.

"See anyone who looks familiar?" asked Boedecker.

Wade stared inside, letting his eyes roam the room full of customers having a good time.

Boedecker looked at Wade. "Alright, let's check the next one."

They walked along the crowded boardwalk to the second saloon, stopping at one of two large windows. Wade looked inside, glancing from table to table, and after several minutes said, "No."

Boedecker gave French a look, and then he looked at Wade. "You sure you know what these fellas look like?"

"I'm positive," said Wade.

"Well," said Sheriff Boedecker, "Let's check the last one."

As they walked away from the window, Wade glanced inside and stopped. "Hold on."

The others stopped and crowded around the window.

"Well?" asked French.

Wade was staring at a man with red hair walking down the stairs with his arm around a heavy set whore.

189

"Well?" repeated French sounding impatient.

"That may be the redhead," replied Wade as he stared through the glass of the window. "I can't be sure."

Sheriff Russell Boedecker looked at Wade. "What the hell you mean you can't be sure?"

Wade ignored the sheriff and watched as the redheaded man walked away from the girl and sat down at a table with two other men who had their backs to the window. "I never got that good a look at any of them up close, damn it."

"Better make a decision Wade," said Seth. "We ain't got all night."

Wade shook his head. "No," he said. "Both men at the table have brown hair. The other two we're after have curly blonde hair and straight black hair."

Boedecker cleared his throat and looked at the table. "I can't tell if I know the others or not with their backs to us."

"Well," replied French sounding disappointed. "Let's check out the last saloon before we go to the whorehouse."

They started to walk away when Wade grabbed French by the arm. "There," he said, looking through the window once again. "The man coming down the stairs with blonde curly hair."

The others stopped and returned to the window.

"One blonde and one redhead," said Seth. Then he looked up and down the street with a worried look. "If it's them, where's the other?"

Frank Wells quickly glanced around town. "That's a good question. Bastard could be anywhere's."

"He could still be upstairs," offered Jewett.

Wade glanced at the hitching rail. "Where are their horses?"

French looked at the horses tied to the hitching rail and wondered the same thing. "Could be the third man's upstairs." Then he looked at Boedecker and the others. "I don't want us running in there scaring them into shooting some drunk or whore."

"This is still my town Billy."

"I realize that, Russell."

"Just so's we're clear on that." Boedecker looked through the window at the men sitting at the table. "However, since you're a United States Marshal, I'm guessing you have a plan."

French glanced at the others. "We go in one or two at a time and spread out." He looked at Frank and then Seth. "When you two get inside, head for the stairs across the room, go up to the second floor by the banister, and try not to look too conspicuous." He paused. "Think you can do that?"

Seth resented the question and said, "What the hell do you think."

French grinned, then told Wade to walk around the room, staying close to the outside wall until he was near the piano, giving him a clear view of the men at the table. He looked at his deputy Todd Jewett. "You and the sheriff go to the bar, order a drink, and I'll follow in a minute or two." He looked at each one. "We wait for the third man to show up."

With everyone understanding what they were supposed to do, Wade pushed the swinging doors open and walked in first while the others waited until he was in position. Then Seth and Frank stepped inside and casually made their way up the stairs to the second floor and stopped at the railing, acting as if they were talking about something.

Todd and the sheriff went in, walked to the bar, and ordered two beers. Being the last one in, Billy made his way past several crowded tables to the bar, seeing if everyone was where they should be. Standing next to the sheriff at the bar, Billy ordered a beer and glanced at the table where the two men were sitting. French took a sip of beer and quietly asked Boedecker if he knew the other two men at the table.

Boedecker sipped his beer. "Never seen either before."

Seth and Frank stood beside the railing with a clear view of the main floor, keeping an eye on the table below. Frank started to say something when a door opened behind them. As they turned, an older man walked out of the room wearing a smile. Seeing Seth and Frank, the man's smile disappeared, replaced by guilt as he hurried down the stairs and out the swinging doors. Seth grinned at Frank and wondered why men always look so guilty.

The minutes passed, and it was clear to French that Boedecker was getting impatient. Billy hoped the old man didn't do anything foolish, glanced at Jewett standing on the other side of Boedecker, and nodded at the sheriff.

Being a smart young man, Jewett looked at Boedecker and knew that French was concerned about the old man.

Without a word to either French or Jewett, Boedecker suddenly stepped away from the bar and walked to the table where the two men were sitting. French straightened up, looking worried, and stepped away from the bar. Watching Boedecker, Billy walked to the stairs leading to the second floor with his hand resting on the butt of his pistol.

191

The place was noisy, and the man at the piano next to Wade pounded the keys as if he wanted to break them. Wade wished he would play a softer song as he watched Boedecker step away from the bar.

Wondering what the sheriff was doing, Todd stepped toward the door while Billy headed for the stairs.

Wade felt something was not right and wondered what the sheriff was doing. His heart pounded as he recalled Billy's words to wait for the third man.

Seth and Frank watched the sheriff from the second floor's railing as he walked up to the table. "What the hell's he doing?" asked Seth.

"I don't know," replied Frank. Then he and Seth watched Billy wondering if the third man had walked in or if Billy's plan was going south.

The Marshal stopped next to the post and railing of the staircase and looked up, and his expression told them it was going south. Billy turned to Boedecker, standing at the table where the man with red hair and the man with blonde hair was sitting, and wondered what the hell he was doing. The smokey room was filled with loud laughter, and piano music. French and the others watched Boedecker as he leaned over and said something that made the man with red hair nervous and fidgety. The man with blonde hair, also appearing nervous, glanced around the room as if looking for someone. When his eyes found Marshal French standing by the stairs watching them, he knew he was the law. He reached across the table, touched the man's arm with red hair, and nodded toward Billy.

The redhead looked at Billy, saw the corner of his badge sticking out from his duster, then noticed Seth and Frank upstairs watching them. Suddenly, he stood drawing his pistol and shot the sheriff in the belly. Boedecker grabbed his stomach and turned, looking at Marshal French with a surprised frightened look on his face as he fell.

In the next instant, the man with blonde hair stood and turned to leave when he saw Jewett going for his gun, shooting Jewett in the shoulder. The man with blonde hair fired at French as he dove for the floor next to the stairs. Everything happened so fast that Wade and the others were unprepared for what followed. Men yelled, and women screamed as both ran in all directions, diving under tables or cramming their way through the swinging doors. The other two men at the table, not knowing what was happening, stood and drew their guns. Seth fired at one, not knowing who they were, hitting him in the chest and knocking him backward onto a table. The other man looked up and got off a shot, grazing the post next to Frank, splattering his face with splinters. Wells grabbed the side of his face fearing his eye was injured, as he dove to the floor.

Seth got off another quick shot just as the man moved, and his bullet hit an innocent man behind the one he meant to shoot. He cursed his poor aim, knelt, and looked at Wells to see if he was okay. Seth looked through the railing's wooden slats at the man he had intended to shoot, backing toward the swinging doors. Seth aimed at the man again, but Billy fired and hit him in the chest. As he fell backward onto a table, mugs of beer, glasses of whiskey, cards, and money spilled all over the floor.

Only seconds had passed when Wade drew his gun and tried to get past the crowd that was now a riot of screaming women, yelling men, gunshots, and tables overturned by those trying to get out of the way. Seeing Todd was shot, he tried making his way through the crowd to him but kept bumping into someone. Hearing glass breaking, Wade turned to see a man jump through the big broken window and disappear into the dark street. Wade looked at Deputy Jewett just as the blonde shot Todd, knocking him back against an overturned table. As the blonde and the redhead ran for the swinging doors, Wade aimed at the redhead and fired just as someone bumped into him, causing his shot to go wild. He cursed his miss, shoved the man out of the way, turned, and ran for the broken window. Jumping through it onto the boardwalk, he saw the two men disappear into an alley across the street.

People were pouring into the street as Wade gave chase, and as he approached the ally, the three men swung up onto their horses. He stopped, took aim, and fired but missed. One of them returned fired, missing Wade but hit a woman behind him who screamed as she fell. Wade turned to her, then back to the three men, and got off a hurried second shot just as they disappeared around a building. Wade stared down the empty dark alley for a moment, turned, and ran to the lady sitting in the street holding her arm. He knelt next to her, looked at her arm, and, seeing it was only a flesh wound, told her that she would be alright. As he helped her to her feet, a man came running up the street yelling, "Janice!"

"I'm alright," she said. "This nice young man was helping me."

"She'll be alright," Wade told him, and as the two walked away, he heard the man scolding her for going outside. A disappointed Wade turned and made his way through the crowd gathered in the street and on the boardwalk. He pushed through the crowd, stepped inside, and looked around the messy room of overturned tables, chairs, and bodies. Seeing

Marshal French kneeling next to Deputy Todd Jewett, bleeding from his right shoulder and left side, he walked toward them.

Seth was at the bar taking a drink of whiskey while standing next to Frank, holding a towel the bartender had given him against his face.

Wade knelt next to Billy to have a look at Todd. "Somebody send for a doctor."

Billy nodded. "Doc's with Russell." Then he looked at Wade. "Hit anyone?"

Wade looked disappointed. "I followed them into an alley across the street, got off a couple of shots as they rode away, but I don't know if I hit anyone."

The marshal sighed. "Too bad." Then he looked across the room at Sheriff Boedecker, lying on the floor while the doc worked on him. "Check on Boedecker."

Wade stood and walked around the overturned tables and chairs past the bodies of the two men who had been sitting at the table with the killers. As he stood over the doctor working on the sheriff, Wade thought of Seth's story about Sheriff Jasper Conners and his yelling in pain from being gutshot. He could see the fear in the old man's teary eyes as he begged the doc not to let him die.

An older woman entered the saloon looking frightened, hurried across the room, knelt beside Doc, and looked at her husband through red, welling eyes. She gently touched his cheek with one hand, held his hand with the other, and looked into Doc's eyes with fear.

"We need to get him to my office." Then he pushed his glasses up his nose with one finger and looked at the bartender. "Jake, you got anything we could use to carry Russel and that one over there (referring to Todd) to my office?"

"Sure, do, Doc," replied Jake. Then he disappeared through a doorway behind the bar and returned with two sturdy planks giving one to Doc and one to Billy. After the sheriff and Todd were placed on the planks, Doc Brewster looked around, amazed that half the town was not dead or wounded. He turned to leave when five town councilmen walked in, looking like they had just got out of bed. "What the hell went on?" asked the tallest of the five.

Doc Brewster was in no mood. "Get the hell out of my way, Paul. I've wounded to take care of." He walked to the swinging doors, pushed them open, and waited while they carried the sheriff and Jewett out. "If you want to find out what happened here, follow me to my office, and you can ask the United States Marshal from Santa Fe."

Wondering who this Marshal fellow was, they followed Doc Brewster and the wounded men up the street to his office. After they carried the sheriff and Todd inside, the doc quickly shut the door, hoping that would keep them out. But to his disappointment, they came inside. "Just stay out of my way," he told them.

The last man inside closed the door, and then all five stood in awe at what they saw. The sheriff was lying on a table, his wife crying as she held his hand while Doc Brewster worked on him. They saw Todd Jewett lying on a table in another room and Wade and Seth looking worried as they stood next to Frank, holding a towel against the side of his face. "We're the town council," said one. "Which of you is the Marshal?" asked another.

Billy French was in no mood for a town council meeting as he walked out of the room where Todd was lying. "I'm Marshal French."

"May we have a minute, Marshal?" asked the tallest of the five as he stepped forward. "I'm Paul Sharpton, Marshal, and this here's—"

Billy interrupted the man, "What's on your mind, Mr. Sharpton?"

"Well," began Paul, "we'd like to know what the hell happened in our town."

French had no patience for this as he quickly glanced at each man. "Your sheriff is gut shot, and my deputy's got two bullets in him." Then he pointed to Frank. "That man there has a face full of splinters from a bullet nicking a post, and those two men are hurt because they were in the wrong place at the wrong time. We also got three dead back at the saloon. That's what happened." He looked at Paul. "Now, if you've nothing else, I'm gonna check on my deputy."

The council members looked around and then at one another, trying to decide what to do. Then Paul said, "Sorry, Marshal, but we ain't used to this much trouble. Pine Springs is a quiet, peaceful little place."

"Well," said Billy with a wry smile. "Guess we changed all that. Now, if you'll excuse me, I'm going to check on my deputy."

Before any of the five men could respond, Sheriff Boedecker called out. "Marshal."

French walked over to the table and looked at Mrs. Boedecker's dress covered in her husband's blood, looked into her worried eyes, and then at Boedecker lying on the table. Billy took the sheriff's hand and held it tight. "You're gonna be alright, Russell."

Russell Boedecker smiled. "Sorry, Billy."

"For what?"

The sheriff grimaced and stiffened in pain, and after his wife wiped the blood from his mouth, he looked up at Marshal French. "Thought I could handle a couple of young pups. Never figured they'd just up and shoot me in a room full of people."

"No one could have figured that one out, Russell. These boys are crazy." Billy held Russell's hand tightly in his. "Any idea who the other two men were?"

Mrs. Boedecker wiped the blood from his mouth again as he stiffened in pain, then relaxed and shook his head. "No idea Billy, probably just a couple of saddle bums caught up in a fight with two men they thought they'd impress."

The doc gently pushed French to one side. "You need to let me do my work, Marshal." Doc knew Billy was worried about Todd and looked at him. "As soon as my wife gets here, she'll see to your deputy. She's a nurse and knows as much about gunshots as most doctors, but right now, I have to tend to Russell here." Then he glanced at Frank. "My wife or I will tend to your face as soon as we can. Sorry for the delay, but these two—"

"That's alright, Doc," interrupted Wells. "I can wait. You take care of the sheriff and Deputy Todd."

The door opened, and a thinly built middle-aged woman with black hair and a worried look hurried across the room. Asking the doctor what he wanted her to do, he quickly introduced his wife and told her to check on the young man in the other room. French followed her as the men of the town council decided to leave.

Twenty

Wade opened his sleepy eyes and looked into the kindly face of Mrs. Brewster, the Doc's wife, asking if he would like a cup of coffee. He said he surely would then lowered the chair's front legs to the floor.

"It's almost seven," she said, figuring he was wondering about the time.

He looked at the cup of coffee she was holding and thanked her as he took it. He felt the warm steam against his face, took a sip, and watched as she went about the business of coffee for the others.

Seth had been asleep on the floor, sat up with his back against the wall, took the cup, and thanked her. As he stared across the room out the window at the morning sun, he took a drink and thought about last night.

Frank sat in a chair next to Seth, trying to sip the hot coffee from his cup while fighting the bandages on the side of his face.

Wells appeared ornery as ever, which brought a smile of relief to Wade. Then he heard Marshal Billy French's voice thanking Mrs. Brewster for the coffee from the other room where Todd Jewett lay.

After checking on Jewett, she walked out of the room carrying the pot of coffee, looking tired.

Billy followed to the doorway, leaned against the doorjamb, took a drink of coffee, and watched her disappear through another door.

"How's Jewett?" asked Wade.

Seth and Frank turned with interest.

French took a drink of coffee and nodded, looking worried. "Doing alright, according to the Doc and Mrs. Brewster. He won't be able to travel for a while."

"You taking him back to Santa Fe?" asked Wade.

197

French took a drink of coffee. "I'll leave him here while I head back to Santa Fe for a wagon."

Seth looked worried. "I sure hope Todd will be alright."

French watched Frank fuss with his bandage while he tried to sip his coffee and grinned. "How are you doing?"

"Sore. Came damn close to ending up with an eye like Seth." Then he chuckled. "One old fart with a bad eye's enough."

The others chuckled, and Frank looked at the table where Sheriff Boedecker had laid wounded and screaming in pain the night before. "Too bad about Boedecker."

Billy French took a drink of coffee while looking at the empty table and nodded. "Russell got a little ahead of himself last night. That's always dangerous."

Seth took a deep breath and blew out a sigh. "What the hell was he thinking?"

French shook his head slowly. "Don't know exactly, but maybe it was as simple as him not wanting any of us arresting someone in his town. He had to do the deed."

Frank looked sad. "It was an old man's mistake, alright."

Wade looked into his empty cup and then at the others. "Now what?"

"We go after the sons-of-bitches" said Seth with an angry look. "Nothing's changed." He looked at Frank. "You up for it?"

Wells tilted his head to see out of the eye that wasn't bandaged. "Hell, yes."

Marshal French took a deep breath, blew it out, and looked at them. "Wish I could come with you boys, but with Todd down, I can't."

Seth looked at him. "We understand, Billy."

"Sure do," said Wells.

Wade just nodded and hoped Todd would recover from his wounds. He had come to like him a lot.

The door that Mrs. Brewster had disappeared through opened, and Doctor Sam Brewster walked in carrying a cup of coffee. His wrinkled white shirt was bloody. Suspenders hung down his pants legs, he had the look of a man who had not slept. Sam Brewster walked to a desk a few feet from where Wade sat down and took a sip of coffee. He looked at each of the four men with a sad face. "Death rode in with you boys yesterday."

"Don't mean any disrespect, Doc," replied Seth. "But death was already here in that saloon. You just didn't know it."

Brewster sat back in his chair. "That's true enough. I can't blame Russell's death on you boys."

Billy looked at Brewster. "What'll become of Mrs. Boedecker?"

Sam Brewster stared into his cup with a thoughtful look. "That'd be up to the town council. The place she and Russell have been living in these past twenty-odd years belongs to the town. Guess the new sheriff will move in as soon as she's out."

Frank Wells leaned forward in his chair, looked at the others, and then at Brewster. "They gonna just kick her out?"

Sam Brewster stared into his cup, looking sad. "More'n likely."

Wade felt sorry for her. "She got family here 'bouts?"

Sam looked up and shook his head no. "They had two children. A son who died in the war and a daughter who died giving birth to a stillborn little girl."

"What about their daughter's husband?" Wade asked. "Can't he help her out?"

The doctor looked sad as he shrugged. "Two weeks after his wife and child died, he got drunk, wandered off during a bad snowstorm, and froze to death."

They sat in silence, contemplating Mrs. Brewster's future in Pine Springs and her hard luck. After several minutes, Billy French walked to the window, looked down the empty street, and thought of his wife. "Seems to me the town should let her stay in that house. Sort of payment for all the years she washed Russell's shirts after drunks vomited on them and the hours she spent alone while he made sure the town was safe and peaceful."

Doc Brewster nodded in agreement. "Ain't getting no argument from me on that accord, Marshal, but that's a decision that's up to the city council members you met last night."

The clock on the far wall chimed nine. Doc Brewster turned, compared his pocket watch to the clock on the wall, and returned the watch to his pocket. "Guess I better check on that young fella in the other room." He stood with his cup and walked toward the room where Todd Jewett was resting.

Wade asked Seth and Frank when they wanted to leave. They looked at one another, and Seth said they needed to head back to Santa Fe to get their packhorses. Wade turned to Marshal French and asked when he was leaving.

"As soon as I talk with Doc Brewster about Todd."

Wade turned to Seth and Frank, suggesting he return to Santa Fe with the Marshal to get their supplies and packhorses. He would return to Pine Springs with Billy.

Seth looked at Frank and then Wade. "Might be a good idea. Frank can let his face heal a bit longer."

French nodded toward the door. "Let's step outside." Once outside, he glanced up and down the street as he reached into his coat pocket, taking out three U.S. Deputy Marshal badges. "I brought these along just in case. I'm deputizing the three of you, but I'm not wasting my time with a big swearing-in ceremony. That'd be like sending a whore to screwing school."

That brought a chuckle from the others.

Billy looked at Wade and smiled wryly. "I figure any man riding with these two is worth his salt." Then he handed badges to each of them. "I don't know how far you plan on chasing these three, but this makes you the law anywhere north of the Rio Grande."

Wade looked at the badge he held and felt proud. "Suppose we have to go further south?"

Seth answered before Billy could. "We won't be the law south of the Rio, but these may help us get help from the locals in bringing the three back across the border." Then he looked at French. "If not, we'll kill them and leave them down there."

French half-smiled. "If it comes to that, be damn careful." Then he lowered his voice, glanced around, and looked at Bowlen. "I want these bastards dead, Seth. I ain't particularly interested in seeing them in my jail getting fed while awaiting trial." Then he looked at Wade. "Let's get our horses and head up to Santa Fe."

Wade and Billy returned from Santa Fe with the wagon, packhorses, and supplies on the second day. When they walked into the office of Doc Brewster, Doc, and Frank Wells were arguing about the necessity of keeping the bandages on his face. As Wade closed the door, they stopped arguing, looked at him for a moment, and then continued the argument. Wade glanced at Seth, who shrugged, rolled his eyes, and shook his head as the argument between Doc and Frank continued. Finally, Frank agreed to leave the bandages and salve on for another day.

Doc Brewster sighed. "Thank you, you stubborn bastard."

Wells grinned and said he knew he was stubborn, but he would have been dead a long time ago if he weren't.

Doc Brewster looked at the others, sat at his desk, opened the bottom drawer, and pulled a small bottle half full of whiskey. "I need a drink."

Wells stared at the bottle as Brewster poured a small amount into his empty cup while Billy asked how Todd was doing.

"He's doing as good as can be expected," said Doc. "Be best if you waited a day or two before taking him back to Santa Fe."

While Billy considered that, Frank looked at Wade and asked the obvious. "Got our stuff?"

Wade nodded at the door. "Outside."

"It's a warm day," offered Seth. "You need to rest that mare of yours and them packhorses. We'll leave this afternoon." Then he stood. "Let's take the horses to the livery and let them rest with some oats and freshwater." He looked at Billy. "You coming?"

Billy shook his head no. "Think I'll stay with Todd until he wakes up and see how he's feeling."

Seth, Frank, and Wade were sitting at a table in a small café next to the window when Billy walked in, took off his hat, and hung it on a peg to the door. Frank pushed a chair out with his boot for Billy, who glanced around at the other tables to see what everyone was eating as he sat down.

Wade leaned on the table with both forearms and looked at French. "How's Todd doing?"

Marshal French looked worried. "Not so good. I guess I'll do as the Doc suggested and stay another day."

A pretty Mexican señorita who wore a floral skirt and white blouse asked if they were ready to order. They did, and minutes later, she placed a dish of beans, chopped beef, and tortillas in front of each of them. As she walked away, Billy looked at Seth and Frank. "Any ideas where you're heading?"

Seth chewed and swallowed. "While you were in Santa Fe and Frank here was goofing off, I saddled up and did some scouting south of town and found the tracks of Wade's friends."

Wade gave Seth an unhappy look, not appreciating him calling them his friends.

"I followed them for a spell," continued Seth. "And it appears they're still heading south."

Wade chewed his food and swallowed. "Looks like they're still heading for the border." He looked at Frank. "Not to change the subject, but we came across that Indian of yours on my way back."

"Dark Cloud?" asked Frank.

Wade shoved a fork full of food in his mouth. "You know any others?"

Frank ignored the question. "Where'd you leave him?"

Wade nodded toward the north. "North of here. It seems he ain't too fond of towns. Said he'd ride on and wait for us further south by the river."

After eating, Billy walked Wade, Seth, and Frank up to the livery and watched as they saddled their horses. He wished he was going with them when he noticed two town council members walking toward the livery.

Dan Hurley and Paul Sharpton of the town council walked in and introduced themselves. "May we have a word with you, gentlemen?"

They stopped what they were doing, looked at one another, and then at Dan Hurley and Paul Sharpton.

Wade placed one hand on the mare's rump and looked at the two men curiously.

"What's on your mind?" asked Billy.

"Well," said Paul Sharpton, "After the death of Sheriff Boedecker, we need a sheriff for Pine Springs. The pay's good includes a house and one meal a day at any of the three cafés in town." He paused as he gestured to Seth and Frank. "We were hoping one of you would consider taking the position."

Seth turned away, pulled the cinch to his horse's saddle a little tighter, and then looked at them. "That a fact?"

Dan Hurley smiled and nodded. "Yes sir."

Wade was concerned about the widow, the same as the others. "What about the widow Boedecker?"

"What about her?" asked Hurley.

Frank chuckled without humor. "So, one of us takes the job, and you good samaritans put her out on the streets of Pine Springs now that her man's dead?" Frank raised his voice. "The wife of the man that took care of this town for some twenty-odd years.

Hurley looked at Sharpton, shrugged his shoulders, and turned to Frank. "Well, we haven't decided what to do about Mrs. Boedecker just yet."

Wade turned away to cinch his saddle. "Well, maybe it's time you bastards started thinking about her."

Surprise and anger filled Dan Hurley's face. "Now look here, young man, you got no reason to talk to Paul and me in such a manner."

Wade gathered the reins to his mare, lead rope to the packhorse, and started toward the livery door. "I ain't gonna stay here and listen to this bullshit."

Dan Hurley yelled after Wade. "By law, we got no obligations to Mrs. Boedecker. It was her husband Russell who was the sheriff."

Wade stopped just outside the livery doors, turned, and glared at Dan Hurley.

Billy tried to keep a lid on a bad situation and stepped away from the big door he was leaning against. "There must be something the town can do for Mrs. Boedecker."

Wade and the others stared at the two men waiting for their reply.

They looked at one another thoughtfully, and then Hurley said, "I suppose the council would agree on her staying in the house until a new sheriff's appointed."

Seth's face filled with disappointing anger. "You're not serious, are you, Mr. Hurley?"

Dan Hurly looked at Seth, shrugged his shoulders but never answered.

Sharpton looked at the three men. "You men still haven't said whether any of you'd be interested in the job as Pine Springs Sheriff."

"Not me," replied Seth.

Frank shook his head. "Not on the worst day of my life."

Billy looked at the two men. "How many years was Boedecker sheriff of this good town?"

"Some twenty-odd years, I believe," said Hurley.

"What about Mrs. Boedecker?" asked Seth. "How many years did she put in?"

Paul Sharpton looked at Seth, feeling embarrassed. "I see your point." Then he looked at Hurley. "A word Dan." The two stepped a few feet away and whispered for several minutes. When they finished, they returned to the others, and Paul looked at each man. "You have our word, gentleman. The town will take care of Mrs. Boedecker." He paused to look into each man's eyes. "We'll see she has a place to stay, perhaps in one of the boarding houses."

Wade looked at them. "I'm holding the two of you and the rest of the council to that, Mr. Sharpton."

He looked at Wade and held out his hand. "I'm sure you will, sir."

Wade looked down at Paul's hand and then into his brown eyes and shook his hand. "I believe you're a man of your word." He climbed up on his horse, settled into his saddle, and wrapped the lead rope of the packhorse around his saddle horn. "If I find out differently, I'll be back." Then he tipped his hat to both men and turned to the Marshal. "Thanks for everything, Billy. I hope Todd recovers from his wounds." Wade pulled at the lead rope of the packhorse and nudged the mare into a walk away from the livery.

Seth climbed onto his horse and looked at the two men. "I don't think you want him coming back to Pine Springs, Mr. Sharpton." Then he smiled. "It's been a pleasure, gentleman." Then he nudged his horse, pulled at the packhorse, said goodbye to Billy, and followed Wade down the street.

"Gentleman," said Frank Wells as he climbed onto his saddle, ignored the others, said goodbye to French, and rode out of the livery.

Twenty-One

Dark Cloud sat on the ground, leaning against a tree, his legs stretched out in front of him, his rifle across his lap, waiting as he told Wade he would. He watched the last of the day go with the large reddish-orange sun slipping behind the mountains to the west, turning the river and landscape the same soft color. It was peaceful. The warmth of the setting sun felt good against his dark skin. He closed his eyes, rested his head against the tree trunk, and remembered the old days. He thought of cold winters in his teepee, sitting by a warm fire while the wind outside moved the snow into deep drifts. On peaceful evenings such as this, the emptiness and sorrow of losing his squaw and son to the white man's disease came to visit. Opening his eyes, he looked toward the setting sun, thought of his son, and wondered what sort of brave he would have grown up to be.

The neigh of horses interrupted his sad memories and looking toward the sound seeing three riders and two packhorses, he knew it was Frank Wells, Seth Bowlen, and Wade Garrison. Standing, he swung up onto the back of the gray, and then with his rifle cradled in the elbow of his left arm, he rode down the hill at a slow walk to meet them.

Seeing the Indian, Frank handed Seth the lead rope to his packhorse and spurred his horse into a trot.

The Indian stopped in the middle of the dirt road that was nothing more than two lines of wagon tracks separated by weeds and waited for his friend, Frank Wells.

Frank grinned as he rode up. "Been waiting long?"

"Not long." After a brief exchange of greetings, the Indian turned and looked south as he pointed with the hand holding his rifle. "The men you hunt go that way." He looked at Wells. "I follow, then come back to wait by river for my friend Frank Wells."

Frank looked in the direction the rifle had pointed. "How far did you follow the tracks?

"Far enough."

"Show us where the tracks are, my friend," said Frank.

Dark Cloud cradled his rifle in his left arm, turned, and rode south at a slow trot sitting tall on the big gray.

Wade leaned closer to Frank as they followed and quietly asked, "What'd he mean by far enough?"

"No one knows what an Indian means but another Indian," replied Frank. "Guess we'll find out eventually." Then he laughed and nudged his horse into a trot.

Wade nudged the mare and followed, remembering the first time he saw Dark Cloud standing on top of the hill in the morning sun.

The sun had disappeared behind the mountains, and the landscape was no longer orange but shades of gray and black. It was getting dark, and the night was engulfing everything, including the road in front of them. Dark Cloud stopped and pointed with his rifle at a grove of trees barely visible in the dim distance. He said something to Frank, who nodded, and then the Indian turned his gray and rode in the direction of the trees.

Frank slowed his horse, and when Wade and Seth caught up, he gestured after the Indian. "We'll make camp by them trees. The Indian says there's a small pond for water and good grass for the horses."

The Indian had already dismounted when Wade and the others rode up. He was kneeling next to a circle made of small rocks, smelling a hand full of ashes as they fell gently through his fingers. He looked up at Frank. "Men camp here." Then he stood and pointed south. "They ride that way."

Frank grinned at Wade. "Guess this was far enough."

Dark Cloud turned and looked up at Frank. "I follow the men who run from you to this place because you are trying to kill them." Then he pointed to his hair and said, "The one with black hair was hurt." Then he put one hand on his shoulder. "Here."

Seth smiled as he looked at Wade. "Looks like you got a piece of that bastard after all."

Wade grinned, wishing he had killed him, but he was not that good of a shot with his pistol, especially when hurried. Accompanied by his new friend's hate, anger, and revenge, Wade climbed down, looked around at the campsite, and imagined the three sitting by the fire, talking and laughing while Emmett lay on the ground. He looked south, wanting to mount his horse and go after them. Instead, he did like the others, loosened the cinch of his saddle, lifted it off the mare, and set it on the ground a few feet from the circle of rocks. While he and the others hobbled their horses and unloaded the supplies from the packhorses, the Indian was busy gathering sticks and wood for a fire.

With their chores done and the fire burning, Frank began cooking a supper of beans and beef while Seth visited the pond to get water for their coffee. Wanting to be alone, Wade carried his saddle a few feet away and dropped it on the ground next to a large rock. He leaned back against his saddle and stared into the fire, thinking of Sarah.

July 4, 1870

Sarah Talbert had become good friends with Hattie Dougherty, the girl whom Emmett Spears had feelings for. Hattie's father, Robert Dougherty, owned a small farm a few miles from the Talbert ranch, and since Sarah and Hattie were the same age, it was only natural they favored one another's company. Wade and Emmett being good friends helped the relationship, giving the two girls a chance to share secrets and dreams that most young girls share.

Wade and Emmett had the good fortune of receiving an invitation to the Talbert ranch for an afternoon picnic and fireworks later that evening. They had showered in cold water, shaved, and wore the new clothes they bought in town just for this occasion. However, Emmett complained that his new shirt was a little stiff and smelled like the General Store. Having already put his new shirt on, Wade smelled his sleeve, agreeing with Emmett. He knelt beside his bunk, pulled out a wooden box of personal items, and lifted the lid. He looked around to see if the other cowhands were watching and took out a small bottle.

Emmett looked on with curiosity while Wade sat beside him on his bunk.

Wade looked at Emmett, glanced around the bunkhouse, making sure no one could listen, and quietly read the label. "LaNeer's Lilac Hair Tonic."

"Where'd you get that?" whispered Emmett.

"From Howard the Barber in Harper," he proudly yet softly replied. "Howard says this is the latest thing for the gentlemen of the east and places such as New Orleans, even San Francisco. He told me it came all the way from France."

Emmett looked at Wade skeptically as he took the bottle and looked at it. "No shit," he said softly. "From Spain?"

"No, you idiot, it's from France."

Emmett looked at Wade, then back at the bottle. "What's the difference?"

"Well, for one thing, in Spain, they speak like the Mexicans, and in France, they speak Frenchman." He paused. "The way Pardee talks at times."

Emmett looked a little confused as he glanced at Pardee sitting at the table playing cards and lowered his voice. "You ever hear anyone else speak Frenchman?"

"No," replied Wade looking irritated. "How would I? I have been in America my whole life."

Emmett raised his brow. "Hmm, you gonna wear any of this today at the picnic?"

Wade lowered his voice once again. "I have been saving it for just an occasion such as today. Do you want some?"

Emmett considered that as he smelled the sleeve of his stiff new shirt. "Might be a good idea."

Wade glanced around as he opened the bottle, poured a small amount into his hands, and then handed the bottle to Emmett. Grinning, he rubbed his hands together and patted them on his shirtsleeves and chest to take away the new shirt smell.

Emmett took a quick whiff, frowned, and said, "Mite strong, don't you think?"

Wade smelled his shirt looking worried. "Sure is. Maybe it'll wear off on the ride to the Talbert's."

"I sure do hope you're right," whispered Emmett as he looked around the bunkhouse with an uncertain expression. Seeing no one was watching, he poured a small amount into one hand and gave the bottle back to Wade. After another quick look around, he rubbed his hands together as Wade had and patted the sweet-smelling fragrance on his shirtsleeves and chest while Wade put the bottle away.

Jessup Haggerty and Johnny Pardee sat at a long wooden table with benches on both sides playing poker for used matchsticks when Johnny Pardee turned and looked toward the two. "What the hell are you two putting all over yourselves?"

Wade and Emmett looked at one another, fearful of being teased, which Emmett hated. Wade turned and told them it was something he got from Howard the Barber in Harper.

Pardee laughed and said it reminded him of a whorehouse in New Orleans.

Haggerty laughed. "You boys, be careful at the Talbert's. You two may come back married to each other."

Pardee laughed so hard that tears rolled down his cheeks. Just then, Bill Dobbs, who was close to forty and stood about six-one was muscular with rusty-colored hair and beard, walked in and asked what was with all the commotion. Before Pardee or Haggerty could tell him, Wade walked past the two on his way out of the bunkhouse, telling them to shut up while Haggerty and Pardee continued to laugh, enjoying the moment.

Emmett walked over to the table and looked at Pardee. "You wanna step outside?"

Pardee stopped laughing and grinned as he looked up at Emmett. "I ain't looking to get married today, but I might next week if you keep wearing that stuff."

Dobbs and Haggerty joined Pardee in laughter.

Emmett stepped toward him with raised fists, but Dobbs grabbed him around the shoulders and chest from behind. "Easy, Emmett," said Dobbs. "They're just funning with you and Wade. Don't go getting yourself all beat up and dirty before the party. These two are just jealous."

Emmett relaxed, so Dobbs let him go, but Haggerty and Pardee were still giggling, trying not to look at Emmett. Neither would have fought with Emmett anyway. They liked the boy far too much, but they did enjoy teasing him.

"He's right," said Johnny Pardee as he fought the urge to laugh while trying to look serious. "Jessup and me are just jealous, like Dobbs said. Now you and Wade, go have a good time."

Emmett looked from one to the other and nodded once, looking stubborn. "I think we will." Then he turned and walked toward the door of the bunkhouse.

Wade was sitting on the porch steps when Emmett walked out of the door. He stood, and they stepped off the porch, headed for the corral and their horses as laughter from the bunkhouse caught up with them.

Emmett gritted his teeth in anger as he turned to go back.

Wade grabbed his arm. "Emmett, take it easy."

"I'm going back in there and kick the shit out of both of them."

"No, you ain't," argued Wade. "You know damn well neither will fight you. It'll be like it always is. They'll run around the bunkhouse till you get tired of chasing them, and everyone, including you, will laugh."

Emmett's face was red and filled with anger. "This is different."

"How's it different?" Wade grinned as he put one arm around Emmett's shoulder. "Forget Jessup, Haggerty, and Johnny Pardee for tonight. Sarah and Hattie are waiting for us."

Emmett looked back at the bunkhouse, then at the corral, and finally at Wade. "C'mon, let's get going."

The Campsite

Dark Cloud interrupted Wade's ride down memory lane as he walked up and sat next to him. "Your eyes tell of the sadness you carry in your heart."

"Just thinking of someone," said Wade without looking up from the fire.

The Indian looked into the dancing flames. "My friend, Frank Wells, told me of the killing of your friend by the men you trail." Then he looked away from the fire at Wade. "How did you call this friend?"

"Emmett Spears was his name. He came west from Ohio."

The Indian looked thoughtful. "I have heard of this place, Ohio." Then he pointed east. "It is a long way beyond where the sun rises."

Wade glanced in the direction he was pointing just as Frank called out that dinner was ready, so Wade and the Indian got up and filled their tin plates with beans and a piece of beef. Dark Cloud sat on a flat rock next to Wade, eating with his fingers, while Wade sat on the ground against his saddle.

The Indian picked up some beans with his fingers, stuck them in his mouth, licked them, and looked at Wade. "Do you believe the killing of the men we follow will take away the sadness and hate you carry in your heart?"

Wade thought about that for a moment. "I can't answer that until they're dead."

"I think it will," said Dark Cloud.

Seth and Frank ate in silence, listening to Wade and the Indian.

Wade shoved a fork full of food into his mouth. "Do you still feel the sadness for your wife and son?"

The question took Frank and Seth by surprise, thinking it was foolish, but it did not seem to bother the Indian.

Dark Cloud placed his half-eaten plate of food on the rock next to him, rested his elbows across his knees, and stared into the fire. "Yes," he said with a soft, sad voice. "My heart is still sad. I felt good when I was with my squaw. I still carry her and our son in my heart." He paused a moment and then gestured with his left hand. "When I die, my spirit would have lived through my son, his sons, and their sons until the end of time. Now my spirit will no longer live in the places I have known. It will not feel the warm sun, night's chill, and winter's white cold." He paused and looked at Wade. "Without a son, that part of my spirit will go with me on my journey to the ancients." He looked around, gesturing with both hands. "I will not be part of this land any longer."

Wade looked at him, considered everything he said, and thought it was different from what he had been taught while growing up. "Why not take another squaw and have more sons?"

"I have thought on this a long time," said the Indian as he turned from the fire, picked up his plate, and looked at the food as if considering another bite. "When the white man's sickness took my woman and son, my heart was heavy with sadness for a long time." He paused in memory. "The time came when I wanted to trade horses and bearskins for a young girl that was beautiful and strong. She would have given me many sons, but she was taken by a band of Bannock and killed when she tried to escape." He shrugged. "I don't think Be He Teiht, our creator, means for me to have another woman or sons."

Wade thought of Frank's story about the Indian's name and a life of hard luck. "What was your son's name?"

Dark Cloud picked up the meat on his plate, bit off a piece, and chewed while looking at the fire in thought. After he swallowed, he

211

looked at Wade. "He died of the white man's sickness before he had a name." He turned back to the fire. "And now I believe he wanders without a name in the spirit valley."

That interested Wade. "Will he wander forever?"

"Not forever, but he will until I die and our spirits meet. Then I will give him his name, his mother will call him, and we will wander the spirit world together."

"Is that what your people believe?"

The Indian thought for a moment, then looked at him. "It is what I believe."

Wade studied him for a moment. "What name will you give your son?"

"It cannot be told until I am with him." Then, Dark Cloud set his plate on the rock next to him. "Do you have a woman waiting for you?"

Wade smiled. "Sarah Talbert."

"Tell me of this woman who waits."

"Not much to tell." He raised one hand to his chest. "She's small-boned and stands up to here. She has brown eyes and light brown hair that shines in the sun but turns darker when evening comes." Wade smiled once again as he pointed to his nose. "She has little freckles on her nose and cheeks."

"What are these things you call freckles?"

"Little brown spots the size of sand."

The Indian nodded his head while considering freckles. "I have seen these things before on other whites." He sat back against a rock with a curious look. "Now tell me about the woman Saha who waits."

"Sarah," corrected Wade.

He looked at Wade and repeated, "Sarah. Is she strong?"

Wade considered that. "Not like a man, but she's strong."

"Is her heart and spirit strong?"

Wade chuckled. "Oh, she's a mite strong-spirited, alright."

"Will you return to Sarah with the strong heart when you have killed these men you hate?"

Wade looked into the fire, thinking of his hate. "I hope so."

"That is good," said Dark Cloud, looking pleased. "When you do, you must lay down with her and plant your seed in her so you will have a son to live on after you die." Then he suddenly stood and gestured to the others. "You are a good man like Frank Wells and Sheriff Bowlen. I like you, Wade Garrison. I will help you find and kill these men. Then he turned, walked to the other side of the campfire, and sat on his haunches, staring into the flames.

As stillness fell on the camp, Seth, and Frank thought about what was said between Wade and the Indian for several moments, then Seth stood, "Let's clean up and get some sleep. I want to get an early start. If one of these bastards is wounded, they'll need a doctor before long."

Twenty-Two

By the time the sun was above the eastern horizon, the four men had eaten breakfast, broke camp, and were riding south with Dark Cloud riding point; his eyes fixed on the ground and the tracks they followed. It was mid-morning, and the horses needed a rest, and so did the riders when Seth told Frank that the Indian was going to run their horses into the ground. Frank gave a whistle, and he stopped, turned, and waited.

"Horses need to rest," Frank told Dark Cloud as they rode up.

The Indian turned and pointed to a group of cottonwoods about five hundred yards to the south. "Trees will give shade, and horses can drink from the stream." He turned from the trees and looked at Seth. "The stream will let Bowlen make white man's bitter black water."

Seth looked at Dark Cloud. "I thought you didn't like my coffee."

"I don't," replied the Indian as he turned his gray horse and rode toward the trees.

Wade nudged his horse closer to Franks. "How does he know there's a stream?"

Frank pointed to the line of cottonwoods. "See the way them trees follow the land and aren't all bunched up?"

Wade looked. "Yeah"

"They're following the stream. Trees need water too."

Wade considered that as he looked toward the trees while Seth and Frank galloped after the Indian. Then, tugging at his tired, protesting packhorse, he followed. Reaching the stream, Wade dismounted and let his horses drink the cold clear water. While he looked around, half-listening to Frank and Seth bicker as they unloaded the satchels from their packhorses, he thought of the things Dark Cloud had told him.

The supplies unloaded, they sat by a fire Seth built and waited for his bitter black water to boil. Frank was cutting up some jerky to put into the beans, saying he was a bit hungry. The fire hissed as the coffee boiled over, and Frank cursed the boiling coffee pot. He lifted it from the rock next to the fire and placed it on a flatter rock to let the coffee grounds settle. When the coffee was ready, he poured a cup, handed it to Seth, did the same for Wade, and poured one for himself. He looked at the Indian setting against a tree a few feet away. "Want some coffee?"

Dark Cloud looked up from the stream he stared into and shook his head no. "No, black water too bitter."

While the three drank their coffee, Seth and Frank talked about old times while Wade sipped his coffee, thinking that the Indian was correct about dark bitter water. He sat back against his saddle, looked at the mare hobbled safely a few yards away nibbling on some grass, and thought about the Fourth of July party a couple of years ago.

Talbert Ranch

When Wade and Emmett rode up to the Talbert ranch, most guests had already arrived. The two hurried to the corral, put their horses away, and walked toward the house, looking for Sarah and Hattie. People were walking around the yard or visiting in small groups in the shade provided by trees lining the yard on the north side of the house. Several long picnic tables occupied the area next to the house, filled with food and pitchers of lemonade, tea, or water. The women seemed to gravitate toward one another in small groups, as did the men, and the whole thing reminded Wade of celebrations back home in South Carolina.

They hung back a bit, looking for the two girls half-listening to some men talking when Wade saw Sarah and Hattie talking with some women. Sarah was wearing a pale yellow dress with a high lace neck and a sash of a lighter shade of yellow wrapped around her waist with a bow in the back. Her long, light brown hair was not in the usual ponytail she favored but hung softly around her face and shoulders. She looked up, saw Wade, smiled, said something to the women they were talking with, and then she and Hattie walked over to Wade and Emmett.

"Hello, Wade," Sarah said with a smile that included her eyes, and then she said hello to Emmett.

Emmett smiled broadly at Hattie and tipped his hat. "Hello, ladies."

215

Wade glanced around. "Looks like a lot of people showed up."

Sarah's smile left her face as she looked around. "Ma was afraid no one would come."

"Looks like she was wrong," replied Wade, then he smiled. "You sure look pretty, Miss Sarah."

She blushed and smiled. "Why thank you, and you look handsome. Is that a new shirt?"

He nodded. "Bought it last month and was saving it for today."

"You look good in blue."

Embarrassed by the compliment, Wade looked away.

Sarah knew she had embarrassed him and smiled.

Meanwhile, Emmett asked Hattie if her parents were at the celebration. She said they were, then she looked around, and seeing them across the yard, she pointed them out to Emmett. He looked over at them just as Mr. Dougherty looked at him. The two nodded, and Emmett looked at Hattie, wearing a light blue dress with white lace around the quarter sleeves and neck. Hattie had dark brown hair and brown eyes. She was big boned and tan from working on her father's farm, yet she was delicate and soft.

"You sure look nice, Hattie," Emmett told her.

She smiled and blushed, looking embarrassed. She raised her nose in the air and asked Sarah if she could smell the lilacs.

Emmett and Wade looked at one another, worried they would know it was them.

Sarah sniffed the air. "The breeze must be carrying the scent from the other side of the house."

Wanting to change the subject, Wade asked the girls if they would like to take a walk, and as they walked around the yard, Wade and Emmett made sure they talked about anything but the smell of lilacs.

The afternoon passed quickly, the sun had set, and evening darkness covered the picnic. Scattered campfires appeared across the yard, with small groups of people sitting around talking and laughing. Wade, Sarah, Emmett, and Hattie were sitting on the blankets Sarah had brought down from her room, and they waited patiently for the fireworks display that Mr. Talbert would soon proudly begin. As they sat watching the fire consume the logs, Wade thought the blanket they were sitting on smelled like Sarah, hoping no one smelled lilacs.

Mrs. Janice Talbert approached and asked if they minded if she sat down with them to enjoy the fireworks.

"No, ma'am," said Wade as he and Emmett stood, then Wade helped her sit next to Sarah. Wade liked Mrs. Talbert, and she often sat between him and Sarah during church, holding both their hands. Whenever the Talbert's invited Wade for Sunday dinner, he felt more at ease with her than with Mr. Talbert. Right now, however, he wished she had sat somewhere other than with them. Suddenly, as if she read his mind, she waved at another woman, excused herself, got up, and walked away.

Glad her mother had left, Sarah moved closer, and as their bodies touched, he put his arm around her, and she laid her head against his shoulder. The minutes passed, and suddenly rockets shot into the air, exploding into magnificent colors of red, green, yellow, and bright white, each so bright it was as if the day had suddenly reappeared. They watched the rockets climb into the air exploding into different colors and shapes, hearing others uttering sounds of excitement and wonder among oohs and aahs.

Neither Sarah nor Wade spoke as they looked up at the display of colors. She placed her hand on his arm and squeezed it. He held her tighter, pulling her against him feeling her warm body relax against his. Concerned that others may be watching, he glanced around, but all eyes were skyward, including Emmett and Hattie. Wade gently kissed Sarah's cheek. She closed her eyes, pressed her head against his, then turned and kissed him. Then she looked skyward, resting her head against his shoulder, and watched the fireworks. Wade glanced at Hattie and Emmett, both having their eyes fixed skyward, and then into the crowd seeing Mrs. Talbert looking at him, and he wondered if she saw them kiss. She smiled and then looked skyward when an explosion burst above them. He looked up as bright masses of red, blue, and white clusters flew across the sky, lighting up the farm as the air filled with oohs and aahs. He turned and looked toward Mrs. Talbert. She looked at him for a moment and then turned to the magnificent show in the sky.

The fireworks display ended, and while the guests were leaving, the four crowded around a small fire, talking and laughing. They enjoyed the evening so much that they had not noticed they were the only ones left. Mrs. Talbert stood inside the back door, telling Sarah that she and Hattie would have to come in. Sarah argued politely with her, and after a

217

moment of consideration, Mrs. Talbert said they could stay outside for a while longer, but then she and Hattie would have to come in. Looking happy, Sarah thanked her mother, smiled at Wade, and asked him to put another log on the fire.

Their time quickly passed, and now Mrs. Talbert called Sarah from the upstairs window. Sarah stood, grabbed her blanket, and they walked toward the house. Rounding the corner, Wade was surprised to see Emmett kissing Hattie on the lips and Hattie responding by putting her arms around Emmett's neck.

Wade turned from them and looked at Sarah, leaning with her back against the house, and smiled. His heart was beating so hard against his chest he thought it would explode like the rockets earlier. Her eyes were barely visible in the darkness, and the smell of her perfume excited him. He lowered his head and kissed her.

Mrs. Talbert called out from an upstairs window, "Sarah, where are you?"

Wade quickly stepped back, looked up at the second-story window above them, and wished she would go elsewhere.

Sarah softly giggled as she looked up. "We're at the back door, Ma, saying goodnight. Be up in just a minute."

Just then, Mr. Talbert yelled out the window. "Well, hurry up girl! Them two boys have to saddle their horses, and then they have a long ride ahead of them in the dark."

"Alright, Pa, we're coming."

"See that you do," replied Mr. Talbert firmly, then he yelled out the window. "Goodnight boys."

"Good night, sir," the two yelled in unison. Wade kissed Sarah, Emmett kissed Hattie, and after the girls went inside, the two hurried toward the corral to saddle their horses.

The Campsite

Wade looked up as Frank's foot poked his leg while asking if he wanted another cup of coffee. Wade nodded and held his cup up while Frank refilled it. Wade thanked him, took a small sip, and wished he were back at the Circle T having some of old Barney's coffee. As he sipped from the tin cup, he thought of Jessup Haggerty, Johnny Pardee, Bill Dobbs, and Stu Parks, wondering how they were getting along and if they ever thought of him or wondered where he was or if he was ever coming back.

Dark Cloud sat against a tree, his rifle resting against it, watching the water rush over and around the small rocks of the stream while his horse fed on the grass a few feet away. He looked up from the stream toward the mountains for several moments. "Thunder clouds over mountains."

The others stopped talking and looked toward the cloud formations along the mountains' peaks and knew from experience that the mountains would not stop the cloud's journey. Soon the thunderclouds would stretch across the sky above them, blocking out the sun.

"We see them," replied Seth.

The Indian raised his head, closed his eyes, smelled the air, and looked at Frank. "Soon, the ground will be muddy from the rain, and the sky full of white thunder."

Frank looked at the gray and white thunderheads that seemed motionless along the mountain range, but he knew better. "The Indian's right," he said. "Smells like rain." Then he turned to the others. "Won't be here for several hours."

"My friend Wells is right," said Dark Cloud. "But rain will cover tracks of men Wade Garrison wants to kill."

Wade thought the words made him sound like a killer rather than a man out for justice. But then he wondered if there was any difference between the two. He turned to the thunderclouds fighting to get over the mountains and thought about the tracks they followed getting washed away.

The Indian looked once more at the gray and white thunderheads dwarfing the mountains. Then he turned to Frank. "I will go ahead and mark trail if rains come early."

"Not a bad idea," agreed Frank. "What mark will we look for?"

Dark Cloud bent down and picked up several small stones, placing them in a straight line. "Look for small trees with a broken branch. I will leave rocks like this at the base of trees for you to follow."

Seth was standing next to Frank. "I think we can follow that."

Dark Cloud smiled at Seth, "Even the white man Bowlen can follow," Then his smile grew larger. "If Bowlen is not blind in both eyes."

Frank chuckled, but Seth saw little humor in the Indian's attempt at a joke.

On the other hand, Wade thought it was downright funny and laughed, bringing an unpleasant look from Seth.

Dark Cloud swung onto his gray, cradled his rifle in his left arm, and looked back at the thunderheads. Thinking they looked darker, he said, "I will wait for you at the flat rock."

With a curious look, Wade quickly asked, "What flat rock?"

"You will see it," replied the Indian.

"Be careful," warned Frank.

Dark Cloud looked like he smiled just a little before turning his big gray horse and rode through the cottonwood trees disappearing over the small hill.

Still curious about the rock, Wade turned to the others. "Do either of you know about this flat rock?"

"How the hell should we know?" replied Wells. "If the Indian says he'll wait for us at flat rock, then there must be a flat rock out there big enough for us to see it from a distance." Then he looked in the direction Dark Cloud had ridden. "With Indians, you have to look like you know what they're talking about. Now let's get these supplies loaded."

Wade thought about the thunderheads in the West as they worked breaking camp and turned to look at them, thinking they were moving north. "Looks like them big clouds are following the mountains and heading north."

Frank turned from what he was doing and looked. "You might be right about that. The Almighty might be giving us a favor."

"What the hell do you know about the Almighty?" asked Seth as he tossed his saddle on his horse.

Wade grinned and thought, *here it comes.*

"About as much as you do, maybe more."

Seth chuckled. "Hell, that ain't saying much."

Frank grinned. "No, I suppose it ain't." He looked at Wade. "How about you Wade? You and the man upstairs on good terms?"

Wade tossed his saddle on his mare, thinking about his hatred, wanting revenge, and what the Indian said about finding the men so he could kill them. "Don't rightly know. Before the war, we used to go to church every Sunday. My granddad would drive his wagon over to our place, pick us up in his wagon, and we'd all ride to church together." He smiled in memory. "Grandpa was a deacon and proud of it. Always carried his Bible with him no matter where he was going." He looked at them, grinning proudly. "He could quote scripture after scripture." He paused as the smile slowly left his face. "After pa got killed at a place called The Wilderness, we stopped going. Grandpa would still come around every Sunday for dinner, but none of us felt like going to church anymore."

Frank and Seth paused in loading the pack animals and listened to Wade.

He tightened the cinch to his saddle. "Grandpa took us all to church the Sunday before I left. We prayed and sang, and it was nice and peaceful." He looked in the direction Dark Cloud had gone, recalled what the Indian had said, and wondered what his grandpa would think about his wanting to kill these men. "That was the last time I was in church." He looked at them. "So, I can't rightly say if the Lord and I are on good terms."

Seth and Frank returned to the business at hand, and when the satchels were on the packhorses, the three mounted up and rode across the small stream, up the embankment, and through the cottonwoods heading south. Seth followed the trail left by the Indian and the three men he was tracking and suggested that Frank ride ahead and look for the flat rock the Indian told them to look for.

Wade took off his hat and held it above his eyes, shading them from the afternoon sun as he looked up. "Figure we got about four hours of light left."

Seth looked up and grunted in agreement as he turned to look at the thunderheads that had moved north.

Wade turned to see what he was looking at. "Looks like we got lucky."

Seth nodded. "Looks like."

When they looked back at Frank in the distance, he disappeared over a hill of sagebrush and rocks.

Several minutes passed when Frank reappeared at the top of the hill, riding toward them as if something was after him. Wondering what was wrong, Wade and Seth pulled up. Seth stood in the stirrups with his hand on the butt of his pistol, wondering if Indians were after Frank. Then he worried over Dark Cloud.

Frank looked worried as he pulled up, looking at Wade. "Hope you're as good with that Sharps as you claim to be."

"Why?" asked Wade.

"What's wrong?" questioned Seth.

Frank looked back at the hill. "Some damn Apaches have Dark Cloud staked out."

Wade looked confused. "But he's an Indian same as them."

Seth looked at Wade. "Apaches and the Arapahoe ain't exactly friendly toward one another." Then he looked at Frank. "How many Apache?"

Frank was unsure. "Four, that I counted. But there could be more. I tried counting the horses, but they's all bunched up by some fir trees."

Wade was worried about Dark Cloud. "What are we gonna do? We can't let them kill him."

Seth looked toward the rise. "They'll kill him for sure if we go riding in there." He looked at Frank. "Can we get close without them seeing us?"

"Not very. Maybe five or six hundred yards."

Seth looked at Wade. "That range good enough?"

Wade considered the distance for a minute. Being unsure and looking worried, he said, "Has to be, I guess."

Seeing he was worried, Frank asked if he could shoot that far.

Wade looked at Seth and then at Frank. "I've hit targets at greater distances before, but never when someone's life depended on it."

Seth looked at him. "We got no choice Wade. You'll have to, or the Indian dies."

Wade looked into Seth's bad eye, toward the hill, and finally at Frank. "Get me as close as you can."

Reaching a hill north of the Apaches, they pulled up and dismounted. While Seth kept the horses out of sight, Wade and Frank crawled up the hill and watched the Indians having fun with Dark Cloud.

Wade was concerned about the distance. "This is closer to seven hundred yards."

"That too far?" asked Frank.

"No, said Wade, I've hit targets further." Then seeing a ridge about a hundred yards east of them, he looked from it to the Apache. "That ridge there looks to be about five hundred yards."

Frank looked at the ridge. "That's about as close as you'll get. Everything else is open ground."

"It'll have to do," said Wade, worried if he could be quick enough to kill all four Apache before they killed the Indian. He looked back at Seth and the horses, and then seeing a gulley that led to the other ridge, he slid down the hill and headed for the horses.

As Frank climbed up on his black and white, he looked at Wade. "Think you can get all four of them from there?"

"We'll soon find out." He swung up onto the mare, and then they rode around the hill into the gully that led to the ridge. Tying their horses to two of the trees, Wade grabbed his Sharps, the metal rod used to steady the barrel and the bandolier of cartridges. Then he followed Frank and Seth to a group of rocks among several fir trees at the edge of the ridge.

As they settled in behind the rocks, Frank looked through his long glass at the Apache camp. "Them four Apaches are standing by the horses, and it appears they're arguing."

"Probably arguing on who gets the gray horse and rifle after they kill him," said a worried Seth.

Wade was busy sticking the rod in the ground. "Can you see Dark Cloud?"

Frank moved the long glass away from the Apache. "He's still staked out on the ground. I can see his head moving." He paused. "We better hurry before they settle the argument and start on our Indian."

Wade held four cartridges while looking at Seth. "Hold these."

Seth took the cartridges. "Like this?"

Wade nodded. "I don't want to have to look for them." He raised the sight of the Sharps. "I'll be a mite busy." He looked through the peep-sight and asked, "How far do you think it is?"

Frank took the long glass from his eye and looked at the expanse between them and the Indians. "Can't be sure, four hundred yards, maybe not more than five."

Wade looked at Frank. "That's a big difference." Then he looked across the expanse at the Indians, took in the nearer trees and those that trailed off in the distance. "I make to be four." He wet his right index finger and held it above his head, testing the wind as he looked at the tree line off to the left that would block any wind. He raised the sight, blew into the tiny hole to clear any dust, cocked the hammer, and looked through the peep-sight at the Apache. "Frank," he said as he pulled the first trigger. "It appears that one of them is standing directly behind the other."

Frank looked through the long glass at the Apache. "He is."

Wade pulled the second trigger. The Sharps kicked as the cartridge exploded, and the sound of thunder traveled over the New Mexico plains.

Frank saw two of the Indians jerk and fall. "Hot damn boy, you got both of them."

Wade had already taken a cartridge from Seth, shoved it in the breech, and got off a second shot, killing a third Apache. The fourth stood frozen for a moment, then ran for the ponies. That gave Wade time to load the Sharps, take aim, and fire. The Indian never made it to the horses that reared up and pulled at their reins, trying to get free. Only the gray managed to pull free and run at full gallop away from Wade and the others.

Seth handed the last cartridge to Wade, patted him on the shoulder, and stood. "Great shooting Wade." He looked at Wells. "I'll get the gray while you check on your Indian."

Wade proudly looked toward the Apache camp hoping Dark Cloud was okay. While Seth rode to get the gray, Frank rode toward Dark Cloud. Wade pulled the rod out of the ground, picked up the bandolier shoved the cartridge in it and hurried to the mare and the two packhorses.

Twenty-Three

When Wade rode into the Apache camp, Dark Cloud was naked and sitting on the ground drinking from Frank's canteen. He dismounted, walked over to the Indian, and asked if he was alright.

Dark Cloud looked tired as he nodded. He took another drink and looked up at Wade. "My friend Frank Wells tells me it was you who killed my enemies, the Apache."

Wade glanced at the bodies of the Apaches lying a few yards away and wondered if they had squaws and children. "Didn't have much choice." Then he grinned. "Your friend Frank Wells was getting worried about you."

Seth rode up with the Indian's gray horse in tow.

Dark Cloud looked up at Seth with a thankful expression. "They argued a long time over my horse and rifle."

"Good thing they did," replied Seth.

The Indian nodded. "Apache know about horses." He looked at their ponies still tied to the tree and then at Wade. "Now their ponies belong to you."

Wade glanced at the ponies. "What the hell am I gonna do with them?"

"Start a ranch," chuckled Seth.

Wade never smiled. "Not likely. I'll turn them loose. They'll eventually find their way back to where they came from."

Dark Cloud took another drink from the canteen and swallowed as he looked around at the dead Apaches. "My enemy wanted to see the strength of my spirit. If it took a long time for me to die, it would prove my spirit was strong, and when death came, my spirit would make them stronger."

Curious about that, Wade looked at him. "And if you died quickly?"

Dark Cloud looked at the distant hills and shrugged. "I would still be dead." He looked up at Wade, pointed to the ridge, and asked, "How far?"

Wade turned to the hill. "A little over four hundred yards."

Not knowing what four hundred yards meant, the Indian looked at the hill in the distance and knew it was a long way. "It is far from there to here."

Wade looked back at the hill. "Yes, it is."

"I know this gun you have," he said. "White men kill many buffalo from far off."

Thinking he would like to see the gun, Wade walked to his horse, took the Sharps from the scabbard, handed it to the Indian, and watched as he closely examined it.

"Heavy," said the Indian as he raised it up and down with both hands.

"It is," agreed Wade. "Weighs thirteen pounds."

The Indian looked up at him with a curious look.

Wade realized the Indian probably had no idea what thirteen pounds meant. "Yes, it is heavy."

Dark Cloud stood, having no sense of embarrassment that he was naked. Wade thought that was a little peculiar, for he would surely be embarrassed standing in the middle of nowhere butt-naked. He watched the Indian as he lifted the rifle to his shoulder and looked down the long barrel as if to shoot it. "It is long."

Wade started to say the barrel was forty-two inches long but figured he could not comprehend measurements of length either. "That's why it shoots a great distance."

Tired of watching a naked Indian stand around holding a Sharps rifle, Frank scowled. "Don't you think it's about time you got dressed?"

The Indian glanced at Frank, handed the rifle to Wade, and turned to look for his clothes. Finding them in a pile a few feet away, he got dressed. Wade untied the Indian ponies, raised both hands and yelled. He watched them gallop away and then turned to Frank and Seth and asked if they were going to bury the dead Apaches.

Frank frowned. "I ain't wasting my strength any. Let the prairie take care of them the way God intended."

Seth scowled, shaking his head. "There you go again, talking about the man upstairs as if you know what he's intending."

Frank turned, giving Seth a dirty look, looked at Dark Cloud, and asked if he wanted any of their belongings.

The Indian looked at the dead Apaches shaking his head no. "Nothing of theirs is for me to take." He looked at Wade. "Their scalps belong to you."

Wade shook his head. "No, thank you." Then he turned, walked back to the mare, and put the Sharps away.

Dressed in his rawhide leggings, red loincloth, and faded dark blue sleeveless shirt, the Indian looked at Wade. "I do not understand why Wade Garrison does not take what belonged to those he killed."

Wade's predicament amused Seth and Frank as they waited for his response.

Wade climbed up into his saddle and glanced around. "Let's find those tracks we been following."

Frank settled into his saddle, turned, and asked Dark Cloud if he could find the trail of the three men he was following before the Apache chased him.

The Indian picked up his rifle, swung up onto his gray thought for a moment, and looked over his right shoulder toward the north. "The Apache chased me from that direction." He pointed with the barrel of his rifle. "That is where we find the tracks. When I heard the war cries of the Apache and saw them riding after me, the tracks not matter, so I ride fast."

"I can understand," smiled Seth. "That would have scared any of us, but do you think you can find them again?"

He looked at Seth's bad eye. "I'm an Arapahoe with two good eyes." Then he spurred the gray with his moccasins and rode north to the chuckles of Frank Wells while Seth had no appreciation for the Indian's further attempt at humor.

It did not take the Arapahoe long to find the big rocks he had ridden past when he heard the Apache war cries. He stopped his horse, climbed down, and knelt to one knee, examining the trampled ground of Indian pony tracks for the tracks of the white men he had been following. Dark Cloud stood and looked south, seeing the others riding at a gallop toward him. Returning his gaze to the ground, he started walking in circles, looking for the tracks of the three men. Finding them, he turned to see how far behind the others were, draped the reins over the big gray's neck and slid off.

227

While the horse fed on the grass, Dark Cloud sat down on a rock and waited. It was peaceful and quiet as he watched the gray feed, and as he turned his face toward the sun, which was low in the western sky, he closed his eyes, took in a deep breath, and slowly exhaled, knowing he had come close to a slow death this day. It felt good to be alive, and as he looked back at the riders and packhorses coming toward him, he knew he would have suffered a long time at the hands of the Apache. He would not have died easily or quickly as the white man Wade Garrison had asked. The gray whinnied, and he turned to look at it while contemplating the white man Wade Garrison and the debt he now owed him. A debt he was not sure he could repay, and that hung heavy on his mind. Seeing the others were almost upon him, he climbed onto the back of the gray and waited. As they approached, he pointed to the ground and let his hand and arm follow the tracks until he pointed to the horizon. "Your enemy ride that way."

The others looked down at the tracks letting their eyes follow them until they disappeared into the distance.

"Well," said Wade looking determined. "Let's get after them." Then he spurred his horse, and they trotted south, tugging at the packhorses.

Dark Cloud nudged his horse and rode next to Wade. The Indian never took his eyes from the trail up ahead as he spoke. "I have thought much about the long rifle that killed my enemy so they could not take my spirit."

Wade looked at him and then at the trail they followed.

Staring at the horizon as he rode, the Indian said, "Dark Cloud, not forget the gift of life. I will help you find the men you want to kill, and when you have done this, you must return to the woman you call Sarah, who waits and have many children. As you sit by the fire with your children at night, you will tell them of me and how I helped you kill those that killed your friend." Then he nudged his gray, rode on ahead, and kept his eyes focused on the ground and the tracks they followed.

Wade stared after the Indian, feeling a little confused.

Frank was riding beside him now. "What'd the Indian have to say?"

Wade shook his head, looking confused. "Says he won't forget me killing them Apaches. Says he'll help me kill these men we're after, and then I should get married, have a passel of kids, and tell them about it." He looked a little bewildered. "I think we're friends."

228

Frank chuckled softly. "Indians remember things that count in life. If things were different and his son hadn't died, he'd do just as he told you. He'd sit by the fire in his lodge or teepee and tell his children and grandchildren how you killed them Apache with the long rifle at a great distance. Then they would tell their children and grandchildren down the generations keeping the memory of you and him alive. Indian's way of being immortal, I suppose." He smiled and patted him on the back. "You've made a friend for life, and he'd give his for you if need be."

Wade considered that as they followed behind the Indian. Once the sun had disappeared behind the mountains, the darkness swallowed up the land. The Indian turned his horse and rode back to meet them. "Too dark to follow."

"Alright," said Seth. "Let's make camp yonder by them boulders. They'll give us shelter and cover in case Frank's other Indian friends come along."

The Indian looked at Frank with a curious expression.

Frank looked at the Indian. "He jokes about the Apache. Seth thinks he's funny at times."

Dark Cloud looked at Seth. "Apache, not funny."

Seth's expression told of his mood. "Let's get to cover and make some coffee."

The formation of boulders gave excellent cover and protection, and plenty of firewood was lying about. After they had unsaddled their horses, the satchels on the pack animals unloaded, and they made camp. Wade and the Indian gathered wood and built a fire while Frank took care of supper, rattling pots, and tin plates.

Seth gave the horses water from his hat when he turned to Frank. "Damn, good thing we aren't trying to hide. You're making enough noise to tell the dead where we are."

Frank stopped what he was doing and looked up. "If you're so damn afraid we might be seen or heard, I'll douse the fire, and you can eat a cold supper."

Wade was in no mood for their bickering and walked to the edge of the boulders, climbed up to the top, and looked back into the dim light of evening in the direction they had come. He sat down to watch the night swallow the hills and trees until they were gone, and soon he looked up into the moonless black sky filled with thousands of stars stretching from horizon to horizon. As Wade looked across the black sky, he wondered if Emmett had been right about the stars being the windows to heaven where angels looked down. He thought of God and the lives he had taken since he left the Circle T and wondered if he would go to hell when he died.

Feeling the need to pray and ask forgiveness, he looked into the night, wishing he could talk to his grandpa, and regretted they never spoke his last day at the train station. A coyote cried out, and then another. He imagined a male and female meeting with tails, wagging and frolicking playfully in the darkness until the female submitted.

"Dinner's ready!" yelled Frank.

Wade took one last look into the sky, then, in the direction of the coyotes, made his way down the boulders and walked toward the fire catching a whiff of the food and coffee. When he got to the fire, Seth was trying to sit back against his saddle with a plate of food in one hand and a cup of coffee in the other, trying not to spill either. Dark Cloud was sitting against a rock, staring into the fire, and Wade wondered what thoughts occupied the Indian's mind, but he was afraid to ask.

Frank filled his plate, walked to his saddle lying on the ground close to Seth's, and sat down.

Wade picked up a plate, filled it, and then filled his cup with coffee. Careful not to spill either, he sat against his saddle and took a sip before placing the cup on the ground next to him and asked Dark Cloud. "You're not hungry?"

The Indian looked up from the fire, picked up a plate, filled it, sat down, and began eating with his fingers.

Wade listened to Frank and Seth talk about the old days in Rio Blanco and Sheriff Danner while watching the Indian. He was curious if coming close to death this day gave him reason to reflect on life and death as it would a white man.

Twenty-four

The sun was about to come up when the Indian opened his eyes to an early morning sky and a scattering of stars. Seeing the others were still sleeping, he quietly got up and walked toward the pile of boulders that Wade had visited the night before. Although the Indian was quiet, Frank Wells opened his eyes and, seeing the dark figure, reached for his pistol. Realizing it was Dark Cloud, he rose onto his elbows and watched as he climbed the boulders and sat down, looking toward the east. Frank figured he must be praying to his ancestors or the Great Spirit, tossed his covers back, sat up, and stretched his stiff back. Quietly he moved next to the ashes from last night's fire and built a warm fire.

Wade opened his eyes, sat up, and glanced around camp seeing the Indian was gone and Frank was busy building a fire. "Where'd the Indian get off to?"

Frank Wells turned and gestured to the boulders. "Up there." Then he grinned at Wade. "Now that you're up, fill the coffee pot with fresh water from one of the water bags while I get breakfast started."

Wade looked in the direction Frank pointed and saw the Indian's silhouette against the eastern horizon's light blue sky, sitting on top of the boulders. Hearing a coyote cry out somewhere to the south, he wondered if it was one of those he heard last night, figuring the other got what it wanted and headed off somewhere to be alone. Tossing his two blankets back, he stood and stretched the stiffness from his back, picked up the coffee pot, and made coffee.

Frank nudged Seth with the toe of his boot and told him to get his lazy ass up and help with breakfast.

Seth raised his head and pushed his hat back from his sleepy eyes. "What's wrong with Wade? He knows how to cook."

"Wade filled the pot with water for our coffee. He ain't as good a cook like you, so get your ass up."

231

Wade took exception to his not being as good a cook, but he diverted the conversation since he did not feel much like cooking anyway. "We only got one water bag and one canteen of water left."

"We ain't far from the Rio," said Frank as he looked toward the west. "It runs from north to south a few miles from here." He pointed southwest and said they would reach it around midday.

Seth stood and started mulling around the fire, banging pans together while mumbling something neither Wade nor Frank understood and didn't much care about anyway.

Wade decided to get away before the argument started and walked toward the rocks and Dark Cloud. Climbing the boulders, Wade found the Indian sitting with his legs crossed, his hands on his knees, staring at the horizon. He sat down a couple of feet away and looked at the beauty of the sunrise on the land. "Seth and Frank will have breakfast cooked soon."

"When I was a small boy," the Indian said, "I would sit in my grandfather's lodge and listen to the stories of the ancient ones before the horse when our people walked great distances using dog sleds to carry their belongings. How they hid under buffalo skins to fool the buffalo so they could crawl into the herd with their lances and bows."

Wade sat in silence, picturing such a scene as he watched the sun make its journey above the hills in the east.

The Indian continued. "My grandfather told me that one day the Great Creator gave his children horses to make their life better, but it created jealousy and greed and that many tribes traveled great distances to steal from one another." He looked at the hobbled gray horse standing a short distance away. "The day my grandfather's spirit left him, he gave me the gray pony that was the grandson of his gray horse. It is a good horse, fast and strong. I would not want the Apache to have him."

Wade looked at the horse, thinking it was a beautiful animal, looking strong and fast. "He's a beautiful horse, alright. I feel much the same about my mare."

"Wade Garrison and the long rifle stopped the Apache from taking my spirit. Dark Cloud owes you much, and the Arapahoe word hahou for thank you is not enough." The Indian stared at the gray horse. "But we talked of this yesterday, and after today we will talk on it no more." He turned from the horse, looked at Wade briefly, and then looked back at the gray horse. "Though I owe you much, I must ask something of you, Wade Garrison."

Curious, Wade waited for the Indian to ask.

232

"If I die on this journey of death, you must take the gray horseback to my brother Two Birds."

Surprised at the request, Wade looked at the animal and then the Indian. "How will I find Two Birds?"

"My friend Frank Wells knows. You will ask him to lead you to my brother, and you will give him my horse and tell him that I died a good death."

Wade knew this was important to the Indian, nodded in agreement, and wondered if he knew he was going to die.

Frank yelled, "Breakfast is ready!"

As Frank had predicted, it was around midday when they reached the Rio Grande River, which flowed south to Mexico's border. They stopped to rest the horses and, after loosening the cinches on their saddles, let them drink, then hobbled them in a shady, grassy area. Dark Cloud found a log next to the riverbank, sat on the ground with his back against it, and watched his gray drink. Seth and Frank filled their canteens, sat down in the shade with their backs against a tree, and closed their eyes while Wade filled the two water bags.

Wade lightened the packhorses' load, sat on the ground next to Frank, leaned toward him, and lowered his voice. "Frank?"

"Yeah?" replied Frank lazily with his eyes closed and his hat pulled down.

"If anything happens to Dark Cloud, he says he wants me to take his gray back to the Arapahoe and find his brother, Two Birds. Why would he ask me to do that? I haven't known him as long as you and Seth have. Shouldn't he be asking one of you?"

Frank opened his eyes, pushed his hat up, and looked at the Rio Grande River. "If memory serves me, that gray of his was a gift from his grandfather." He looked over at the Indian sitting against the log. "He holds that gray in high esteem, and that's why he wants you to take it to his younger brother, Two Birds."

"Do you know this, Two Birds?"

Frank rested his head against the tree, closed his eyes wishing Wade would be quiet, and pulled his hat down. "Not like I know Dark Cloud, but I've met him."

Wade sighed, looking relieved. "That's good 'cause he said you'd help me."

Frank pushed up his hat and opened his eyes, looking irritated. "I ain't sure I'd know him if I saw him. Besides, this is your problem."

Sounding irritated, Seth said, "Would you two shut the hell up for five minutes?"

Looking frustrated, Frank leaned toward Wade and spoke in a whisper. "This is your problem, not mine. You're just gonna have to figure it out." He pulled his hat down over his eyes and leaned his head against the trunk. "Why worry over something that ain't even happened? Damn Wade, he'll probably outlive the bunch of us. Wake Seth and me in a while and make sure them horses are hobbled good.

Wade looked at the horses feeling sure they were hobbled good enough. He looked toward Dark Cloud, who had moved from the log to a tree, his rifle leaning against it and the gray tied to a small bush next to him. Wade considered going over and talking to the Indian but remembering what happened the last time the two talked, he leaned back against the tree, closed his eyes, and thought of Sarah.

Two hours later, they were on the trail of the three men heading south toward Mexico. The Indian had ridden ahead, needing to be alone and away from the white men for a while. Wade turned to Frank and Seth, asking if they had any idea where the three they were chasing would cross the border.

Seth quickly considered. "They won't head for El Paso. It's too busy, and I believe there's a United States Marshal there. My guess is either Rio Blanco, where Sheriff Danner killed himself, or Paso Del Rio, a few miles to the west."

"My guess is Paso Del Rio," offered Frank.

Wade asked with a worried look, "What's to stop them from just riding across the border someplace else?"

Seth looked at Wade. "Guys like them need a town for whores and drinking, and Paso Del Rio has both and a sheriff that doesn't ask questions unless you're a Mex."

Wade looked hopeful. "If you know the sheriff, maybe we can ask his help."

Frank and Seth looked at one another, and then Seth explained. "Andy Hayes and his son pretty much ran Paso Del Rio a few years back. Sheriff Danner didn't think too kindly of the elder Hayes and his son, saying they were just a couple of crooks with badges."

234

Wade considered that. "Sounds like the place they'd head for sure."

"Another good reason for Paso Del Rio," said Frank. "It's easy to cross into Mexico. There's no river, and all you have to do is walk across the street. Half the town's in Mexico."

"We'll know soon enough," Seth said, and as he started to explain, Dark Cloud appeared at the top of a hill about three hundred yards to the south, signaling for them to come.

"He's found something," Seth said, then he spurred his horse into a gallop toward the Indian.

Frank and Wade followed as fast as the packhorses would let them and watched Seth and the Indian disappear over the hill.

Frank knew something was wrong and tossed the lead rope of his packhorse to Wade. "Take care of the horses." Then he spurred his horse into a gallop and rode toward the top of the hill.

It took Wade a moment to gather the lead ropes of both pack animals, and when he turned the mare to follow Frank, he saw him disappear over the hill, and a moment later, three gunshots broke the quiet afternoon. Wondering if it were Indians or maybe the three men they were after, he drew his Colt pistol and spurred the mare toward the top of the hill tugging at the two packhorses. As he crested the hill, he pulled up as Seth climbed down from his horse next to a covered wagon. The Indian was sitting on his horse a few yards away, and Frank rode toward the wagon. Not sure what was happening, Wade sat on his mare and watched Seth take off his hat and drop to his knees with his head down. Frank dismounted and knelt next to something lying on the ground. He watched as Frank stood and walked to the rear of the wagon, looked inside, took his hat off, turned away, and dropped to his knees.

Knowing they had found something terrible, Wade holstered his pistol, tugged at the two packhorses, and spurred the mare into a gallop down the hill. Dark Cloud had dismounted and was sitting on a rock, staring at the ground. Frank was sitting on the ground leaning against the spoked wheel, his hat beside him. Seth was still on his knees near the front of the wagon, looking down at something. Wade jumped down, dropping the reins to the mare and lead rope of the packhorses as visions of the cabin and the farm ran through his mind.

As he walked toward Seth, he was holding the body of a little girl of five or six. Seth wiped the tears from his eyes, fussed with her dress,

235

gently brushed her red hair from her face, then looked up at Wade. "Sons of bitches."

Seeing the canvas pulled back from the first metal hoop in the front of the wagon, Wade stepped closer. He was startled by the limp body of a half-naked man tied to the metal hoop by his wrists, facing the inside of the wagon. He could see the man had been severely beaten, and as he climbed onto the wagon to see if he was still alive, he found the man's throat cut.

Turning from the dead man, he saw the body of a naked woman at the rear of the wagon and knew what she had gone through. Feeling sick, he climbed down, held onto the front wheel of the wagon, and fought the urge to vomit. He looked at the scene of overturned trunks, scattered clothing, and two dead horses imagining the terrible things this family went through. Seeing what looked like the body of a young boy lying next to the horses, he walked to the body seeing the boy had been shot several times in the back with one bullet in the back of his head.

Unable to fight the urge any longer, Wade turned and vomited everything in his stomach. Gagging and coughing to clear his throat and mouth, he knelt to one knee and spat to rid the taste from his mouth. Then he looked at the Indian sitting on the rock, staring off into the distance. Frank sat on the ground at the rear of the wagon, with his elbows on his knees, his head in his hands, crying.

No one spoke as the warm, dry air filled with the soft breeze mixed with flapping wings, faint cries of waiting vultures, and large black crows. Wade wiped the tears from his face and sat next to Frank by the rear wagon wheel.

Seth stood, walked to the wagon, got on his hands and knees, reached under it, and pulled out a shovel attached to the wagon's underside. Then, he stood, walked several yards, and started digging.

Hearing the sound of shovel and dirt, Frank turned and watched Seth for a few moments, got up and walked to his horse, took off his brown duster, and lay it across his saddle. He knelt beside the wagon, reached under it, pulled out a pickax, and walked to help Seth dig four graves.

Wade watched the two for a few minutes, stood, walked to one of the open trunks, and started looking for blankets to wrap the bodies.

Paso Del Rio

On the Border of New Mexico and Mexico

The sun had set hours ago on the border town of Paso Del Rio when three men slowly rode up the dark dirt street, passing in and out of the islands of light from windows and open doorways. Mexican music flowed from the cantinas on the Mexican side of the street, mixing with a piano and guitars from the American side. They rode in silence, giving little or no heed to the laughter and voices pouring out of the cantinas and saloons. Stopping at the hitching rail in front of the sheriff's office, they climbed down, tied their horses to the rail, and went inside.

A man of forty, heavyset with brown balding hair and brown eyes wearing a sheriff's badge, looked up from behind an old wooden desk. He looked surprised as a broad smile filled his acne-scarred face. "I'll be damned." Then he got up and walked around the desk.

"Hello, Uncle," said the taller man as he extended his right hand. Paul Bradley needed a shave, stood six feet, and had blue eyes and blonde curly hair.

The sheriff grinned while shaking Paul's hand firmly. "Paul Bradley, you little son of a gun." Then he shook the hand of the man with red hair. "Hello, Kevin." Then he grinned at Paul. "You're still better looking than your brother here."

Kevin, the younger brother, stood five feet eight with a lean body, red hair, green eyes, and red beard firmly shook his uncle's hand.

"Good to see you, boys," said the sheriff as he looked at the third man and gestured to his bandaged shoulder and arm in a sling. "What happened to you? A jealous husband catch you in bed with his wife?" Then he laughed.

Steve Hardy was a big man who stood six-two with broad shoulders, black hair, and beard. "Nothing that serious, Mr. Hayes." He grinned as they shook hands. "You're looking good. How've you been?"

The sheriff shrugged. "Oh, I been alright, ornery as ever, I guess, and you can stop with the Mr. stuff and call me Todd." Then he looked from one to the other. "What brings you boys so far south? I thought you were working on a big spread up in Wyoming."

"That's a long story, Uncle," said Paul. "We'll tell you all about it later."

Hayes wondered if they were in some kind of trouble. "Well, when you're ready, I'll listen." Then he glanced at their tired faces. "You boys look hungry."

They all said they were, and Sheriff Hayes walked to the door, took his coat off the peg, and shrugged into it as he turned to them. "Your

Aunt Anna will be right happy to see you, boys." They walked out the door and stopped at the boardwalk's edge, where Sheriff Hayes asked, "Them your horses?"

"Yeah," said Paul. "I think they're as tired as we are. Been a long ride from Wyoming."

Sheriff Todd Hayes gestured up the street. "The liveries on the way to my place. We'll drop them off and let George take care of them for a few days." Then he winked. "We'll let George worry about the costs."

Paul grinned. "I see things haven't changed any since we left."

The sheriff grinned, "Why would they? George is an understanding man." He walked down the steps to the dirt street and waited while they got their horses, and then they walked up the street to the livery. Then they walked to the sheriff's house north of the town. Greeted with hugs, kisses on the cheeks, and tears from Mrs. Anna Hayes, she fixed a nice meal of beef stew and fresh bread. After dinner, while Anna cleaned the kitchen, the men sat on the back porch and sipped homemade whiskey from one of Uncle Todd's jugs.

Hayes sat in the only chair and filled his pipe with tobacco, then put a match to it. Puffing smoke, he blew a big puff into the air and looked at Paul. "What happened up in Wyoming?"

Paul glanced at the others as he leaned forward, looking past his uncle through the window's lace curtains into the house, making sure their aunt wasn't listening. "Truth of it is, the law up in Wyoming thinks we done killed Mr. Hoffman and raped his pretty young wife he brought from Kansas City."

Sheriff Hayes pulled the pipe from his mouth, looking surprised. "Why would they think that?"

Paul Bradley glanced around and lowered his voice. "There were four of us working for Jessup Hoffman. Us three and a half colored half Pawnee by the name of 'Charlie Two Skins.' That's what the Pawnee called him; we just called him Charlie. Anyways, me Paul and Steve there were hunting strays one day, and when we got back to the corral late that evening, the house's front door was open, and the inside was dark as all get out."

"That's a fact, Uncle," said Kevin. "Me and Paul got worried, went up to the house, and knocked on the door calling out. No one answered, so Paul pushed the door open, and we went inside. Mr. Hoffman was dead, and his young wife raped and murdered."

"Did you get the sheriff?" asked Sheriff Hayes.

Kevin shook his head no. "We know we should have, but we got scared, figuring we'd get blamed."

"We should have, Uncle," said Paul. "But we just took what money we could find thinking they owed us wages anyway, and high-tailed it out of there." He looked at his Uncle Hayes. "I know what we did was wrong, Uncle, but we were scared as hell and wanted to get out of Wyoming before we got hung for something neither of us did."

Sheriff Hayes took the pipe out of his mouth. "What about the half-breed? Where was he?"

"Don't rightly know," said Kevin. "When we left that morning to hunt strays and ride the line like we did every day, he was working in the barn."

Sheriff Hayes thought about that a moment. "Think it was him that did the killing and the raping?"

The three looked at one another. "Could have, I suppose," said Paul as he lowered his voice, making sure their aunt wouldn't hear. "We were sitting in a saloon south of Rawlins when Charlie the half-breed walked through the door. Seeing us, he came over, sat down, and asked if we heard what happened to old man Hoffman. We said we did, and we told him that we found them and high-tailed it. Charlie ordered a drink, but before it came, the sheriff and his deputy busted in, saying we's all under arrest." Paul looked troubled. "That's when Charlie drew his gun and killed them both."

Sheriff Hayes frowned as he puffed on his pipe, listening while Paul told the rest of the story.

"When Charlie ran out of the saloon, the bartender reached for his shotgun, and that's when Steve there put one through his chest." He looked at his uncle. "It was his life or ours, Uncle. After that, we ran out, climbed on our horses, and headed south."

Sheriff Todd Hayes looked worried as he stared at his nephew. "Maybe you boys should have shot Charlie instead."

"Ain't arguing that none," said Kevin. "But the fact is we didn't even think about it. We were going to turn ourselves in as soon as we got to a town in the Colorado Territory. But I guess the word spread, and every sheriff in the territory started taking shots at us." He paused. "Never had a chance to tell our side of the story."

"That's a fact, Uncle," said Kevin. "We have been blamed for every robbery, killing, and rape between here and Wyoming. The truth," Kevin said, looking worried. "Some men have been trailing us since we stopped at a town called Harper up in the Colorado Territory."

Hayes looked at Kevin. "What happened in this town of Harper?"

"Some drunken showoff got into a disagreement with Paul over some whore and tried to shoot him, but Paul was quicker and shot the fool."

Paul looked at his uncle. "I had no choice but to kill him."

Sheriff Hayes stared across the porch into the night and thought these boys sure had a mess on their hands. "Well," he said, "if it's the town sheriff after you boys, he's a little out of his jurisdiction." Then he looked at Paul. "You know how many are trailing after you?"

"Four, five maybe," replied Kevin.

"We stopped in a little town called Pine Springs for a drink," said Paul. "Thought we'd get a beer or maybe a poke from a couple of whores when they came in the saloon blasting away at us. We weren't about to be arrested and hung for something we didn't do, so we shot back in self-defense, hitting the Sheriff of Pine Springs."

Sheriff Todd looked concerned. "Well, that sure as hell ain't good." Then he looked at Steve Hardy. "Is that where you got hurt?"

Steve nodded. "Guess we were damn lucky they didn't kill us all." He paused. "They killed these two fellas we were having a quiet drink with. Guess they must have thought they's with us."

"Sounds more like friends and family than the law," Hayes said thoughtfully. "They kill the half-breed in Pine Springs?"

Paul shook his head no. "Us and Charlie split up in Colorado. He headed east, and we rode over Raton Pass and then down into Santa Fe."

Sheriff Todd Hayes sat up in his chair. "If they're family, they won't stop." Then he looked at his nephews. "We sure as hell wouldn't if someone were to kill one of our family."

Paul nodded toward the south. "That's why we're heading into Mexico. We plan on heading east to Juarez, follow the Rio for a spell, and back into Texas somewhere near the gulf." He shrugged. "After that, we ain't got no plans."

Sheriff Hayes nodded his head thoughtfully. "Sounds like a good plan. When are you thinking of leaving?"

Paul looked at the others. "Day or two, maybe three at the most."

Sheriff Todd Hayes puffed his pipe while considering all he had heard from his nephews. "You're welcome to stay here. We got a spare room upstairs, but one of you will have to sleep on the floor. I know my

Anna would love to visit with you boys before you take off again. And I think your cousins, the Wilkins boys, will want to drop by and visit." Then he looked at Paul. "You boys got any money?"

Paul grinned as he lied about what they had stolen from the families they killed. "Not much."

"I'll see what I can do about that tomorrow," said Hayes. "Some folks around here owe me a favor or two. I'll see if I can collect a little cash for you boys."

Paul smiled with an appreciative look. "We surely appreciate that, Uncle Todd."

Kevin nodded. "Paul's right, Uncle Todd. We surely do."

Hayes looked at his two nephews affectionately. "Shit, boys, my dead sister, your mother would send me to hell if I didn't help her two boys." Then he stood. "Now, if you don't mind, I'm tired and have to make my rounds before I turn in. You can fight over who gets the floor." He stepped off the porch to head for the sheriff's office but paused a few feet from the porch and looked back. "Ain't no one gonna bring any harm to my kin in my town."

Rio Grande River Northwest of the Town of Rio Delanco

Wade and the others had followed the three men's trail that disappeared into the stage road leading east to Rio Delanco and west to Paso Del Rio. Sitting in their saddles, staring at the two dirt lines separated by weeds and wildflowers, Frank climbed down from his horse and knelt to one knee. He picked up a hand full of small stones and studied the dirt and gravel road while playing with the stones in his hand. "We've been on the road for an hour now." Then he tossed the pebbles across the stage trail in frustration while looking up at Seth. "There's no sign on this road that I can find, Seth."

Bowlen looked disappointed. "Then the bastards could be in either Rio Delanco or Paso Del Rio."

Frank nodded. "That's the look of it. Rio Delanco's about five miles southeast, and I ain't sure how far it is to Paso Del Rio."

"I say we split up," said Wade.

Seth and Frank looked at one another, considering Wade's suggestion, and then Seth shook his head. "No, we stay together." He took off his hat to shade his eyes as he looked up at the cloudless blue sky. "Still, plenty of daylight left," he said as he looked in the direction of Rio

241

Delanco and then toward Paso Del Rio, then at Frank. "I'm betting they're in Paso Del Rio right now." He put on his hat. "As you said, Frank, the town is half in Mexico and half in the New Mexico Territory."

Wade was worried. "What if they aren't there? Then what?"

Seth stared at him for a few moments. "I've trailed a few men in my day, and I have a pretty good feel for what they'll do." He glanced up the road and then looked at Wade. "If I'm wrong, I'll help you trail these bastards through Mexico and into hell if need be."

"I think Seth's right, Wade, but if he's wrong, we'll both live that promise." Frank thought about the family they found a few miles from here. "I swear on my mother's grave, these men are gonna pay for all they've done." He looked at Seth and then Wade. "Now, let's get after them." Then he swung up onto his horse and looked at Dark Cloud. "We're going to a place called Paso Del Rio, my friend."

Twenty-Five

Paso Del Rio

Like many border towns, Paso Del Rio consisted of Mexican adobe and Anglo-American wooden buildings. Because the middle of the street was the border between the United States and Mexico, the Mexicans controlled the south side of the street, the Americans the north, which often brought about conflicts.

It was dark when Wade and the others rode their horses at a walk up the deserted street in silence, in and out of the lighted images of windows and open doorways. Their eyes searched each hitching rail for the horses belonging to the men they had trailed from Colorado. Mexican music and laughter spilled from the open doorway as they rode past the first cantina on the south side of the street. Seeing that most of the horses had fancy Mexican saddles, they continued their journey along the dirt street when they came to a narrow alleyway. Sitting just beyond the end of the alley stood a two-story adobe building with several girls scantily dressed sitting on the porch in the dim light of kerosene lanterns.

Frank looked at Wade. "Must be a slow night."

Wade gave Frank a quick grin as they continued up the street, passing in and out of islands of light left by windows and doorways. They rode past the general store, barbershop, land office, and women's dress shop. The voice of a woman singing off-key to loud piano music flooded the street through the saloon's swinging doors. Wade looked up at a sign painted in faded red letters on a weathered white background, 'Rio Saloon Prop Red Hayes,' and wondered if this was the same Hayes Seth and Frank mentioned earlier.

They eyed the horses at the hitching rail, and after stopping to give the saloon a quick look, they continued up the street. They rode past the sheriff's office, an empty lot, a bank, and a crowded cafe. The smell of cooked food suddenly escaped from the café when a man and woman opened the door and stepped onto the boardwalk. Feeling hungry, they turned their horses around, stopped, and looked back at the town and street they had just ridden up. Each considered the café while watching a dark figure, here and there, cross the street or walk along the boardwalk.

A disappointed Wade stared back along the dirt street. "What now?"

Seth looked up at the dark, star-filled sky and then back along the street of lights, music, and laughter as he considered the question. "Let's check out the livery," he said. "Maybe they put their horses up for the night, and our boys are in one of the cantinas or the saloon." Then he took a deep breath and let out a soft sigh. "If not, we'll put the horses up, get something to eat, and then a couple of rooms and get a fresh start in the morning." He paused, then said, "I'm tired."

The livery was dark when Seth climbed down from his horse and banged on the big, closed doors while the others waited in their saddles.

A husky voice on the other side of the weathered doors asked, "Who's there?"

Seth leaned closer to the doors and said, "Need to put our stock up for the night."

"Just a moment," said the husky voice as he lifted the board holding the doors closed. The door opened, and a big burly man with black, curly hair and beard stepped outside. He held a lantern in one hand while pulling his suspenders up with the other. He looked at Seth and then the others with dark, curious eyes. "Evening." Then he noticed the Indian sitting on his horse behind Wade. "Don't see many Indians in town."

Frank glanced back at Dark Cloud, feeling a bit offended by the comment. "He's with us. I hope you don't have a problem with that."

The blacksmith looked at Frank. "Makes no difference to me, mister. I was saying we don't see many Indians in town." He paused. "See no use in making anything out of it."

Wanting to cool the situation down, Seth smiled. "Neither do we." He gestured back down the street. "That hotel we rode past, I believe the name was the Border Hotel. What's it like?"

The blacksmith glanced at Frank, looked at Seth, then shrugged as he hung the lantern on one of the big doors. "Ain't bad, I guess. I've lived here most of my life and never stepped inside, so I can't say for sure." Then he glanced at the others. "You boys come far?"

"Far," replied Frank as he climbed down. Hearing a commotion erupt from outside the Rio Saloon farther back along the street, everyone turned.

Several men stood on the boardwalk in the light from the saloon, laughing as another kicked a man in the ass knocking him down the steps into the dirt street. The man who did the kicking picked up the man's hat from the boardwalk, tossed it into the street, and said something that brought laughter from the others.

Seth looked away from the scene to the blacksmith. "Looks like a busy night for the sheriff."

The livery owner frowned. "Sheriff Todd Hayes is more'n likely inside getting drunk with the rest of them." They were too far away to see who it was they kicked down the steps into the street, but the blacksmith shook his head in disgust. "That's more'n likely old Barney."

"And who might this Barney be?" Wade asked as he climbed down from his horse, thinking of Curley back in Raton.

"A good man that Sheriff Hayes likes to pick on," replied the big man.

"I take it that you don't think much of the sheriff," said Frank."

The big man gave Frank a quick look. "He's a bully, same as his pa was. A few years back, Todd Hayes and his pa Andy, the sheriff at the time, got drunk and, for no reason other than for the pure pleasure of it, beat up an old man I had working for me." The blacksmith shook his head with a sorry look. "Damn near killed the old man."

"Where's the old man now?" asked Seth.

"After my missus patched him up, he left town. He was afraid the next time they'd kill him." He paused. "And they might have at that."

"Is the elder Hayes still around?" asked Seth remembering the stories he had heard about him when he and Frank were deputies for Sheriff Donner in Rio Del Blanco.

The blacksmith shook his head. "No. The Good Lord smiled down on the town of Paso Del Rio one night a few years back and took Andy Hayes from us."

"Heart attack?" asked Frank.

"No," replied the blacksmith. "Someone put a bullet in the back of his head one night while making his rounds."

"Ever find out who did the deed?" asked Seth.

"No. But most believe it was a drifter he knocked around and ran out of town."

Frank chuckled. "That's been known to happen now and again. One of the dangers of being an officer of the law."

The blacksmith grinned. "I'll take your word on that, mister, but I ain't got much use for Sheriff Todd Hayes, and the truth is most of the honest people around here don't either."

"Why not vote him out of office and run him out of town?" asked Wade.

The blacksmith looked at him. "That's not so easy. Sheriff Todd Hayes's cousin Red Hayes owns the Rio Saloon and is also on the town council. That's why there's only one saloon on the American side. And if that ain't enough, he has a sister who married into the Wilkins family of three brothers. She has two sons, Jake, and Norman Wilkins, who ain't much better than their uncle Todd Hayes. He also had another sister who died shortly after a mule kicked her husband in the head. She had two sons, Paul, and Kevin Bradley. And they've got a few more cousins, so you see, there's not a lot of men in town having the guts to run for office."

While the blacksmith was talking, Seth looked at Frank and nodded toward the livery, then turned and quietly stepped inside while Frank and Wade kept the blacksmith talking. Dark Cloud sat on his gray horse, watching the strange mixture of talk and secrecy of the white man's world.

Seth quietly stepped past the lantern hanging on the door that gave little light inside. He paused at the door, glanced back at the others, then stepped deeper into the dim light of the livery. While Frank and the blacksmith talked about boarding their horses for the night, he saw a sorrel in the first stall. It turned its head and looked at him with big dark eyes reflecting the lantern hanging on the door, then turned away. Seth stepped

246

into the stall, put his hand on the horse's neck, and spoke softly to calm him. He glanced back at the open door, then bent down and lifted the sorrel's right front leg. It was too dark to see the mark, so Seth rubbed his index finger over the shoe, trying to feel the imperfection but couldn't. He stood, patted the sorrel's neck, and looked into the next stall seeing a spotted gray and a black in the last stall. Knowing they had caught up with the men they had been trailing, he stepped out of the stall and walked outside.

As Seth walked out of the livery, the blacksmith stopped talking and looked at him. "Don't much like folks snooping around my place, mister."

Seth pulled his coat lapel to one side, showing his Deputy Marshal's badge. "We're Deputy Marshals. The Indian is our scout, and we been trailing the three men who own them horses you have inside."

"Why didn't you just say who you were and then ask me to look inside?"

Seth smiled. "I guess I should have, and I apologize." He gestured to the doors of the livery. "Do you know who owns the sorrel, spotted gray, and the black inside?"

"They belong to the Bradley boys. Paul and Kevin and that no-good friend of theirs, Steve Hardy." He frowned with an angry look. "If it's them you're after, I ain't surprised any. I wondered about Hardy's right arm being in a sling." He looked at Seth. "Mind me asking what it is you're after them for?"

"Murder," replied Seth, not wanting to get further into the details. "Are they staying at the hotel?"

The blacksmith shook his head. "More than likely, they're staying at the sheriff's place up the street past the bank." He paused. "They're probably all in the saloon celebrating."

"Celebrating what?" asked Frank.

"The Bradley boy's return," responded the blacksmith. "They have been gone for almost three years. I heard they were working on a big ranch somewhere's up in Wyoming."

Figuring that's why they passed through Harper, Wade became excited. "We going after them?"

"Soon," answered Seth as he looked at the blacksmith. "You said earlier that most of the honest people don't care for the sheriff. Any idea how many do?"

Wade became impatient. "What difference does that make?"

247

Seth glared at him and lowered his voice. "Because I want to know what the hell we're up against here, and I don't aim to fight the whole damn town."

Wade looked apologetic as Seth turned back to the blacksmith for an answer.

"Well," said the blacksmith. "Most of the town wishes the Hayes family and their cousins would go someplace else, but there ain't much chance in that ever happening. As far as the Mexicans, I think they don't have much use for the sheriff or his family. And since they're across the border, they got their own law that doesn't take a lot of crap off Sheriff Hayes and his family."

Bowlen looked toward the Rio Saloon. "Tell me about the family."

The blacksmith scratched his jaw thoughtfully and then lowered his voice. "Besides Sheriff Hayes, there's Red Hayes, Jake, and Norm Wilkins, their pa Howard Wilkins, and the Bradley boys, Paul, and Kevin. Paul is the older of the two."

"If they're all in there," said Wade. "That brings the number to nine."

Frank looked at Seth. "Ten counting that Hardy fellah." He paused with concern. "Your call Seth."

Bowlen looked at him in thought. "I didn't come all this way to ride back without these bastards." Seth stared along the street at the saloon as his right hand instinctively settled on the butt of his forty-four pistol as he calmly said, "Hell, there could be twenty to thirty inside the saloon."

Wade was getting desperate, and so was his common sense. "This may be our last chance, Seth. If they cross over into Mexico, we may never find them."

"You forgetting Pine Springs?" asked Seth irritably.

"No," replied Wade. "I ain't forgot Pine Springs, but---"

"Good," interrupted Bowlen. "We were six then and damn near got ourselves killed. Since they know what we look like, it ain't likely we'll surprise these boys a second time."

The blacksmith wondered what happened in Pine Springs but decided not to ask.

"Well," Frank said. "We sure as hell can't walk in there blasting away."

"No," replied Seth softly. "We can't, but we can sure as hell wait." Then he turned to the blacksmith. "When did you say the Bradley boys rode in?"

"I ain't sure, but when Sheriff Hayes and them others brought their horses to me for boarding just after dark yesterday."

Wells stepped closer to Seth. "They've probably been in there drinking and buying other assholes a drink for a spell."

The blacksmith looked toward the saloon. "Free drinks buys a lot of useless friends."

Seth smiled. "You got that right." Then he looked at the others. "Let's give them a while longer."

"Fine by me," said Frank, then he chuckled, "A few more drinks might affect their aim."

Seth smiled as she found humor in what Frank said but was doubtful of that as he stared down the street at the saloon. "Wouldn't count on that too much. But I sure would like to know how many are in there."

"How long we gonna wait?" asked Wade impatiently.

Seth considered that for a moment. "Couple hours, maybe."

The blacksmith hoped these men would rid the town of the Hayes and Wilkins families, smiled, and introduced himself. "George Johnson, blacksmith handyman, and jack of all trades." After he shook their hands, he nodded toward the livery. "I have a little place behind the livery, and I'm sure my missus wouldn't mind fix'n you boys some coffee while you wait." Then he looked apologetic. "I ain't got anything stronger. My missus won't allow whiskey in the house."

"I could use a cup of coffee," said Frank with a hopeful look.

Seth smiled, appreciating the offer. "Coffee sounds good right now, Mr. Johnson." Then he and Frank led their horses to the corral, tied them to the top rail, and loosened the saddles' cinch.

Wade looked toward the saloon while reluctantly agreeing, tied his mare to the corral rail, and helped lighten the packhorses' load.

Dark Cloud had no desire for the bitter drink the white man called coffee, so he jumped down from his gray and sat on a bundle of hay against the livery wall. "I wait here."

The blacksmith looked at the Indian. "You may as well tie your gray up and come along. I'm sure my missus won't mind."

The Indian looked at Frank.

Wells grinned. "You may as well come along. No sense in you sitting out here in the dark all by yourself."

The Indian quickly considered what Frank said, and curious about what lay beyond the livery, he tied his gray to the corral rail.

George led them through the livery and out the back door to a small two-story house. He opened the door, stuck his head inside, and asked his wife if she was decent. They heard her say she was, and then the blacksmith stepped inside, saying they had company as he motioned them inside. Kerosene lamps filled the room, which was clean and comfortably decorated. A rose-colored floral loveseat sat in front of the fireplace and bookshelf, and a small rolltop desk took up the far wall.

A woman in her mid to late thirties, barely five feet three, with short black hair, walked into the room. She was plain but pretty, with soft brown eyes wearing a faded dark red housedress and soiled white apron. When she saw the Indian, fear quickly replaced the smile.

Her husband looked from her to the Indian and lowered his voice. "It's alright, Izzy. He means us no harm." Then he nodded at the others. "These three men are Deputy U.S. Marshals, and the Indian is their tracker."

She blushed with embarrassment, looked at the Indian, and apologized. "Forgive me, but I didn't expect to see an Indian standing in my living room."

Dark Cloud stood like a statue, stared at her in silence, and thought white women scare easily.

George looked at the others. "This here's my wife, Isabelle Johnson. I call her Izzy."

Wade, Frank, and Seth stood bunched up with their hats off as Bowlen smiled. "Seth Bowlen, Mrs. Johnson."

Then Wade introduced himself, then Frank, who also introduced Dark Cloud.

Feeling nervous about the Indian, she smiled. "What a peculiar name." Then fearing she may have insulted the Indian, she said, "What I mean is it's not a name you hear every day."

The Indian stared at her without emotion as he stood straight and proud while Frank assured her that he was a good and honorable Indian.

She looked at Dark Cloud, feeling nervous but not afraid, stepped closer and extended her hand. "Welcome to our home, Mr. Dark Cloud."

He looked down at her tiny hand of white skin and then into her soft brown eyes, took her hand, and shook it firmly, yet gently.

She turned to the others and smiled. "May I ask what brings three U.S. Marshals and their tracker to our little town?"

George looked at his wife. "They come to arrest the Hardy Boy's Izzy." Then he asked her if she would make a pot of coffee for their guests.

Wanting to know more about them arresting the Hardy boys, she said she would be happy to fix coffee, turned, and walked toward the kitchen doorway. "George," she said, "show the gentlemen back here to the kitchen where there's more room." Then she stopped, turned, and gestured to the chairs. "Bring them two chairs as well." Then she looked at the four men. "You all look like you could use a bite to eat."

Seth wondered how women always know when a man is hungry. Then he and Wade picked up the two chairs and followed George into the kitchen where a smiling Mrs. Johnson was already busy making the coffee. George moved two chairs to the long table so Seth and Wade could fit the extra chairs. He stepped back, thought it looked a little crowded, and told them to sit down.

Meanwhile, Dark Cloud had quietly moved to the corner next to the back door and stood against the wall as he curiously glanced around the crowded room.

Breaking the awkward silence, Wade asked, "How long have you folks lived in Paso Del Rio?"

"Most of our lives," replied George, then he explained that the livery and blacksmith belonged to his pa, and when he passed away a few years back, it became his.

"Hope you don't think I'm nosey," said Frank. "How long have you two been married?"

Johnson smiled proudly. "Fifteen years last May."

"Any children?" asked Seth.

Isabelle turned from what she was doing. "We had a daughter, but she died of pneumonia when she was only three."

"My apologies for asking Mrs. Johnson."

"No need to apologize, Mr. Bowlen," she said with a small smile. "The Good Lord gave her to us for a while, and we're both grateful for that." Then she turned back to the stove. "Baked a couple of apple pies today." Then she turned and looked at the four men. "When was the last time you men ate?"

They looked at one another. "About noon, I reckon," replied Frank thinking of what they had, then he grinned. "Wasn't much of a meal, though."

"Well, for heaven's sake," she said. "You can't just have pie and coffee then. We still have plenty left over from supper. There's enough to go around."

"No need for that, ma'am," said Seth, to Wade's displeasure.

"Nonsense," she said. "Men such as you can't go around the country being hungry. Won't take but a minute to heat up."

Wade felt happy and smiled at the thought of eating. And since they weren't going down to the saloon to arrest the three men, he looked forward to eating and having a piece of apple pie.

Isabelle told her husband to set the table, and while he went about the business of plates and cups, she gestured toward the back door. "You'll find a pitcher of water, soap, and a towel just outside."

Wade was the first to get up, followed by Seth and then Frank, while the Indian stayed where he was. The men found the washbasin, a pitcher of water, soap, and towel, just as she said. They quickly washed and returned to the kitchen, finding Dark Cloud sitting at the head of the table. After Mrs. Johnson placed a plate in front of him, he leaned over, smelled the food with a curious face, and began eating with his fingers. That amused Isabelle Johnson, so she picked up a spoon and showed him how to use it. She filled plates for the others and sat across from her husband between Wade and Seth, enjoying the pleasant conversation with these strange but likable men. After dinner, Mrs. Johnson filled everyone's cup with hot coffee and surprised them with a slice of pie.

Dark Cloud looked at the pie of apples and syrupy liquid oozing from under the hard brown crust onto his plate. He looked at Frank eating his pie with a fork and Wade stuffing a fork filled with pie into his mouth. He picked up his spoon, cut into the edge of the pie, and put the spoon of pie into his mouth. Tasting apple pie for the first time in his life, Dark Cloud stared at Mrs. Johnson while concentrating on the sweet taste as he chewed. After swallowing, he smiled, nodded, and then continued eating."

Wade looked at his pocket watch, and, seeing it was after nine, he looked at Seth. "You said you wanted to give the Bradleys time to do a little more drinking. It's after nine. How much longer are we gonna wait?"

Seth drank the last of his warm coffee, set the cup down, pulled out his pocket watch, and checked the time. "Another hour should do it. I wish we knew how many of their friends were in the saloon before we barged in."

"I can go down and peek in from the street," offered Frank Wells.

Bowlen thought about that for a quick moment. "S'pose you could, but if they see you, they'd know we were here, then they'd skedaddle into Mexico."

Frank considered that and nodded. "There's that chance, I guess."

"I'll go," volunteered Wade.

Seth shook his head. "No, they'd recognize you also." Then he grinned and pointed to the Indian. "We can always send him."

Dark Cloud quickly looked from Seth to Frank Wells.

Bowlen looked at the Indian and chuckled. "Just joking."

The Indian thought of Seth's joke about the Apache and didn't think this was funny, either.

George Johnson was listening while he was helping his wife with the dishes. "I can go." He looked at Seth. "I could go in, buy a beer and look around for you boys."

Mrs. Johnson turned from the sink. "George, do you think that'd be a good idea? I have been listening to Marshal Bowlen and these others talking, and that could be dangerous."

"For them, not me, Izzy," he said. "Nothing dangerous about having a beer after a hard day's work. I've done it lots of times."

"Not with killers, you ain't," she said with concern.

Seth liked the idea. "I doubt any harm will come to your husband, Mrs. Johnson." Then he looked at George with a stern face. "As long as you have one beer and come directly home."

George looked at his wife. "That's all I'm gonna do, Izzy. Have one beer, see how many are in the place, and come directly home."

Mrs. Johnson's expression said she was not convinced but reluctantly gave up the argument.

Wade recognized the fear on her face. "Nothing will happen to your man Mrs. Johnson. They wouldn't hurt anyone living here."

She looked at Wade with an unsure look. "They might if they're mean from drinking."

George turned to his wife. "Izzy, no one's gonna bother me." Then he turned to Seth. "I'll count how many are in the saloon."

Seth looked at Frank, then at George Johnson. "Alright, Mr. Johnson. If you're sure, this is something you want to do."

"It is," he replied with an excited look and a small smile. "Anything to put one over on the Sheriff."

Seth leaned forward in his chair, elbows on the table, and spoke in a soft determined voice. "When you get inside, go straight to the bar. Is there a big mirror on the wall behind the bar?"

George shook his head. "No."

Disappointed, Seth sighed. "Alright then. When you get to the bar, order your beer, take a sip, and casually turn around. Count how many are in the place and where they're sitting." He paused. "Especially the sheriff, Bradley boys, and anyone else you think will side with them." Then without thinking of his Mrs. Johnson, he smiled and jokingly asked, "Think you can do that without getting shot?"

Mrs. Johnson stopped what she was doing, turned, and looked at her husband with a worried look.

"Sorry, ma'am," apologized Seth. "It was meant as a joke to help your husband relax a bit." He smiled. "Your man's gonna be just fine, Mrs. Johnson."

She put her hand over her heart and smiled dryly. "Perhaps we can do without the humor, Mr. Bowlen." Then she gave her husband another worried look. "You do as Mr. Bowlen tells you, George."

"I will Izzy." George stood from the table, took his hat from a hook on the wall next to the back door, smiled at his wife then kissed her on the cheek. "I'm gonna be alright, Izzy."

Wade, Seth, and Frank left the Indian at the table, followed him out the front door through the livery, and went over what they had discussed at the kitchen table.

George glanced down the street toward the saloon, looked at Seth, and grinned childlike. "Be back soon." Then he turned and walked toward the Rio Saloon.

They watched George Johnson as he walked away from the livery down the dark street toward the saloon.

Wade was concerned while watching Johnson disappear into the darkness. "Think he'll be alright?"

Seth considered. "He'll be just fine. The Sheriff would have no reason to suspect Mr. Johnson of doing anything but having a beer, as he said he sometimes does. Come on, let's get back inside and see what trouble the Indian has gotten into with the missus."

Twenty-Six

As planned, George Johnson walked into the Rio Saloon unnoticed, found a spot at the bar, said hello to John, the bartender, asked for a beer, and tossed a coin on the bar. After getting his beer, he turned and stood with his back against the bar to see the entire room and casually sipped his beer. The saloon was busy but not crowded, filled with piano music, loud talking, and laughter. He eyed each table nonchalantly while making mental notes of who sat with who and where.

"Hey, George," Sheriff Todd Hayes suddenly called out. "Bring that beer over here and have a seat." Then the sheriff told his uncle Red Hayes to grab an empty chair at the table behind him so George could sit down.

George did not know what else to do, so he forced a smile, walked to their table, and sat down.

Red Hayes was a short heavyset man of sixty with white hair and beard, thick lips, and an oversized nose. He laughed as he slapped George on the back. "Does that little woman of yours know you snuck out?"

That brought laughter from several of the other men.

George had always hated Red Hayes, but he grinned and forced a laugh showing his embarrassment. "She lets me out of the house now and again."

Steve Hardy sat at the next table with a whore on his lap. "You shoe that horse of mine like I told ya?"

George didn't have any use for Steve Hardy, but he forced another smile and thought he'd be happy when all three were arrested. "Sure did, Mr. Hardy. She's good as new."

Sheriff Hayes looked at Hardy. "George ain't one to shirk his duties, Steve." Then he turned to George with a big grin. "Yes sir.

255

George, here's a hard worker." Then Hayes turned and yelled at the bartender. "Bring us another round on, good old George."

George felt the sudden urge to get out of there and smiled. "Sorry, Sheriff, but I can't stay."

"Ah, nonsense," said Todd Hayes, his words slightly slurred from the liquor he had been drinking. He put one hand on George's shoulder and squeezed. "Buy a round, George, and then you can go back to that little barn you call a livery and that fine little wife you have." Hayes found humor in his words, looked at the others, and laughed.

"I really can't stay, Sheriff," said George Johnson as he stood.

"Sit down," said Todd Hayes, looking angry. "You ain't too good to have a drink with my family and me, are you?" Hayes looked around the saloon gesturing at the others. "We're all your friends George and customers at that." He nodded his head once. "Don't forget that."

George wanted to get up and leave, but the sheriff was drunk and persistent, and when he got drunk, he got mean. Johnson was confident he could take the sheriff in a fair fight, but he was alone and outnumbered. "Alright," he said with another forced smile. "One drink, and then I have to go." He turned to the bartender. "Bring this table a round and put it on my bill."

"What about the others?" Todd said as he gestured to the rest of the room with one hand.

George glanced around the room with a worried look. "Shit, Todd, I can't afford to buy drinks for this many."

Sheriff Todd Hayes looked at his uncle. "How about it, Red? Can old George run a tab for a few drinks?"

"I can't afford that many drinks," George argued with a smile as he started to get up.

"Alright," Todd said as he pulled him back into his chair. "Buy a round for my uncle here and me."

George Johnson had been gone for more than an hour on what was to be a quick scouting expedition. Now, Seth and the others were getting a little worried that something must have gone wrong. Seth looked at Wade, thinking he was young and fleet of foot. "Sneak down to the Rio, take a peek in a window, and see what the hell's going on." Seth looked at Mrs. Johnson and knew she was worried.

Frank grabbed Wade's arm. "Be careful. The Bradleys know what you look like."

Mrs. Johnson abruptly said, "I'll go."

Seth turned to her and said, "You can't go in there, Mrs. Johnson. That's no place for a lady such as yourself."

"I heard what you told my husband about these men, and if they recognize Mr. Garrison, my man could get hurt just for being there." She paused with a worried yet determined look. "I've gone in there plenty in the past after my George, same as a lot of wives in town. So, they won't think anything of it." She looked at Seth with worry on her face. "Please, Mr. Bowlen. Let me get my George out of that damn saloon before something happens."

Seth smiled at her and nodded. "Alright, Mrs. Johnson. Go get your husband. But we're gonna walk a ways behind just in case." Then they followed her out of the house and through the livery.

While the Indian sat on a bale of hay next to the livery door, Seth and the others followed Mrs. Johnson at a safe distance down the street, where they waited in the shadows of a nearby building. They watched as she walked up the steps and went inside the saloon. Moments later, laughter erupted from the saloon doors just before she and her husband walked out the swinging doors.

Red Hayes got up from his chair, hurried to the door, and smiled as he looked over the swinging doors as the Johnsons hurried up the street and yelled, "Don't be too hard on him, Isabel." Then he laughed, returned to the table, and took a drink of beer.

Seth stepped out from the shadows to make sure whoever was at the saloon's door was gone. Then seeing a lonely rider coming up the street, he stepped back into the shadows and softly said, "Rider coming up the Mexican side."

As the Johnsons headed for the livery, Wade and the others stepped back into the shadows beside the bank, watching a rider pass in and out of the light from the windows.

Seth grinned. "It's French."

"I wonder how the heck he knew we were in Paso Del Rio," asked Frank.

"Beats the shit out of me," replied Seth as they watched French ride by at a walk toward the livery. "Let's ask him." Seth stepped out of the shadows and quietly asked, "You lost again?"

French turned in the saddle as his hand went for the butt of his pistol. Seeing who it was, he turned his horse and pulled up. "What the hell are you three doing standing out here in the dark?"

Seth looked toward the saloon, worried that someone was to come out. "Come over here, Billy."

French nudged his mare toward them, pulled up, and got down. "You boys thinking of robbing the bank?"

Seth turned, looked at the bank, and chuckled. "Long story."

Wade looked concerned and asked how Todd Jewett was doing.

The smile left Marshal French's face. "Todd died the night you boys left."

"Died," replied a surprised Wade. "How?"

French shook his head. "Infection. Least that's what Doc Brewster said killed him, but I say it was these boys we're after."

"Sorry to hear that," said Wells. "I know you were fond of the boy."

Billy French shook his head with a sad look. "Gonna miss the dumb shit, that's for sure."

Seth glanced back along the street to the saloon and pointed toward the livery. "How'd you know we were in Paso Del Rio?"

Billy French looked sad. "I came across a wagon about dusk and figured you boys dug the graves and buried them poor folk. I followed your trail until it got dark, but I knew you were headed here, so I kept to the stage road letting the moonlight guide me."

Wade glanced back at the saloon. "Maybe we should get back to the livery before someone see's us."

Seth nodded in agreement. "Our stock's up the street at the livery. Let's walk, and I'll explain what's been going on." Seth told Billy French about the Bradley boys, the sheriff, and the others in the Rio Saloon as they walked. Then he told him about the blacksmith George Johnson, his wife, and how George went to the saloon to see how many were inside.

Billy French was surprised at seeing Dark Cloud sitting comfortably on the bale of hay, his back against the livery wall, his rifle leaning against his shoulder. "Howdy, Chief."

Dark Cloud considered being called "Chief" an insult by most men, but he liked Marshal French, so he smiled and gave him a quick, friendly wave.

French tied his horse at the railing and followed them through the livery to the house behind it. As they approached the door, they could hear Mrs. Johnson questioning her husband's intelligence, and not in a nice way. That brought grins to their otherwise somber faces as Seth knocked softly on the door. The loud talking suddenly became a whisper, and while they could not make out the words, they had a good idea of who was winning the argument. A couple of moments passed, and then the door opened.

George had that look all husbands have after a lost argument, but he managed a smile, stepped back, and motioned them inside. "It's the deputies and another fella, Izzy!"

"Bring them into the kitchen so's you can talk. I'll put on a pot of coffee and then go upstairs so you men can discuss how they're gonna get you killed."

George Johnson gave Seth a small grin and raised brow, and then he and the others walked into the kitchen where Isabelle was busy making coffee.

She never looked up. "You men have a seat. The coffee will be ready soon."

"Thank you, ma'am," Seth said, gesturing to the marshal. "This here's United States Marshal Billy French from Santa Fe, Mrs. Johnson."

She turned, having the face of a woman upset about something, and cleaned her hands on her apron as she walked across the room to shake his hand. "We have some apple pie leftover from supper if you're hungry."

Marshal French combed his hair back with the fingers of his right hand and smiled. "Pie sounds mighty good right now, thank you."

She gestured to the table. "You have a seat at the head of the table." Then she walked toward the stove while talking to her husband. "George, take their hats and set them on that table in the corner." When she got to the stove, she stopped and turned. "Ain't had this many men in my house all at once since George's Pa died." She smiled. "Sort of warms up the kitchen." Then she gestured around the table. "You others sit where you can while George pours the coffee, and I give a piece of pie to the marshal."

"Hope it's not your last piece," said Billy French as he sat down.

"No, it ain't." Then she glanced around at the others. "We killed the other pie earlier this evening." Setting the plate and pie with a fork in front of him, she looked at her husband and then at Billy. "I'm mad at George right now, Marshal, in case you were wondering about the loud talking as you walked up to the door." Then she looked at Dark Cloud standing in the corner by the back door, watching them, and smiled. "Would you like a cup of coffee?"

He thought about that and quickly answered, "Coffee bitter."

She smiled. "Maybe I can fix that for you." She turned and poured a cup of coffee, added some honey she had in a jar, stirred it a few times, and handed it to the Indian while the others watched with interest.

The Indian took the cup, looked at the black coffee, held the cup to his lips, and felt the steam against his skin while smelling the aroma.

"It's hot," Isabelle warned. "Drink it slow and in small sips." Then she imitated sipping.

He looked at her with a puzzled expression, put the cup to his lips, took a small drink, and at tasting the honey, grinned. "White man's coffee not bitter."

The others laughed.

While the Indian enjoyed the coffee with honey, Seth turned to George Johnson sitting between him and Billy French. "How many inside?"

George looked at Seth. "Close to fifteen, maybe more. I ain't sure."

French had just put a fork full of apple pie into his mouth, stopped chewing, looked at Seth, and raised a worried brow.

"Two, three each," Frank said with a concerned look.

"Can you show us on the table here where everyone's sitting?" asked Seth.

"You bet," said George, then he moved the plates, cups, and saucers on the table. "This here's the door," he said as he placed a saltshaker on the table. Then he took a butter knife from the table. "This here's the bar where John Hart, the bartender, works."

Billy shoved the last of his pie into his mouth. "Has he a gun tucked away behind the bar?"

"Shotgun," said George as he pointed to a spot on the knife. "Keeps it just about here, which is where he usually stands."

Marshal Billy French shook his head thoughtfully as he looked at Wells. "Frank, you keep your eyes on the bartender. If you think he's going for the shotgun, kill him. Don't think about it. Just do it. I don't want a twelve-gauge cutting a couple of us in half." He leaned forward while looking at Frank. "You're gonna have to keep an eye on the Wilkins boys as well, so position yourself where you can see both."

Frank raised his brow. "Hope there's a big post by the door."

"There is." Replied Johnson.

260

Seth grinned at Frank and then turned to George. "How many whores?" Then he looked at Mrs. Johnson. "Sorry for the crudeness Mrs. Johnson."

"I've heard worse, Mr. Bowlen."

George glanced at his wife and looked at Seth. "Three. One on Steve Hardy's lap, two others are sitting with Josh and Greg Thornton at another table about here."

Billy looked at Seth. "We'll have to get them out of the way soon as we walk in."

Seth nodded in agreement while Mr. Johnson continued.

George picked up a pepper shaker and placed it close to the saltshaker he used as the door. "Sheriff Hayes, Red Hayes, Ike Wilkins, and their brother-in-law, Harry, are sitting at the first table." Then he placed a cup on the table. "This here is where the two Bradley boys and that damn Steve Hardy were sitting along with the whore Jolene." He paused in thought and then moved another empty cup next to the salt and paper shakers. "The two Wilkins boys are sitting here with a couple of rowdies named Josh and Greg Thornton and two girls."

"That makes eleven," Wade said.

Everyone was quiet as they studied the bar's layout on the table.

Seth looked at George. "You said close to fifteen. Who are we missing?"

"I can't think," replied George with a frustrated look.

Billy put his hand on George's shoulder. "This is important, Mr. Johnson. Try clearing your head and picture the rest of the saloon."

He thought for a moment, picked up another cup, placed it on the table, and then another. I think these two tables had three each, but I ain't positive." He looked at Billy and then Seth. "I was a little busy trying to get out of having to buy the whole place a drink." He looked down at the table. "Oh yeah, the piano player sits here against the far wall under the stairs."

"What about the piano player?" asked Seth.

George looked at him. "What do you mean?"

Billy French leaned closer to George. "He means, does he own a gun, and how loyal is he to the owner, Red Hayes?"

"Loyal?"

French was frustrated. "Is he willing to die for Red or any of the others?"

George shrugged. "Can't say for certain. Pete's been around a while, but I can't answer for sure."

Billy turned to Wade. "You watch the player and the last two tables."

Disappointed, Wade nodded and looked down at the mock saloon on the table, wishing he could keep an eye on the Bradly brothers instead.

Billy turned to Seth. "The Bradley and Hardy table is yours."

"Let me have the Bradleys," asked Wade.

French looked at Seth and then Wade. "I know you want to get the men who killed your friend back in Harper, and I want to get them for killing Todd Jewett and Sheriff Boedecker. Nothing personal, Wade, but I know Seth and Frank. You've still to prove yourself."

"I understand," said Wade.

French stood and looked down at the silverware cups and shakers thoughtfully. "We'll stop at our mounts and get our Winchesters. I'll deal with the sheriff. Maybe he'll side with us once he knows I'm a United States Marshal and you're my deputies."

Doubtful, Frank nodded to the Indian. "What about him?"

Billy French looked at Dark Cloud. "We're leaving you outside, Chief."

Frank saw the disappointment on the Indian's face. "You know what the Bradley boys and this Hardy fella look like from when they tried to sell them two little gals to you. After the shooting starts, if either walk out those swinging doors, we're more'n likely dead. Kill them, get out of town, and head north as fast as that big gray of yours will run." Frank paused. "Think you can handle that?"

Dark Cloud looked at Frank, smiled as he stood with his rifle across his belly, and nodded.

"It's almost midnight," Billy French said. "Let's get to it."

George got up from the table. "I'll get my shotgun."

Mrs. Johnson looked at him with a shocked and worried look.

Seth held up one hand. "No," he said, shaking his head. "This isn't your fight, Mr. Johnson, but it is ours."

Billy turned. "What gauge?" he asked, referring to the shotgun.

"Twelve."

French looked at Wade. "I left my shotgun in Santa Fe when we returned for the wagon, and that Sharps of yours is no good in tight quarters." Then he looked at George Johnson. "Can Wade borrow the twelve-gauge?"

"He sure as hell can." Then George hurried into another room and returned with the shotgun and a box of shells. "There's already two in it and eight more in this box."

Wade took the gun and the box of shells while the others walked outside. "I'll see you get the shotgun back, Mr. Johnson." He grinned. "But you probably won't get the shells back." Then Wade turned and followed the others outside to the livery.

When George and Wade got to the open doors of the livery, no one was talking while taking off their spurs. He watched as Billy French pulled his rifle out of the scabbard of his saddle and made sure a shell was in the chamber. Frank did the same while Wade put on his black duster and emptied the box of shells into his right coat pocket.

Seth was the last to pull his rifle out of its scabbard, and after he made sure a shell was in the chamber, he looked at the others. "Ready?"

Twenty-Seven

The town was otherwise quiet, its good citizens at home with their families peacefully sleeping, unaware that a small war was about to occur in their peaceful little town. Billy French, Seth Bowlen, Frank Wells, Wade Garrison, and the Indian walked shoulder to shoulder down the dark street with all eyes fixed on the lighted windows and door of the Rio Saloon. Though words flowed through their heads, no one spoke as the adrenaline flowing through each of their bodies caused their hearts to beat a little faster. Music spilled from the cantinas on the Mexican side of the street, mixing with the drunken laughter and loud piano music from the Rio Saloon on the American side.

Wade looked up into the full moon and night sky boasting a thousand stars and wondered if Emmett and the others these men had killed were watching. His heartbeat was fast, and his hands were sweaty. Wiping them on his pants as he walked, he hoped he would make a good accounting of himself and not let the others down. Laughter from the saloon made him look from the heavens to the lighted doorway and windows reflecting across the boardwalk and into the dark street.

When the group stopped at the corner of the saloon building, Wade stared at the lighted windows and knew that either death or life awaited them just inside. Suddenly visions of Sarah crying over his death filled his mind.

Frank looked at Dark Cloud and nodded to the corner of the building.

The Indian quietly melted into the dark shadows against the corner wall of the saloon.

As the others stepped onto the boardwalk and walked to the doors, they paused while Billy French looked over the top of the swinging doors into the saloon. Seeing everything was as Mr. Johnson had said, he put the nose of the barrel of his rifle against the swinging doors, pushed them open, and walked in, followed by Seth, Frank, and then Wade.

Everyone inside the saloon turned and looked up in silence as Frank moved to the left, giving him a clear view of the bartender and Wilkins' table. Wade made his way across the room with the shotgun toward the piano player who had stopped playing.

Seth and Billy's boots on the hardwood floor broke the silence as the two walked toward the table where Sheriff Todd Hayes sat.

The sheriff glanced from one man to the other. "What the hell's going on here?" he asked as he looked up at Seth and then Billy.

Billy quickly glanced around the room. "Everyone, just keep your hands on the tables where we can see them." Then he looked at the women. "You girls, get up and go on now."

Irritated by their hesitation, Billy yelled, "Now!"

Reluctantly the three girls got up and hurried up the stairs, where they stood on the balcony and watched.

Sheriff Todd Hayes watched the three girls hurry away from the tables, then looked at the four men and figured they came for his nephews. "I'm Todd Hayes, Sheriff of Paso Del Rio. Something we can do for you boys?"

The Bradley brothers recognized Billy French, Seth, and Frank from Pine Springs.

Billy French moved the lapel of his coat so they could see his Marshal's badge pinned to the pocket of his shirt. "Name's Billy French," he said with authority. "I'm a United States Marshal from Santa Fe, and these men are my deputies."

Sheriff Hayes looked at his uncle Red Hayes, the Bradley boys, and then at Billy standing a few feet from the table. Experience told the sheriff not to make any sudden moves, so he sat back with a relaxed and unthreatening look. "As I said, Marshal, I'm Todd Hayes, Sheriff of Paso Del Rio." Then he nodded to his uncle. "This here's my uncle Red Hayes, the owner of this fine establishment and a member of the City Council." Then Sheriff Hayes looked at the Winchester the marshal held across his belly and the rifles the others held. "Santa Fe's a far piece," he said. "What brings you, boys, to Paso Del Rio?"

Marshal French glanced around the room, stopping at the Bradley boys' and Steve Hardy's table. "We've been trailing you boys and burying bodies for quite a spell, and now that we've caught up to you, we're gonna arrest you."

Sheriff Hayes thought about that as he glanced at his nephews and then looked up at Billy. "Mind telling me what for?"

"Murder and rape," said Billy as he looked at Sheriff Hayes. "Since you're the town sheriff, I'm officially advising you of our intentions."

Sheriff Todd Hayes leaned forward, rested his elbows on the table, and looked thoughtful as his left hand scratched his white beard. He started to say something when the legs of Paul Bradley's chair scraped across the floor as he slowly pushed it away from the table.

Seth pointed his Winchester at him. "That's far enough, Son. We'd like to take you alive, but dead's less trouble and just as good."

Paul looked at Seth and the Winchester he was holding and sat back, gesturing submission by placing both hands back on the table.

Sheriff Hayes turned and looked at his nephews and Steve Hardy recalling their story of being falsely accused. Then he glanced at the table next to his nephews, where Jake and Norm Wilkins sat with Greg and Josh Thornton. He turned to the marshal and asked, "Mind me asking where your deputies are from?"

"What difference does that make?" answered French.

"Just curious," replied the Sheriff.

Billy thought that was a strange question but answered anyway. "Colorado."

Todd Hayes nodded at Seth and Frank. "They from Harper?"

"I'm from Harper," said Wade.

Sheriff Hayes looked at Wade standing several feet away, holding a shotgun. Then he looked at Billy. "I heard some men were looking to revenge a dead family member of theirs---"

"Friend," interrupted Wade.

Hayes looked at Wade. "Alright, a friend." Then he turned back to French. "The way I heard it, you and these Colorado deputies have been chasing the wrong bunch."

Billy was sitting on a short fuse as he looked at the Sheriff. "We're here to take them back to Santa Fe to stand trial for rape and murder of a family near Pine Springs, another north of Santa Fe, and a family not far from here traveling in a covered wagon." He looked at the two Bradley brothers and then at Steve Hardy. "The trail of their terrible deeds leads here to Paso Del Rio." He gave Sheriff Hayes a stern look. "We mean to take them back with us, and I ain't asking your permission."

Sheriff Hayes glanced back at his nephews, wondered about their story, and then looked at Billy French. "Mind if I get up?"

"Just do it slow like," replied Billy.

Sheriff Hayes slowly stood and looked at Paul and Kevin Bradley while thinking of his dear dead sister. Remembering his promise to do his best and watch out for her two sons as she lay dying, he wanted to believe them. But he was having doubts as he looked at them, wondering if they were rapists and murderers. "These boys say they're innocent, Marshal." Then he turned to Billy. "The first thing they did was tell me about being falsely blamed for a killing up north in Harper, Colorado."

"They did the killing," Wade said in anger. "A saloon full of people saw it and described them as the men that shot an unarmed drover by the name of Emmett Spears five times."

Marshal French looked at the sheriff. "Did they tell you about them raping women and killing their entire families, including children? Did they say anything about kidnapping two little girls or stealing horses, and only God knows what else?"

Sheriff Hayes looked at his nephews for a long moment wondering which was the truth. "They also mentioned that they were blamed for a thing or two after the Harper incident." He turned back to French. "But that doesn't make them guilty."

Billy was getting impatient with the sheriff. "I understand those two are family, Sheriff, and I can appreciate your feelings, but they're going back to Santa Fe with us." He paused. "It would be a mistake if you doubted that."

Frank was watching Paul when he saw movement out of the corner of his eyes and turned, seeing the bartender John Hart raising the shotgun over the top of the bar.

At the same instant, Red Hayes saw him and yelled, "No!"

Frank Wells had already turned, and before he realized Red Hayes had yelled at the bartender, he pulled the trigger of his Winchester, hitting him in the chest shattering his breastbone. The force of the bullet knocked the man back against the counter behind the bar, knocking over stacks of empty beer mugs and bottles of whiskey. As the bartender slid to the floor with a surprised look, he pulled both triggers of the shotgun and blew out the front of the bar.

While everyone was looking at the bartender, Steve Hardy drew his gun and shot Seth in the right side. Seth managed to get off a shot hitting Hardy in the left chest, knocking him back onto an empty table falling to the floor.

Suddenly, and against all reasoning, the piano player reached for the pistol he kept above the piano. As he turned with the gun in his hand to fire at Billy, Wade pulled one of the two triggers of the shotgun. The force of the buckshot slammed the player against the wall next to the piano. As he slid down the wall leaving a trail of blood, Wade turned to three men that leaped from their chairs under a table, yelling, "Don't shoot! Don't shoot!" Believing they were no threat, Wade looked from them to the Thornton and Wilkins boys, who turned their table over. He pulled the second trigger that misfired, and while he reloaded, both men got off a shot, hitting Frank Wells in the right shoulder and stomach. As Frank fell back against the wall between the window and doorway, he fired his Winchester, narrowly missing the Thornton boy. With the shotgun loaded, Wade pulled one trigger and then the other, hitting Josh Thornton in the chest, knocking him back several feet, and ending up under a window. A bullet hit the large post supporting the second-floor balcony next to Wade, who dove for cover behind a table and chairs.

Greg Thornton rose, fired, and hit Billy in the upper-left arm. Billy managed to get off a quick shot but missed Greg Thornton, who quickly ducked behind an overturned table.

Sheriff Todd Hayes stood with hands raised, yelling at his nephews, "You're gonna get killed, boys. Drop your guns and give yourselves up!"

Kevin Bradley rose from behind the overturned table and yelled, "Go to hell!" Then he shot his uncle in the chest.

Sheriff Hayes grabbed his chest with both hands as he fell back into his chair, where he died looking up at Billy French.

Billy got off a shot, hitting Kevin Bradley in the left shoulder, knocking him backward onto another table, tipping it over.

Paul Bradley rose from behind the table, fired at Billy French, then helped his brother get behind the table.

Billy ran toward the bar, diving over the counter in a hail of bullets landing next to the dead bartender. He quickly examined the wound in his left arm, drew his pistol, and got on his knees. Taking a quick look over the bar, he fired, then quickly crouched down while bullets passed over his head breaking the glasses and bottles on the shelf behind the bar.

Red Hayes was hit in the back of the head and slumped across the table. Ike Wilkins sat at the same table as Sheriff Todd Hayes and Red

Hayes and dove from his chair to the floor. He yelled at his nephews to stop shooting before they both got killed.

Seth saw Frank sitting on the floor, leaning against the wall holding his stomach and fired twice at an overturned table while crawling toward Frank. Grabbing his arm, Seth pulled him onto the floor, shielding him as best he could while firing blindly at the overturned tables.

Wade loaded the shotgun and blasted a table with both barrels, not knowing if anyone was behind it.

A wounded Norm Wilkins stood up from behind the overturned table and ran toward the broken window, firing blindly behind him. French rose above the bar, fired, and hit Norm in the side, spinning him around as he crashed through the window onto the boardwalk.

Jake Wilkins stood and ran for the window, and while Billy French and Seth managed to get off a shot, but both missed. Jake fired blindly as he jumped through the broken window onto the boardwalk. Moments later, a single Winchester sounded, and Wade knew that Dark Cloud would not have missed.

Paul and Kevin Bradley reloaded their guns, stood, and fired as they ran and jumped through a broken window onto the boardwalk, followed by Greg Thornton.

Afraid the Bradley boys were getting away, Wade ran out the swinging doors finding Norm Wilkins lying face down across the boardwalk stairs and the body of Jake Wilkins lying on his back in the middle of the street. Wade turned, seeing the Indian sitting on the boardwalk, his back against the saloon wall, his rifle on the boardwalk next to him. Wade knew he was shot, ran to the Indian, knelt next to him, and examined the wound he knew was bad. While Dark Cloud coughed up blood, he turned his head and pointed a finger toward the livery. "They go."

Hearing horses, Wade turned in time to see two riders disappear behind a building into Mexico and knew it was the Bradley brothers. Disappointed, Wade turned back to Dark Cloud, whose eyes had closed, and his head turned slightly to one side, looking as if he were sleeping. Wade felt bad about Dark Cloud and wished the Indian had stayed in Colorado. The night was eerily silent as Wade noticed the people gathered in the street and on the boardwalks. As he stood, he knew what happened in the saloon was over and hoped Seth and the others were okay. He looked at Dark Cloud for a long moment, picked up the Indian's rifle, and walked along the boardwalk toward the swinging doors. A gun fired, and a bullet hit the wall of the saloon next to him. He drew his gun as he turned and saw a man on his knees trying to fire an unloaded weapon. Wade stepped into the street, keeping his gun pointed at the man, and walked toward him. "Drop it."

Greg Thornton smiled as he dropped his unloaded gun and collapsed onto his back. As Wade approached, he looked up at him. "You killed my brother with that damn shotgun."

Wade knelt next to Greg Thornton and set the Indian's rifle on the ground. "You and your brother should have stayed out of it."

Thornton grimaced and stiffened in pain as he nodded toward the Indian. "I killed that friend of yours who was waiting outside."

Wade glanced back at Dark Cloud in the shadows of the saloon and then at Greg Thornton. Seeing he was gutshot, Wade knew it was Dark Cloud's bullet and smiled. "Looks like you did alright, but from the way you're bleeding, I'd say that Indian killed you as well."

Thornton looked surprised. "Indian?" Then he smiled ironically. "Be damned. I didn't see who was shooting." Thornton looked up at Wade as he coughed up blood. "You and that damn Indian can both go to hell."

"I'm sure we will." Wade placed the barrel of his pistol under Thornton's chin, looked into his terrified eyes, and pulled the trigger. He picked up the Indian's gun, slowly stood, and walked back into the Rio Saloon. Inside, he paused to look around at the carnage that took less than thirty seconds.

A wounded Marshal, Billy French, stood behind the bar, his rifle lying on the counter. Seeing Wade, he raised his glass, looked at him for a long moment, then gulped his whiskey.

Wade glanced around the saloon of overturned tables, chairs, and bodies. A few feet away, Sheriff Hayes' lifeless body sat slumped in a chair as if he were sleeping, his uncle Red Hayes sprawled on top of the table. Ike Wilkins sat on the floor next to Sheriff Hayes's chair with his head buried in his hands, sobbing.

Seth was sitting on the floor a few feet away, leaning back against the wall next to Frank, lying on the floor with his head on Seth's leg. Wade walked over, knelt, put one hand on Seth's shoulder, and asked if he was alright.

Seth looked up with red, teary eyes. "Frank's gone." Then he closed his eyes, lowered his head, and quietly wept.

Wade looked down at the face of Frank Wells and thought of Dark Cloud and Deputy Jewett. As guilt found him, he remembered Seth's words of warning that day in sisters. Maybe they'd all be alive if he had just stayed in Harper as Sarah had asked.

Marshal French poured another whiskey, gulped it down, picked up his Winchester, walked over to Wade, Seth, and Frank, and knelt next to Seth. Knowing Frank was dead, he put one hand on Seth's shoulder. "He was a hell of a good man."

Seth simply nodded.

Billy thought about the Indian, stood, and glanced around, looking for Dark Cloud. "Has anyone seen the Chief?"

"He didn't make it," said Wade sadly. "But he got two."

Billy looked sad about that and asked, "Any sign of the Bradleys?"

George Johnson stepped forward. "The Bradley boys took off on a couple of your horses."

"Which two?" asked Wade.

"The big gray and the black and white." He looked regretful. "I'd have stopped them, but you had my shotgun."

Wade thought it was best George never had the shotgun and said, "Frank's and the Indian's horses," while remembering his promise to Dark Cloud.

An angry Billy French turned, kicked at an overturned chair, and raised his voice, "Damn it to hell!" Then he turned a chair upright, sat down, and looked at Frank and Seth.

A middle-aged man dressed in his nightshirt and dark pants with suspenders hanging at his side paused at the door and looked at the carnage. He stepped inside and walked over to Ike Wilkins, still sitting on the floor. "What the hell happened here, Ike?"

Ike looked up, his eyes red and teary, and then he stood from the floor and sat down in his chair. "It all happened so fast." He nodded at Marshal French. "The marshal was trying to get Todd to arrest his two nephews and a friend of theirs for murder and rape so they could take them back to Santa Fe to stand trial." He looked at the lifeless body of Sheriff Hayes in the chair next to him. "But all hell broke loose when Kevin Bradley up and shot his uncle. I can't believe he just up and killed him. The sheriff died just as you see him."

The man in the nightshirt and suspenders was short, heavyset, bald, and looked a little afraid as he approached Billy and, in a soft voice, said, "Excuse me, Marshal."

Billy French looked up and waited for the man to speak.

The man leaned closer and whispered, "I'm Jeb Smith Marshal. I own the General Store, and I was wondering what the Bradley boys are wanted for?"

Anger filled Billy as he looked up at the man, thinking he was a fool. He started to tell him to get away from him when George Johnson and the doctor pushed their way through the small crowd that had gathered just inside the door.

Doc Abernathy paused to look around the saloon at overturned chairs and tables with bullet holes, bodies, and blood on the floor. He was young with black hair, brown eyes, and a thin mustache looking like he belonged in a big city back east instead of a border town like Paso Del Rio. He knelt next to Marshal French. "I'm Doc Abernathy. Let me take a look at this arm of yours."

French pulled away. "It'll wait." Then he nodded at Seth. "Take a look at Seth Doc. I think he got one in the stomach."

Seth looked up. "Side. Went clean through." He looked at the Doc. "I'll be alright."

The doc knelt next to Frank Wells, moved his coat to one side, and, seeing the holes in his blood-soaked shirt, knew he was dead.

"He's gone," said Seth.

Marshal Billy French stood, looked at Wade, and said, "Let's get a drink." They walked to the bar, where French poured two drinks and handed one to Wade. He turned to look at the scene that quickly played through his mind, gulped down the drink, slammed the glass down on the bar, and looked at Wade. "Frank's dead, and so's the Indian. Seth's wounded pretty bad, but I think he'll make it, and my arm's not much use to me right now." He looked at Wade. "You've got to go it alone now." He paused with a determined look and lowered his voice. "You can't let these two live." He paused. "Understand what I'm saying?"

Wade nodded while glancing around at the slaughter.

Billy gulped another whiskey. "You'll be alone in Mexico, and that badge you're wearing won't do you much good once you ride across that street outside. Just the same, it might be best if you keep it in plain sight. Stay clear of the Mexican army," Warned French. "I suggest you try and get a couple of hours sleep and head out just before sunup."

Seeing George Johnson standing nearby, Billy called him over. "Would it be alright if Wade slept at your place for a couple of hours?"

George looked at Wade and then Billy. "He sure can." He looked at Wade. "As long as you need Mr. Garrison."

Wade smiled. "Appreciate it, Mr. Johnson."

Doc Abernathy finished tending Seth, walked over to French, and looked at his arm. "I best get you and that other one over there," he said, nodding at Seth. "To my office down the street." Then he looked at the man in the nightshirt. "Jeb, see these two get to my office. The door's unlocked."

Jeb nodded. "Sure thing Doc."

Then, Doc Abernathy looked around. "Nothing more I can do here. The rest need burying." Then he looked at Jeb. "I'll be along directly."

Billy French, Wade, and George Johnson walked over to Seth and helped him up, and as they walked toward the door, Billy told Seth that Wade was going it alone.

Seth stopped and looked at Wade. "Go easy. Don't go rushing after them. Take your time and do as Billy here told you. And try and get some rest before you leave. I doubt they've had much time to rest, and they'll have to stop sooner or later."

"Alright, Seth," said Wade.

Billy held his wounded arm and looked at Wade. "Don't rush into anything and do as Seth said." Then he leaned closer and lowered his voice. "Do like I said. They can't get away."

Wade gave Billy a long look considering what he said. "They won't."

Seth Bowlen and Jeb walked out the swinging doors heading for the Doc's office.

Wade turned to take one last look around before picking up the shotgun and followed George Johnson out the swinging doors to the boardwalk, where he handed Johnson the shotgun.

Wade tossed and turned, trying to sleep, but the events of the night kept getting in the way, and he only managed little naps. Sleep and exhaustion finally won the battle, and he slept for a couple of hours. He was looking up at George Johnson, gently shaking his shoulder, when he opened his eyes.

"It'll be light soon, Mr. Garrison," said Johnson.

Wade felt tired as he sat up, put both feet on the cold floor, and sat on the edge of the bed with his head in his hands. Again, the memories of Frank, the Indian, and Todd Jewett raced through his mind. He looked out the window into the darkness and knew they would be alive had it not been for his promise of revenge.

"I done saddled that mare of yours, Mr. Garrison."

Wade looked up at George, nodded, and shoved his left foot into his boot. "Thanks, George. I'm a lot younger than you, so please, call me Wade."

George grinned. "Part of being in business, I guess. My missus is fixing you something to eat. When you're ready, come into the kitchen."

As George closed the door, Wade put on his other boot as he looked around the small, meagerly furnished bedroom and thought it must have been for their daughter, who had passed away. Still tired, he retrieved his hat from the short bedpost of the narrow, single bed and walked out of the room.

George Johnson was sitting at the table nursing a cup of coffee, and Mrs. Johnson, dressed in an old faded pink cotton robe, was busy over the stove when Wade walked into the kitchen. She looked up from what she was doing, smiled, and gestured to the back door. "You can wash up outside, Mr. Garrison, and I'll pour you a cup of coffee."

"Wade, please, Mrs. Johnson." He thought she looked tired. "Hope I wasn't a bother to you and Mr. Johnson last night."

"No bother at all," replied George.

Izzy smiled. "You weren't no bother, Mr. Garrison. Go on now, wash up, then come in and eat your breakfast."

"Yes ma'am." Wade walked outside, washed his face and hands in cold water, dried them on a damp towel, and stepped back inside the kitchen. Sitting down, he looked around the table and thought of the Indian getting his first and last taste of apple pie and honey coffee. Of Frank Wells with that big laugh of his.

Mrs. Johnson placed a plate of eggs, a slice of beef, and fried potatoes on the table and then sat across from him, looking worried. "George tells me you're going after those two men alone?"

He looked into her soft eyes. "Yes ma'am"

She thought of the men that had died in the saloon, looking concerned. "You don't have to go."

George looked at his wife. "Man does what he has to, Izzy."

Wade looked at her and remembered Sarah asking him not to go. "These are terrible men, Mrs. Johnson. I can't tell you all the bad things they have done to good families."

"It's almost sunup," warned Mr. Johnson.

She knew she could not stop him, so she turned away from the table.

Wade looked at George, nodded, took another bite of food, drank the last of his coffee, and looked at Mrs. Johnson as she sat across from him. "I can't let them ride away to continue doing such deplorable things to people, even in Mexico."

She looked disappointed. "No, I suppose not." She got up from the table, picked up a small burlap sack, and handed it to him. "Some food so's you won't go hungry."

"Thank you." Wade smiled as he took the sack and followed George out the door to the livery.

Wade tied the burlap sack to the saddle horn, checked the two canteens, made sure they were full, and then led his mare outside into the cool morning air. He slipped into his black duster, looked down the street at the Rio Saloon, and thought of Frank Wells and the Indian Dark Cloud. He looked up at the light blue eastern horizon, knew the sun would be up soon, turned, and offered his hand to George Johnson. "Thanks for your hospitality, Mr. Johnson, and the use of your shotgun."

"My pleasure Mr. Garrison." They shook hands then Wade led the mare into the street and climbed up onto his saddle.

"Be careful, and good luck to you."

He felt he could use some luck, pulled his hat down, and nudged the mare into a walk. The warm sun crested the hills to the east, spreading its warmth on the empty street of Paso Del Rio as Wade rode toward the Rio Saloon. He thought of Seth, sitting next to Frank on the saloon floor with tears in his eyes. He remembered the Indian dying as he sat against the building corner in the dark, hoping to get the gray back and fulfill his promise to the Indian. George Johnson's words, be careful and good luck kept repeating themselves over and over in Wade's mind. Being careful was something he planned on doing now that he would be alone in Mexico. As he turned his mare south across the street, he glanced toward the Rio Saloon and nudged the horse into a trot.

Unable to sleep, Seth got out of bed, walked to the window, opened the curtain, and looked down on the dirt street just as Wade rode into Mexico and whispered, "Vaya Con Dios, son."

Twenty-Eight

A small, yellow dog was lying on the porch of Gil Robinson's house enjoying the late afternoon sun when it suddenly sat up with ears alert, staring at the tree line at the edge of the canyon. After a moment of watching the tree line, the dog lay back down, rested his head on his front paws, and closed his eyes. Something he heard disturbed his nap, and he sat up, staring at the tree line at the base of the hill where Roscoe's Creek flows quietly from the mouth of the canyon. Excited, the little yellow dog sat up, tail wagging as it whined and then barked.

Gil stopped chopping wood, turned to look at what the dog barked at, and, seeing nothing, told him to be quiet. As he went back to the task of chopping firewood, the dog continued barking. Gil turned and yelled at the dog, but he just ignored Gil and jumped off the porch. Watching the dog run toward the trees and Roscoe's Creek barking, he heard the neigh of a horse. Gil raised one hand shading his eyes from the low sun, fearing for the little dog that kept running toward the tree line. Then Gil saw a solitary rider emerge from the canyon's trees at a slow walk.

When the dog got to the rider, it jumped up and down, barking and whining as it ran alongside the red sorrel horse. The rider pulled up, climbed down, and picked up the dog that continued to whine. Gil watched as the dog squirmed and licked the rider's face with such enthusiasm it almost knocked off the rider's black hat. Seeing the rider was Wade Garrison, Gil smiled and whispered, "Glory be dear Lord." Setting the ax against the stump, he pulled a rag from his back pocket and wiped his hands as he walked toward Wade and the dog.

The small dog had settled down, looking happy and content in Wade's arms as they walked toward Gil. Wade grinned. "You ain't planning on licking my face, are you, Gil?"

276

Gil Robinson grinned and walked a little faster. "Seth came back months ago saying you went into Mexico after them two no goods" Then, holding out an open hand, he looked into Wade's tired eyes. His long hair bulged from under his black Texas flat hat, his face covered with a dark brown beard, and his clothes showed the wear of a long trip. "Did you get them?"

Wade shook Gil's hand while holding the dog cradled in his left arm. "You look like you've recovered from your wounds. How is Bowlen?"

"I have, and Seth's doing just fine keeping a tight clamp on Sisters." Then worried about how Wade looked, he asked, "How're you doing, Wade?"

He looked down at the small dog and gently petted its head. "I'm doing alright."

As Gil watched him with the little yellow dog, he thought he was different somehow.

Wade smiled. "A mite tired."

"Did you get them, bastards?" asked Gil once again.

Wade nodded, and then he noticed the girls playing behind the house. "How are them two young gals doing?"

Gil looked toward them and smiled. "They're fine."

Wade looked puzzled. "What are their names?"

Gil looked at Wade with a worried look. "Why, they're Jessie and Clementine."

"Oh yeah," Wade said as he watched them play, then he looked at Gil. "Dark Cloud told us about running into you, saying you had a fever."

"I was sick for a while, but as you can see, we made it." Gil looked sad. "Too bad about Frank and the Indian."

Wade slowly nodded and looked down at the dog. "Yeah, it is. They were good men."

Gil took off his hat, scratched his head, and looked at the girls. "After we got home and I got well enough to ride, I drove a wagon out to the Miller place, gathered up the girls' belongings, then closed the place up." He looked back toward the house. "My wife Annie and our Annabelle sure have taken a liking to them two, and it appears the little gals have settled right in."

Wade smiled, looking pleased. "That's good." Then he handed him the little dog, climbed up on his horse, and settled into his saddle. He looked around at the small house and yard, then at the edge of the town of

Roscoe's Creek, sitting a couple hundred yards to the east. "You have done well, Gil."

Gil stared at Wade with a worried look and thought he looked tired and could use a good meal and rest. "Wanna stay for a day or two? It looks like you could use a good home-cooked meal. I'm sure my missus and them two little gals would like to visit with you a spell."

Wade smiled softly as he looked at the house listening to the inaudible words and laughter from the girls as they played. Then he looked at the little dog staring up at him with big dark eyes while Gil held it in his arms. "I appreciate the offer, but I still have a ways to go." He bent down and held out his hand. "Good seeing you, Gil. I'm glad you and them little gals made it back in one piece."

Gil shook Wade's hand. "Wish you'd stay and have supper with us and visit some."

Wade looked toward the town of Roscoe's Creek. "Who's sheriff'n here now?"

Robinson grinned and looked embarrassed. "That'd be me."

Wade smiled, feeling happy for him. "Good choice. You'll make a damned fine sheriff."

Gil's face turned sad. "Not as good as Frank. Sure, do miss that ornery cuss."

Wade looked at the mountains in the distance and pictured Frank lying on the Rio saloon. "Yeah, so do I." said Wade, still blaming himself for the deaths of Frank, Todd, and the Indian." He looked down at Gil and the dog. "Well, I best be on my way."

"Can I ask you something?"

Wade nodded with a curious look.

"Did it take you all this time to find them two and kill them?"

"No, it didn't. I found them soon after leaving Paso Del Rio."

Gil stepped closer as he held the dog that watched Wade with its big black eyes. "Where the hell have you been all this time?"

Wade smiled. "Looking for an Indian over on the western slope."

Robinson looked puzzled. "An Indian? What in blazes for?"

Not wanting to discuss it, Wade looked down at Gil. "I Best be going. It's getting late, and like I said, I have a ways to go." Wade smiled at the dog. "Take care of the dog."

Wade nudged his mare gently into a walk along the trail that led to Roscoe's Creek. Without looking back, he said, "Take care, Gil, and tell the girls I asked after them."

Gil stared after Wade with the unanswered question on his mind. "I'll do that," said Gil wishing he would stay. "You take care of yerself."

Without turning, Wade raised his right hand, gave a small wave, and rode at a walk toward town, looking like a man carrying a heavy burden.

The little dog fought to get out of Gil's hands, but he held him tight while watching Wade ride away. Still holding the dog, he turned and walked to the porch, tied the dog to the porch post, and returned to the woodpile. Picking up the ax, he looked toward town in time to see Wade disappear around the corner of a building.

As he stared at the emptiness, he recalled their first meeting in the sheriff's office when Wade tried to explain how he came by the little dog he held. Gil smiled, bent down, grabbed a piece of wood, set it on the chopping block, and split it in two with the ax. Looking toward the house, he saw the dog was gone and the chewed rope dangling from the porch post. He looked in the direction Wade had gone, grinned, and thought the dog belonged to him anyway.

Wade rode quietly through Roscoe's Creek to the trail that led past the Barton's cabin. He pulled up and looked in the direction of the cabin, remembering that terrible day. Hearing the familiar sound of a dog barking, he turned in the saddle and looked back along the street of buildings. It took a moment to see the little yellow dog running after him with his tongue hanging out one side of its mouth. He grinned at the sight, stepped down, and knelt to one knee just as the dog jumped into his arms. As it whined and licked his face, Wade laughed as he closed his eyes and moved his head in a vain attempt to dodge the dog's quick tongue. "Alright," he said softly. He took the chewed rope from around the dog's neck, held him up with both hands and looked into its dark eyes. "You should stay here with Gil and the little girls, where you'd have a nice warm home and plenty of food." He tucked the dog under his arm, climbed back onto his horse, and let the dog settle comfortably between him and the saddle horn. "Maybe they don't need a scruffy little yellow dog." Then he nudged the mare and rode at a walk toward the Barton cabin to visit the graves he dug those many months ago.

A few hours later, they were sitting on Wade's horse, looking at the familiar cabin, standing ghostlike in the shadows of the tall trees. The garden the boy's mother had cared for was overgrown with weeds and the crops wilted. The dog whined as it looked at where Wade had buried the boy and his parents. Thinking it wouldn't hurt any, Wade held the dog by the nape of the neck, bent down, and gently dropped him to the ground. The dog took off at a run to the graves and started digging. Realizing his mistake, Wade climbed down, picked the dog up as it growled and kicked to get free, and looked into its black eyes. "Maybe this wasn't such a good idea."

Wade kicked the dirt back onto the grave with his boot, and as he stood over the graves petting the little dog, he said, "Just stopped by to tell you, folks, I sent the men that did this to you to hell." He paused a moment. "I hope you rest easy now." He turned and climbed back into the saddle, held the dog tightly against him, and nudged the mare into a walk. The dog fought and whined for a few minutes but soon settled down and began licking Wade's hand as if to say he was sorry. He looked down, felt sorry for the dog, and regretted coming this way, but he wanted to visit the Barton graves. "I know," he said as he gently petted him. "I know."

They had ridden several miles down the trail he had traveled up at the beginning of his long journey. The sun had long since set, and it was beginning to get dark. As he rode around a bend on the trail, he saw the Colorado plains stretch out before him and remembered stopping here before finding the cabin. He paused to take a long look at the scene, and remembering a creek not far from the trail, he turned the mare and rode through the thick underbrush.

Reaching the creek, he pulled up, let the mare have a drink, then followed the creek back the way he had come all those months ago. Enjoying the stillness and sounds of the small creek mixing with the mare's hooves against the rocky bank, he thought of seeing Sarah again. After several minutes, he was at a familiar campsite where he once ate breakfast while watching the sunrise. He climbed down, set the dog on the ground, and as it looked for a place to do his business, Wade started on the cinch to his saddle.

The mare unsaddled and hobbled a few feet away, he gathered firewood, built a fire, and leaned back against his saddle, staring into the red and orange flames wishing he had food for the dog. His mind found the breakfast Big Gus had fixed him a few days ago, and he remembered the jerky Gus had shoved into his saddlebags.

He opened the saddlebags, and after finding the last two pieces, he sat back against his saddle, gave one to the dog, and ate the other. While staring into the fire, he thought of Frank Wells, Todd Jewett, and Dark Cloud. Their images quickly disappeared, replaced by the images of the Bradley brothers.

The dog licking his hand saved him from those visions and troubled thoughts. He looked down at the dog and apologized for not having anything better than jerky to feed him. The dog looked up as if to say he understood, put his head on Wade's leg, and closed its eyes, content with where he was. Feeling the weight of the day, Wade's eyes grew heavy wanting sleep, so he slid down, resting his head against his saddle. After the dog curled up next to him, he covered up with the one blanket, then pulled his hat over his eyes. Feeling the friendly warmth of the fire and the comfort of the dog resting against him, he closed his eyes and drifted into a restless sleep of faceless men and death.

Sisters Colorado

It was late afternoon when Wade and the little yellow dog rode into the town of Sisters. The sun was at their backs, casting long shadows along the wagon-rutted street. Riding at a walk toward the familiar sign, Sheriff, hanging from the roof of the boardwalk, the smell of cooked food found them. As they passed Moly's Restaurant, the dog raised his head, whined, and sniffed the air.

Wade smiled. "I smell it too."

The main street of Sisters was busy with riders, wagons, and the boardwalks even busier with mixtures of women and men hurrying along their way. The little dog sat on Wade's lap behind the saddle horn, watching everything with curiosity. Wade pulled up outside the sheriff's office, held the dog in one hand, and dismounted. Tying the horse to the hitching rail and anxious to see his friend, he walked up the steps to the boardwalk toward the door. He paused at the door for a moment holding the dog in one arm against his stomach, then opened the door and stepped inside.

Seth was sitting behind his desk, busy cleaning his rifle just as he had been the day the two first met. He looked up and grinned. "I'll be damned."

Wade smiled as he thought of that first day and Seth's warning. "You sure you can see well enough to clean that rifle?"

Still grinning, Seth set the rifle down, tossed the dirty cloth on the desk, and stood. "I was thinking maybe you fell in love with some pretty señorita and was busy repopulating Mexico with half-breeds."

Wade grinned. "I was a little too busy to do any populating."

Seth walked from behind the desk with an outstretched hand and a big smile. "Hardly recognized you with the long hair and beard." They shook hands as Seth looked at the dog. "That the same dog you took into Roscoe's Creek all them months ago?"

Wade looked down at the dog and smiled. "Same one."

Seth pointed to a chair and thought Wade looked older. "Have a seat."

Wade sat down, held the dog on his lap, and eyed the coffee pot on the stove behind Seth. "Any coffee in that old pot?"

Bowlen turned, looked at it, and shook his head no. "I drank the last of it an hour ago." Seeing the disappointment on Wade's face, he asked, "Hungry?"

"Ain't ate anything other than jerky since Gus Parker fed me early yesterday." He paused in thought. "Leastways, I believe it was yesterday. It may have been two or three days. Ain't sure." Then he looked at the dog. "Can't say when he last ate something other than a piece of jerky." He glanced out the window as he smiled. "I stopped to see Gil and the little shit up and followed me."

Seth looked at the dog. "Looks better fed than you do." Then he slapped the top of the desk with both hands, stood, and walked to his hat hanging from a peg on the wall. "C'mon. I'll buy you supper."

Wade grinned as he stood. "Best invite I've had today." "Truth is, it's the only invite I've had in quite a spell." Cradling the dog in his left arm, he followed Bowlen toward the door.

Seth looked him up and down. "From the way you look and smell, I can understand that." He grinned, opened the door, and looked at the dog as Wade stepped outside. "You taking the dog to the restaurant with us?"

Wade looked at Seth. "Why not? I'm sure he smells better'n I do."

Seth frowned and then shrugged, wishing he would leave the dog in one of the cells. "I can't argue that, but I ain't never sat at a table with a dog before."

"Didn't think you were all that particular."

"Being particular ain't got nothing to do with it. I ain't sure Molly's gonna like us bringing a dog inside her place while her customers are trying to eat."

Wade looked down at the dog he carried in his left arm. "He's small, and he won't bother anyone. Besides, ain't you the sheriff?"

Seth never answered and knew what he was getting at. As they walked into Molly's, heads turned, and people stared while whispering something the two figured was about the dog.

Seth leaned closer and whispered, "Don't let him shit."

Molly Charles walked out of the kitchen carrying a tray with two plates of food and hesitated as she looked at the dog, Wade, and Seth. Molly put the plates of food down in front of two customers, told them to enjoy their meal, and approached Seth and Wade while staring at the dog.

Seth smiled a nervous smile. "Hello, Molly." Then he pointed at an empty table next to the wall. "That table over there, alright?"

Molly Charles was a middle-aged woman recently widowed. She was big-boned, standing five feet two, a little on the heavy side but not fat. Her long hair was a mixture of black and gray, big brown eyes, and she wore no makeup. Taking her eyes from the dog, she smiled affectionately at Seth and showed them to the table.

Seth forced a smile. "Molly, this here's Wade Garrison, that friend of mine from Harper I told you about."

She smiled while thinking he would be a nice looking man if he cleaned himself up. "Nice to meet you, Mr. Garrison. Seth's talked about you so much it seems I already know you."

Wade gently took her hand, wondering what Seth had told her. "I wouldn't put too much stock in what Seth says, ma'am."

As the two sat down, Wade glanced around at the other customers seeing they weren't all that happy about a dog in the café and thought it might have been better if he had left it in a cell while they ate.

She gently put her hand on Seth's shoulder and smiled. "How about some coffee before you order?"

"That'd be great," said Wade, thinking the two were a little friendly.

Seth looked up at her. "Just bring us the special."

"I'll be right back with your coffee." Then she turned and disappeared into the kitchen.

Wade looked at Seth. "You two appear a might friendly."

Bowlen squirmed in his chair, looking embarrassed. "We're friends if that's what you mean."

Wade chuckled. "Don't get upset, Seth. She's a nice-looking lady."

Seth glanced around, wishing Wade would stop talking about him and Molly.

Wade knew Seth was embarrassed and grinned as he petted the dog. "Don't think I ever seen you blush." Then he chuckled.

Molly returned to the table with two cups and a small pot of coffee.

Bowlen glanced at Wade and then looked up at Molly. "Thanks Mrs. Charles."

Surprise filled her pretty face. "Since when did you start calling me Mrs. Charles?" Then looking a little irritated, she turned and walked away.

Seth turned and looked after her with a nervous smile, stood, said he'd be back in a minute, and followed her into the kitchen.

The dog began to whine, and believing he had to go to the bathroom, Wade stood and walked toward the door carrying the dog past three men sitting at a table near the door. One of them said something that caused the others to laugh, and as Wade opened the door and stepped outside, he glanced at them, seeing one of them mimicking him carrying the dog. Ignoring them, he closed the door, stepped into the street, and put the dog down. While the dog sniffed the hitching post, Wade leaned back against it as his mind drifted to Sarah. He thought of how pretty she looked the last time he saw her standing on Mason's General Store steps in Harper. Wade was anxious to see her, hold her in his arms, and feel her soft, warm body against his. The dog's whining interrupted those thoughts, and looking down, Wade saw he had finished.

Seth was at the table wearing a big smile, looking happy when Wade and the dog returned.

"Everything alright," asked Wade as he sat down and placed the dog on the chair next to him, where it curled into a little ball and closed his eyes.

Bowlen looked toward the kitchen, then at Wade, and lowered his voice. "Had to apologize to Molly." He looked down at the table while his index finger followed a crease in the tablecloth. "Truth is," he said with a grin. "We are friends. Have been for a spell now."

Wade was happy for him. "That's good, Seth. I'm glad for you."

Seth squirmed in his chair, looking both embarrassed and pleased. "She's a nice lady. Lost her husband while we were in New Mexico."

"What from?"

"Oh, he'd been sick for a spell with cancer. Anyway, when I got back, I started coming in for breakfast as I always had." He shrugged while gesturing with his hands. "One thing led to another, and she started sitting down having coffee with me, and we'd talk. The next thing I knew, we were going for buggy rides and such things."

Wade started to say something when Molly walked out of the kitchen carrying their dinner.

She put the plates on the table, and to Wade's surprise, she set a small plate of cooked beef on the chair next to the little dog.

"What's its name?" she asked.

Wade looked at the dog as he ate with some enthusiasm. "Don't rightly know. I came by him a while back." He looked up at her and shrugged. "I just call him Dog."

"Cute little fella," she said. "You should give him a proper name."

Laughter came from the table where the three men were sitting.

Wade turned his head and looked at them over his shoulder, and as they looked at him, they laughed at something one of them said.

"Pay them no mind," said Seth. "The one with curly black hair is Daniel Hoskins, and that's his younger brother Pete sitting across from him."

Wade turned from them to Molly. "Appreciate your kindness, Mrs. Charles."

She quickly corrected him. "Call me Molly, and we wouldn't want the little fella going hungry." Then she looked at the three men. "Seth's right Wade. Pay them no mind."

Wade smiled and shook his head. "I don't intend to, Molly."

"Well," she said so the three men could hear, "the dog has better manners than them three, and that's a plus in my book." She glanced at Seth and smiled. "You could always name him after the sheriff."

Wade chuckled, but Seth only smiled as Molly turned and walked toward the kitchen.

The three men stood and started toward the door when Daniel Hoskins turned and said, "Little Rat would be a good name," bringing laughter from the other two as they followed Dan Hoskins outside.

Wade turned his head, watched them walk out the door, and then looked at Seth. "They always act like assholes?"

Seth grinned. "Pretty much." He stared at the door the three had just walked out. "Most of it's harmless, but they do have a way of getting on your nerves." Seth paused a moment. "Pay them no mind. The two Hoskins brothers think they're something special."

Wade looked at the door. "The name Hoskins sounds familiar."

"It should. They own a big spread between here and Harper."

Wade considered the name as he shoved a fork of mashed potatoes into his mouth. I remember now. It's a big spread southwest of Harper.

After the two finished eating, Wade took the dog outside while Seth paid for dinner. While the dog took care of business, Wade looked through the restaurant's window and watched Seth and Molly talking and smiling at one another. He felt happy for Seth, thought of Sarah, and wondered if she had found someone else. Thinking he couldn't blame her if she had, he turned away from the window and watched the little dog sniff at the boardwalk post and then raise his leg.

Seth opened the door, walked out of the restaurant, down the steps to the dirt street, put his hand on Wade's shoulder, and gently pushed him toward the sheriff's office. "Now that your little dog's done with his needs, we'll drop him off at my office, put him in a cell, and I'll buy you a drink. Then you can tell me what happened in Mexico and where you have been all this time."

Wade didn't want to talk about what happened but knew it was only fair that Seth knew. They dropped the dog off at the jail and made sure he was comfortable on a cot in one of the cells. Wade started to close the cell door but realized the dog could walk between the bars, so they left it open.

Walking into the saloon, Seth paused, looking for a table. Seeing an empty table in the back of the saloon, away from the piano, they sat down, and Seth ordered a bottle of whiskey and two glasses. Seth poured two drinks, shoved one toward Wade, and picked up the other. "To Frank and the Indian."

"And Todd Jewett," added Wade.

Seth took a drink, and anxious to know what happened after Wade rode out of Paso Del Rio, he asked, "What happened in Mexico?"

Wade picked up the glass, took a sip, set it down, and looked at it for a long moment as if recalling the past months from some hidden place in his mind. Then he took another sip, sat back, and told the story.

Twenty-Nine

As Paso Del Rio slowly disappeared behind him, Wade thought it ironic that, in the end, he was alone, just as he had started. He rode deeper into Mexico at a trot as the sun climbed higher into the clear blue Mexican sky. Vigilant in his quest for the men he had been hunting for weeks, he kept his eyes focused on the hoof prints in the sandy soil. Mental pictures of Emmett, Frank, Todd, the Indian, and the families he had helped bury raced across his memory.

The border town of Paso Del Rio had long ago disappeared behind him, and the mare's breathing was becoming labored in the mid-morning heat. He knew she was getting tired, and he needed to stop so she could rest and drink some water. The trail he followed led to a grove of trees, a small stream of water, and grass for his horse. Wade stopped in the shade of a small group of trees, climbed down, and let the mare take a good drink of cool water while he took off his black duster and tied it behind his saddle. He untied the small burlap bag Mrs. Johnson had filled with food, placed the bag on the rocks, took the saddle off the mare, and led her to a spot of grass where he hobbled her. While she nibbled on the tall grass, he sat down on the ground next to his saddle and wondered how far ahead of him the Bradley's were.

He untied the burlap bag and peered inside as he reached in, took out one of the white cloth wrappers, unfolded it, and found a large piece of cooked beef. He unwrapped the second, containing a half loaf of bread, and the third two boiled potatoes. He smiled at the thoughtfulness of Mrs. Johnson, began to eat, and made sure he left enough for tomorrow. When

287

he finished, he wrapped the food, put it back in the burlap bag, laid his head against his saddle, and closed his eyes. His mind drifted from the gunfight in the Rio Saloon to the families they had found, then buried, and finally to Sarah. He thought it seemed like years since he left her standing on the steps to the Mason's with her eyes welling as she asked him not to go. Missing her, he wondered if he would ever see her again.

The mare's soft nicker interrupted his thoughts of Sarah, and when he turned to look at the mare, she appeared rested and eager to continue the hunt. He considered the small bag of oats George Johnson had given him but decided to save it for later. He stood, held his hat above his face, and looked up at the sun high in a cloudless sky.

An hour passed, and Wade saddled the mare, and as he was about to climb up, he noticed something lying next to the rocks on the other side of the small stream. Filled with curiosity, he led the mare across the stream and picked up a bloody brown shirt sleeve. Recalling that Kevin Bradley was wearing a brown shirt, Wade looked in the direction they had ridden, smiled, and dropped the bloody sleeve. He hoped that Kevin's wound would slow them up a bit, swung up onto the saddle, and followed their tracks at an easy gallop.

The trail led him to the outskirts of a small Mexican village of adobe buildings and small adobe houses lining the dirt street. It was late afternoon when he pulled up and guided the mare into a grove of scraggly trees, cactus, and rocks where it was shady and cool, giving relief from the hot afternoon sun. He climbed down, took off his hat, and wiped the sweat from his forehead with his shirt sleeve. Thinking it was hot, he took the water bag from the saddle, poured water into his hat, and held it so the mare could drink. When she finished, he put his hat on, took a small drink from the water bag, then tied it to the saddle. Curious about the small village, he pulled the long glass from his saddlebag that he had taken from Frank's saddlebags before leaving Paso Del Rio. Pulling the long glass apart, he looked up the village's dusty dirt street and saw a half dozen men dressed in white cotton shirts and pants with straw hats walking along the street. Two women dressed in white peasant blouses and colorful skirts tended the goats in the corral next to the hut at the edge of the village closest to him. Three more women dressed in the same attire filled jugs with water at the well in the village center, but he saw no sign of the horses he followed. The village appeared quiet and peaceful as the goats crying mixed with the tiny bells that hung from their necks. A young boy dressed in the same clothing as the men walked out of a small adobe church, filled a jug with water, and returned to the church.

The slight breeze coming from the villages carried the smell of cooking, and suddenly he was hungry. He gave the village another quick look with the long glass before returning it to his saddlebag. Thinking it would be safe to enter, he climbed up on the mare and rode out of the cool shade into the hot sun toward the village. He rode at a walk up the dusty street while holding his hand on the butt of his pistol. Seeing the sign, Cantina, above an open doorway, he guided the mare to the empty hitching rail and climbed down.

He glanced around as he dusted himself off, then stepped through the narrow doorway. Once inside, he paused in the dim light letting his eyes adjust from the hot, bright sun outside and saw two men at the bar talking to the barkeep. Seeing no one else in the place, he walked past several small empty tables and chairs to the other end of the bar. He leaned against it, gave the two men a friendly nod, then looked at the barkeep. "Cerveza."

The man shook his head and then spoke in English. "Sorry, señor. No Cerveza, no beer. Tequila or mescal."

Wade pursed his lips as he considered both drinks. "Mescal." He looked at the other two men who were still staring at him. "Buenas Tarde."

The man, nearest Wade, noticed the badge on his shirt, turned to the other, and said something Wade could not hear.

The bartender placed a glass of mescal on the bar. "Tres pesos señor."

Wade looked down at the milky liquid, nodded, and, not having any Mexican currency, put some American coins on the bar. "I'm looking for two Americano hombres who rode through here earlier today. One may be badly hurt."

The bartender glanced at the Marshal's badge on Wade's shirt, picked up the money, and glanced at the other two men as he nodded at Wade. "Policia." The two men gave Wade a long look, then turned away. The bartender rubbed the bar with a dirty, damp towel. "Si dos gringos rode in Esta mañana looking for a doctor."

"This morning?"

"Si."

"Where is this doctor?"

"There is no doctor in our small village, señor." Then he pointed. "There is an old woman that lives at the end of the street on the left who is wise in healing."

Wade turned and started to walk away when the man behind the bar called out, "Señor, your drink."

"You drink it," Wade said over his shoulder as he hurried out of the cantina into the hot sun. Untying the mare, he looked in the direction the bartender had pointed and led her along the hot, dusty street, looking for the last house on the left. Minutes later, Wade tied the mare in the shade of a tree in front of a small adobe house. Carefully he pushed the flimsy gate open of a fence made from thin pieces of tree limbs tied together and stepped into the small yard. Catching a whiff of something cooking inside, he knocked on the door.

A small older woman with gray hair appeared at the door, looking frail and fearful. Her face was dark and wrinkled, yet she had a softness about her. Her once bright eyes carried the years in them, and the whites were no longer white but a mixture of gray and red.

Wade thought of his grandmother as he smiled, trying to look unthreatening, and asked if she had helped two men.

She stared at him for a moment as if she had not heard him, and then a woman's voice from inside spoke to her in Spanish. The old woman nodded and smiled as she stepped away from the door and motioned him to come inside.

He entered the small house, finding a pretty, fifteen-year-old girl dressed in a white blouse, a bright red and orange skirt, with long black hair standing barefooted next to the old woman. She looked at him with curious big dark eyes. "Buenas tardes," she said without smiling.

Wade smiled and nodded. "Buenas tardes. Hablas ingles?"

She smiled proudly. "Si." Noticing his badge, she looked at the older woman and spoke in a low voice. "Americano Policia."

The elderly woman looked frightened as she stared at him.

"Tell your Madre not to be afraid."

"She is my Abuela, my grandmother." She turned to the old woman telling her not to be afraid, and then she looked at Wade. "I am Maria. What can my grandmother do for you, señor?"

"My name is Wade Garrison, and I'm a United States Deputy Marshal."

"Wade Garrison," she repeated thoughtfully.

He nodded. "Were dos hombres here today?"

She nodded, looking angry. "Si señor dos americanos. Uno americano hurt very bad."

Wade thought about that for another second. "Did your grandmother help them?"

The girl's pretty face held fear or worry; he was unsure which. "It's all right if she did. I'm trying to catch up with them." He looked at her. "Bad hombres."

The girl smiled and nodded but still looked fearful. "Si. My grandmother put medicina, and" she paused in thought, then said, "How do you say." Then she smiled. "Bandages on the man's chest where he had been shot." Then she looked sad. "He was not well and had much loss of blood." She looked at her grandmother. "My poor Abuela was frightened by the Americanos." Then she looked angry. "They left without paying."

Not surprised, Wade reached into his pocket, took out some money, and handed it to the young girl. She looked at it briefly and then at him with a curious look.

He smiled. "Take it, please."

The young girl smiled, took the money looked at her grandmother, and said something in Spanish that Wade didn't understand. The grandmother smiled as she nodded her head he presumed was in thanks.

Wade thanked the girl and turned to leave when she asked if he was hungry. The smell of food rushed at him from the open stove in the corner, where a black pot sat next to a fire in a small open fire pit. He smiled and nodded. "Si."

The girl walked to the pot, took off the lid, picked up a flour tortilla, spread a little shredded beef and beans onto it, rolled it up, and handed it to him. She smiled and softly said, "Eat, señor."

He took a big bite, and as he reached into his pocket for more money, she quickly placed one hand on his arm and shook her head no. He smiled, thanked her, then the old woman, and hurried out the door. Climbing onto the mare with the tortilla in one hand, he turned her south and rode out of the small village.

Wade followed the tracks of the Bradley brothers for two hours into a grove of trees that led to a clearing and a small mud house with a thatched roof. Pulling up beside a large berry bush next to two trees, he saw the two horses he had been trailing tied to a tree a few feet away from the corner of the house. Besides the smoke rising lazily from an open cooking pit at the rear of the house, Wade saw no other sign of life and worried for the people living there. He backed the mare further into the trees, took the long glass out of the saddlebags, and looked at the open windows. The inside of the house was too dark to see anything. Taking the glass from his eye, he looked at a large black pot sitting on a fire pit. Being hungry, he wondered what was inside.

Wondering where the woman was and who should be doing the cooking, he returned the long glass to his eye and looked at the small corral containing a horse and mule, both busy eating hay from a bin separating the two animals. Next, the glass found the outhouse halfway between him and the house, the door halfway open, appearing to be empty. Then he moved the glass to the dim light of the back window. He saw movement and thought of the other families they found after the Bradley brothers had visited. He pushed the long glass together, put it back in his saddlebag, and climbed down. He tied his mare to a tree, took off his black hat, and hung it on the saddle horn. As he pulled his forty-four Colt pistol from its holster, he wished Seth and Billy were with him. He glanced around to see if anyone else were about, then made certain each of the cylinders of his pistol had a shell in them. Then he crouched down and ran across the open ground to the back of the outhouse.

As he peered past the outhouse wall to the door and window of the small mud house, he heard a woman crying and voices filled with anger. Fear of what may be happening inside, he considered running across the yard and bursting inside. Just then, a young girl dressed in a white blouse and dress with a red sash came out of the door and walked to the cooking pit. She wiped the tears from her eyes and cheeks with her hands, and he could tell she looked frightened as she looked back at the house. The door opened, and Paul Bradley stood in the open doorway, yelling for her to hurry up with the food.

Wade wanted to put a bullet in Bradley's head right then, but he didn't know what shape Kevin was in and figured Kevin would kill whoever was inside the house. He watched as Paul Bradley walked across the small yard and slapped the young girl on the side of her face knocking her back into the cooking pit and burning her arm. Bradley grabbed her by her arms and pushed her against the pit. "Bring the damn food inside bitch, or I'll shoot that old man you're so worried about." Then he turned and disappeared through the doorway.

Wade couldn't chance her seeing him, so he ducked back behind the outhouse, and when he looked again, she entered the house with two plates of food. Wade knew time was running out. He looked down at his trembling hands and thought about dying alone in Mexico and Sarah, never knowing what happened to him. Then Wade peered around the corner of the outhouse at the closed door of the mud house. He wished he knew where everyone was sitting so he would not shoot someone by accident if he rushed inside blindly or get himself killed. He considered waiting until the Bradley brothers came out, but that would be too late for the family inside. Then Wade thought that if he could make it to the open window without being seen, he might be able to tell where everyone was by the sound of their voices. It was dangerous at best but worth taking the risk. Crouching down, he ran to the corner of the house and knelt under the open window. Moments of silence passed, and then he heard a woman crying and a man pleading. "Señor, please, I beg of you, we are a poor family. Take what you want and leave us."

"You sure are poor, you dumb Mexican," said a voice Wade believed to be that of Paul Bradley. "You may be poor, but you got one hell of a good-looking daughter."

"Paul," said Kevin, sounding tired and sickly. "I've got to get to a doctor." Then he coughed several times. "I ain't gonna last long if we don't."

Wade could tell Kevin was near the window and thought he was probably lying on a bed.

"Just lay there, little brother. We'll be on our way just as soon as I finish here."

Kevin's coughing escaped through the open window as he pleaded with his brother. "We've got to get the hell out of here now." Then he coughed several times. "Just kill the others, and we'll take the bitch with us."

Wade heard something creak, then Paul's voice close to the window. Kevin coughed several times. "Paul, we have to get going. I need a doctor."

"We'll be on our way soon, little brother."

Wade knew it was now or never, so he quietly moved to the door that was slightly ajar. He paused a moment, thought of all the things that could happen, then pushed the door open and rushed inside. He fired toward the sounds of Kevin's coughing while diving to the dirt floor, ending up under the table. Paul ran toward the door getting off two quick shots that missed Wade but hit the table. Wade fired twice as he disappeared through the open doorway. Hearing the sound of a pistol cocking, Wade turned to Kevin and fired twice, hitting him once in the chest just below his neck and another on the right cheek.

Jumping up, he ran outside just as Paul Bradley rode the gray through the small stream and up an embankment. Afraid he'd hit the gray, Wade turned and hurried back inside, facing the young girl he watched outside, pointing Kevin's gun at him.

Afraid she was going to pull the trigger, he held up both hands and said, "Amigo." Then he pointed at his badge and yelled, "Americano Policia."

The man tied to the chair said something to her, and she dropped the gun and rushed to help her mother untie her father from the chair. Wade felt Kevin's neck to make sure he was dead, then turned seeing to an old man lying on the floor, dead from a gunshot to the chest. Wade knelt, felt the man's neck, looked at the older woman kneeling beside him, shook his head, and softly said, "I'm sorry."

The man, the girl untied, fell to his knees, took Wade's hand, and kissed it. "Gracias señor, gracias."

"Everything is alright now," said Wade as he slowly pulled his hand away. Thinking of Paul Bradley getting away, he looked at the two, smiled, and hurried out the door reloading his pistol as he ran to get the mare. Swinging up onto the saddle, he nudged her into a gallop past the small mud house across the creek and up the embankment after Paul Bradley.

It was easy trailing the big gray in the hard sandy soil, and Wade figured time was on his side, believing Paul had ridden the gray hard before they stopped at the farm. The minutes passed, and the mare's breathing was getting labored. He recalled Seth telling him slow and steady would get the job done. Wade pulled her up by a small group of trees next to a large rock formation to let her cool in the shade and let her drink from his hat. He took the long glass from his saddlebags, climbed to the top of the rocks, and looked in the direction Bradley had ridden. The expanse before him was empty except for cacti, a few trees, and rock formations.

Thinking this was a lonely place to die, he pushed the long glass together, turned, and looked in the direction he had come, seeing the sun was low in the sky. He looked down at the mare resting in the cool afternoon shade and decided to let her rest a little longer.

He put the glass to his eye, looked toward the horizon, and to his surprise, there was the gray standing near some cacti about five or six hundred yards up ahead without Paul Bradley. While wondering where Paul was, he suddenly appeared and slowly climbed onto the gray. "I got you now, you son-of-bitch," Wade said in a whisper. As he lowered the glass, he thought one of his shots back at the house must have hit him. He glanced back at the sun and knew it would be dark in a couple of hours, jumped down from the rock he was standing on, swung up on the mare, and followed the trail of the big gray.

The sun was just above the western horizon as Wade rode to the top of a small hill and stopped. He took out the long glass and saw Paul Bradley about three hundred yards due east, hunched over in the saddle. Wade pushed the long glass together, put it away, and pulled the Sharps from the sheath in the front of his saddle. He took a fifty-caliber cartridge from the bandolier, shoved the lever forward, and shoved the shell into the breech. "Let's get this over with," he said to know one and closed the breech. He pulled the hammer back, raised and adjusted the sight, and put the butt of the rifle to his shoulder. Looking at Paul through the tiny hole of the peep sight, Wade pulled the first trigger, and before he could pull the second trigger, Paul Bradley fell off the gray. Watching the gray walk a few yards and stop, he wondered if this was some trick by Paul. After giving it some thought, he put the Sharps away, took the long glass out, and watched the big gray as she lowered her head to feed off what little grass there was.

Drawing his pistol, Wade cautiously walked a few steps, then stopped several yards from Dark Cloud's gray horse. Hearing coughing off to his left, he turned and saw Bradley crawling toward some rocks. Wade tied the mare to a small bush, walked to where Paul lay, bent down, pulled his pistol, and tossed it away. Wade grabbed him by the collar of his coat and moved him onto a nearby flat rock. From the amount of blood, he was coughing up, Wade knew the bullet had punctured his lung. Seeing the knife in time, Wade grabbed his arm, took the knife, and stepped back. "You're a tricky one."

Bradley smiled as he coughed blood. "Had to try," he said in a weak, exhausted voice.

"I guess you did at that." Wade stood back and looked into the evil brown eyes of the man he had been trailing through two territories and part of Mexico.

Bradley moaned in pain as he looked up at Wade. "You got me good," he said just above a whisper. "I need to get to a doctor, or I'll never make it back for a trial."

Wade remembered Billy's words, looked at Paul's bloody side, and knew he was getting weaker by the minute, would bleed out soon or choke on his own blood. Either way, he would die right here. "Who said anything about taking you back?"

Beads of sweat formed on Paul's face as he looked at the badge. "You're the law. You have to take me back."

"Hate to tell you this, Paul, but you are wrong about that."

"Who the hell are you?"

Wade shrugged. "The man that killed you and your brother."

Bradley looked at him for a long moment in curiosity. "That dumb little bastard we killed in the saloon was family?"

"A Friend."

Paul coughed, grimaced in pain, and his breath became shallower as he looked at Wade. "I recall you saying that in the saloon before the ruckus." His coughing sounded more like choking. "You trail us all this way over, a friend?"

"I wouldn't expect you to understand such a thing, but yes, I did. I shot that half-breed friend of yours, watched him die, and left him for the vultures and the crows."

"We were wondering about him." Paul looked at the blood on his hand as he took it away from his side. "Kevin dead?"

Wade nodded yes.

"I need a doctor."

Wade knew Bradley wasn't going anywhere, walked to the gray, brought it over by the mare, and tied it to the same bush. When he finished, he watched Paul trying to sit a little higher against the rock.

"I wouldn't move around too much if I were you."

"Can I have some water?"

Wade considered that and decided no use in wasting it. "Sorry, but the horses may need it."

Wade never understood how Paul found humor in that as he chuckled, coughed, and spat up blood.

Wade noticed the vultures gathering in the nearby trees, talking to one another in loud screeches. As he watched them covered in the red glow of sunset, he marveled at how quickly they had arrived.

Paul Bradley turned his head and looked at several big ugly birds sitting in the tangled branches of an old leafless tree. "Scare them, bastards, away."

Wade considered that for only a moment as he looked at the birds and thought of all the people Paul, his brother, and their friends had raped, beaten, and murdered. Seeing the large birds were gaining in number, he said, "I think it's the blood."

Paul looked at Wade, the birds, and then at his bloody clothes. "Scare them away, damn you."

Becoming noisier with their chattering and screeching, the horses were getting nervous. Wade walked over, made sure they wouldn't get loose, and knelt on his haunches a few feet from Paul. "I don't think your new friends will wait much longer. It's getting dark."

Fear and terror filled Bradley's face as a large vulture flew from a branch of that leafless tree to the ground several yards away, his wings raised, his neck stretched, with his black eyes staring at him.

"Like I said before, Paul. It's your blood. Makes them hungry." Wade glanced around at the big, ugly birds, and then he looked at Paul. "I think the ugly bastards are getting impatient."

Looking afraid, Paul tried to get up, but the pain was too much, and he collapsed against the white rock covered with his blood.

Wade knew it wouldn't be long now, and he was glad Paul Bradley was dying, but he wanted him to suffer like the people he tortured. He looked at the big bird a few yards away with wings spread and head moving from side to side, chattering as it looked at Paul. Wade looked down at Bradley for a moment, almost feeling sorry for him. As images of the bodies, he and the others had buried ran through his mind, he walked to the mare. Pausing, Wade looked back at the vultures and then at Paul lying on the ground watching him with frightened eyes. Wade took the rope from his saddle, walked back to Paul, and tied both wrists together.

Paul looked up at him. "What are you doing?"

Wade never answered as he pulled the rope tight, wrapped the rope around Paul's ankles, and made sure the rope was secure.

"What are you doing?" asked Paul again as he looked at his wrists and feet.

Wade sat back on his haunches and looked into Paul's brown eyes, sweaty face, and wet hair. "Most people believe they wait until you die before they start." He paused to look into the big black eyes of the two nearest to them. Wade turned to Paul. "I always heard if they think you're helpless, they'll start early."

Though Paul was weak from losing blood, he fought against the ropes. Feeling too tired to fight any longer, he looked at the two larger

297

vultures staring at him, turned, and yelled at Wade, "Cut me loose!" He coughed up blood and then cried out, "You can't leave me here like this, for god's sake!"

"Is that the way the people you tortured, raped, and killed begged? Wade walked to the grey, untied it, untied the mare., and looked at Paul, begging him not to leave. Turning away, he put one foot in the stirrups, swung up into his saddle, and looked at Bradley. "You can yell, but they'll soon find out that's harmless. After I leave, that big one over there will test your strength before he invites his family and friends." Wade turned away, nudged the mare into a walk, and pulled at the gray's reins.

A terrified Paul Bradley tugged at the ropes trying to get free, while the closest bird spread its wings of seven feet and hopped a little closer. He knew what would happen in a few minutes, looked at Wade riding away, and cried like a child as he screamed, "You can't leave me here like this!"

Wade never looked back as Paul Bradley screamed, "Come back here, you son-of-bitch!" Paul's screaming softened to sobs as he begged, "Please come back. I don't want to die like this."

As the birds screeching mixed with the cries and screams of Paul Bradley, Wade pulled his hat down, nudged the mare, and never looked back.

Thirty

Wade gulped his whiskey, set the glass down, and looked into it, afraid to tell Seth the truth about Bradley. "After I shot Paul Bradley, I left him for the vultures, climbed on my horse, and headed back to the border with the Indian's big gray horse. I left Frank's horse with the family in Mexico."

Seth watched Wade stare into his empty glass, a changed man. Silence hung heavy around them as if they were the only two in the saloon. Seth picked up the whiskey bottle, poured two drinks, and set the bottle on the table. Wade stared into his glass in silence while Seth took a drink and sat back in his chair, wondering what it was that had ahold of Wade. "You didn't have any trouble getting back across the border into Paso Del Rio, did you."

Wade looked up as if he had just awoken from sleeping, shook his head, leaned forward, picked up his glass, and gulped it down. "No trouble." Then he said, "I stopped at Johnson's livery to let the mare rest a couple of days and got a room in the hotel. After the mare had rested, I rode north to Santa Fe with the Indian's big gray. Billy bought me dinner and put me up in one of the cells for the night." He grinned. "Seems I've spent a lot of nights in cells these past months."

Seth smiled and picked up the bottle to pour them another drink.

Wade put his hand over the glass, leaned back in his chair, and looked at Seth. "French asked me to stay on and take Jewett's place as his deputy."

Seth grinned. "You'd make a damn good Deputy United States Marshal." He paused and leaned forward in his chair, his forearms on the table. "What'd you tell Billy?"

Wade looked unsure. "Told Billy I'd think on it, but first, I had to find an Indian and give him that big gray that belonged to his brother."

Seth remembered the promise. "Since you no longer have the gray, I take it you found the brother."

Wade looked at Seth with a small grin. "Tweren't an easy task."

Seth chuckled. "S'posen not." He looked at the troubled face of Wade Garrison. "What now?"

Wade looked uncertain. "I don't know Seth. Everything seems different."

Thinking he understood, Seth asked, "Different how?"

Wade looked at Seth across the table and shrugged. "Different."

"A thing like what you've been through the past months is certain to affect you. But they'll pass in time." Seth thought about the vultures feeding on Paul Bradley's body. "If it's the vultures feeding on Bradley that's bothering you, don't let it. Bastard got just what he deserved."

Wade thought about the screams, flapping wings, and vultures screeching as he rode away that day, knowing Paul while he was still alive when they started on him.

"Everything we do brings about a change in us. Some a little more than others, and some a whole lot more. Some are good changes and some bad."

Wade stared across the room, thinking of the violence and death the past months had brought into his life and knows now that Seth had been right in his warning.

Seth sipped his drink. "Feeling guilty?"

Wade looked regretful and nodded. "I've killed a lot of men in a short time. It seems to come easy, and that scares the hell out of me."

"I'm sure it does, and that's a good thing. Time to worry is if you enjoy it."

Wade stared at the wall across the room. "I enjoyed the killing of the Bradley brothers."

Seth leaned forward in his chair, reached across the table, and gently grabbed Wade's forearm. "We all wanted to kill those boys. You just happened to be the one that got to do it." Seeing Wade was still bothered, Seth sat back. "I can't explain it all to you. Some men are so bad it pleasures a good man like yourself to kill them." He watched Wade hoping he was making sense to him. "Remember me telling you about Jasper Collins?"

Wade nodded. "That sheriff you knew back in Kansas when you were a kid?"

Seth sat back. "Well, Jasper was always telling me stories or giving me advice in case I grew up wanting to be a lawman." Seth paused in memory. "Only two kinds of men that like to kill, he once told me. Over the years, I've come to understand that he was right. There are men like Billy French and Frank Wells, may God rest his soul, and me that love to rid the world of trash. Then there are men like the Bradley boys and that half-breed you left on the plains near Raton Pass that are just plain evil. Good, peaceable folks like that Sarah of yours and her family live in fear of both kinds, knowing that when the two meet, innocent folks have a way of dying." He paused to pour a little whiskey into his glass. "The only real difference is those peace-loving people tolerate men like Billy French and me because they have to."

Wade considered that for a moment. "But what if the killing comes easy? What about losing one's morality, or his soul even?"

Seth took another drink and sat back in his chair. "You regretful about killing Paul Bradley for what he did?"

"I guess." Wade could hear the screams of Paul in his mind as he looked at Seth. He wanted to tell him what he did but was afraid.

"You could argue that it would have been more humane to bury the bastard rather than leave him to the vultures. But Paul Bradley was one evil person." Seth paused, staring at him. "I wouldn't let it get under your skin any. Forget the Bradleys." Seth smiled. "I think you need a good night's sleep, and when you wake up in the morning, a hot bath and a shave. Be a good idea to have them dirty-smelling clothes washed as well. Afterward, we'll have breakfast at Molly's, then you, that scruffy little dog and that mare you prize so much, can head up to Harper and that soft little gal that's still waiting."

Wade wondered if Sarah was still waiting, then he grinned as he looked at Seth. "I could use a good night's sleep and a bath." He smiled in memory. "Hadn't had a bath since Raton."

Seth smiled, missing his old friend Frank Wells. "Better get back to that dog of yours before he shits all over that cell you're sleeping in."

Wade smiled, pushed his chair back, stood, and followed Seth toward the swinging doors wondering if the dog was okay.

Dan and Pete Hoskins walked in, and Dan quickly raised his arm and put his hand against his brother's chest, blocking the doorway. "Lookie here, Pete, if it ain't the man with the rat for a pet."

Pete laughed. "Maybe some cats already got the little shit."

"Nah," said Dan. "A cat wouldn't bother a tiny piece of shit like that.

"You're blocking the way," said Seth.

Dan looked past Seth to Wade as he smiled, apologized, and stepped aside. "Sorry, Sheriff."

Seth gave Dan, and Pete stern looks as he stepped toward the door, thinking he'd arrest them if Wade and the dog weren't sleeping in the jailhouse.

Dan stepped in front of Wade, leaned closer, and lowered his voice. "Hope no one shoots that little rat before you leave town."

Before the laughter had time to leave the mouth of Dan Hoskins, Wade pulled his pistol, placed the barrel under his chin, and cocked it.

Surprised by the quickness of what happened, Seth drew his pistol and shoved it into Pete's stomach. "Take it easy Pete. I wouldn't want to tell your pa he has to bury two sons." Then, with his free hand, he took Pete's gun and tossed it on the floor. As he looked at Wade, he saw something that worried him. "Let's go Wade."

Wade stared into Dan Hoskins's eyes with the same hate and contempt he held for Paul Bradley. He wanted to pull the trigger and splatter Dan's brains all over his brother's gray shirt.

Seth's calm voice brought him back from that dark place he had gone. "Wade," Seth said as he reached out, took Dan's gun, and tossed it across the floor. "Let it go."

Wade looked into Dan Hoskins's eyes, released the pistol's hammer, slowly lowered it, and pushed the barrel into Dan's stomach. "The trouble with a man like you is, you're just too stupid to know when to keep your mouth shut." Wade holstered his pistol, stepped around Seth, walked outside, and headed for the jailhouse.

Seth looked at the two brothers. "You boys go on home."

"Tell your friend this ain't over," said Dan Hoskins.

Seth let out a long sigh and looked at him in disappointment. "You dumb bastard. That man has killed more men than both of you know, and if I were you, I wouldn't push him any."

"Who is he?" asked Pete.

"His name's Wade Garrison. Now, go home." Seth pushed through the swinging doors and hurried after Wade.

After bathing in a hot tub of soapy water and putting on clean clothes, Wade sat in the barber's chair with his eyes closed. As the razor glided down his neck, his mind raced south to Raton and the Chinese bathhouse. He smiled in memory of Frank and Seth's water fight and the anger on Mrs. Kim's face as she raced in, yelling at them in Chinese. Those images gave way to the Rio Saloon and Frank's death. That image led to the screams of Paul Bradley, causing Wade to move, getting nicked by the razor.

"Sorry, mister," apologized the barber.

"My fault," said Wade softly.

When the barber finished, he held out a small white bottle. "Care for some fragrance, Mr. Garrison? Comes with the shave."

As he looked at the bottle, memories of lilacs and a 4th of July celebration at the Talbert's came to mind. "No thanks." He stood, picked up his gun belt, strapped it on, and reached for his wallet.

"Sheriff Bowlen's already taken care of it, Mr. Garrison," said the man. "The bath too."

Wade smiled as he put on his battered Texas flat hat, picked up the package containing his old shirt and pants, and stepped outside. Feeling the bright warm sun on his face, he walked toward the sheriff's office with his mind full of thoughts of Sarah. Wade felt a hot sting in the back near his right shoulder and, at the same time, heard a loud explosion. Dropping the package, his hand went to the butt of the forty-four pistol, turned in a crouch as he drew the pistol, and fired at Dan Hoskins as he got off a second shot that hit the storefront behind Wade.

Wade fired, hitting Dan Hoskins in the chest knocking him backward into the alley. He cocked his pistol and carefully walked toward the alley where Dan Hoskins lay.

Seth ran out of the sheriff's office with a gun in his hand and looked up and down the street for where the shots had come from. Seeing Wade a few doors down with his gun drawn, he ran to him. "What the hell's going on?"

Wade looked down at the body of Dan Hoskins sprawled on his back, his green shirt soaked with blood.

Seth looked down. "Damn it to hell," he said as he knelt next to the body, thinking of what Dan had said in the saloon last night. "I should have seen this coming." Then he touched Dan's neck for a pulse. "He's gone." Seth stood and looked at Wade. "What the hell happened?"

"Bastard shot at me as I was walking across the street." He turned so Seth could see his shirt. "Nicked me on the back." He touched the flesh wound on his upper back and then looked at the blood on his fingers. "Brand new shirt, damn it."

Seth looked at the bloody wound cutting Wade's brown shirt at the shoulder. "Lucky he was a lousy shot."

A man in his thirties stepped out of a small crowd. "He's right, Sheriff. I saw the whole thing." He pointed to Dan Hoskins. "That one there took a shot at this man while he was walking along the boardwalk, minding his own business."

"Thanks, Mr. Thorne." Then Seth looked down at Hoskins. "Damn it. Now I've got to tell his pa that his oldest son's dead."

"I should do it," offered Wade as he holstered his Colt. "I did the killing."

"No," said Seth shaking his head and looking sad. "I want you to go see the doc and then saddle up and get your ass to Harper."

Wade looked worried. "You expecting trouble from this?"

Seth shook his head. "Don't think so. Hoskins seems like a good man. It's his two sons who are the idiots of the family. He'll be mad at first, but with witnesses saying Dan tried to dry gulch you, he'll bury his boy and get on with life." He paused. "I just don't think it'd be a good time for you and him to talk about you killing his son."

"Maybe you're right."

Seth stared down the street thoughtfully. "Can't be sure about anything these days." Then he looked at Wade. "I'm pretty certain about Mr. Hoskins, but I ain't sure about his other idiot son and some of the Hoskins' hands. That's why I want you out of town pronto."

Wade glanced around, wondering where the brother was. "Maybe I should stay."

Seth shook his head. "Go see Doc, and I'll meet you back at the jailhouse."

Wade walked into the jailhouse with a bandage under his new bloody shirt finding Seth sitting at his desk reading the town newspaper. Dog jumped off the cot in the cell and ran to greet him. Wade bent down, picked him up, sat in one of three chairs in front of Seth's desk, and remembered the first time he looked at Seth across his desk.

"Coffee?" asked Seth.

Wade shook his head. "No, I best be heading out."

Bowlen set the newspaper on the side of his desk and stood. "I'll help you with your belongings."

Wade set Dog down, walked into the cell, and opened his saddlebags. He took out a faded blue shirt that had been washed and ironed while he bathed and put it on. Wade picked up the Sharps and his saddlebags, stepped out of the cell, and walked to the potbellied stove in the corner. He opened the small metal door, stuffed the new bloody shirt into it, and then looked at Seth. "You can burn that for me."

Seth looked at the shirt and grinned. "Ready?"

"Guess so." Wade slung the saddlebags over his shoulder while Seth bent down and picked up the little dog.

Wade went about saddling his mare while Seth sat on a bale of hay holding Dog, and though Seth would not admit it or say so, he hated to see Wade leave. After the mare was saddled, he led her outside into the warm, midmorning sun.

Seth got up from the bale of hay, stopped just outside the door next to Wade, and looked down the street. While he petted Dog, he wished Wade would get on his way before any of Hoskins' hands came looking.

Wade climbed up onto the saddle and settled in as he looked around the town and then at Seth.

Bowlen handed the dog to him and grinned. "Hope he pisses all over you."

Wade chuckled as he took the dog that settled behind the saddle horn. Feeling bad about riding out and leaving this mess for Seth to clean up, he looked down at his friend, tipped his hat, and nudged the mare into a walk. "Be seeing you Seth."

"Think about the offer from Billy. You'd make one hell of a deputy."

Wade wasn't sure he would after what he did to Paul Bradley, turned in the saddle, and said, "Maybe. Take care of yourself and tell that lady friend of yours I said goodbye."

Embarrassed by that, Seth glanced around to see if anyone was listening. "You do the same." Seth watched as Wade and the dog rode at a walk along the dirt street toward the end of town, then turned the mare towards Harper. Seth watched his friend for a few moments, then he turned, walked toward the sheriff's office, and wondered how Mr. Hoskins would take the news about his son. With the Hoskins' ranch close to Harper, Bowlen hoped Wade would take Billy's offer and head south to

Santa Fe. He stepped onto the boardwalk, paused with worry as he looked down the empty street, and knew the man who rode out of Sisters toward Harper was not the same Wade Garrison that first rode into Sisters a few months earlier.

Thirty-One

Harper Colorado

The mountains west of the Circle T were about to swallow the evening sun when Wade stopped his mare atop the hill, overlooking the familiar scene below. Long shadows of the house, outbuildings, and trees covered the red sandy Colorado soil that now held the sun's reddish-orange color. Smoke taking on the sunset colors rose from the chimneys of the bunkhouse and mess hall.

Smoke floated lazily from the chimney of the big house where Bertha, the Indian housekeeper, was busy preparing the evening meal that Mr. Grimes would eat alone. Wade's gaze went from the house to the mess hall behind the bunkhouse, where he imagined the heavyset Juan Gonzales, the Mexican cook, busy with the evening meal for the hungry hands. Wade sat in silence, petting the head of the little dog, reminiscing about the days before he left, knowing that those times were gone forever.

From where he sat on his horse, he could see the corral and the black that had belonged to Mr. Grimes' son Charles. Emmett's big black horse stood alone in the far corner of the corral as if waiting for Emmett to toss a saddle on him. A figure walked out of the barn toward the bunkhouse, and he could tell it was Stu by the way he walked. Recalling how badly Stu had wanted to go after the Bradleys, Wade thought about Frank Wells, Deputy Todd Jewett, the Indian, and he was glad Stu never came along.

A coyote's cry broke the stillness causing the small dog sitting between Wade and the saddle horn to stiffen with ears alert and let out a soft little growl. Anxious to see Mr. Grimes, Wade nudged the mare into a walk down the hill toward the big house.

He dismounted, put the dog down, and while it took relief on a small bush, Wade tied the mare to the railing of the hitching post, pulled the Sharps from the scabbard, and took the bandolier with only a handful of cartridges left from the saddle horn. He reached down, picked up the dog, walked up the three creaky steps of the porch, and wondered what he would find inside. Wade crossed the porch to the sound of loose boards and knocked on the door. It was getting dark, and the kerosene lamps inside the windows cast a yellow glow across the porch. He looked through the white lace curtains of the door window at Bertha's unsmiling face as she walked toward the front door.

Bertha opened the door, looked at him for a long moment, and then stared at the dog he was holding. She stepped to one side and gestured him inside with an expressionless face.

He stepped into the house, thanked her, and asked if he could see Mr. Grimes.

She looked at the dog and gave Wade a stern look she always wore when he visited the big house. Without a word, she walked away and disappeared through a doorway he knew was the library.

He leaned the Sharps against the wall next to the front door and set the bandolier on the floor next to it. While waiting, he petted the little dog as he glanced around the familiar room of expensive furniture, oil paintings, and other things Mrs. Grimes had brought with her from back east after she and Mr. Grimes were married.

The library door opened, and Tolliver Grimes stepped out wearing a smile and hurried across the room with an outstretched arm and open hand.

Wade grinned as he took the open hand and firmly shook it.

To Wade's surprise, Mr. Grimes pushed it away and hugged him. Stepping back, the old man grinned. "Was about to give up on you, boy." Then he noticed the dog. "What the hell is that?"

"That's a good question," said Bertha as she walked toward the kitchen.

Both looked at her as she walked past, then Wade looked at Tolliver. "A dog."

308

Tolliver Grimes looked confused. "I can damn well see that, but what the hell are you doing with a little dog?"

Wade looked down at the dog and smiled. "I'll explain it all later." Then he looked at Mr. Grimes. "Almost gave up on myself a time or two."

Tolliver stepped back, looked at the dog, and grinned. "Looks like a mean little shit. What's its name?"

"I just call him Dog."

Tolliver chuckled as he put his hands on Wade's shoulders and squeezed with his big strong hands. "Have supper with me, and you can tell me about those men you went after and that damn little dog you came back with."

Wade looked at the dog. "I think both of us could eat a good meal if it isn't no trouble."

"No trouble Son." Mr. Grimes smiled and asked, "He gonna eat with us?"

Wade looked down at Dog's dark eyes and thought of Molly's Cafe. "Guess I could leave him outside."

"Ah, what the hell," replied Grimes seeing Wade didn't want to do that, and turned toward the kitchen, yelling, "Bertha, we've two guests for dinner!" Then he laughed, looking happy.

Wade pointed to the Sharps rifle and bandolier next to the door. "I took good care of the Sharps, but it needs to be cleaned and oiled."

Mr. Grimes looked at both and then at Wade. "Hell, there'll be time enough to sort all that out, but right now, I'm hungrier than hell. Just leave them by the door for now." Tolliver looked at Wade, thinking he looked different. Older than his years. "Where's your horse?"

Wade nodded toward the door. "She's outside." He paused. "It's been a long ride."

Mr. Grimes looked at the Sharps and knew it no longer belonged to him. "I suppose it has." He pointed to a stuffed chair. "Have a seat. After Bertha gets our dinner on the table, I'll have her run down to the bunkhouse and have one of the boys take care of your mare." Then he turned and walked toward a liquor cabinet against the far wall while talking over his shoulder. "How about a drink before dinner?"

"Yes, sir," replied Wade. "If it's no trouble."

Grimes turned and smiled. "No trouble at all, Son."

Wade eased into an overstuffed chair with the dog on his lap while Tolliver Grimes opened the doors of the liquor cabinet.

Tolliver turned and looked at him. "I think it's about time you stopped calling me Sir or Mr. Grimes. Name's Tolliver." Then he turned back to the cabinet, took out a bottle of whiskey and two glasses, walked to the sofa across from Wade, and sat down. He placed the bottle and glasses on the table between them, looked at the dog on Wade's lap, and chuckled. "Bet my wife's turning over about now."

Wade smiled softly. "Maybe I should put him on the porch with a rope."

"Ah hell," replied Grimes. "Leave the little fella be. He ain't bothering nothing." He pulled the cork from the whiskey bottle and filled the two glasses to the brim. After setting the bottle down, he handed a glass to Wade and sat back on the dark green sofa holding the other. After Tolliver was comfortable, he grinned and held his glass up in front of him. "Can't tell you, Son, how glad I am you're back." He sipped his drink and watched as Wade drank more than just a sip. "Careful with that stuff, your stomach's still empty."

Bertha walked into the room. "Dinner's on the table." She looked at Wade and then at the dog. "Don't know if there's enough. I didn't know we'd be having company."

Tolliver stood. "We'll make do, Bertha. Thank you."

She looked at the dog. "He eating at the table?"

"No," replied Grimes with a small smile wishing she'd go about her business. "He'll eat on the floor next to the table." Then he gestured to a door leading to the dining room. "In there Wade."

As they walked into the dining room, Mr. Grimes asked Bertha to go down to the bunkhouse and have one of the boys come up and take care of Wade's horse.

She looked unhappy about that as she looked at Wade and then Tolliver. "Why not bring the horse in to keep the dog company?"

Wade couldn't help but smile.

"That'll do, Bertha," said Grimes. "Thank you."

She turned away and walked toward the front door while Wade followed Mr. Grimes into the dining room. A long dark cherrywood table and twelve chairs, five on each side and two at either end, occupied the center of the room under a glass chandelier of five small kerosene lamps. A China cabinet of the same dark wood sat against one wall, a six-foot buffet chest against the other. He imagined Mrs. Grimes proudly sitting at one side of the table, Mr. Grimes at the head, and their son across from her.

"Have a seat Wade," said Tolliver as he gestured to a chair while sitting in his usual spot at the head of the table.

Wade thought this room must be lonely and quiet for Tolliver as he put the dog on the floor, pulled a chair from the table, and sat down while the dog curled up under his chair. He glanced around the room and couldn't help but feel a little uncomfortable.

Tolliver Grimes picked up a steaming bowl of sliced skinless boiled potatoes covered with melting butter and handed it to Wade. While filling his plate, Mr. Grimes picked up a plate of fried pork chops sticking his fork into one before passing the plate to Wade.

Wade looked down at the dog sitting next to his chair, his dark eyes staring up at him, whining.

Mr. Grimes looked down at the dog, feeling sorry for it, and stood. "Hang on a minute." Then he disappeared into the kitchen and returned with an empty plate he handed to Wade. "Fill this with some potatoes, gravy, and a small piece of pork."

Wade and Mr. Grimes ate while making small talk about the ranch, Harper, and the other hands.

About halfway through dinner, Grimes looked at Wade. "Had a visit from Seth Bowlen over in Sisters a while back. He told me you parted company in some shit town on the border where you headed into Mexico after them that killed Emmett. Have to ask, did you get them, bastards? All of them?"

Wade swallowed his food, looked down at his plate, and thought about Paul Bradley. Pushing him aside, he looked at Tolliver. "All four."

Grimes smiled and looked relieved. "I knew you would." Then he pushed his chair back, stood, walked to a bottle of whiskey, and overturned glasses on a nearby table. Setting two glasses upright, he poured two drinks, sat one in front of Wade, and returned to his chair. He looked at his glass and then at Wade. "Mind telling me what happened out there?"

Mr. Grimes listened as Wade ate and told the story of finding the first family and taking the little yellow dog with him. He glanced down at the dog, lying on the floor next to an empty plate, sleeping, and smiled. "Cute little guy."

Getting comfortable, Wade told of Show he met Seth Bowlen, Gil Robinson, Frank Wells, and the Indian Dark Cloud. He told of the families, rescuing the girls, and killing the half-breed with the Sharps.

Tolliver looked pleased. "That's one. Go on."

Wade told him everything after they left Raton, including getting arrested and rescued by Marshall Billy French from Santa Fe. He told about the gunfight in Pine Springs, Sheriff Boedecker getting shot and later dying, and the death of Deputy Todd Jewett.

Tolliver took a drink. "That's too bad about them two."

Wade told about the gunfight at the Rio saloon in a border town called Paso Del Rio, where another of the men they hunted, Steve Hardy, was killed.

Grimes took a drink and smiled. "That's two."

Sadly, he told him about Frank Wells, the Indian getting killed, and Seth and Billy wounded and unable to go on. Then Billy told him it was up to him to finish the job. He told of trailing the two Bradley brothers into Mexico and killing them, leaving out how Paul Bradley died. Then Wade told of looking for Two Birds, the brother of Dark Cloud, and giving him the gray horse. Wade sat back, took a small drink, and stared into the glass, still hearing the screams of Paul Bradley. "That's about it."

Tolliver Grimes took a drink of whiskey, thinking Wade was deeply troubled over something. "You ain't staying, are you?"

Wade took a sip of whiskey and looked at Mr. Grimes for a long moment. It was hard to tell him he was leaving because he liked the old man as a son would a father. But something in him was different, and punching cattle would never be the same. "No sir," he said sadly.

Grimes looked disappointed. "You taking that job as a deputy in Santa Fe?"

Wade sighed. "I haven't made up my mind yet. I only know I can't stay here."

Tolliver drew in a deep breath, feeling sad and a bit lonely. He was happy when he saw Wade for the first time in months, and him leaving again never entered his mind until now. "What about Miss Sarah Talbert?"

"I love her, alright. But everything is a little confusing right now."

The room was silent as Tolliver watched Wade staring into the half glass of whiskey. Moments passed, then he leaned forward with his forearms on the table and folded his hands, looking sad. "I got no one left in this world. My wife killed herself after the death of our son Charles. My only brother died at the hands of rustlers just after the two of us laid claim to this here place back in fifty-one."

Wade sat back in his chair and stared at his glass.

"The thing of it is," said Tolliver, "I got no one to leave this place to." He let out a soft sigh and looked across the room as if looking at

312

someone. "Emmett was like a son to me, but them bastards...." He let the sentence die, took a drink of whiskey, and looked at Wade. "I'd like you to stay on, Son. Guess what I'm trying to say is that I'd like you to take over this here place after I'm gone." A heavy silence hung over the room while Grimes waited for an answer.

"Don't know if I can do that." Wade saw the disappointment on his face and said, "Leastways, not right now."

Mr. Grimes looked at Wade, knowing something sad and terrible held him in its grasp. "What's got a hold of you, Wade?"

Not knowing how to answer, Wade sat in silence and thought of those he had left behind.

Mr. Grimes wondered if he had seen too much death and killed one too many men. He thought about the promise Wade made to Emmett when they laid him in the ground and him giving Wade money and supplies to hunt the men down that he couldn't. "Too much killing has a way of changing a man." The room was silent as Mr. Grimes stared at him. "You look tired. It might be best if you stayed the night here in this house so's you won't have to answer a lot of questions from the others in the bunkhouse."

"If it's no trouble."

"No trouble," said Mr. Grimes, looking at the dog. "He sleep inside?"

Wade looked down at Dog and smiled. "If you wouldn't mind."

Grimes chuckled. "Why would I mind? I just had dinner with the little shit."

Wade chuckled.

Mr. Grimes stood in disappointment. "After we take the dog outside to do his business, I'll show you and the little fella to your room."

Wade stood, unbuttoned his shirt, and took out the wallet Mr. Grimes had given him filled with money the day he left. "I almost forgot. Here's your wallet. There's only a little money left."

Grimes took the wallet, looked at it for a moment, and then at Wade. "You've still a couple of months' wages coming. They'll be waiting for you on the table when you come down for breakfast." He smiled as he started for the door. "Let's take that little shit dog of yours outside first."

Wade stood next to the bed and looked around the room in the dim light of the one kerosene lamp. He sat the little dog on the bed and glanced around

313

the room that once belonged to Mr. Grimes's son Charles. Several photographs of Mrs. Grimes, Mr. Grimes, and Charles were on the dresser, wall, and nightstand. The room smelled stuffy and unused, so he opened the window and let in the fresh air and the night sounds of crickets and an owl. Lights in the bunkhouse brought back memories of the ranch hands playing cards or checkers while reading Moby Dick to Emmett. He turned from the window in sadness and sat on the edge of the bed next to the dog. As Wade petted him, he wiped the tears from his face with his other hand. Unable to push the sadness away, he took off his boots, pants, and shirt. After blowing out the lamp, he climbed between the cool sheets and rested his head on the soft cool pillow. Dog walked in a small circle, curled up next to him, and closed his eyes. It wasn't long before sleep found them both, and for the first time in days, Wade slept without seeing the faces of the men he had killed or hearing vultures and the screams of Paul Bradley.

Wade walked into the dining room carrying the little dog finding Tolliver Grimes sitting at the head of the table drinking a cup of coffee. "Good morning."

Mr. Grimes thought Wade looked rested, smiled, and nodded at the dog. "He need to go out?"

"Already been."

Grimes nodded to the same chair Wade sat in the night before. "Have a seat. I had Bertha bring in an extra plate."

Wade placed the animal on the floor between him and Mr. Grimes, then sat down at a table of fresh biscuits, scrambled eggs, and sausage. The wallet he had given back to Mr. Grimes was sitting next to his silverware filled with money.

"There's four hundred dollars in it."

Wade picked up the wallet and looked at the money. "Seems like an awful lot."

Mr. Grimes smiled. "Just take it, Son."

"Thank you." Wade set it down in front of his plate and felt embarrassed by the generosity. Then he picked up his plate and filled it with scrambled eggs and fried potatoes.

Mr. Grimes filled a plate with eggs and sausage and put it on the floor for the dog, then smiled as the dog ate with much enthusiasm. Then he watched Wade shove a fork of food into his mouth. "Give any thought to our conversation last evening?"

"Yes sir, I have. I thought a whole lot about it last night."

Mr. Grimes leaned forward, rested his elbows on the table, fork in one hand and a knife in the other, looking anxious.

"The thing of it is, Mr. Grimes---"

"Tolliver boy. Tolliver," he corrected.

Wade smiled with a nod. "Well, Tolliver, the thing is, I think it'd be best if I go away for a spell."

The old man looked disappointed as he sat back in his chair, but he understood. "Guess I figured as much." Mr. Grimes knew he would miss seeing Wade around the place. "How long a spell?"

Wade put his fork down and sat back in his chair, staring down at the uneaten food on his plate. "I ain't exactly sure about that." Then he looked at Mr. Grimes. "All I know is that I can't stay around these parts right now." Then he leaned forward. "I hope you understand, sir."

Tolliver Grimes looked down at his half-eaten breakfast, having lost his appetite. "Too bad." Then he smiled. "I'm not happy with your decision, but I understand."

Wade saw the sadness in his smile and thought of his grandfather when Wade left South Carolina for the West. "I'm sorry, sir," he said softly. "I don't want to punch cattle right now. I think a year away will do me some good."

Tolliver looked up. "Maybe so. A year's not that long. You gonna see that little gal before you leave?"

Wade smiled. "Soon as I finish here."

"Sarah Talbert's not going to like you leaving again." He paused. "She'll take it hard."

Wade looked down at the uneaten food on his plate, knowing she would.

Moments of silence passed, and having lost his appetite Mr. Grimes gently slapped his big hands on the top of the table and forced a small smile. "Well, I guess you best be on your way to the Talbert's' place before that little gal hears you're back and comes riding over here after you." He stood pushing his chair away from the table with the back of his legs. "I'll go see your mare's saddled and ready. Go on and finish your breakfast." As he walked past the little dog licking an empty plate, he stopped at Wade's chair and put a hand on his shoulder. "I'm sure the boys are still at the bunkhouse waiting for you to come by. They won't get a darn thing done until you do, so I'd appreciate it if you'd go on down there and say your goodbyes. I'll be waiting in the barn."

"Yes sir." Wade listened to the heavy footsteps, then the front door opening and closing. He thought he'd miss the old man and his grumpy ways. He pushed his chair back as he stood, reached down, picked up the dog, and walked out of the dining room.

Bertha was at the front window holding the lace curtain back with one hand, staring out the window. "You broke that old man's heart," she said without looking away from Tolliver Grimes as he walked toward the barn.

Knowing she spoke the truth, he opened the door and stepped past her. He paused at the edge of the porch taking in the buildings and the land. Hearing Bertha close the door, he stepped off the porch and walked toward the bunkhouse. Stepping inside, he was greeted by familiar smells he had forgotten. Seeing the familiar faces of Jessup Haggerty, Johnny Pardee, Bill Dobbs, and Stu.

Jessup was the first to stand with a grin as Wade walked to greet him. After the hellos and shaking of hands, he gave them a brief accounting of the past months and explained about the dog. When Wade finished, he told them that he wasn't staying and offered no explanation as to why or where he was going. He shook their hands, said goodbye, and walked out of the bunkhouse carrying the small yellow dog.

Tolliver Grimes stood at the corral fence with an apple cut in half and waited for the big black horse that once belonged to his son and Emmett's black horse. Both horses leisurely walked to the fence, gently took a piece of apple, and walked away. Hearing Wade, Tolliver turned and smiled. "Say your goodbyes?"

"Yes sir."

Mr. Grimes put a hand on Wade's shoulder as they walked toward the barn, knowing he was carrying a heavy burden. "What you did out there was a good thing, Son. Don't ever let anyone tell you different. Those men weren't just bad, they were pure evil and needed killing. In my way of thinking, it doesn't matter how the killing was done, and I think the Good Lord sent you after those men to stop them." He paused. "I truly believe you were the instrument he used to send those evil young men to hell."

Wade considered all that Mr. Grimes said as they walked into the barn finding his horse saddled and a packhorse loaded with supplies waiting.

"Thought you could use some supplies to take you wherever it is you're going." Grimes held out his hand, and as they shook hands, Mr. Grimes smiled sadly. "You've always a place here."

Wade could see the sadness in the old man's eyes and felt regret about leaving.

Tolliver Grimes fought the tears in his eyes and smiled. "You take care of yourself and that little dog that now owns you."

Wade smiled, thought that was pretty much the truth, and was glad he did. Then as he started to climb up onto the saddle, he saw the bandolier of cartridges and the stock of the Sharps rifle sticking out of the scabbard, and looking surprised, he turned to Mr. Grimes.

The old man smiled as he gently patted him on the back. "It's yours now. I figure the Good Lord would want you to keep it. You'll do more good with it where you're going than I ever will here." Then the smile left his weathered face. "Now get the hell over to the Talbert place and break that little gal's heart." Then he turned and walked out of the barn toward the big house.

Wade watched him for a moment, took the lead rope of the packhorse, climbed up onto his mare, and settled the dog between him and the saddle horn. He glanced around the barn and thought of those Saturday mornings cleaning the stalls with Emmett Spears. He felt sad and missed his friend, nudged the mare into a walk out of the barn, and turned her toward the Talbert ranch.

Thirty-Two

The ride to the Talbert ranch took Wade past the rock formation and shack where he and Sarah had taken shelter from the storm and had become their secret meeting place. He could not see the shack, but he knew it was there, and his memory still held the sounds of pounding rain and wind that blew the door open, frightening the horses, as well as Sarah. It all seemed like such a long time ago.

Stopping at the top of the hill overlooking the Talbert ranch, he looked down at the white two-story house nestled among poplar and cottonwood trees. Excited at seeing Sarah, he nudged the mare down the dusty hill. Struggling with the lead rope of the packhorse, he rode under the archway with two wooden J's and nudged the mare into a faster trot.

Sarah stepped out of the house and stood at the porch's railing, holding one hand above her eyes to shade them from the sun. Recognizing the mare and how the rider sat in his saddle, Sarah's hand went to her heart, knowing it was Wade. Filled with excitement, she had never known, she waved, lifted her floral, white, and pink dress above her shoes, and ran down the steps into the yard to meet him while calling out his name.

Wade pulled up, wrapped the reins to the mare around the saddle horn, tossed the lead rope over the neck of the packhorse, jumped down, and set Dog on the ground.

Sarah ran into his arms with such force it almost knocked him over. Oh, Wade," she whispered as he held her. "Where have you been?"

Ignoring Dog jumping on his legs, whining, and growling, he held Sarah in his arms, smelling the familiar odors of perfume and soap.

Hearing Dog whine and bark, she looked down. "Where did you get the cute dog?"

Wade looked down at him. "I'll explain later."

"What's his name?" she asked.

"I just call him Dog."

She smiled with a puzzled look. "What a strange name. Is it okay if I hold him?"

He reached down, picked the animal up, and handed him to her.

She cradled it in her arms while looking at Wade, thinking he looked different. "You're not hurt, are you?"

He smiled. "No. I'm not hurt."

Relieved, she petted the dog. "I've been so worried. We knew the sheriff of Sisters came back, and we waited and waited, but you never came." She paused to look at the dog. "I was afraid I'd never see you again."

Mrs. Talbert came out of the house and stood on the porch with one hand on the porch post and the other shading her eyes from the sun.

Wade waved and hollered. "Morning, Mrs. Talbert."

"Morning yourself" she yelled.

"Thank you," then he asked about Mr. Talbert.

She gestured with one hand and yelled, "Round here someplace. You had us all worried." Then she raised her voice even louder. "Especially my Sarah!" Then Mrs. Talbert called out, "Come on inside! It's almost lunchtime."

Wade shook his head, looking regretful. "Wish I could, Mrs. Talbert, but I can't stay."

Surprise and anger filled Sarah as she stepped backward. "What do you mean that you can't stay? You only just got back."

"Nonsense" yelled Mrs. Talbert. "You come on into the house."

"Sorry, Mrs. Talbert," he replied. "I really can't stay."

Mrs. Talbert looked from him to her daughter, hoping he would not break her heart. Angry at Wade, she turned to go inside, stopped, turned, and hollered, "Seems to me you could give Sarah a little more than a few minutes of your time." Then she stepped into the house, closed the door, and watched them through the lace curtains.

"Looks like I made your ma mad."

"She ain't the only one." Sarah looked at him with welling eyes as she held Dog. "Why can't you stay?"

He wanted to take her in his arms, but instead, he turned and looked toward the snowcapped Rocky Mountains in the distance beyond the split rail fence.

In a choked voice, Sarah asked, "Why can't you stay? What is it?"

He turned and looked past Sarah toward the house, thinking he saw Mrs. Talbert standing in the window, and her presence there made him feel uncomfortable.

"Wade, why can't you stay?" Sarah asked again.

Knowing he was about to break her heart, he looked away toward the barn and bunkhouse. "I have to leave the territory for a while."

She set the dog down, put one hand on the side of Wade's face, and turned it so she could look into his eyes. "You've changed. I can see it in your face and your eyes. What happened out there?"

Wade looked into her soft brown eyes wanting to stay, but something bigger than her love was pulling at him. He couldn't explain it to her or anyone. He took her hand. "Walk with me."

Holding hands, she gripped his arm with her other hand and pulled herself into him as they walked toward the split rail fence that led to the archway. Dog was happily running behind them, paused now and again to smell the clumps of grass, wildflowers, and weeds.

When they reached the fence, Dog was at Wade's feet whining, so Sarah reached down, picked him up, and held him in her arms so he'd be quiet. She fought the need to cry, waiting for Wade to tell her why he had to leave. He took off his hat and fidgeted with it nervously as he leaned back against the fence. He talked for the better part of an hour, briefly telling her everything that had happened since he left that July day except how Paul Bradley died.

Sarah put the dog down, turned to the mountains, and stood with her hands on the top railing of the fence. Her voice was soft, as it broke with emotion while looking at the snowcapped peaks. "Seems to me you did what you set out to do. You kept your promise to Emmett, and you stopped those terrible men from killing other families." She turned and looked at him. "All of that is over now. Emmett and the families those men killed are resting in peace because of what you and the others did."

He looked away at the distant mountains wishing it could be that simple. But it wasn't simple, not for him. He was different inside, and no matter what she did or said, he would never again be that young man she begged not to go. He felt he was missing part of himself and couldn't explain what. "Maybe what you say is true, Sarah. Maybe those people are resting in peace because those men are dead now, and I hope each one is burning in hell for what they did."

She looked into his face and saw something she had never seen before.

"I never realized it until now, but after a killing, you can't go back to being the man you were before. That man is gone, and I can't get him back." He hit the fence railing with his hand in anger. "I'm not sure I know who the hell I am anymore."

"The others who were with you came back," Sarah said while trying to understand. "You said that the man in Roscoe's Creek who got shot came back to his wife and family with them two little girls." She looked away for a moment trying to understand, and then hope filled her. "It sounds to me like that sheriff you liked so much came back to Sisters, and maybe he'll marry that widow you told me about." Her eyes welled, and tears ran down her face. "So why can't you come back to me?"

He had no answers for her as he looked from the mountains into her soft, brown eyes, thinking of how much he loved her. "You're the only reason I did come back." He knew that Seth Bowlen, Frank Wells, and Marshal Billy French had learned to come to terms with the killing years ago. Each knew that to save a life, sometimes you had to take a life. He had to find out how they got used to living with a killing and the violence. "I need some time to find myself, Sarah. I'm asking that you give that time to me."

She put the dog down and turned away, trying not to cry.

He gently took her small hands from the railing and looked into her soft brown eyes, filled with the sadness he had brought back. He let go of her hands and turned to the mountains once again. "After I killed Paul Bradley in Mexico, something inside me changed. I couldn't figure out what it was. I thought for a long time that maybe I left my soul in Mexico."

"Why?"

He wanted to tell her the truth about Paul but didn't dare. "Maybe it's just all the violence and killing I've done and seen." He paused. "People do terrible things to one another, Sarah. Things people like you, your ma and pa would never think of." He paused to look at her. "It's like we live in a fairy tale here in Harper. This place, the town, they aren't the real world."

She reached down, picked up Dog, and held him in her arms as tears ran down her cheeks.

"While I searched for Dark Cloud's brother, Two Birds, to give him the gray horse, I remembered the Bible lessons taught to me by my grandfather when I was a young boy back in South Carolina. I felt God had damned me for being filled with so much hate and revenge while I showed those men no mercy." He looked into her welling red eyes. "It wasn't until I got back to the Circle T and was getting ready to ride over here today when something Mr. Grimes said made sense."

Sarah wiped the tears from her face. "What'd he say?"

"He said that he believed the Good Lord used me as an instrument and sent me after those men."

Sarah wiped the tears from her eyes. "Maybe he's right Wade. Maybe God did choose you. They say the Lord works in mysterious ways."

"That's what I been thinking all the way over here."

"So, you don't feel lost no more?"

"I'm not sure if it's lost or empty."

She looked hopeful. "Then you'll stay?"

He sighed with a regretful look. "No. I'm sorry, but I can't stay."

"But why?" she asked in a voice filled with desperation. "Those terrible men are dead, Emmett's revenged, and them that they killed are resting in peace because of you and the others."

He hoped she would understand. "I believe it's my purpose in life to help protect good people from men like the Bradleys and help uphold the law. The only way I can do that is to return to Santa Fe and be a deputy for Marshal Billy French."

Sarah pulled away, turned in anger, and softly asked, "How long will you be gone?"

"I don't know."

She looked at him for a moment. "I won't wait forever. You could be gone for years. No matter how much I love you, I won't waste my life watching for you to ride over that damn hill anymore. I thought you loved me."

He stepped toward her. "I do love you, Sarah. Truly, I do love you with all my heart."

She looked into his sad blue eyes. "Then take me with you to Santa Fe."

Surprise filled his face. "Take you with me?"

"Yes." She smiled, looking happy. "We'll get married, and I'll go with you."

He shook his head. "We can't just up and get married."

"Why not?"

Wade took off his hat and thought on that as he wiped his brow, half expecting to see Mr. Talbert staring at him from some corner of the ranch. "I haven't even asked your ma and pa for your hand yet. We just can't up and get married like that. I don't have a job, and the only money I have is what Mr. Grimes paid me in back pay this morning." He looked at her with hope on his face. "Will you give me one year?"

"A year?" she asked with a disappointed look.

"Yes. Give me a year. Let me get settled in Santa Fe, find a place for us to live, and I'll come back and ask your ma and pa properly if you'll still have me."

"But Wade, ---"

He put his hand on her mouth to stop her from talking. "I need this year, Sarah, to sort things out."

Looking determined, she wiped the tears from her face with both hands. "You'll have your year, Wade Garrison. One year and no more."

He sighed with relief. "Will you write to me?"

Sarah wiped the tears from her cheeks, smiled, and softly said, "I'll write to you."

He took her in his arms and kissed her, careful not to crush Dog. "Wait for me. When the year is up, I'll come back for you and prove how much I love you."

"I'll wait for you, I promise." Then she made a fist and shook it at him while speaking through clenched teeth. "But if you're not back by then, don't ever come back."

He smiled at the angry expression she wore. "I'll be back. You're the only reason I came back this time."

She smiled, finding pleasure in what he said.

He put his arm around her, and then they walked back to the mare and packhorse. He kissed her, then turned, climbed up on the mare, reached down, and took the small dog. When the dog was settled in, Wade reached down and gently touched Sarah's face. "I'll be back. Wait for me." He nudged the mare into a walk and tugged at the lead rope of the packhorse. "I'll be back, Sarah."

She hollered after him, "I'll wait one year, Wade, no longer." Standing alone in the yard, she watched as he rode under the archway disappearing over the hill. Wishing he would turn around and come back for her, she wiped the tears from her face and walked back to the house. Crying, she rushed into her mother's arms.

Mrs. Talbert tried to comfort her daughter as best she could where there was no comfort. She listened as Sarah told her why Wade had to leave. Mrs. Talbert looked out the front window at the archway and knew there was nothing she could do to ease her daughter's broken heart.

As she looked out the living room window toward the archway and the hill, Sarah wiped the tears from her eyes and cheeks. After a few moments of staring out the window, she put her shoulders back, turned, and walked toward the stairs.

"Where are you going, child?" asked Mrs. Talbert.

"To Santa Fe, Mother." Then she climbed the stairs disappearing down the hall to her room.

Mrs. Talbert stared at the empty staircase for several moments with the realization that her daughter loved Wade Garrison as she would no other man. She loved him so much that she would give up every possession she had and follow him across two territories. Mrs. Talbert smiled affectionately yet proudly, remembering another young girl who had followed the man she loved to Colorado from Pittsburgh. She sighed, smiled broadly, gently slapped her knees with both hands and stood. Janice Talbert walked out of the front door to tell her husband that his daughter was not at all like him but more like her mother.

The Wade Garrison Saga continues in the next book of the series 'God's Coffin.'

Other books by Richard Greene

<u>Death of Innocence</u>

The book Death of Innocence is about five families of my ancestors who lived during the Civil War. The story is based on fact, along with fiction and family lore. For the most part, what happened to these families is true, but I also added some fiction to fill in the gaps. Joseph Samuel Greene, the main character, was my great-grandfather. I think you will find the story interesting as well as entertaining.

Befriended by a slave and the captain of a riverboat, a young runaway named Joseph Samuel Greene finds adventure on the river and the love of a young Mary McAlexander. The Civil War will not only test their love for one another but the faith of the McAlexander Chrisman and Patterson families as each endures the war's death and destruction.

Death rides across the South in the guise of the southern home guard, taking the innocent without hesitation or regret. The sorrow they leave will last forever as each proud family endures while losing their innocence.

God's Coffin

Sequel to Wade Garrison's Promise

Wade Garrison rides out of Harper, Colorado, into the New Mexico Territory in 1872, believing he rides away from a troubled past.

Now six years later, his old friend Sheriff Seth Bowlen in Sisters, Colorado, is in trouble and needs help. Sheriff Bowlen sends a wire to United States Marshal Billy French in Santa Fe, who sends Deputy Marshal Wade Garrison to help their old friend.

Innocently Wade decides to take his wife Sarah and son Emmett to visit her family in Harper, a small town northeast of Sisters. As he and his family board the train in Santa Fe, he could not have known that a terrible storm of violence was already brewing, and this fateful decision could destroy his wife and child.

Atonement

Sequel to God's Coffin

In August 1878, Wade Garrison took his vengeance against the men who took his unborn daughter's life while trying to kill his wife and son to settle a score. When the last man was dead from Wade's Sharps Rifle, he rode out of Harper, Colorado, a wanted man, and disappeared into the Montana Territory.

Morgan Hunter was a forty-eight-year-old gunman from West Texas wanted for the killing of a sheriff and his deputy. He rode into the Montana Territory, fleeing from those killings and riding away from the sorrow that caused them. Unaware of the other, both men rode toward the same destiny.

Sarah looked toward the top of the hill every day, waiting for Wade and his red sorrel mare to come home. The days turned into weeks and then into months, and still no word of him or from him.

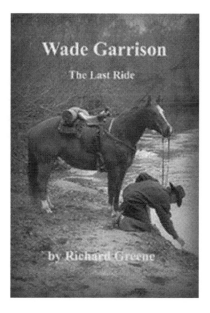

Wade Garrison

The Last Ride

Sequel to Atonement

It has been a year since Wade was shot and nearly died after being found innocent of murder at his trial in Harper, Colorado. While he misses the life of a United States Deputy Marshal, he is content being with his wife Sarah, son Emmett and daughter Mary Louise on their ranch. Keeping his promise to God and Sarah, his Colt pistol lies tucked away in the bottom drawer of a chest in his bedroom, and the Sharps rifle, covered in a rawhide sheath, stands in a corner behind the chest.

Unknown to Wade and Sarah, he is about to be thrust into a life of violence once again by events in the small town of Harper, Colorado. When the people of Harper seek his help for justice, the old life pulls at him. Resisting those old ways, he fears the town and his son will think he is a coward. How can he break his promise to not only Sarah but to God?

<u>Feeding the Beast</u>

1951

The Second World War has been over for six years, and the United States is now involved militarily in Korea, termed a Police Action rather than a war. On April 10, President Harry S. Truman fires General Douglas MacArthur, commander of the United States forces in Korea. This action resulted in the president's lowest approval rating of 23%, which remains the lowest of any serving president.

The Denver Police Department protecting a population of fewer than 415000 residents, was small compared to Chicago, New York, and Los Angeles.

The use of DNA by the judicial system is far in the future. Electric-powered streetcars were the primary source of transportation and were soon to be replaced by electric buses. Computers were in their infancy, and while most old newspapers and other public records are on microfilm, thousands of documents are not. Not every home could afford a television, so the radio remained the household's nightly entertainment. The closest thing to a cellular telephone was Dick Tracy's two-way wristwatch found in the comics, so the police had to rely on rotary phones and shortwave radios. Being Mirandized was not an option criminals were given in 1951 and would not be until 1966.

The term Serial Killer would not be coined until 1970 by FBI Special Agent Robert Reesler.

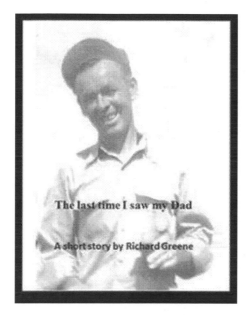

The last time I saw my Dad

A short story by Richard Greene

The Last Time I Saw My Dad

This short story is about my last trip to Houston, Texas, to visit my Dad and the memories it brought back of the summers I spent in Houston as a young boy growing up.